Discover the series

'A high level of realism . . . the action
fast. Like the father of the modern thriller, Frederick Forsyth, Mariani has a knack for embedding his plots in the fears and preoccupations of their time'

Shots Magazine

'The plot was thrilling . . . but what is all the more thrilling is the fantastic way Mariani moulds historical events into his story'

Guardian

'Scott Mariani is an ebook powerhouse'

The Bookseller

'Hums with energy and pace . . . If you like your conspiracies twisty, your action bone-jarring, and your heroes impossibly dashing, then look no further. The Ben Hope series is exactly what you need'

Mark Dawson

'Slick, serpentine, sharp, and very, very entertaining. If you've got a pulse, you'll love Scott Mariani; if you haven't, then maybe you crossed Ben Hope'

Simon Toyne

'Hits thrilling, suspenseful notes . . . a rollickingly good way to spend some time in an easy chair'

USA Today

‘Mariani constructs the thriller with skill and intelligence, staging some good action scenes, and Hope is an appealing protagonist’

Kirkus Reviews

‘If you haven’t read any Mariani before but love fast-paced action with a historical reference, maybe this one won’t be your last’

LibraryThing

‘A breathtaking ride through England and Europe’

Suspense Magazine

‘This is my first Scott Mariani book . . . and I totally loved it. It goes on at a good pace, and for me Ben Hope was brilliant, the ultimate decent good guy that you are rooting for’

AlwaysReading.net

‘Scott Mariani writes fantastic thrillers. His series of Ben Hope books shows no sign of slowing down’

Ben Peyton, actor (*Bridget Jones’s Diary, Band of Brothers, Nine Lives*)

‘A really excellent series of books, and would make a wonderful television series as well!’

Breakaway Reviews

‘Scott Mariani seamlessly weaves the history and action together. His descriptive passages are highly visual, and no word is superfluous. The storyline flows from beginning to end; I couldn’t put it down’

Off the Shelf Books

THE TEMPLAR SECRET

Scott Mariani is the author of the worldwide-acclaimed action-adventure thriller series featuring ex-SAS hero Ben Hope, which has sold millions of copies in Scott's native UK alone. His books have been described as 'James Bond meets Jason Bourne, with a historical twist'. The first Ben Hope book, *The Alchemist's Secret*, spent six straight weeks at number one on Amazon's Kindle chart, and all the others have been *Sunday Times* bestsellers, most recently with *The Tudor Deception* being an instant number one. Scott was born in Scotland, studied in Oxford and now lives and writes in a remote setting in rural west Wales. You can find out more about Scott and his work on his official website: www.scottmariani.com

By the same author:

Ben Hope series

The Alchemist's Secret
The Mozart Conspiracy
The Doomsday Prophecy
The Heretic's Treasure
The Shadow Project
The Lost Relic
The Sacred Sword
The Armada Legacy
The Nemesis Program
The Forgotten Holocaust
The Martyr's Curse
The Cassandra Sanction
Star of Africa
The Devil's Kingdom
The Babylon Idol
The Bach Manuscript
The Moscow Cipher
The Rebel's Revenge
Valley of Death
House of War
The Pretender's Gold
The Demon Club
The Pandemic Plot
The Crusader's Cross
The Silver Serpent
Graveyard of Empires
The White Knight
The Tudor Deception
The Golden Library

To find out more visit **www.scottmariani.com**

SCOTT
MARIANI

THE
TEMPLAR
SECRET

HarperNorth
Windmill Green
24 Mount Street
Manchester M2 3NX

A division of
HarperCollins*Publishers*
1 London Bridge Street
London SE1 9GF

www.harpercollins.co.uk

HarperCollins*Publishers*
Macken House
39/40 Mayor Street Upper
Dublin 1
D01 C9W8

First published by HarperNorth in 2024

1 3 5 7 9 10 8 6 4 2

A catalogue record for this book
is available from the British Library

ISBN: 978-0-00-860118-8
Printed and bound in the UK using 100% renewable electricity at
CPI Group (UK) Ltd, Croydon

PROLOGUE

Southern France,
April 1308

The soldiers were still out there hunting for him, he knew it. And they wouldn't give up their search until he was their prisoner, covered in chains and hurled into a dungeon awaiting the most torturous execution it was possible for a man to suffer.

The fugitive's name was Thibault. Twice that day he'd been convinced he could feel the pounding of hooves resonating through the cold stone floor on which he crouched down here in the darkness, and that he could hear the whinny of horses and men's muffled voices coming from outside.

Or perhaps he was just imagining it, he tried to tell himself. Hunger could play strange tricks on the mind, and he hadn't eaten anything since his last near-disastrous venture out of the crypt to forage for food. He was losing count of the days but it must have been a week ago at least. On that occasion, having crawled through the narrow escape passage that tunnelled below the outer wall of the manor house, he'd wandered for nearly half a mile through the woods before he'd spotted the family of rabbits running over a grassy knoll. He'd used his slingshot to kill one of them, gutted and skinned it with his dagger; and he'd been in the process of gathering dry twigs to build a fire over which to roast his catch when the thunder of approaching horsemen had alerted him.

Peering through the foliage he'd watched the troop of soldiers gallop by. If they'd turned up just minutes later than they had, they would have smelled the smoke of his fire, and it was unlikely that one man on foot, even a knight as skilled in warfare as he was, could have evaded eight well-fed and determined king's men on horseback. More of them were sure to be scouring the countryside for him – and so, unwilling to risk staying out in the open, Thibault had crept back through the woods to his secret refuge and devoured the rabbit uncooked.

Since that anxious day he hadn't dared to venture out again a single time, though he knew he couldn't stay for ever. His meagre water supply was dwindling fast. How long had he been living down here now, three weeks? A month? He was losing track.

His temporary abode was a small, dank stone crypt secretly located below the floor of the rambling great manor house. Though it was far from comfortable as a hideout, he was fortunate to have one at all. Many of his fellow knights had been far less lucky, rounded up, incarcerated and executed in the weeks and months following the joint royal and papal decree, announced during the autumn of the previous year, that had made outlaws of them literally overnight. And Thibault was deeply grateful to the sympathetic noble family who had allowed him to take refuge in the crypt of their country home. They were risking a great deal by offering protection to a member of a condemned military order whose extermination had been sanctioned at the very highest level. For their own sakes the family had travelled north to their residence near Paris for the season, taking all their staff and servants with them: that way, if Thibault was caught, they could deny all knowledge of his having been here. He couldn't blame them for being cautious in these dangerous times.

As he'd slowly adapted to his new life as a hunted outlaw, Thibault had had plenty of time to reflect on the dramatic and utterly unforeseen turn of events that had reduced a hitherto powerful and respected order of knights to a scattered band of renegades, accused of the most terrible forms of heresy against God and the Church. The persecution had been as ruthless as it was sudden, and he had no doubt the authorities intended to continue it until every last one of them was dead. Never before in their long and successful history, through all the wars and conquests in which they'd so loyally defended Christendom against its foes, had they been threatened with such total extinction. That they should be facing that grim prospect now seemed unthinkable. Yet it was true; and in his darker moments, of which there were many, Thibault feared that this was truly the end for his kind.

It wasn't so much the fear of his own death that haunted him – God knew he'd faced that enough times in the past – nor even that of the pain and torture inflicted at the hands of his would-be executioners. What troubled him far more was that if he and all his fellow knights were to die, then so too would die their sacred legacy, the precious secret that every member of their order was sworn to uphold. The secret could not, *must not*, be allowed to pass into obscurity and be forgotten. And recently, over the course of these endless days and nights that Thibault had spent hiding in the darkness of the crypt like an animal in its burrow, he'd become increasingly convinced that he must do something to prevent that from happening.

But what, and how? The answer was clear to him now, after so much reflection and prayer. If he was indeed doomed to perish – and after all, wasn't that the fate of every mortal man sooner or later? – then it was his duty to leave behind some kind of message for posterity. After that, if the Lord Almighty in His wisdom should see fit that he and all his fellows were to meet the same cruel end, at least Thibault could go to his death with hope and faith that the holy secret could be preserved for the benefit of future generations.

'That is what I must do,' Thibault said to himself.

His eyes had become quite accustomed to the darkness of the crypt, but for this important task he needed a little light. He still possessed one tallow candle, the last of those he'd brought with him. Gathering a sufficient quantity of dry moss from the stonework and a few pieces of twig and root from the mouth of the escape tunnel, he made them into a small pile near the wall. Then crouching over it, he used his flint striker and the tiny amount of tinder and wood shavings he had left in his fire-making pouch to kindle a flame, and blew gently on it and built it up with scraps of moss and twigs until the crackling little blaze was strong enough to light the wick of his candle. He set it on the floor close to the wall, so that its soft flicker glowed on an area of stonework. The candle spat and sizzled and gave off a stench of burning animal fat. It wouldn't last long, but long enough.

Working quickly, Thibault drew out his dagger, pressed its sharp tip against the stone wall and began to carve.

Chapter 1

'See, what did I tell you? It's perfect for us. Just bloody perfect!'

Jeff Dekker might be sometimes prone to gloom and pessimism, but he was also well known for his bouts of irrepressible, almost boyish eagerness – and this was certainly one of them. On this occasion, though, neither Ben Hope nor even the normally ultra-buoyant Tuesday Fletcher was quite sure if they could share their friend's enthusiasm.

The three friends had flown south across France to the Languedoc region in Jeff's Cessna Skyhawk the day before, and had driven up into the hills on this clear, sunny Monday morning in September to view a property for sale. The slightly rundown house, bordering on if not quite worthy of being called a château, was situated deep in the tall, rugged Pyrenees foothills a few miles south-west of the small commune of Quillan. The medieval citadel town of Carcassonne lay some forty-five minutes to the north, and the vibrant regional capital, Toulouse, could be reached in just an hour and a half. France's southern border with Andorra wasn't far beyond the mountains.

All in all, such a spot was a world away from the cooler, often wetter and decidedly less visually dramatic corner of rural Normandy Ben and his companions were used to, which had been their home and base for quite some years.

The business that Ben and Jeff had co-founded there in a sleepy patch of countryside called Le Val had been gaining so much success and reputation within its specialised field that the time had now come for them to consider expanding to a second location.

It was a major step for them to take, and only after months of discussions had they now finally bitten the bullet and started scouting for likely properties. So far the search had been narrowed down to two possible options, both situated within a few kilometres of one another in the heart of the Languedoc region.

Of those two candidates the older property, the Manoir du Col, seemed especially attractive to them, and it was the one they'd elected to see first. Its location perched above the spectacular Boulzan valley with the ridges of the Pyrenees behind was remote but still easily accessible. Their research had shown that the local climate could get exceedingly cold in winter but enjoyed long, balmy summer seasons that would be a positive asset to their business, while the reasonable proximity of Toulouse's nightlife and international airport would be attractive to those clients who tended to feel somewhat isolated in the admittedly less exciting surroundings of Le Val. The Manoir was also a considerably larger property with a good deal more land than they currently possessed, which would allow them elbow room to develop amenities they'd not been able to before.

The main downside, as far as Ben could see, was the old manor house's state of repair. It had lain empty for years and suffered the ravages of neglect, so much so that some fairly major and extensive renovations would be needed to make the place habitable, let alone in a condition ready to open their doors to paying clients.

'But you see the potential,' Jeff had kept telling them on the journey here, and was reiterating now, just in case they'd missed it the first fifty or sixty times. 'Once the house is all done up we could house twice as many delegates, and we wouldn't neehald to make them all kip in prefab barrack huts any more. Then we'd have all this space around us. Think what we could do with it, stuff we could barely dream of at Le Val. Expanding the rifle range from six hundred yards to over a thousand, for starters. How many of our competitors can offer their trainees the chance to plink at proper anti-materiel targets a mile away with a Barrett fifty-cal?'

'None,' Tuesday had to admit. Put that way, he was beginning to warm to the idea himself.

It wasn't every business that needed wide enough open spaces to accommodate such things as long-distance sniper practice ranges, private road circuits on which to hone the techniques of high-speed pursuit and defensive driving, and areas of dense wilderness where delegates could be taught to track and hunt human targets. But those, among many others, were the kinds of skills that Ben, Jeff, Tuesday and their associates taught at Le Val, forging the reputation of being one of the most elite tactical training facilities in Europe, maybe in the world. Their international clients included police SWAT teams, paramilitary units and hostage rescue specialists looking to take their capabilities to the next level, and private close protection firms who wanted to maximise the quality of their VIP bodyguard services by learning from the best. And ex-SAS major Ben Hope, his fellow former Special Forces commander Jeff Dekker and their indispensable associate Tuesday Fletcher, once among the finest master snipers the British army could boast, *were* indisputably the best.

Not that they generally revealed too much about the nature of their profession or their past experience to people on the outside, knowing that a lot of ordinary folks could easily get the jitters over such things. For that reason they were exercising their usual discretion with the local property agent who'd met them here at the Manoir du Col this morning to give them the guided tour.

His name was Matthew Sadler, a half-French British expatriate who'd resettled in his mother's homeland and made money selling prestige villas, stately homes and even castles to droves of wealthy buyers leaving the UK in search of cultural wealth and better lifestyles. It was Jeff who'd picked out his agency, partly because in all the years they'd lived and worked in France, Jeff had never really applied himself to learning the language and was drawn to Sadler's being a Brit. By contrast Ben was perfectly fluent, having a natural talent for languages that he'd developed in the military and later, during his years as a freelance 'kidnap and ransom consultant', mostly around Europe. Even Tuesday, a relative newcomer to the country, could nonetheless get by much better than Jeff in French, albeit with the same Jamaican lilt that also accented his spoken English.

Sadler was a lively and likeable man who clearly enjoyed his own existence here in France's deep south. His classic open-topped Delahaye roadster was already sitting gleaming in the front courtyard when they'd turned up at nine a.m.

sharp in their rental car. Their own mode of transport was an unexciting and sedate Renault Espace; Ben might have chosen something a little spicier but he was glad of the freedom of not having to hire a vehicle in his own name, having long ago become blacklisted by all but the most forgiving of car rental firms for his unfortunate and frequent tendency to turn their expensive property into scrap metal.

As they stepped out of the Espace into the warm sunshine and the chirping of the cicadas, Sadler appeared from the house's ivied stone entrance to greet them with warm smiles and handshakes. 'Welcome to the Manoir du Col! What do you think of these views?' he asked, merrily waving down the steep hillside to the valley below. 'Stunning, no?'

They were certainly a revelation for Tuesday and Jeff, neither of whom had travelled as much around France as Ben. He was familiar with the rugged, spectacular Languedoc area from his visits to local scenic spots like Rennes-le-Château and Esperaza some years earlier. It hadn't been exactly a pleasure trip, and at times had come close to being his last – but the beauty of the place had made a deep impression on him and he'd often thought about coming back.

'Let's go inside and get started,' Sadler said, ushering them through the entrance. 'There's a wealth of unique features I'm dying to show you.'

The tour began, moving from the grandiose vaulted entrance hall through the many cavernous reception rooms, Sadler waxing lyrical about the potential for redevelopment. As bare, empty and in need of restoration as they were, the images on the agency website hadn't been able to do them justice.

'Fuck my boots, that's a fireplace and a half,' Jeff marvelled at the enormous carved stone mantelpiece in the banquet room.

If Sadler was bothered by Jeff's colourful way of expressing himself, he didn't show it. 'I could just see a big tapestry hanging there,' he said, motioning at a vast expanse of stone wall. 'And a couple of armoured knights in the corners to set it off. Give them shields and halberds, hang up a few candelabras and throw down a fur rug here and there, and you could be right back in medieval times when this place was built.'

Tuesday was similarly impressed by the scale of the rooms and their period features, which combined to show up their beloved home at Le Val as the simple, humble little farmhouse that it really was. Even Ben, who'd been the most sceptical of the three, was soon finding it hard not to be won over.

Seeing he was making all the right impressions, Sadler pushed even harder to convince them. 'It's really not that often that a gem of a place like this comes up for sale, what with its rich history and a whopping sixty hectares of prime land. And certainly not at this silly price.'

As they already knew, the last owner had died intestate and heirless more than a decade ago, and Sadler was handling the sale through the government officials who really just wanted shot of it. 'It's an unbeatable investment,' he assured them. 'Frankly, I'm amazed that nobody's snapped it up yet. But I can't see it staying on the market much longer,' he added, perhaps by way of a sly hint.

The agent's skills at salesmanship were having their desired effect on Jeff, who scowled at the thought of another buyer beating them to it. No question, Jeff was hooked.

‘Have you anyone else interested in the place?’ Ben asked Sadler.

‘The last potential buyers to view it were a couple from the States, just last week actually. It seems they’ve been thinking of moving to France for a while. Can’t recall the lady’s name but he’s Brad someone.’

‘Aren’t they all,’ Jeff growled, instantly marking this Brad guy as a sworn enemy.

‘I get the impression they’re quite well-heeled,’ Sadler said airily, pouring fuel on the fire of Jeff’s belligerent attitude. ‘They’re renting a villa in Tarascon-sur-Ariège while they scout around possible properties. Nice little pad, actually,’ he added half to himself. ‘I wouldn’t have minded handling that deal myself.’

‘Looks like we’ve got competition, then, boys,’ Jeff said with the look of a crocodile about to chomp down on a nice young gnu. There was nothing Jeff Dekker loved more than a good fierce contest. And he usually won them.

‘So that pretty much wraps it up for the groundfloor rooms,’ Sadler said. ‘Still got three upper floors to take you around. But before we go upstairs, I really must show you the *pièce de résistance*, and that’s the wine cellar.’

‘Of course,’ laughed Tuesday. ‘Most important room of the house.’ Tuesday had developed quite a taste for red wine since moving to France.

Sadler led them down a narrow passage and a flight of stone steps worn smooth in the middle by the passage of a million feet throughout the centuries, at the bottom of which was a barred iron door. Producing an enormous key and a torch, he showed them through into the shadows of the dusty cellar with its great curved vaults. ‘There’s no electricity down here. It's basically unchanged since the Middle Ages. Look, it even still has the original iron fittings where you'd hang your candle lanterns while sampling the vintage.'

'I could see myself doing a lot of that,' Jeff mused. By Sadler's torch beam he reached up to grasp one of the ancient iron lantern hooks. To his surprise it waggled sideways away from the wall, and he quickly withdrew his hand. 'Christ, I didn't mean to do that. It just came loose.'

'Can't take him anywhere,' Tuesday said, shaking his head. 'Clumsy git, now look what you've gone and done.'

'No, it's not broken,' Ben said, looking at it more closely. The lantern hook had sprung back into position when Jeff let it go. 'It looks like it's actually some kind of concealed lever.'

'Well I never,' Sadler exclaimed. 'So it is! But what could it be for?'

Then, in the thin light of his torch, they saw that the lever had activated an internal mechanism within the wall, releasing a hidden catch that allowed a section of the stonework to swing open. Until that moment it had blended invisibly with the rest of the wall. The craftsmanship was ingenious.

'My sainted aunt,' said Sadler. 'It's a secret doorway! I had no idea this even existed . . .'

'Wow, this is just the absolute dog's bollocks,' Jeff chuckled, his embarrassment totally forgotten. 'I want to see inside.'

Ben wondered for a moment whether this might be some clever new sales trick of the property agent's, intended to appeal to his already smitten prospective client and make buying the place even more irresistible. But no, the look of astonishment on Sadler's face was quite genuine.

The secret doorway was low and arched and they had to duck their heads to pass through. The other side was a short, narrow stone passage, which then widened out, and Sadler's torch shone on the dusty stonework of a second basement room, a hidden crypt, low-ceilinged and rough-walled. It could have been centuries since anyone else had entered this space.

Or perhaps not. Because as they realised in the next moment, the four of them weren't alone in here.

Chapter 2

At first all they could see of the crypt's fifth occupant was the small rectangular glow of a mobile phone light shining on a small area of the far wall. The person holding it was obviously so intently focused on whatever it was that was occupying them to have noticed that they had company. But the moment was short-lived, as Sadler's torch beam swept over the crouching figure and he – being a man, as they could now suddenly see – twisted away startled from the wall to face them. Behind the expression of surprise and horror he was about forty, white, somewhat on the plump side, clean-shaven and wearing a battered old leather hat with a broad brim.

That was all Ben and his companions were able to make out of him before he jumped to his feet, ran like a madman straight for Sadler and crashed into him, making him fall and drop his torch. It landed on the stone floor and went out; and suddenly the crypt was pitch dark except for the man's phone light, which darted back away from them, flashed quickly across the room and disappeared.

In a voice fit for a battlefield Jeff roared out, 'Hoi! You! Come back here!' But the escaping intruder clearly had no intention of hanging around to explain his presence.

There were a few moments of confusion – a stunned and disoriented Sadler scrabbling upright with the help of Jeff while Tuesday went hunting for the fallen torch only to find it was indeed broken, the bulb smashed from the impact – before Ben got out his own phone and activated its light function. He shone it around the crypt but nothing could be seen in its faint glow except bare stone walls.

'Who the bloody hell was that guy?' Jeff burst out angrily, getting Sadler back on his feet.

Whoever he was, he seemed to have disappeared without a trace.

'He's run off,' Tuesday said.

'Not past me, he hasn't,' Jeff said. 'There's no chance he got out this way. You okay, mate?' he asked Sadler.

'Y-yes . . . I'm all right . . . at least I think so . . .'

'So where'd he go? Just upped and vanished like a ghost?'

'Maybe he was one,' Tuesday said.

'Oh, give me a break, Tues,' Jeff shot back at him. 'A medieval ghost with a mobile phone and a silly bloody hat?'

'This is where he went,' said Ben, who'd been tracing his light around the walls in the direction the man had disappeared. 'There's another way out of here.'

The others gathered closer as Ben shone his light through a smaller arched doorway half-hidden by cobwebs in a corner recess. Beyond it was a twisting, narrow flight of stone steps coated in moss. 'Where does it lead to?' Jeff muttered, mystified.

Ben hopped up the steps and came face to face with a blank wall, with no apparent way further. Then he shone his light upwards at the centuries-thick matting of cobwebs that had been disturbed and hung down like rags of dirty silk. Reaching overhead, he pushed his fingers through the webs and felt a craggy stone panel that moved when he pushed against it. He pushed a little more, and a shaft of daylight appeared around the edges of what he realised was a flagstone trapdoor lid. Dust and dirt rained down on him from the hole. Judging by all the growth of moss around its edges, until very recently it hadn't been opened for a long, long time.

'It's an escape hatch,' he called down to the others. He debated for a moment whether or not to climb out through it after the guy – then dropped the idea. The mystery intruder could have gone off in any direction, and what was the point anyway? Brushing cobwebs and dead insects from his head he returned back down the steps to rejoin the others.

'A hidden trapdoor, eh? So much for ghosts,' Jeff said scathingly. 'Meanwhile it seems like this place has even more strange and unusual period features than we thought. First a hidden entrance from within the house, and now a secret escape route out of it. What's that about?'

'I'm truly at a loss,' Sadler replied, sounding dazed. 'I mean, it's not unusual for very old buildings like this one to hold all kinds of surprises. One house I sold had a hidden room where the French Resistance had a radio set-up for secret communications during the war. The buyer had been living there for a year before he even stumbled across it. And of course, when this place was built times were no less turbulent. medieval castles and monasteries often had hidden chambers and escape tunnels and the like.' He shrugged. 'All I can say is, if there are any other concealed ways into the Manoir du Col, please rest assured that my agency will make it a top priority to find them and make them all secure. We've never had to worry about such things in the past, this being such a low crime area. In the meantime, please accept my humble apologies.'

'Here we go,' Tuesday said. In his practical way he'd been fiddling with Sadler's torch and found a spare bulb inside the screw-on cap of the battery compartment. A few moments later the torch was working again.

If the guy wasn't a ghost, Ben found it hard to believe he was a burglar either. Short of making off with a three-ton medieval iron fireplace there was literally nothing to steal in this big old empty manor. So who was he, and what had he wanted?

'Pass me that torch a minute, will you?' he asked, and Tuesday handed it to him. Ben shone it along the area of wall that the intruder seemed to have been examining before they'd interrupted him.

'What's up, Ben?'

'I think this must be what he came looking for,' Ben said, pointing the torch at something he'd found. 'Carvings in the stonework.'

'What kind of carvings?' Jeff said, coming closer for a look.

'Old ones,' Ben replied. 'Looks like they were made a long time ago. I'd say they could even date back to around the time this place was built.'

Before he'd been interrupted, the mystery intruder had been scraping away at the dust and dirt to make the carvings more legible. Ben used his finger to clear away more of it. The carvings appeared to be a strange mixture of symbols, Latin numerals and letters, but no complete or intelligible words that he could make out. 'I can't say they mean much to me.'

'medieval graffiti,' Jeff grunted. 'How fucking fascinating, I don't think.'

'Or the marks of the masons who cut the stones,' Ben said. 'Back in those times, every piece had to be chiselled to size by hand. Who knows? Whatever these markings are, whoever carved them, this has to be what our man came here to check out.'

'So maybe he's an eccentric archaeologist, or something,' Tuesday suggested cheerfully. 'Or someone interested in how they used to build old houses. An architect, or a historian.'

'If that's what he is, he's got a pretty funny way of going about his business,' Ben said.

'Takes all sorts,' Jeff said dismissively. 'Anyway, who gives a toss about him or what he was doing here? We've got business of our own to be getting on with. What do you blokes say we forget all about the silly bastard and finish looking around the house, eh?'

Ben was curious about the markings on the stonework, but all the same he tended to agree with Jeff. They were wasting time here. Maybe if they'd been able to stop the guy from running off, they could have found out more. Too late now.

Later on, Ben would find himself wishing that they had.

Chapter 3

'I still can't understand it,' Sadler said. A quick check of the grounds outside the main entrance had shown no sign of the mystery intruder. The cars hadn't been touched. Back inside the house, they headed up the grand staircase to resume their tour. But Sadler was still shaken from the strange incident, and his mind was distracted. 'I can understand if some of the local kids with nothing better to do were inclined to hang around an old empty property like this, with so many nooks and crannies to explore. But a grown man?'

Ben, like Jeff, was beginning to wish that they could just move on from the episode and focus on more important matters. Yet Sadler wasn't ready yet to leave it alone. 'I'm in two minds whether or not to call the police about it,' he went on. 'We don't want anything like this happening again.'

'I'm sure the police have better things to do,' Ben said.

'Anyhow, I'd like to see the guy try to sneak back in if we take the place,' added Jeff. 'If the guard dogs and the security fences don't put a stop to his shenanigans, I sure as hell will.'

Only half listening, Sadler mused, 'The oddest thing of all is, now I come to think of it, I'm certain I've seen that fellow somewhere before. He seemed familiar somehow. But from where?'

At last the agent was able to return his attention to the task at hand, and for the next half-hour they explored the upper floors of the manor. Ben and his friends carefully inspected every inch. A surveyor might be able to spot what they missed but as far as they could tell the timbers seemed sound enough, the roof appeared to be in decent condition and there were no obvious structural nightmares to contend with. The tour finally concluded, they were on their way back downstairs when Sadler suddenly stopped dead in mid-stride on the staircase, snapped his fingers and exclaimed, 'I've got it now! *That's* who he is! Of course!'

'Who?' said Jeff, who'd managed to totally dismiss the earlier incident from his thoughts.

'I knew I'd seen him somewhere before; just couldn't remember when or where. He's the American chap who was here viewing the place with his wife. That is,' Sadler added, 'I assumed she was his wife.'

'Brad,' Ben said.

'Yes, it was definitely him. Brad Harrison, or Harrington, or something. Very odd indeed. Perhaps I *should* report it to the police, after all.'

Happily, by the time they'd covered as much of the grounds as they could on foot and returned to convene in front of the house, the subject of conversation had moved on again. Jeff's eyes were bright with enthusiasm and Tuesday seemed to be approving of what he'd seen.

'So what d'you reckon, mate?' Jeff asked, looking expectantly at Ben. It had been agreed between them in advance that a decision of this magnitude needed everyone to be unanimous, or the deal was off.

Ben was thoughtfully silent for a moment before replying. Then he nodded. 'It's certainly got promise,' he conceded. 'It's more than big enough to do all the kinds of things we wouldn't have space for at Le Val. My only concern is the extent of the renovations we'd need to do.'

'Money's not an issue,' Jeff said carelessly. He was clearly so taken with the idea that he'd probably have agreed to twice the asking price. But to some extent he was right. Business had been booming and there was plenty in the bank. However their real nest egg was the very much larger sum that had come to them some years back, the reward offered by an Omani prince called Tarik Al Bu Said in exchange for the safe return of a spectacular diamond, the legendary Star of Africa. Even after deducting many various expenses and donating hefty chunks of the money to as many deserving individuals and causes as they could think of, Ben and his friends had been left with a more sizeable fortune than they could even count, let alone spend at the time. Prince Tarik's mountain of cash had been sitting pretty in an investment account ever since, untouched by mutual consent, largely forgotten about and waiting for the day when it would come in useful. That day might just have arrived.

'It's not the money,' Ben told them. 'It's the length of time it could take to do the place up. What with all the other building work, we could be looking at months. A year, or longer. Do we really want to be tied up with such an extensive project, having to travel up and down between here and Normandy to oversee every last little detail?'

'So you want to give it a miss, then?' Tuesday said, suddenly bereft of his almost perpetual bright smile. The sunshine seemed to have dimmed a fraction as a result. Jeff was frowning and working up a suitable counter-argument.

'I didn't say that,' Ben assured them. 'I just think we should stick to the original plan and go and take a look at Domaine Lauriac first like we said we would, before we make a decision either way. All right?'

Domaine Lauriac was the second of the two properties to which they'd narrowed down their search. A former wine-making establishment situated to the west of Quillan, it was somewhat less grandiose in terms of both the house and the land, but a couple of centuries more modern and considerably less in need of work than the Manoir. Given that they'd all agreed to go and view it in any case, Ben's suggestion seemed like a reasonable one.

'Okay, but I can't see it being anything like as good,' Jeff grumbled.

'Absolutely fine by me,' said Sadler, looking at his watch. Thanks mainly to the unexpected discoveries and events of the morning, their tour of the Manoir and its grounds had taken longer than anticipated. 'Only thing is, by the time we've driven over to Domaine Lauriac and started looking around the place, the day will be almost over and I'd really like you to get a proper tour. How about we leave it for today and make a fresh start bright and early in the morning?'

'Not a problem,' Ben said. 'Our work schedule means we need to get back to Normandy pretty soon, but I think we can squeeze in an extra day for you.'

Sadler beamed. 'Excellent. And in the meantime, gentlemen, by way of a further apology for the embarrassment earlier, may I invite you all to be my guests for dinner tonight?'

Chapter 4

Hot damn, that was a close one!

Brad Hutchison's heart was thumping fast as he made his escape through the grounds of the old manor house. He was almost drunk from elation, fuelled by the adrenalin rush from having been taken by surprise like that, mixed with the dizzying excitement of what he'd found back there.

This was hardly the first time in his career that he'd come within a hair's breadth of getting caught, and had to make a run for it. Such rough and tumble was all in a day's work for an international adventurer, as he proudly regarded himself. His life was one of intrigues and discoveries, though seldom had one this sensational come his way. It was exactly what he'd been hoping to come across. The confirmation that they were definitely on the right track.

Brad only wished he'd picked a better moment for his reconnaissance mission, though it had been pure bad luck and not his fault that someone else just happened to be poking around the old empty house at the very same time. He fully intended to revisit the crypt. He'd be more careful next time. Maybe she'd come with him now they knew it was the right place. She could stand guard outside while he snuck back inside and resumed his inspection of the markings. There might be more critical clues hidden waiting to be discovered.

Still, what he had already was mind-blowing enough for the moment. He pressed on through the grounds. The land around the Manoir du Col was part woodland, thick and tangled and overgrown from years of abandonment, and part open scrub – the typical kind of garrigue terrain found in dry Mediterranean regions like this. He stumbled over rocks and through thorny bushes, scrambled up and down slopes and paused now and then to catch his breath. He wasn't quite as fit and athletic as he'd once been. But hey, he was still a hero in his own eyes. First chance he got, he was gonna buy himself a drink and celebrate his own brilliance.

Nobody was coming after him. Once he'd put enough distance between himself and the house, he decided he couldn't wait any longer to take a peek at what he'd found. A nearby cluster of rocks was all overgrown with scrubby bushes; panting, heart thudding, he nestled among them to yank out his phone and examine the snaps he'd taken of the old wall carvings. As he scrolled through the images he saw to his delight that they'd come out even better than expected.

Someone else would be happy, too. 'Boy, wait till she gets a load of these,' he chuckled to himself. But then he thought, *why wait?* His phone screen was telling him he was picking up just about enough mobile reception out here to ping the images off to her right away. He attached the best of them to an email with the header BINGO!!, adding a brief line below saying, 'Who's your Daddy? Catch ya later. B.'

Feeling even more pleased with himself, he stuffed the phone back in his pocket and continued on his way. A few hundred metres further on was the brow of a tree-dotted hill, beyond which he'd left his hired 4x4 hidden carefully out of sight at the side of one of the narrow winding roads that skirted the boundaries of the Manoir du Col's land. In just a couple of minutes he'd be out of here and speeding back to base with his trophy.

But Brad would never make it to the car. As he reached the top of the rise and started scrambling down the thinly forested slope towards it, a movement among the trees behind him caught his eye. He turned, saw the three men coming after him, and the elated beat of his heart turned to one of sudden terror.

The men had been tracking him all that morning. They were expert in many things, one of them being the art of covert surveillance. At no time had any one of them been more than fifty metres away, in constant radio contact with his two associates. They could have closed in and caught him at any time, but had wanted to hold back until the moment was right – that was to say, until he'd obtained the evidence that was about to become his downfall.

That moment had come. The men emerged from cover and spread quickly out in a pincer movement to surround and cut him off before he reached the safety of his vehicle. He'd spotted them now, and had begun darting this way and that through the trees in the hope of evading them, like a rabbit suddenly startled at the sight of a pack of stalking predators. But he knew as well as they did that there *was* no hope of escape.

Brad let out a whimper of fear as he ran. He was no longer even trying to get to the car, because one of his pursuers had flanked his route to it and blocked off any chance of reaching the road. He glanced around him for something, anything, he could use to defend himself against them: a stick, a rock. But that was as futile a hope as getting away. He wanted to yell at them, '*What do you want from me? Why are you doing this?*' That would have been futile, too, because Brad understood all too well what they wanted from him. Just as he also understood what was probably about to happen to him.

He would not be their only victim. Once they'd finished with him they'd come for her, too. If he could no longer save himself, then perhaps he could at least do something to try to warn her.

They were closing in now, having managed to encircle him from all directions: one racing up the slope towards him, one directly behind and the third blocking off any chance of retreating back the way he'd come. Still running, he yanked out his phone again. It wasn't easy to key in a message while fleeing for your life, even if his hands hadn't been shaking so badly that he could barely control them. In a breathless rush he stabbed out the letters *D-A-N-G-W-E-R*. There was no time to correct the fluffed spelling. She'd understand. She'd have to. And then it would be up to her to get away to safety, if it wasn't already too late.

Brad hit SEND and the message was safely flying through the ether.

And in the next moment, the three men were on him. The one who'd been tearing down the hillside reached him first, and made a grab for his jacket collar. Brad dropped his phone. He lashed out at his attacker with such force that he lost balance on the slope and went tumbling down it. He rolled helplessly over and over, coming to a tangled and bruised halt right at the feet of the second attacker who'd blocked off his path to the car and was heading up the slope to intercept him. The third joined them moments later. Brad tried to scramble to his feet but fell back with a cry of fear as the muzzle of a handgun poked into his face.

'Please,' he tried to cry out, his voice sounding warbly and quavering. 'Please don't do this.'

Brad was so transfixed in horror at the sight of the gun that he never even saw the telescopic baton coming down in an arc towards his head. Its impact cracked against his skull and his vision flashed blinding white and filled with spangling stars. Then the world went dark and he knew nothing more.

The three men stood on the hillside and looked down at the limp body at their feet. 'You'd better not have killed him,' said the one with the gun. 'We need him to talk.'

The one who'd coshed Brad over the head closed up his weapon and put it away, then crouched down by the body and felt for a pulse. He looked up at his associates and said, 'He's alive.'

'For the moment,' the third man said.

The one with the gun stepped over to where Brad's phone had fallen into the scrubby, dry grass. He stooped down and picked it up and spent a moment examining it. 'We were right,' he told the others, holding it up to show them the images. 'He found what he was looking for. And it's too late,' he added a moment later when he checked the messages. 'He's already texted the woman and sent her the pictures. Messaged her again just now, to warn her.'

'We should have grabbed him sooner,' said the third man.

'Yes, well, we talked about that,' the one with the gun said impatiently. 'Nothing we can do about it now.'

'Except find the woman,' said the one with the cosh. 'And anyone else who's working with them.'

The one with the gun nodded. 'Right. So now we take this one back to base, and make him tell us everything he knows.'

Chapter 5

The restaurant Matthew Sadler had chosen for dinner that evening was reputed to be the finest in Quillan, and it also happened to be conveniently within walking distance of their hotel, so that Ben wouldn't have too far to help Jeff stagger home afterwards. They started in the proper way with apéritifs in the bar lounge. Sadler contented himself with a demi of bière blonde to kick off with, while Ben and Jeff did the compulsory Midi thing with pastis – served the proper way in a tall glass, topped up with ice water – while Tuesday, apparently in an adventurous mood, opted for a Kir Royale, a blend of crème de cassis and champagne regarded by his friends as a nauseating sticky mess not fit for consumption. Tuesday liked it so much that he ordered another.

'You're going to make yourself sick as a dog if you carry on like that, mate,' Jeff said with a nasty grin. 'Anyhow that's a woman's drink. You big girl's blouse.'

'Up yours, moron,' Tuesday replied with his brightest, sweetest smile.

They were called to their table and the meal got started, promising to be one of those hearty Gallic feasts that went on until late. They attacked the entrée menu with gusto: being so close to the Spanish border there was an Iberian touch to the opening course, with small plates of tapas and miniature pâtés baked into little pies that were another speciality of the deep southern region, as well as a dish of *cargolade*, which consisted of escargots done in the Catalan way, grilled over a wood fire and stuffed with herb-scented bacon lard and Languedoc sausage meat, then covered with creamy aioli sauce. Ben and Tuesday shared most of the platter, while Jeff (who just wasn't Francophile enough yet for such delicacies) declared flatly that he was having none of that there fucking snaily shit and stuck with the safer option of a fish soup.

As the first course wound to an end and plates of rare steak and grilled lamb shanks appeared on the table together with three bottles of an excellent local wine especially recommended by their knowledgeable host, the conversation inevitably turned to property matters. Ben was relieved that the subject of the strange American, Brad whatever-his-name-was, seemed to have been laid to rest. Sadler filled them in on many of the details and features of Domaine Lauriac that they'd be seeing for themselves in the morning. 'Of course, as you know, the estate isn't quite as extensive as the Manoir du Col's, but it's still a good few hectares, and all excellent land, being a former vineyard property.'

'Remind me again what a hectare is in real money,' said Jeff, not a fan of the metric system.

'Just under two and a half acres,' Tuesday instantly informed him.

Jeff did the mental calculation and pulled a face at the result. 'Christ. We're talking pocket hanky compared to what we saw today. It's not much bigger than Le Val.'

'There could be an option to extend,' Sadler explained. 'If extra space really was an issue.'

'Yup. The more the better,' Jeff said emphatically through a mouthful of steak.

'I understand that the nature of your business requires a lot of, what should we say, *elbow room*,' Sadler said. 'Though I must confess I'm a little hazy on what exactly it is you do. You're in the security industry, is that correct?'

'Education, mostly,' Ben said.

'But of a rather specialised kind, I gather?'

Tuesday chuckled. 'You might say that. The stuff we teach can't always be confined to your average-sized classroom.'

Sadler was fascinated to hear more, and having outlined the basics of what went on at Le Val – the practical training in long-range rifle marksmanship that was Tuesday's particular area of expertise, the live-fire pistol and submachine-gun shooting exercises designed to replicate real combat situations as faithfully as possible, their exact replica of the SAS 'killing house' at Hereford used for hostage rescue and anti-terror operations training, the skid pan and defensive driving elements of their teaching programme and all the other explosive fun and games of their daily routine – they moved on to talking about the unavoidable bureaucratic nitty-gritty of setting up a sister operation down here in the south.

'Yeah, it's going to be a nightmare of red tape convincing the local powers-that-be that we're all kosher and not a bunch of trigger-happy nutters,' Jeff said. 'The insurance requirements are insane. But it's nothing we haven't been through before.'

'It helps having two bona fide Special Forces guys with amazing service records as our directors,' Tuesday said, pointing at Ben and Jeff.

'Especially me,' Jeff said.

'You're a director too,' Ben reminded Tuesday with a smile.

'And we have a perfect safety record at Le Val,' Tuesday told Sadler. 'Nobody's ever been shot, or blown up, barely even singed. At least, none of the clients have.'

'I'm pleased to hear it,' Sadler laughed. 'So you're not intending on selling up the business in Normandy and moving down here lock, stock and barrel, to use a shooting-related expression?'

'Le Val is home to us,' Ben replied, shaking his head. 'And it always will be. The idea is to run both side by side. Which of course means a lot of travelling between the two, and taking on extra people as instructors, security staff and so on. It's a big undertaking but we're confident it'll work for us.'

'Well, I have to say that either of these two properties sounds ideal for your purposes,' Sadler said. 'I flatter myself that I'm pretty good at spotting a plum deal, and that's even more true of the Manoir, at the price it's being offered at.'

'I'll say,' Jeff cut in, knocking back more wine.

'Plus you'd be surprised how fast the renovations could be done. I happen to know some excellent local tradesmen. Used them myself, when I moved into my place. It was in a real mess, I can tell you. But you should see it now.'

'Another rustic property?' Tuesday asked him.

'No, it's an apartment in town. Fifteenth-century, lovely building. Nice thing about being in the property business is that you get to pick out some of the better bargains for yourself.'

The main course eventually gave way to a giant cheeseboard and a fourth bottle, which went on flowing as freely as the conversation while the restaurant gradually began emptying of diners. Their host's face was a rosy pink and the wine had loosened him up nicely, though not as nicely as Jeff, who'd consumed twice as much and was ready for more. Tuesday, by contrast, was showing no sign of being as sick as a dog. As for Ben, one of the few positive benefits of too many years of indulgence in alcohol was that he could comfortably sink a couple of bottles of heady red wine without showing any appreciable effect.

'Now let me ask you something,' Sadler said, leaning across the table with a smile directed at Ben. 'Jeff tells me that you're a rather useful chess player.'

'Am I?' Ben replied, taken by surprise at the sudden change of subject. 'Where did he get that idea?'

'He's being modest,' Jeff said as he topped up their glasses with the remnants of the wine. 'He's pretty damn good. Beats the crap out of everyone he plays.'

'Not everyone,' Ben protested.

'That being the case,' Sadler said, 'here's a proposition for you. It so happens I'm a chess player too. I gave up competitive tournaments after I got to grandmaster level, but I love to push a pawn now and again.'

'Way out of my class, that's for sure,' Ben said. 'I'm only a rank amateur compared to you. But all the same I'd be curious to hear your proposition.'

Sadler's eyes twinkled. 'That you and I pit our wits against one another in a game, just for a bit of fun. It's not often I get the chance to face a decent opponent over the board these days. If you win, I'll agree to knock a percentage off my commission.'

'I see. And if you beat me, you hike it another thousand?'

Sadler laughed and shook his head. 'Nothing of the sort. All I want is the pleasure of the contest. Come on, what do you say?'

'Whoa,' Tuesday said. 'The pressure's on.'

'Go for it, Ben,' Jeff urged him. 'What's there to lose?'

Ben smiled politely and shook his head. 'Thanks, Matthew, but no thanks. I had my work cut out for me in Rome with Scarpa that time. Long story, but the upshot is that I promised myself never to play for bets again, win or lose.'

Sadler's eyebrows shot skywards. 'Scarpa? You mean the great Silvano Scarpa? The former world champion? You played him? Beat him?'

'Kicked his arse,' Jeff said. 'Big time. Wish I'd been there to see it.'

'I got lucky, that's all,' Ben said. 'And the game was a lot tighter than the end position made it look.'

'Well, I do hope you'll change your mind,' Sadler said. 'Think about it.'

'You know what I'm thinking?' Jeff asked, trying to wring the last drops out of the empty wine bottle. 'I'm thinking we need another one of these.'

'And I'm thinking it's time for us to go,' Tuesday said. Sure enough, they'd been the last diners in the place for some time and now the waiting staff were hovering closer and closer, while the manager had started pointedly looking at his watch.

Sadler insisted on settling the bill. 'Gents, it's been a delightful evening. If there was a Mrs Sadler I'm sure I'd be in trouble for staying out so late. Now, there's a nice little café-bistro across the street from my offices, where I often have breakfast. Perhaps we could meet there tomorrow at nine-thirty, grab a quick coffee and a croissant, and then we'll jump in our cars and I'll lead you along the scenic route to Domaine Lauriac.'

Ben smiled. 'The scenic route?'

'It's actually quicker that way. Instead of heading up the main street and picking up the Nationale, you take a left two blocks up from my office and head out of town along the old west road. It's a much nicer drive, passing through Sainte-Clothilde-du-Roussillon, as lovely a little Provençal village as you'll ever see, and then over the river by the Roman aqueduct bridge, which is known locally as the Pont de Clothilde. It's not as impressive or as well known as the Pont du Gard, but the view from the top is quite spectacular. On a really clear day you can actually see the western edge of Domaine Lauriac's estate from there, with the mountains behind. So, nine-thirty sharp?'

'Sounds like a plan,' Ben said. 'I look forward to it.'

Chapter 6

The regional base that was being used by the three men had belonged for centuries to the much larger, well-organised but very secretive group to which they belonged and whose orders they unquestioningly followed. Built long, long ago by experts in the construction of impregnable defences, the old fortress stood alone in the remote hills, an hour's drive from the spot where they'd captured the American.

The main part of the building was still in good order and served as a temporary dormitory and living quarters for the three men. Its amenities remained unchanged since medieval times, with only a basic open fire for cooking on. The windows were small, glassless and shuttered as they had been in the thirteenth century. Of the four squat round towers that had originally stood at the corners of its thick stone defensive outer wall, only one remained intact.

That was where they were keeping him.

It had been a long and gruelling day for their captive, and it still wasn't over yet. Come nightfall, with no electric lighting in the place the men had lit oil lamps that cast a flickering light across the craggy stone floor, at whose centre the American sat helplessly bound to a wooden chair in a pool of his own blood.

He'd absorbed a great deal of punishment, actually more than they'd expected he'd be able to withstand and still be breathing. To begin with, the three had taken turns battering him with leather-gloved fists until his face was a bloody pulp. Cheekbones broken, nose crushed, teeth mostly gone, one eye completely swollen shut and probably destroyed. When they'd grown tired of hitting him, they'd used a blowtorch on his feet. In their experience that was a very effective method. In this remote rural location nobody could hear his screams of agony.

Needless to say, by the time they'd finished with him the American would be too badly harmed to survive. Not that that mattered to them: it had been a foregone conclusion from the start that he wasn't getting out of here alive. Their only concern was to extract as much information out of him as possible before he finally expired.

He'd been admirably resilient at the start, refusing to tell them anything. However even the most foolhardy courage had its limits, and they'd never yet come across a man who didn't reach his breaking point sooner or later. When the American finally reached his – this was after one foot was a blackened burnt sizzling mess and the other soon to follow suit – the information had begun to flow out of him. In a garbled stream of words he'd blurted out the name and address of the property agent, one Matthew Sadler, who had apparently discovered the existence of the secret crypt beneath the Manoir du Col.

It wasn't just Sadler, either. As his flesh went on frying and the inside of the tower filled with the stench, the American revealed to them that three more players had also somehow become involved in the game, who'd been with Sadler inside the crypt. He claimed not to know their names or the reason they'd somehow come into this. When they tried to learn more by applying more heat to the second foot, the American had fainted, leaving them short of information.

'This Sadler might not have learned much,' one of the men said. 'Isn't it possible that nobody told him what the carvings mean, or who put them there?'

'Don't be so sure about that,' said another. 'For all we know, Sadler knows as much as this one does. He could have been in on it too.'

'Doesn't sound that way to me.'

'But we can't afford to assume otherwise,' the second man said.

The third man snapped impatiently, 'It doesn't matter whether Sadler was in on it or not. However he might have learned about the crypt and what's inside it, he's a witness to the secret. And we're not to leave any witnesses. Those are our instructions. We must stick to them, no matter what.'

'And what about these other three?'

'The same applies to them.'

'Even if they know nothing?'

'Even if they know nothing,' said the third man. Then, reminding them of an ancient piece of wisdom, he quoted the Latin phrases: 'Caedite eos omnes. Novit enim Dominus qui sunt eius.' *Kill them all. The Lord knows which ones are his own.*

It was agreed. 'Very well. Then let's wake him up and see if we can't make him tell us their names.'

But when they returned to their victim and tried to revive him by applying yet more of the same hideous pain, they found that his heartbeat had become very weak and faint, his breathing almost imperceptible.

'He's near the end,' said the first man. 'We don't have a lot of time.'

'Turn up the heat. Whatever it takes. We need those names.'

'No,' said the third. 'We already know to find Sadler. We can get the names from him easily enough. The woman is more important. She has the pictures of the carvings, and she's clever enough to use them to get closer to the truth. If we can learn only one more thing from him before he dies, it's got to be her whereabouts.'

'You're right. Then wake him up and let's do it.'

And that's exactly what they did. By the time they'd finished pressing him for the address where they could find her, the American was so badly damaged that they finally gave up trying to learn more and put an end to his suffering with a bullet to the head.

The battered, burnt corpse was removed from the tower and transported into the remote hills, to be interred in the lime pit they'd already prepared earlier. Nobody would ever find him out here among the rocks and the scrubland. The three men returned to the fortress, cleaned themselves up and ate their late dinner in silence by the light of the fire. When they'd finished eating they knelt and said a prayer, asking God's forgiveness for the terrible things they'd already been required to do, and the things they would have to do next.

And then they climbed back into their vehicle and drove off to get the woman.

Chapter 7

When they left the restaurant the night was balmy and starlit, and the narrow streets of the little town were empty but for a few late-night strollers and courting couples. Jeff insisted he needed no help to stagger the short distance back to their hotel, though he did seem to have some trouble holding a straight line. 'Can't hold his grog,' Tuesday laughed. 'Who's the big girl's blouse now, eh?'

It was after one by the time they said goodnight and split up to go to their rooms, which just happened to be consecutive numbers on the first floor. Ben's had a small balcony overlooking the street, and he stood for a while under the neon hotel sign, leaning on the railing and smoking a Gauloise, drinking in the perfect warmth and stillness of the night. After a final visit to the mini-bar (which he'd been pleased to find contained a miniature bottle of his favourite scotch, Laphroaig) he took a quick, cool shower, pulled on a T-shirt and loose jogging bottoms and clambered into the soft bed.

He hadn't been asleep more than an hour or so when the sudden commotion of banging doors and raised voices in the corridor woke him with a start. Trained by experience to be able to go from a dead sleep to full battle-ready alertness in half a heartbeat, he instinctively felt under the pillow for his pistol before he remembered that, of course, he'd left it in the armoury back home at Le Val. Who needed to bring a weapon on a routine business trip? He bounded out of bed and hurried over to the door to see what was happening. Outside in the corridor he met a sleepy-looking Tuesday, who blinked and muttered, 'What the hell's going on?'

The hotel wasn't on fire or under attack by terrorists. It soon transpired that one of the guests, the ninety-something male half of an elderly Danish holiday couple whom Ben had encountered in the lift earlier that day, had wandered confusedly from their room on the floor below and managed to get himself totally lost and bewildered. Poor Arne suffered from dementia, and it seemed he'd forgotten to take his medication that day. By the time he'd started calling out in confusion and randomly banging on room doors the poor man no longer had any idea where he was and had worked himself up into a terrible state, before capping his performance by tumbling noisily down the stairs.

Guests were peering from their doorways and the hotel manager had been summoned. Ben was one of the first people to tend to Arne, who'd become subdued by his fall and was sitting on the stair landing muttering in Danish. 'Are you a doctor?' asked the hotel manager as Ben checked the old man over for anything broken.

'Army medic,' Ben replied, for want of a more detailed explanation. After a thorough examination he was confident that the old man had suffered no more than a few minor bruises and didn't need to be rushed to hospital. By now Arne's wife had appeared in dressing gown and slippers, rollers in her hair, clutching a bottle of his pills and angrily remonstrating with him for wandering off like that. 'He does this kind of thing all the time, the silly fool,' she complained to Ben and Jeff, the latter having finally been roused from his inebriated slumber and emerged from his own room. She added bitterly, 'What am I going to do with him? The bastard's becoming more and more impossible to live with.'

'Maybe you need to keep him on a leash or something,' Jeff suggested helpfully.

It took some time to get Arne recovered and tucked back up in bed, scolded and berated every step of the way by his dear wife. 'Poor sod,' Tuesday said to Ben, shaking his head. 'No wonder he's lost his mind, married to an old cow like that. I'd have cut my throat.'

At last the show was over, and the manager thanked Ben profusely for his help and apologised to everyone for the disruption. By quarter past three, the hotel had settled down again and Ben returned to his room. He rolled into bed and was drifting off again within minutes.

But Ben had always been a light sleeper, and an early riser by long habit. He was up again soon after dawn had broken over the mountains, pounded out a hundred press-ups and sit-ups on the floor next to his bed, pulled on shorts and training shoes and went for his usual five-mile run around the still half-deserted streets. He loved this time of the morning when the world was just waking up. It was already getting warm, shaping up to be another typical day in Paradise. Back at the hotel he quickly showered, changed into his black jeans and denim shirt, slurped a coffee and lit up his first Gauloise of the morning out on his balcony, watching the town come to life and an outdoor market with stripy-awninged food stalls being set up down below. Gradually the street began to fill with life, and the delicious aromas of warm baguettes, ripe melons and fresh fish and charcuterie.

Sometime after nine a.m. he met Tuesday and Jeff down in the hotel bar. If Jeff was a little hung over from last night, he wasn't complaining. They ambled out to the car and drove across Quillan, heading for the main street in which Matthew Sadler's agency offices were situated, opposite the little café-bistro at which they agreed to meet.

It was precisely nine-thirty as they walked into the café and glanced around the tables expecting to see him there waiting for them. No sign of him yet, so they grabbed a table in the corner by the window and ordered coffees. Ben sat with his back to the wall, where he could watch the street through the window and keep an eye on the entrance. That was another long-established habit of his, even when travelling to places where he didn't need to keep a loaded semiautomatic under his pillow.

The coffee was great, but their conversation and relaxed mood began to run thin when Sadler still hadn't appeared after ten minutes. After fifteen, Jeff asked irritably, 'What the hell's keeping him?' Ben kept watching the agency office across the street and could see no movement happening in or out.

'Maybe he got held up with another client or something,' Tuesday wondered. 'Odd, though. He strikes me as a reliable sort of bloke.'

'Yeah, well, he should know we don't have time to faff around,' Jeff grumbled. 'What if someone else decided to snap the Manoir du Col up from under us in the meantime?' Still holding out for his first choice.

'I don't think anyone's falling over themselves in a rush to buy it,' Tuesday said with a grin.

'No? What about this freaky American guy, this Brad what's-his-name and his wife who're obviously dead keen on the place?'

Ben was saying nothing, but he was beginning to wonder if they ought to give Sadler a nudge and find out what the hold-up was. And as the offices were only just across the street, he decided on walking over there and doing it in person. They paid for their coffees and headed back out into the rising heat. 9.47 a.m. and already the sun's glare on the pavements was dazzling white.

By contrast, the reception area of Sadler's property agency offices was cool and airy, filled with the scent of flowers. But there was nothing pleasant about the atmosphere in the place. The instant the three of them walked inside, Ben sensed the tension and could tell something was wrong.

Chapter 8

Ben looked around the office space. A broad reception desk was flanked by inner doors on both sides, with a client seating area opposite, complete with chilled water dispenser, a burbling ornamental fountain and some low tables bearing colourful property leaflets and adverts for homes for sale or rent in the region. The client area was empty. The inner doors kept opening and closing as staff members popped in and out, looking agitated and fraught. As did the plump middle-aged receptionist sitting behind the desk. Her face was puffy and her eyes were red. There was a box of tissues on the desk in front of her, and she didn't seem to be getting a lot of work done. Ben didn't understand what the matter was, but he was about to find out.

Speaking in his easy, fluent French to the receptionist he introduced himself and his companions. 'My colleagues and I had a rendezvous with Monsieur Sadler this morning, but he seems to have been delayed. Do you know if he's about?'

She looked up at him and blinked a tear from her eye. Her voice sounded thick with emotion as she replied, 'I'm so sorry, someone should have called you to say.'

'To say what?'

She blinked again, and more tears welled up and rolled down her cheeks making little streaks of mascara. 'Something awful has happened. Monsieur Sadler . . . he's in hospital. He's in a terrible state. Oh, poor Monsieur Sadler!' The floodgates opened and she started weeping so hard that her shoulders quaked.

Ben glanced at his friends, both suddenly very serious-looking. 'We're extremely sorry to hear that,' he said to the receptionist. 'What happened?' The first image that had jumped into his head was of the dapper little Delahaye roadster wrapped crumpled around a tree or upside down in a ditch. It must have happened last night after leaving the restaurant. But he was wrong.

'We don't really know what happened,' she sniffed, plucking another tissue from the box and dabbing the corners of her eyes. 'Only that someone broke into his apartment during the early hours of this morning and attacked him.'

'Attacked him? A robbery?'

She threw a sideways look at her two staff colleagues who'd emerged from one of the side doors and were having a whispered, agitated conference in the corner. It was clear now that they must be talking about the same thing. She said in a low voice, 'It doesn't seem that way. The police don't think anything was stolen. I'm not even sure I should be telling you this.'

'Please,' Ben said. 'We'd like to know.'

'They pulled him out of bed and beat him up. I'm sure they'd have killed him, if a neighbour in the next apartment hadn't heard the commotion and raised the alarm. Luckily there happened to be a police patrol car in the area. They found Monsieur Sadler unconscious on the floor and badly hurt . . . oh, it's so awful!'

'So I'm assuming that the attackers were gone by the time the police got there. Did anyone see them?'

'The neighbour said he saw them running away at the sound of the police siren. But he didn't get a very good description.' She looked as if she was about to start crying again. 'Who would have done this? Monsieur Sadler gets on so well with everybody and is so well liked. We're all in complete shock.'

'So are we,' Ben told her. Which was half true, in that this was a deeply unpleasant bit of news and for such a thing to happen seemed completely out of place in this quiet little town. But the reality was that such incidents were too common in their experience for it to be truly shocking. And as unfortunate as it was, the world couldn't grind to a halt over it.

Ben could feel Jeff's eye on him. They'd been close friends for so many years that each could tell what the other was thinking, without even needing to look at each other.

Ben hesitated, measuring up his words before he said to the woman, 'You have our deepest commiserations, and we all truly hope that Monsieur Sadler recovers quickly. In the meantime, I'm sure you know he was due to show us Domaine Lauriac this morning. Might anyone else at the agency be available to take his place?'

It was the most tactful way he could put it, but the receptionist clearly didn't take it as such. Seeing her stung reaction he added, 'I hate to put pressure on you at such a difficult moment, but my colleagues and I are here on important business and our time is limited.'

'Yes, yes, of course,' she said a little stiffly. 'Excuse me just a moment.' She bustled away from the desk and went over to confer with the two colleagues in the corner, who threw glances their way. One of them looked at his watch and said something in reply. She nodded and returned to the desk. 'I'm so sorry. As you can imagine, this has thrown us into a bit of confusion. But Monsieur Sadler's partner, Monsieur Xavier, will be free to meet you later and show you around the property. Could you call in a couple of hours, around eleven?'

Ben looked at the others. Jeff shrugged. Tuesday's expression was uncharacteristically blank. 'We'll do that,' he replied to the receptionist. He repeated their sympathies for Sadler and the hope that he'd get well soon, and they left the office.

Back outside, Ben sensed that Tuesday was unhappy with what he'd said. He wasn't surprised when his friend challenged him. 'That was a bit rough, wasn't it? Putting them on the spot like that. They're upset, and who wouldn't be after what's happened?'

'Business is business,' Jeff said gruffly. 'You said the right thing, mate.'

All the same, though, Ben was sorry if he'd come over as hard and unfeeling. He felt bad for poor Sadler and was relieved that the incident hadn't ended much worse for him. It could only have been a random attack. Or could it?

'Anyway, looks like we've got a couple of hours to kill,' Jeff said. 'Don't know about you guys, but I'm not inclined to spend it sitting around drinking coffee.'

'Maybe we don't need to wait for Xavier,' Ben said. 'Sadler gave us some directions to get to Domaine Lauriac, so how about we head over there, just the three of us? Even if we can't get inside the place, we should be able to get enough of an idea whether it'd suit us or not. Then if we're still interested, Xavier can give us the rest of the tour later.'

'Okay,' Tuesday said, softening. Jeff nodded. 'Fine by me. Let's hit the road.'

They recrossed the street and walked back to the car, got in and set off with Ben at the wheel. Following Sadler's directions from last night, instead of following the main street in the direction of the Nationale they took the left turn after the estate agency offices to take the quicker scenic route he'd told them about.

As they'd been climbing into the Espace and driving away, none of the three had noticed the man who was loitering in a shop doorway a little way down the street, pretending to be looking at something in the window display. He'd been watching, from different points up and down the street, as they'd arrived earlier and gone into the café-bistro; then a few minutes later when they'd walked across to the agency offices and re-emerged shortly afterwards. He'd known their faces because he'd been sitting near to their table in the bar lounge of the restaurant the night before, while they'd been having their pre-dinner drinks. Their names he now knew from the information his three associates had beaten out of Matthew Sadler some hours later.

Now as the Renault Espace took off down the main street and rounded the left-hand corner, the man reached for his phone.

'Hope, Dekker and Fletcher are on the move. Not back towards their hotel, and not heading for the Nationale. Looks like they've taken the old west road out of town.'

'Copy that,' said the voice of his associate, who was the nominal team leader. The man in the street knew him and the others only by the adopted identities Jacques, Bertrand and Chrétien. Those, like the one he'd been allocated for himself, were not their real names.

Jacques, the team leader, said, 'We're rolling.'

Chapter 9

The countryside flashed by as they left Quillan behind them. The old west road out of town was twisty and narrow, but even a mundane sort of car like the Renault Espace could be pushed a little sportingly through its paces in the hands of a driver like Ben and the absence of any other traffic allowed him to take the racing line through the tight bends.

'Hey, take it easy,' said Tuesday, getting thrown around in the back seat by Ben's high-speed cornering. 'You're not in your Alpina rocket ship now, you know.'

'He can't help himself,' Jeff commented. 'Never happy unless he's dicing with death and destruction. Anyway, the quicker we get there and give this place the once-over, the better. My feeling is it's not going to be a good fit for us.'

'Yeah, yeah, we know that,' Tuesday replied.

Matthew Sadler's directions had been clear and accurate. After a few kilometres they passed through the village of Sainte-Clothilde-du-Roussillon that he'd told them about, every bit as picturesque as his description. 'So that'd be our local,' Tuesday observed as they drove past the village's only bar, where a group of leathery-skinned old men were engaged in a leisurely game of pétanque outside in the sunshine and already enjoying their first pastis of the morning.

But sadly, not everyone was having such a good time of it. Speeding past the village the conversation soon returned to the unfortunate incident that had befallen the property agent in the wee small hours of that morning. 'Bit of a shocker, you have to say,' Jeff said. 'What's the bloody world coming to with all these lowlife home invaders thinking they can go around beating the shit out of honest, decent folks? Tell you what, I'd just love them to try that on with me. Hoo, hoo.' He laughed darkly at the thought of what he'd do to them.

But Ben wasn't so sure the case was that straightforward. 'You don't think it's a little strange that they didn't steal anything?'

'Do we know that for sure?' Tuesday asked. 'How can the police really tell? He could've had a load of cash lying around. You wouldn't know once it was gone.'

'You're right,' Ben agreed. 'I just have a funny feeling about it, that's all. Like we're missing something.'

'Here we go with the funny feelings again,' Jeff chuckled. 'So what's your theory, Sherlock?'

'I don't have one,' Ben replied. 'It's probably nothing. Just a random incident, like you say.'

They drove on in silence, each mulling over the matter privately. Then as they curved around another tight bend the road straightened out and they caught sight of the old Roman aqueduct bridge a quarter of a mile ahead, the sunlight glittering and spangling on the blue water of the river below and the mountains towering grandly in the background. The breathtaking beauty of the landscape was enough to push the topic of Sadler's attack out of their minds. Jeff said, 'Well, the poor bastard wasn't wrong about the view.'

'He mentioned you could see part of Domaine Lauriac from here,' Tuesday said. 'I wonder if that's it across there.' He pointed towards the horizon. Though with Tuesday's almost preternaturally sharp sniper's eyes, whatever he'd spotted in the distance could have been halfway across France.

But as they started out along the tall, ancient aqueduct bridge Ben wasn't watching where Tuesday was pointing, nor was he admiring the glorious view up and down the river valley. His attention was split between the road and the rear-view mirror, in which he could see the pair of fast-moving sports motorcycles that had been on their tail for the last couple of kilometres come slicing around the bend behind them, hit the straight and accelerate hard to catch up. They were the kind of race-bred machines that could blast from zero to sixty in the blink of an eye, effortlessly eclipsing the performance of most cars. The gap between themselves and the Espace was shrinking rapidly. One bike was being ridden solo, the other carrying a pillion passenger clad in the same armoured leathers and black-tinted visor as the rider.

Ben anticipated that in just a matter of seconds, they'd come screaming past the car like rockets. These empty, fantastically scenic roads were ideal for some high-octane fun and games, whether on two wheels or four. Given a machine like that to play with, he'd no doubt have been tempted himself to whack open the throttle and see what it could do.

But just instants later, Ben realised that he was wrong. As the motorbikes swiftly caught up with them, instead of shooting straight past they backed off their throttles and drew level with the car. That was strange enough, Ben thought – but what happened next was even stranger. The rider carrying the pillion passenger dabbed his brakes just enough to scrub off a little more speed, then accelerated again to come up the car's other flank.

Now Ben was driving along with a bike to each side of him, forcing him to steer closer to the middle of the road to allow them more space. *Fools*, he thought. This wasn't the kind of fun and games he could so easily approve of. Even though they'd slowed right down to match the car's velocity they were still doing a steady 135 kilometres an hour. Messing around like this at such speeds was taking silly risks that could end up with someone getting hurt.

'What the fuck are these numpties up to?' Jeff grumbled, staring out of the window. The riders and the pillion passenger seemed to stare back, their faces obscured behind their black visors.

By this time the speeding vehicles had hit the aqueduct bridge and the view opened up spectacularly all around, the glittering blue water to both sides far below. Ben had had enough of this tomfoolery. He eased off the gas and toed the brake pedal to let the motorcycles overtake. But as he decelerated to below 120 kilometres an hour, the riders did the same, remaining exactly level to each side of the car. The solo rider to their right, the two-up machine to their left.

'These are the kind of bikers that give bikers a bad name,' Tuesday said. 'Slow down more, Ben. Let them by.'

But the bikers didn't want to go by. They were about a third of the way across the aqueduct bridge by now. And then, just as Ben suddenly realised this wasn't any kind of game at all, that was when it happened.

Defensive driving was an important part of the training programme that the Le Val team drummed into their students. Ben was the lead instructor for that course, an expert in the sometimes dark art of evading attack on the road. A bodyguard team charged with transporting a VIP principal would be always on their guard in case of such attacks, which weren't entirely unpredictable or unexpected. Three business travellers innocently driving out to explore a property for sale would not be, and were rather more vulnerable to being taken by surprise.

And that, to Ben's sudden horror, was exactly the case here. *Caught napping, despite all his instincts, skill and experience.*

Even as his mind was still processing what was going on, he saw the pillion passenger on the left-side motorbike reach into his jacket with a gloved hand and pull out a micro-sized submachine pistol. A boxy black ultra-compact assassination tool. A short stubby barrel adapted to close-range execution. An extended pistol grip magazine filled with twenty rounds of lethal 9mm power.

Now Ben's instincts and training came rushing into play and his mind focused. He didn't know why this was happening, and right now it didn't matter. What mattered was getting out of this alive. Before the shooter could pull the trigger, he slammed on the brakes and simultaneously twisted the wheel, veering the car violently left to swipe the motorcycle with his wing as he decelerated harshly past it.

But the rider's instincts and reflexes were pretty sharp, too, and he managed to wobble his machine out of the way to avoid being taken out. These were fantastically agile machines, as instantly manoeuvrable as they were blisteringly fast. They could lose speed much faster than the car, while if Ben braked any harder he risked going into a skid. Clutching the machine's rear grab rail with one hand and pointing his weapon with the other, the pillion passenger sprayed rounds into the side of the Espace. Windows burst into fragments and bullets punched through the doors and bodyshell.

Then Ben deployed the opposite tactic and hit the gas, surging forward with all the power the car could muster. The engine howled. Jeff and Tuesday had thrown themselves down low into their footwells. Ben grappled with the wheel as the wildly accelerating Espace weaved and swayed all over the bridge road on its wallowy suspension. They'd made it halfway across the bridge by now, racing towards the opposite river bank with the aluminium safety barriers streaking by to the left and right. The engine was being pushed to its limits and the speedometer was climbing back towards its upper reaches, revs into the red.

But only a fool would have held out any hope of outrunning the sports bikes in a vehicle like this. They came charging up behind the car's tail, catching up as though it had been standing still. The pillion passenger leaned past the rider in front of him and let off another burst of gunfire that peppered the back of the Espace and blew out its rear screen.

In the kind of scenario that Le Val schooled its trainees in, normally the occupants of the car would be returning fire at this point. That was, if they'd been armed and ready for trouble: in which case Ben would have brought them to a screeching halt in the middle of the road and the tables would have been turned as the attackers suddenly faced being outgunned by determined professional resistance. As things were, though, all Ben could do was to try to get away – but he was caught in a bad situation and he knew it. Another rattle of fire and the tiny hammer blows of bullets perforating metal and chewing up plastic; and this time he felt the back tyres blow out, both at once, and the rear of the car beginning to drift out of control.

He couldn't hold it. Nobody could have, not at this speed, not in this car. Despite everything Ben could do the front wheels broke their grip on the road and the vehicle started to slide, then spin around. The crash barrier at the edge of the bridge flashed towards them. He heard Jeff yell something. He braced for impact.

And then the car hit the barrier, went smashing straight through with a crunch of buckling aluminium and hurtled off the edge of the aqueduct and into empty air with nothing but blue water below.

Chapter 10

Jacques and Bertrand braked their motorcycles to a halt next to the ragged hole in the safety barrier. Chrétien, who had been the pillion passenger, hopped off the back of the machine as the two riders quickly dismounted, killed their engines and rested the bikes on their sidestands. The three of them hurried over to the smashed barrier just in time to see the falling car hit the water with a thunderous splash, the white spray flying almost to the top of the aqueduct. They removed their helmets, leaned out over the railing and watched the ripples spread outward in a wide circle. The rear of the car bobbed clear of the water, slowly beginning to sink deeper and rotate roof-down as it disappeared.

'They're finished,' Bertrand said. 'Surely nobody could have survived that fall.'

Jacques's face was hard. 'You may be right, Brother. But I'd rather make sure. Chrétien, give them another burst.'

Chrétien glanced up and down the empty road to ensure they still had no witnesses. Then clapped a fresh magazine into the butt of his submachine pistol, aimed down at the sinking car and let off a long, loud stream of gunfire until the magazine was empty again. The noise echoed off the tall aqueduct and rolled across the river valley. Some of his bullets holed the back of the vehicle, while others struck the water around it. There was no telling how effective or necessary they might have been. The three men stood in silence and watched impassively as the car sank out of sight. Then it was gone, leaving just a circle of broken water.

'That's it, then,' Bertrand said. 'Come on, let's get out of here before someone comes.'

Jacques shook his head. 'No, wait a minute or so. If nobody comes up, *then* we can get out of here. And only then.'

And so they went on watching the wide ring of empty river where the car had vanished. None of them really expected to see any survivors appear, but just in case they did, Chrétien had another full magazine ready to pepper them with. Bertrand was keeping one eye on his watch. After sixty silent seconds and no sign of life below he called out, 'One minute.'

'Give it one more,' Jacques said. 'Just to be absolutely certain.'

They gave it another full rotation of Bertrand's second hand. Still no movement from below. 'That's it,' Bertrand said. 'Any of them who weren't already dead must have drowned by now. Our job is done here.'

Jacques nodded. 'Our job here, yes. But we have more work to do, Brothers. Next we have to go back to the villa and take care of the woman.'

'We already tried, remember?' Chrétien reminded him. 'The American lied to us. She's not there any longer.'

'Perhaps he did, perhaps not. Either way, we have no choice but to keep trying until we get her. Now let's go.'

Chrétien replaced his weapon in its shoulder holster beneath his armoured leather jacket. The three of them donned their helmets, flipped down the black visors, then walked back to the motorcycles. Jacques and Bertrand climbed on and restarted their engines and Chrétien hopped on behind Bertrand. They U-turned on the bridge and then accelerated hard away with a howl that echoed over the river.

Chapter 11

Two minutes earlier

It was more than a two-hundred-foot drop. For the occupants of the falling car the long, curving, almost graceful nose-dive towards the water seemed to last for ever, a surreal moment suspended in time making them feel strangely weightless.

But they weren't weightless. They were trapped inside a steel cage weighing one and a half tons and plummeting downwards at terminal velocity as the surface of the river rushed up to meet them. Ben had time to yell 'Hold on!' Then came the massive, wrenching, bone-jarring impact as they hit the water with a splash like a bomb exploding, and the force deployed the front airbags to prevent the sudden, total deceleration from tearing him and Jeff out of their seats and through the windscreen. Shattered water and a torrent of bubbles rushed up the sides of the car and the river engulfed them. The vehicle bobbed up briefly with its tail in the air, then rapidly began to sink back down as the river flooded in through the broken windows and the nose-heavy weight of the engine dragged it into the depths.

For the first few instants Ben was still stunned by the impact, disorientated and not even sure if he was dead or alive. But he was quickly brought to his senses as the cold water climbed up his body, reached his chest, then his chin, then closed over his nose. Bubbles streamed from his mouth as he struggled to undo his seatbelt and then push himself out from behind the spent airbag. To his right in the front passenger seat, Jeff was hanging limply against his belt and all but unconscious as the water swallowed him up. Ben released the clasp of the belt and tried to grapple Jeff out of his seat, but he was a dead weight and almost impossible to move. The car was submerging fast, gradually turning roof-down as it slipped below the surface. The attackers were still firing on it from the bridge above. Bullets smacked the water and spiralled past leaving little silvery trails of bubbles in their wake.

Ben swallowed a last lungful of air as the car went under. Twisting around, he peered into the back seats at Tuesday. Tuesday was an excellent swimmer. Ben was thinking that two of them could help Jeff out of the car and get him safely up to the surface.

Tuesday was leaning sideways against the inside of the rear door. The growing murk made it hard to see, and at first Ben thought he was trying to shoulder it open to make his escape. But he wasn't moving. Then Ben saw the brownish cloud drifting like smoke around Tuesday's upper half.

Understanding hit him harder than the impact of the crash and chilled his blood colder than the water. Because the brownish cloud was blood. It was coming from where a bullet had struck Tuesday fatally in the back of the head. His eyes stared unblinking at Ben and no bubbles came from his open mouth. He'd been dead before they hit the river, probably even before they flew off the edge of the bridge.

In that moment of horrified realisation Ben knew he faced the same grim choice he'd faced before on the battlefield, when all hell was breaking loose and the close comrade with whom he'd been fighting side by side was suddenly, bloodily cut down right next to him. He could let shock and despair overwhelm him, and then he would die too. Or he could focus, close his mind to it for the moment and concentrate on saving himself and Jeff. Even a fit, trained man could last only a minute or so underwater without breathing gear and that limited time was slipping away fast. Seconds counted for those who needed to survive. The dead were past caring.

Ben turned away from his friend's body. He reached across Jeff and tried to open his door, but as the car sank deeper the force of the water pressure made the door as immovable as if it had been welded shut. It was getting darker and darker inside the cabin as they slipped further from the surface. How deep the river was, Ben had no idea and he had no intention of sticking around to find out. Already his lungs felt ready to explode. He used his elbow to smash away the window glass instead, and with a sinew-ripping effort born out of desperation and panic managed to heave Jeff's limp upper half out of the window, then shove him out the rest of the way. The moment he was free of the car he began to sink, a stream of bubbles coming from his mouth. If he wasn't half-drowned already he soon would be.

Ben gave Tuesday in the back a last regretful glance, said a quick goodbye and then piled out of the smashed window after Jeff, swimming hard to grab him before he sank completely out of sight. Wrapping one arm around his friend's waist Ben kicked upwards for the shimmer of milky sunlight that penetrated the surface above them. To rescue an unconscious man in deep water, swimming one-armed with your boots on and barely enough oxygen left in your own body to stay conscious: it was tough, but it was among the many tough jobs Ben had been trained for.

A few moments longer, and he was sure his lungs would have burst. He broke the surface and sucked in the fresh air with a hissing gasp. They'd emerged a few metres from where the car had hit the water. Directly above them was the underside of the bridge, its massive ancient arched supports resting on great plinths of stone that jutted from the water. It was towards one of those that Ben dragged Jeff's limp form through the water, keeping his head above the surface with an arm around his chest and paddling hard.

The firing from the top of the bridge had stopped. Ben guessed that the attackers were still up there, peering down at the wide circle of white ripples that were the only visible trace of the sunken car. A few moments later, as he was heaving Jeff bodily up onto the stone plinth, he heard the sound of the motorcycles taking off the way they'd come at high speed. Then they were gone.

Ben had thought that his days of praying to God were behind him. But he prayed fervently again now, that he hadn't just lost both of his best friends in the world. And as he dragged Jeff clear of the river and laid him down on his side to let the water drain from his lungs, he realised that his prayer had been answered. Jeff's pulse was faint, but he was still alive. And nothing mattered more to Ben at this moment than keeping him that way.

For the next several minutes Ben relentlessly performed all the resuscitation techniques he'd ever learned, speaking to his friend the whole time. Gradually Jeff's pulse began to beat more strongly and some of the colour returned to his face. Then his eyes fluttered open, he began to cough violently and Ben rolled him back over onto his side so that he could retch up the last of the river water he'd swallowed. He tried to say something, but he was too weak.

As an additional first-aid method they didn't teach in official classes, Ben fed Jeff a few gulps of whisky from the battered old hip flask he carried. Then he took some for himself. They both needed it.

'You're okay,' Ben told him. 'You made it. Take it easy and rest, now. I'm going to call for help as fast as I can.' His phone was totally waterlogged and useless. Their only means of assistance would be to find a nearby farmhouse or stop a passing motorist.

Jeff tried again to speak and was racked by a fit of coughing. Struggling to sit upright he stared urgently around him, scanning first the stone bridge support and then the water around it as if searching for something. Ben knew very well what he was searching for. Then Jeff's bloodshot eyes fixed on Ben with an agonised look, he gripped his arm tightly and managed at last to get out some words. 'Where's Tuesday? Where is he?'

And Ben had to tell him.

Chapter 12

Tuesday Fletcher was a man with whom Ben had had a deep and close friendship for a long time. With his warm, generous heart and that irrepressible cheery smile that nothing seemed to be able to dampen, he'd become far more than just another member of the gang. Now that that heart had beat its last and the dazzling smile would never be seen again, a light had gone out within Ben's soul that couldn't be relit.

But in some ways the connection between Tuesday and Jeff had been even tighter. Behind the banter and the occasional bickering was that special kind of bond of comradeship and total, unquestioning mutual trust that could only really be understood by men who depended on one another for their very lives. All those times that Ben had been absent from Le Val while off on some escapade, Jeff and Tuesday had been left to forge that friendship even more strongly. And on many occasions the pair had rallied to Ben's aid when situations proved to be more than one man could handle on his own.

As brutally hard as this was going to hit Ben when the full reality sank in, he knew that it was going to affect Jeff even more.

Jeff's first reaction to being told was to refuse to accept it. 'No. *No.*' The colour that had returned to his face was suddenly drained away again and he looked grey and utterly empty.

'He's gone, Jeff,' Ben repeated softly, laying a hand on his friend's shoulder. His own words sounded so surreal and impossible to him that he could barely believe them either. 'He took a bullet. It was quick. He wouldn't have suffered.' As though that were any consolation.

Jeff just shook his head. 'It's not true. It can't be.' But the look in Ben's eyes told him that it was.

Both of them had experienced serious losses before. But this was too much to bear, and as they digested the news a pall of something like despair came over them. There were no words, nothing to be said. Not even to ask who had done this, and why. Those questions would inevitably follow soon enough.

They sat for a while and just gazed at the spot where the car had sunk. Tuesday was down there somewhere, so close by and yet so irretrievably beyond reach. Then, slowly, doggedly, dazed and numb like two men in a trance they made their way up the embankment to where a little service road ran alongside the foot of the bridge. Jeff was limping from an ankle injury sustained in the crash, though at this moment his leg could have been hanging off and he wouldn't have given a damn about it. Nonetheless, when they reached level ground Ben made him sit so that he could inspect the swollen, angrily reddened ankle. 'Looks like you've got a nasty sprain, that's all. But you can't be walking on it. You'd better stay here while I go for help.'

Ben reluctantly left his friend alone and still staring disconsolately down at the water, and set off. The cicadas sang their chirping chorus from the yellowed grass by the roadsides and the sun burned down more fiercely, already beginning to dry off his clothes as he walked. The service road climbed up to eventually rejoin the main route along which they'd come. He paused to look around at the scene of the attack, in case some fresh clue might jump out at him.

There were a lot of black tyre marks on the road, and fragments of glass and shattered taillight from where bullets had struck the car. But apart from those, the smashed safety barrier and the scattered empty brass cartridge cases that the motorcycle pillion shooter had left strewn along the bridge there was little trace of what had happened here that morning, let alone any evidence that might point to the reason behind it. The attackers on their motorcycles could be anywhere by now.

Still feeling utterly numb, Ben walked the empty road for two kilometres under the hot sun before he saw a car approaching and flagged it down. By now it was getting towards noon. The driver and passenger were an older couple who lived locally, and were horrified to hear about the accident. He told them none of what had really happened, only that the car had spun out of control and gone off the bridge. They willingly offered the use of a phone to call emergency services, and gave Ben a lift back down the road. They would have hung around waiting with them for the police and ambulance to arrive if Ben hadn't gently insisted otherwise. The last thing he and his friend needed right now was company, however sympathetic.

It was a very different Jeff that he found sitting there on his return. During the time he'd been left by himself the initial shock had begun to subside and his friend's face reflected the same hard, cold fury that had begun to well up inside Ben, too. Jeff was so choked with emotion that he could barely speak. He blinked away tears of rage and grief as he managed to say, 'The bastards who did this had better pray we never find them. But we will, mate. We will.'

Ben and Jeff had crossed paths with a lot of very nasty characters in their day, and some old scores from the past had never been settled. Even when the original bad guys were no longer around, there was always the possibility of a vengeful associate, a brother, a sister, a son, a daughter. Was that what they had to thank for this? But who would have known they were even here? How could such a precise attack, in this place, at that moment, have been orchestrated?

Neither of them had the remotest idea. For the moment there seemed little point in asking the questions that were burning inside each of their heads. But Ben knew they'd be hearing them over and over again before long.

'The police will be here soon,' he said. 'They're going to be wanting a lot of answers when they pull that car out of the water and realise this was no accident. Not to mention when they find the rest of these.'

He showed Jeff the spent shell cases he'd picked off the road. They were standard nine-millimetre rounds, suited for pistols and pistol-calibre submachine guns and carbines, manufactured by the same ammunition manufacturer based in Užice, Serbia, from whom Le Val also made bulk orders. There was nothing in any way distinctive about them, and Ben very much doubted whether any would show fingerprint evidence. These shooters were too professional for that. Not that you had to be a genius to pull on a pair of gloves to load ammo from its box into a weapon magazine. In all kinds of other ways, the slickness and efficiency of the attack bore the hallmarks of expertise. Whoever they were, they'd done this kind of thing before.

'Give me a fucking cigarette,' Jeff muttered.

'You don't smoke. And they're wet anyway.' Or else Ben would have been smoking his way through them already.

'Then let me have another drink from that flask.'

They shared the rest of the whisky between them while the hot sun dried off their clothes and they waited for the sound of sirens to come wailing down the valley. It wasn't too long before a pair of police cars, one marked and the other unmarked, came swooping down the service road and pulled up at the base of the aqueduct. 'That all we get?' Jeff muttered.

'Be careful what you wish for,' Ben said. As a rule, the fewer cops he had to deal with, the better.

From the unmarked car stepped a small plain-clothes officer who introduced himself as Gardien-brigadier Pierre Grosjean of the Police Municipale. He might have been only a small-time rural cop with generally little to do and pretty much at the bottom rung of the detective ladder, but Ben instantly twigged him as the ambitious type set on proving himself. He took their details and those of the deceased and asked a few preliminary questions about what had happened, to which Ben did all the answering in French while Jeff just glared quietly, then set about organising the recovery of the sunken car. A pair of ambulances arrived soon afterwards.

It took much longer for the necessary diver team and underwater salvage equipment to be sent out from the gendarmerie in Limoux. The police sealed off the aqueduct and a section of the road in both directions while a crane lorry lowered a cable from the top of the bridge, which the police divers attached to the sunken car. Then the crane ground into action and, inch by inch, the cable reeled the Renault Espace from the water.

Gardien-brigadier Grosjean placed himself at the heart of all this activity like a general commanding his troops, though in fact he contributed very little other than a lot of strutting about and shouting into a radio. The real work was carried out by the diver and paramedic team whose job it was to extract Tuesday's body from the wreck. He was pronounced dead at the scene by a medical examiner, zipped into a bodybag and then transferred into a waiting ambulance, which drove off with no need for siren or flashing lights.

Ben and Jeff watched the entire torturous, hours-long process from the sidelines. Another paramedic had examined Jeff's injured ankle and agreed with Ben's diagnosis of a sprain rather than a fracture, although they recommended that Jeff let himself be carried off to the local hospital by the second ambulance. He staunchly refused any medical treatment, as Ben had known he would.

With the body removed from the scene and the wreck of the car loaded onto a flatbed trailer, it was time at last for Gardien-brigadier Grosjean to turn his attention back to the two survivors. The cops had been counting the bullet holes in the recovered vehicle, while others had been scouring the roadside and gathered up a large collection of recently-fired empty shell casings. This was by far the most sensational incident of Grosjean's career, and he was jumping with barely-contained excitement. 'Messieurs, it seems there is much more to this situation than a mere tragic road accident. I suggest we continue this conversation back at the station.'

Chapter 13

The headquarters of the Police Municipale de Quillan were in a small, shabby and very unostentatious building in a narrow dingy street of the town. After being made to wait for nearly two hours in an interview room that smelled of disinfectant, Ben and Jeff were joined by Grosjean and another officer and made to go through the whole story again. As the interview was being conducted in French, it fell on Ben to do most of the talking like before. It was excruciatingly painful to have to relive all the details but he laid it all out for them, leaving nothing out. The second cop took notes while Grosjean listened with a sardonic expression that Ben disliked intensely. His first impressions of the man weren't getting any better.

'It's suddenly all happening in my sleepy little district,' Grosjean said, looking at them beadily with a raised eyebrow. 'First a man, a compatriot of yours, gets beaten almost to death in his apartment. Now we have what looks like a partially successful assassination attempt aimed at disposing of three more. And it all begins with the sudden appearance of you gentlemen on the scene. I'm wondering why that should be.'

This was a line of questioning Ben disliked even more, and it took him aback. 'You're talking about Sadler? Yes, we know about him. But—'

'Indeed you do,' Grosjean interrupted. 'You were seen dining out together just hours before three violent intruders broke into his home. It's also come to my attention that you paid a visit to Monsieur Sadler's offices this morning.'

'Well, ain't this one well informed,' Jeff muttered, getting the gist and not liking it any more than Ben. He was looking at Grosjean as though at any moment he might lunge across the table and rip that officious little look off his face.

'I've told you that we're here in the south to look at properties,' Ben re-explained as patiently as he could. 'Matthew Sadler is the agent handling the sale. That's as far as our connection with him goes. We never met him until yesterday, and before that we only spoke a couple of times on the phone. As to why anyone would want to hurt him, I have no idea. As I understand it, he's been the victim of a home invasion, or a robbery. I see no connection to the attack on us this morning.'

Grosjean considered that for a moment, drumming his fingers on the table and looking unconvinced. 'A robbery in which nothing was stolen. Curious, *non*? It leaves one wondering about other possible motives.'

This was wasting time. Ben said, 'He's a man of taste who likes expensive things. That fifteenth-century apartment of his is probably full of items that would tempt a thief. If nothing was taken, maybe that's because the neighbour raised the alarm.'

'Believe me, Monsieur 'Ope' – like many native French speakers Grosjean had the habit of dropping the H, unless he was doing it just to annoy – 'I am fully aware of the particulars. I make it my business to know all that happens in my little town.'

'Then let me remind you that you also have a murder victim lying in the morgue with a bullet in his head. I thought that's what we were here to talk about.'

'I had not forgotten that, I assure you. Nonetheless it's my job to investigate the evidence before me and probe for possible connections.' Grosjean shrugged. 'Now here we are, dealing with two very serious and dramatic incidents that have occurred seemingly out of the blue and in very close time proximity. You say they are unrelated; and perhaps they are, although that would seem to be a remarkable coincidence, don't you think? And such coincidences get me curious. Which is the reason I have looked into your records: that is to say, your own, Monsieur Dekker's and those of the deceased.'

Ben found it hard to hear Tuesday being referred to as 'the deceased'. He also found it hard to believe that this jumped-up low-ranking provincial cop would have the authority to access their military files – especially his and Jeff's, whose sensitive nature made them accessible to only a very few. More likely, all Grosjean had done was read their brief, sketchy bio details on the Le Val website. That would explain what he'd been doing while keeping them waiting in this poky room. It wasn't an interview. It was an interrogation, and Grosjean seemed to think he was onto something.

'Fine,' Ben said. 'Then you know what line of business we're in. How is that relevant here?'

Grosjean gave another insouciant shrug. 'Only insofar as men of your training and background are known, are they not, to have a certain propensity for violent action. A certain willingness to inflict harm. For instance, I imagine it would present no problems for someone like that to force their way into a man's home in the middle of the night, drag him from his bed, beat him to a bloody pulp and confine him to the hospital.'

'If I didn't know better, I'd think that sounded like an accusation,' Ben said. He was beginning to worry about the way Jeff was looking at Grosjean. If the Gardien-brigadier didn't watch out, he might be about to get a taste of violent action himself.

Grosjean smiled thinly. 'Here's another curious coincidence that has caught my attention. After Monsieur Sadler's neighbour raised the alarm at around three o'clock this morning, certainly saving him from being beaten to death, three men were seen running from the building. *Three* men,' he repeated for emphasis.

'And there were three of us,' Ben said. 'I get it.'

'I've had it with listening to this shit,' Jeff said to Ben, his anger suddenly flaring and his fists clenching. 'Is this bastard actually saying that you, me and Tuesday broke into Sadler's place and beat him half to death, just after we'd all been sitting having dinner? And were set to meet him for coffee next morning? Is he out of his fucking mind?' Jeff turned on Grosjean with thunder in his eyes.

'Take it easy, Jeff,' Ben warned his friend, before he did something stupid. One punch from Jeff, and the cop would find himself in the hospital alongside Sadler – while they went straight off to jail. That wasn't going to help them find the people who'd shot Tuesday.

Grosjean's smile dropped and he leaned across the table, pointing at them. 'I too have had enough of this *merde*. So let us get down to the straight talk, as you say in English.

Where were each of you, as well as the deceased, between two-thirty and three this morning?'

'I suggest you go and speak to the manager at our hotel,' Ben said coolly. 'He'll tell you that we were there at that time.'

'And how would he know that?' Grosjean scoffed. 'Was he sleeping in the same bed with you?' He burst out laughing at his own joke and nudged the uniformed officer beside him, who seemed to find his boss's wit no less amusing.

Ben replied, 'No, he was with us while we had to attend to another of the guests, an elderly Danish gentleman who suffered from some health issues during the night and woke up the whole hotel. It went on for quite a while and we didn't get back to bed until around three-fifteen. Now, I'm not a professional detective, but I'd say that makes it fairly unlikely that at the same time the three of us were also on the other side of town, breaking into the apartment of the man we came all this way to do business with, and beating the hell out of him. Does that satisfy you?'

From the look on his face, Grosjean seemed more disappointed than satisfied, now that his budding little crime theory had just gone *pop*. 'Very well,' he said gruffly. 'But I will be sure to ascertain that with the hotel manager. I happen to know him personally.'

'Probably members of the same golf club,' Jeff growled.

'You do that,' Ben said. 'And now that we've cleared up the matter of our innocence, perhaps you might also try to ascertain who shot our friend and tried to kill us. Or better still, maybe you should just stick to rescuing kittens out of trees and catching pickpockets.'

Grosjean flushed. 'And what is that supposed to mean?'

'It means, Monsieur le Gardien-brigadier, that we don't have an awful lot of faith in your policing abilities. Wouldn't want you to go accusing the wrong person, now would we?'

'That wouldn't do at all,' said Jeff, still looking as though he wanted to knock the cop into next week.

Grosjean looked at them and pursed his lips. 'Please rest assured,' he said officiously, 'that the Police Municipale will be doing all we can to get to the bottom of this tragic incident.'

'And what about placing a couple of men on guard at the hospital for the victim's protection?' Ben asked.

'I hardly think that anyone is going to make a further attempt on his life as he lies there surrounded by doctors and nurses,' Grosjean sneered. 'In any case my department is short-staffed enough as it is without wasting manpower.' He stood. 'Thank you, Messieurs. I think that will be all for now. However I would request that you don't leave town for the next couple of days, in case I require to speak with you again.'

'Oh, we'll be around, all right,' Jeff said. 'We're not going anywhere.'

They were shown out of the police station and back out into the narrow, dingy street. It was after six in the afternoon, but even in the shade of the close-set buildings the sun was baking down on them. 'Fuck that Grosjean and his "tragic incident",' Jeff said sourly. 'Someone did this. It didn't just *happen*.'

'He's just trying to do his job,' Ben said. 'No surprises that a guy like that is way out of his depth.'

'Yeah, well, fuck him anyway. He's not going to be any help to us.'

'Nope,' Ben agreed. 'And I wouldn't have it any other way. He'd only get under our feet.'

Jeff nodded. He closed his eyes and leaned against the pitted stone wall. 'Christ, Ben. Tell me this is just some screwed-up dream I'm having.'

'If that's what it is,' Ben said, 'I wouldn't mind waking up out of it myself.'

The sun had dried out his remaining Gauloises. He lit one for himself and one for Jeff, and they stood and smoked in silence. Then with nowhere to go, the two of them started walking slowly up the street. Jeff was still hobbling badly on his damaged ankle. 'You need a doctor to look at that,' Ben said.

'Fuck doctors too,' Jeff muttered. 'Fuck everything. I need a drink, is what I need.'

And at this moment Ben couldn't think of a much better idea. Finding a little bar a little way further up the street, they headed for the coolest and shadiest part of the lounge. Neither had eaten all day but they weren't interested in food. Only in blasting the sense of acute grief from their heads. Which would only be delaying the onset of the worst of the pain, but they didn't care.

'What can I offer you, Messieurs?' said the beaming waiter, walking over to the table.

'Whisky,' Ben said.

'Certainly. We have a wide selection.'

'Just bring whisky,' Ben said.

'Very well. Two glasses? Would you like ice? Water?'

'Two bottles,' Ben said. 'You can bring glasses as well, but no ice, no water.'

The waiter baulked a little at the order, then saw the two pairs of gaunt, hollow eyes looking back up at him and said hesitantly, 'Uh, you're not going to cause any trouble in here, are you?'

'Not unless you cause it first,' Ben told him, lighting another cigarette. The waiter stared, disappeared and came back with their two bottles and a pair of empty tumblers.

Ben filled them up. The first of many. Then he shook his head and sighed. The words he was about to say, he'd never thought he would hear from his own lips. Raising his glass, he said, 'Here's to our friend Tuesday. Gone but never forgotten.'

'To Tuesday,' Jeff said. They raised their glasses, clinked, and drained them empty in one swallow. Ben instantly snatched up the bottle and refilled them to the brim.

Starting as they meant to go on. It was going to be a long evening.

Chapter 14

Earlier that day

The three men going by the names of Jacques, Bertrand and Chrétien hustled away from the scene of the crash. Not returning to Quillan, instead the motorcycles sped off on the most direct route through the rugged Languedoc countryside to the village of Tarascon-sur-Ariège. Their business didn't concern the sleepy little hamlet itself, with its traditional red-roofed houses, the nearby vineyards, the old stone bridge over the river and the twelfth-century abbey whose tower dominated the landscape. They rode on through the village and continued up the steep, winding hill road beyond it for two kilometres, where the house called Villa Blanche was situated.

They had been here before, because it was the base that the American and his woman had been using during their stay in the region, and the same address they'd beaten and tortured out of him before they killed him. Their first visit to the place, in the hope of finding her and dealing with her in the same way, had proved fruitless. But as Jacques had said, they needed to keep trying until they got her. Nothing could deter them from fulfilling their mission.

So as not to draw attention to themselves they left the motorcycles hidden and made their final approach to the villa on foot, sweltering in their heavy leathers under the hot sun. It was a forested area and the side of the property's walled grounds facing the village below was screened from view of the house by a stretch of coniferous oak woodland. Like before, the three men trudged along a path through the trees where wild boar tracks were visible in the dry earth. When they'd skirted the perimeter right around to the rear, they used the same crumbled hole in the stone wall to enter the grounds. From there they sneaked across to the house. Chrétien was ready with his submachine pistol and his companions had their knives. There had been no need to bring along the other tools of the trade, like thin rope to bind the woman up with, a roll of broad tape and a cloth bag to gag and blindfold her. Capture was not their plan; their purpose was simply to kill.

But once again, they were to be disappointed. 'Her car's still not here,' Bertrand said, eyeing the empty garage.

'Just as I suspected, we're wasting our time,' complained Chrétien. 'She won't be back. Not after finding the lock forced. I told you it was a mistake to leave traces like that.'

'She could still be inside.'

Jacques led them around to the conservatory entrance where they'd already jemmied their way in on their earlier visit. But as they entered the villa and checked from room to room, just like before the only signs of her were the articles of female clothing in the wardrobe and some toiletries in the bathroom. Items like a toothbrush and hairbrush were still missing as they'd been on their first tour of the house, suggesting that she'd gone off somewhere for a few days.

'What do we do now?' Bertrand asked. 'I think the American's warning must have frightened her away. If she's even still in France, we have no hope of finding her.'

'She's left her things here. That means she'll be back,' Jacques insisted. 'Be patient, Brother. We'll get her soon enough.'

The same long, hot trudge back along the wild boar path through the trees to where they'd left the bikes; then they strapped on their helmets, sped back down the hill to Tarascon-sur-Ariège and from there to their remote fortress in the hills. Once they'd gratefully stripped off their stifling leathers, quenched their thirst and cooled down a little, they knelt together on the stone floor in front of the plain wooden cross on a low bench that served them as an altar. They bowed their heads, closed their eyes and clasped their hands. Jacques led the prayer, speaking solemnly in Latin as they made their thanks to God for the successful outcome of their morning's mission.

'Amen.'

'Amen.'

When their prayers were over, they sat at an outside terrace under the shade of an awning to eat a simple meal of bread and cheese. A modest cupful of wine was allowed, as the strictures of their religion fell short of complete asceticism. As they ate and drank, they discussed the progress of their mission so far.

'We have done well, Brothers. Now that three of the four witnesses have been eliminated, that leaves only the matter of the other Englishman, Sadler.'

'How can we get to him again?' Chrétien wondered out loud.

'I've been pondering the best way,' Jacques said. 'We can't risk doing it in the hospital. It's too public, too obvious, and we must be cautious to cover our tracks as much as possible. We've already drawn a great deal of attention to ourselves this morning.'

'We were foolish not to kill him when we had the chance,' grunted Bertrand, carving another slice of cheese.

Jacques shook his head. 'We were unlucky, that's all. We couldn't afford to be caught in the act. But have faith. Another chance will come.'

'You always say that, Brother,' Chrétien said with a snort. 'Like with the woman. What makes you think she'll be so easy to catch?'

'I'm in charge of this operation,' Jacques reminded him. 'And it would benefit you not to question my authority. Regarding Sadler, our plan now is to bide our time until he recovers and is sent home. Then we'll arrange for some accident to befall him. As for the woman, we can't assume she has fled in response to the American's warning, and so we must keep trying. My belief is that wherever she has gone, her absence is only temporary and she will soon return to the villa if only to collect her things. Let's finish our meal, rest for a few hours and go back there again tonight.'

Bertrand shrugged. 'Fine. But not on motorcycles this time. The nights are cold. And I suggest we should take along more than just one gun. It's not as if we don't have plenty more. If we're going to do it, let's do it properly.'

'Are you saying I can't shoot?' Chrétien snapped at his colleague. Turning to Jacques he said, 'Very well, Brother. But if she still isn't there?'

‘If she still isn’t there, we’ll try again the following night. For as long as it takes.’ Jacques finished his cup of wine, then leaned forward across the table to fix his two associates with a steely, penetrating eye. ‘As I’m sure I need not remind either of you, this is a sacred mission that has been entrusted to us in the names of our venerated brethren of the past. You and I have sworn an oath to protect the holy secret that our forebears have fought and died to keep safe for over nine hundred years. And our mission isn’t complete until all those who stand to threaten it are rotting in their graves.’

Chapter 15

They say that first night is always the worst, when the grief is at its rawest. The reality for Ben and Jeff was that the many more to follow wouldn't be appreciably any better, and that their loss was a shared wound that would never fully heal if they lived to be a hundred years old. But whatever lay in store for them, this first stage of acute mourning would have to be brief, because now they had unfinished business to attend to.

It had been after midnight by the time the bar staff finally tossed them out. There'd been no trouble and they weren't even drunk. All the whisky in the world couldn't have dulled the edge of what they were feeling. The same barman who'd been worried about them earlier now took pity on them and called for a taxi to take them home, seeing as both their phones had stopped working after their dunking in the river that morning.

Returning to his room, Ben collapsed fully clothed on the bed and didn't so much fall asleep as pass out from exhaustion. The light of dawn streaming through his window woke him, along with the cold hard realisation that yesterday hadn't been a dream. He felt headachey and nauseous after last night's extended drinking session but his memory was painfully clear.

He sat on the edge of the bed and worked on focusing his thoughts until the deep sadness that threatened to overwhelm him faded somewhat into the background and he was as ready as he could be to face the day. Life had to go on somehow, and so he forced himself to grind through his exercise routine even more savagely than usual. After a coffee and a Gauloise, neither of which tasted of anything to him, he went to Jeff's room, expecting him to be up. But Jeff hadn't yet managed to get out of bed. He'd awoken that morning to find his injured ankle swollen and purple and hurting so badly he could barely move, let alone put any weight on it.

'I told you you should have had it seen to,' Ben reminded him.

'Oh, hark at the wise virgin,' Jeff snapped. 'Screw it. I'll cut the bloody thing off if I have to. Nothing's gonna stop me.'

'Maybe common sense won't stop you,' Ben warned his friend. 'But I will. I'm getting the hotel to call a doctor and one peep of protest from you, I'll break both your legs so you can't even try to walk. Got it?'

'I can't fucking believe this has happened to me. I got things to do!'

'Yes, you have,' Ben said. 'Number one is to get that thing into a plaster and healed up properly. Number two, there are a lot of shitty details to attend to which I frankly don't have the courage to do myself. Such as calling Le Val and telling them what's happened and arranging for Tuesday's things to be taken home. Then someone's got to break the news to his family in Jamaica. Once the cops have finished with him we're going to fly his body there to be buried with his kinfolks. You and I will be there to lay him to rest, and I expect you to be standing on your own two feet by then. Because woe betide you if you're not.'

Jeff struggled to get out of bed, but the pain was too much and he fell back with a stifled moan of agony. 'All right. I'll take care of it. What about you?'

'Me? I'm going to do what I always do, when someone harms someone I cared about. Take it easy, Jeff. I'll see you when I see you.'

Ben closed Jeff's door without waiting for a reply and strode away down the corridor, filled with a dark energy to face whatever was coming next. He loved his old friend as much as he'd loved Tuesday and wouldn't have willingly chosen to leave him behind like this – but in his heart he was glad at the opportunity. He'd always worked best when he worked alone. It gave him the space to operate his own way unimpeded.

And when Ben operated his own way unimpeded, that meant the as-yet-unknown enemy were about to encounter something they couldn't have imagined in their worst nightmares. Whoever they were, however he was to find them, their fate was sealed because he was coming for them now. He wouldn't rest until this was over. And when it was over, they'd be the ones resting. For all eternity.

He gathered his belongings from his room. There wasn't much, because he always travelled as light as possible and had only his old green military haversack for luggage. Downstairs in the lobby, he spoke to the manager – who'd already been on the phone to Gardien-brigadier Grosjean that morning to corroborate their alibi for the night before – and arranged for a doctor and an ambulance to be sent over to attend to Jeff. News of the fatal crash had seemingly yet to reach the manager's ears, though no doubt it soon would. Ben said nothing about what had happened, only that neither he nor Monsieur Fletcher would be needing their rooms any longer, and settled the two bills in cash while asking to keep the third room on for an extra day or two.

Then he stepped outside into the bright sun, took a deep breath, looked around him, and said out loud, 'Right. Let's get moving.'

There were certain things he was going to need before he could progress to the next stage, and he'd already decided on the quickest and most efficient way to get them. But first things first. He walked to the nearby square where a corner brasserie with tables and parasols out on the street offered cheap, basic food, and without caring much what he ate he devoured a large breakfast just to replenish his energy levels. Then he grabbed a taxi from a cab stand and drove out to the private aerodrome a few kilometres away where they'd left Jeff's plane.

Ben didn't have the official pilot's licence that his friend had gone through all the necessary processes to obtain. But he'd learned the skills while in the military, flown everything in his day from seaplanes to jets to helicopter gunships, and he'd never crashed an aircraft except on purpose or after being shot down by fighters. He reckoned he was safe enough for the five-hundred-nautical-mile one-way trip he was about to make.

Without reporting to the airfield's reception office he headed straight for the hangar where the Skyhawk was stored. 'Flying coffin' was one of the kinder expressions Tuesday had used to describe Jeff's pride and joy, as Ben now remembered with a pang, though they'd all flown around in it many times and the old girl had never let them down.

Sunlight flooded inside the metal building as Ben rolled aside the sliding doors. Then after a quick glance to make sure he was unobserved – though they'd find out soon enough from their CCTV footage – he clambered into the plane's cockpit, buckled himself in behind the controls and got started. Throttle a touch open; master switch ON; fuel pump ON; set fuel mixture to rich; then a positive turn of the ignition switch, and the flat-six piston engine fired up instantly. Moments later Ben was rolling out of the hangar and taxiing towards the strip. He was up in the air before anyone could come rushing out to stop him.

The journey was uneventful as he crossed over the better part of France, catching glimpses now and then through the fluffy white clouds from nine and a half thousand feet. He relished the sense of freedom that came with flying a small plane, and would have enjoyed the trip if it hadn't been for the leaden feeling in his heart and the grim sense of purpose that drove him on. Cruising at a steady 120 knots he reached Normandy in just over four hours. He overflew the small aviation establishment where Jeff normally kept the plane, instead setting a course for Le Val itself. As the familiar landscape came into view below – the woods and fields, the yard with its various teaching and accommodation blocks, and the dear old farmhouse itself – he dropped altitude, aimed for the long green stretch of grass that had been Tuesday's classroom, the rifle range, and came in to land.

That was really the moment when it hit him that Tuesday wouldn't ever return to this beautiful place that they'd all called home. His eyes began to sting and burn. He was relieved – and a little ashamed – that Jeff had agreed to the awful task of breaking the news to Tuesday's family. But he knew that at some point he would have to tell Jude. Jude was Ben's son, in his twenties and currently living in New Zealand where he'd started up a boat charter business. Jude and Tuesday had become good friends during the same mission to Africa that had resulted in the recovery of Prince Tarik's diamond. He'd be deeply upset by the news.

That phone call was another unpleasant task ahead. But there would be worse to come beforehand.

As Ben jumped down from the landed plane, a couple of the Le Val instructors, Paul Bonnard and SAS veteran Jimmy Moody, who had spotted the Cessna come over, were already driving out in a golf cart to meet him. The moment Ben saw their devastated, shell-shocked faces he knew that Jeff had been on the phone to break the news. 'It can't be true,' was all Bonnard could say. He'd been one of the team for as long as Tuesday had, and thought of him as a brother.

Ben just put a hand on each of their shoulders and let his own expression tell them the rest. Tears rolled down Bonnard's face and his chin sank to his chest.

'What are we gonna do?' Moody asked disconsolately. A former gunnery sergeant, as tough a man as Ben had ever known, who had once been crouched next to him under heavy fire in the killing fields of Afghanistan when one of their close comrades had caught a direct hit from a rocket-propelled grenade and been blown to pieces just feet away. Experiences like that were liable to harden a man. Here he was, though, looking as forlorn as a little child whose pet kitten had died.

Ben said nothing. He already knew the answer.

Reaching the house, he heard a lively, happy bark and turned to see Storm, his old favourite of Le Val's pack of guard dogs, coming running to greet his master. Storm was an eighty-pound German Shepherd with long, thick fur, boundless energy and an undying attachment to his humans. Tuesday had loved the dog too, but the most special bond was that between him and Ben. He felt an almost irrepressible welling of emotion as he hugged the German Shepherd tight and let him slobber all over his face and hands.

'I'm sorry, boy. I can't stay with you. I've got to go away again.'

'Then take me with you,' Storm said, or at any rate the look in his deep amber-brown eyes communicated just as clearly. But he was used to his master's ways and would always wait patiently for his return.

More of the team gathered by the house as word of Ben's unexpected arrival spread around the compound. Some were openly weeping, and everyone looked as pale and desolate as if they'd lost a close family member of their own. He couldn't bring himself to tell them too many of the upsetting details, and spoke little. Bonnard had fetched a bottle of something suitably potent from his quarters, but as much as Ben would have loved to join them in drowning their sorrows, he had more pressing matters to attend to.

If his colleagues hadn't been so overwhelmed with fresh grief, they would soon have guessed the purpose of his return to Le Val and his intentions for what he needed to do next. Being the loyal comrades and experienced military veterans they were, it would have been difficult to dissuade them from joining him on this mission. Which was deeply touching – but it was the opposite of what he wanted, because he had to do this his own way, alone and unfettered. Leaving them to their commiserations he slipped away and went over to the office building to grab a ring of keys.

From there he headed unnoticed to the armoury, a highly secure underground vault in which Le Val's extensive arsenal of weapons was kept away from the reach of the many criminal and terrorist gangs who would have loved to get their hands on them – and once or twice had tried to. Ben unlocked the several layers of impregnable steel door and turned on the lights, and the scores of military-grade weapons glinted freshly oiled from their racks around the walls.

The contents of the armoury had been Ben's first reason for his flying visit back home: in particular, just a few items that he now picked out and stuffed into a black canvas NATO-issue holdall. Technically speaking, going by the stringent regulations that sought to control every aspect of Le Val's training operations, this equipment was strictly prohibited from ever leaving the compound, on pain of severe repercussions. Technically speaking, Ben didn't give a damn. His first pick was the nine-millimetre pistol with which he did most of his close-quarter battle teaching. It was an old all-steel Browning, the same model he'd carried with him in his Special Forces days and innumerable times since, and which had saved his life more often than he cared to remember. It was impossible to shut out the thought that if he'd had it with him on the trip south, Tuesday might be alive now.

Ben's second pick of the arsenal was another reliable veteran tool of his trade, one of the dozen stubby black

Heckler and Koch MP-5 submachine guns that had been a mainstay of combat operations back in the day and ran on the same ammunition as his Browning. The one he selected had been so well used that most of its black finish was worn to the bare metal, but not because the Le Val team didn't look after their kit. From a separate locker he transferred ten pre-loaded magazines for the MP-5 into his holdall, along with another six for the Browning. That amounted to 378 rounds of ammo between the two weapons, enough to fight your way through the average military skirmish.

He wasn't done yet. From another rack opposite he selected an AR-15 rifle fitted with an underbarrel grenade launcher. Any human or materiel target you couldn't perforate like a colander at up to a thousand yards with the rifle, you could blast apart by lobbing 40mm grenades at it. He quickly, expertly stripped the weapon down into its component sections and stowed it into the bag with the rest, together with two hundred rounds of shiny bottle-necked 5.56 NATO and a box of grenades. Maybe he was overdoing it, but he had no intention of being undergunned for his next encounter with the men who'd attacked them on the bridge.

Finally, he went to the cabinet where the knives were kept. Most of the ones used at Le Val were blunt plastic training blades, for obvious reasons; but some were the real thing. He favoured the old Fairbairn-Sykes fighting knife that had been meeting the gruesome requirements of British commando soldiers since 1941 and remained just as valuable as a killing tool to the modern-day warrior. Because, as Ben knew from his own experience, you never knew when you might have to take out some murdering piece of trash without making a sound. He tossed the knife and scabbard into his bulging, heavy holdall, zipped it shut and slung it over his shoulder from its carry strap.

Back at the farmhouse, he left the holdall in the hallway while he ran upstairs with his green bag to his personal quarters on the top floor. He lived simply up there, with a small bedroom so sparsely furnished that it was almost monastic. From the bedside safe he removed an envelope containing his collection of fake passports and ID papers in a variety of names, all created for him years earlier by a master forger. Along with those he pulled out a thick stack of banknotes sealed in plastic shrink wrap. He'd always carried a useful amount of cash on past missions, to cover all those unforeseen expenses. Another handy item was a burner phone, prepaid in cash and not registered to him. His main phone still wasn't working after its dunking in the river, so he grabbed the burner as a replacement.

He packed everything up in his green bag with another basic change of clothes, then hurried back down the stairs. A gulped mug of strong black coffee and, with Storm trotting hopefully at his heel, he left the house and strode across the yard to the outbuilding where he kept his car.

That was his second reason for the detour to Le Val. The BMW Alpina was the latest in a line of almost identical high-performance saloons that he'd owned, its predecessors having been variously crushed, burnt or shot to pieces. They'd all been the same shade of metallic blue, not because he liked the colour but because he was in many ways a creature of habit. And they were all extremely fast, this one being no exception.

He dumped the heavy holdall onto the back seat, instead of into the boot, in case he might need access to it in a hurry.

Then chucked his green bag into the passenger footwell, gave Storm a wistful goodbye hug and dived behind the wheel. The 4.4 litre V8 bi-turbo engine roared into life and moments later Ben was tearing up the driveway towards the main gates.

So many times before now, he'd left his home to embark on what could turn out to be his last ever journey into danger. He'd always willingly embraced the risk, along with the possibility that he might not return. This time was the same, and yet it was different. Because if there had ever been some deep inner part of him that feared that potential outcome in the past, now it was gone. His own personal safety no longer mattered to him in the slightest. He would see this through come what may, and either succeed or die trying without an ounce of regret.

He owed at least that much to his friend Tuesday Fletcher.

Chapter 16

It was going to take about twice as long as the flight northwards to retrace his steps by road, but Ben was in no desperate hurry. Though the Alpina was one of the fastest production saloons in existence with the world's angriest man at the wheel, his fury was cold, calm and methodical and he had no intention of causing himself problems by getting caught speeding on his way back down across France. Especially not with a bagful of military weapons on his back seat. He drove steadily, comfortably reclined, smoking a continual chain of cigarettes, blasting along mile after mile, town after town, but always keeping enough of a margin beyond the speed limits so as not to draw undue attention.

He'd always had on loud music when he was driving alone, whatever his mood; today, instead of the edgy modern jazz that normally blasted through his speakers he kept replaying a favourite album of Tuesday's, *Blackheart Man* by Bunny Wailer, which he'd picked up from the CD stack in the kitchen at Le Val. The sound of the lilting reggae brought his friend's face, his smile and the memory of his voice and laugh as sharply into focus in Ben's mind as if he'd been sitting right there in the passenger seat next to him.

Don't do this for my sake, Ben. It's not what I want.

That was what Tuesday would have said, if he'd been here. And Ben could hear it so vividly in his head that maybe Tuesday *was* telling him so, from wherever he was now.

But then, Ben thought, that was only because Tuesday had been a better man than he was.

He arrived in Quillan long after midnight, but he didn't return to the hotel to check on Jeff. Something else was on his mind. Two things, in fact, which were the only answers he'd as yet come up with to the question 'where to start?'

The first was Matthew Sadler, because the more Ben pondered over the matter the more he was beginning to wonder if Gardien-brigadier Grosjean, in his accidental wisdom, might actually have been onto something in connecting the assault on the property agent's home to the attack on the bridge. During the long drive southwards Ben had been toying with the prospect of paying Sadler a sneaky visit in the hospital when he reached Quillan, in case the guy might be able to shed more light on who'd broken into his apartment. The problem with that plan was the high chance of getting caught in the act by some night nurse or porter, combined with the realistic probability that Sadler might still not be in a fit state to talk to him, doped up to the eyeballs on painkillers with his jaw wired shut. If the home invaders really had done such a job on him, it could be days before he'd be able to talk to anyone.

And so, shelving that idea for later, Ben had refocused on the other matter that had been bugging him. That was the American.

When you were forced to work things out the old-fashioned detective way and all you had to go on were a few scanty clues, anything – anything at all – out of the ordinary had to be worth investigating. So who exactly, Ben wondered, was this 'Brad' character who'd been hanging around the Manoir du Col? Putting the pieces together, it seemed that first he'd turned up there with his female companion, likely just pretending to be an interested buyer in order to scout the place out. Then he'd come creeping back in secret to check out whatever it was that really interested him. He'd clearly known things about the architecture of the house that Sadler hadn't, like the existence of the hidden vault and the escape passage. Then when surprised, he'd made a run for it as if caught red-handed committing a crime.

What was it all about? The whole thing seemed to revolve around the strange, indecipherable markings on the crypt wall that were of such interest to the American – maybe to both Americans, as his female companion must have some role to play here. Brad and his lady friend were hunting for something. It was quite possible, even quite likely, that one or both of them had already since returned to the Manoir du Col to resume their snooping around.

As Ben had reflected on that, a hypothesis had formed in his mind. What if, just supposing, the thing that Brad and the woman were searching for was also, for some unknown reason, of interest to someone else? And what if, again just supposing, the only common denominator linking himself, Jeff, Tuesday and Matthew Sadler was simply the fact that they'd stumbled on Brad in the course of his search?

Tenuous, maybe. But Ben could think of no other logical connection between all these different players. And allowing for the possibility that his hypothesis was right, that would make the four of them witnesses. Witnesses to what, he had no idea. But maybe that part of the puzzle could be left blank for now, until he learned more. What mattered was that those four witnesses had all become targets for attack within a short space of time after the incident. Which would imply that whatever they'd seen in the crypt under the Manoir du Col, or perhaps just the very fact of their having been there, had inadvertently put all four of them in harm's way.

Which in turn would lead to two logical conclusions. Firstly, that the three witnesses whom the attackers hadn't yet managed to eradicate were still targets for death. None of them was safe, including Sadler in the hospital. And secondly, that the two Americans, Brad and the woman, might also be in serious danger. If that was the case, they might already be dead by now.

Unless, of course, if Brad and the woman *were* the danger. Maybe it was Brad himself who didn't want witnesses to his little exploration of the crypt. Or maybe Brad and the woman were working for someone else, someone with a secret to protect. Targeting Sadler would have been a no-brainer for them, since he was the only agent involved. Then the paid thugs who'd beaten him up in his home could easily have extracted the information they needed to get to Ben, Jeff and Tuesday.

And though Ben had thought nothing of the incident with the American at the time, with hindsight he now wanted to know more. Much more. Which gave him a starting point to begin his search for answers – and if all that proved was that his hypothesis was wrong, then at least he'd have learned something.

He drove through the sleeping town, parked the car a five-minute walk from Matthew Sadler's office, and made his way there on foot. Another hot day had turned into a sultry and humid night, and there was a burning electric smell in the air that signalled a coming thunderstorm.

Reaching the agency, he saw that the double-frontage windows with the colourful property ads on display were covered over by a steel shutter. He kept walking along the empty street until he reached the narrow avenue at the corner of the agency building, and turned into it. Away from the streetlights the alley was dark. Beyond a row of tall plastic wheelie-bins he arrived at a side entrance to the building that was much less secure and offered a far more discreet way in.

Ben was an old hand at slipping undetected into locked buildings, a skill learned in the SAS and much refined over the years since. He always carried a set of lock picks for that purpose, and it took him only a few moments to get through the side door and defeat the rudimentary alarm system. Once inside, he waited for his vision to adapt to the darkness. Then he padded softly through the reception area and began exploring.

The nearest of the two internal doors either side of the main desk led through to a staff bathroom and a small kitchen area. The other opened into a corridor flanked with little offices. The absence of any filing cabinets told him all their records were computerised, and presumably accessible from any of the offices. In one of them he pulled the blinds shut, settled at a desk, fired up the terminal and spent a few moments penetrating their database. It was password-protected, but he discovered the magic code scribbled on a Post-It note and stuck to the inside of the desk drawer. People really should be more careful.

Clicking open the file menu, Ben saw that the agency kept separate lists for clients who had purchased or rented houses and apartments in the area, and for others who had so far only prospectively arranged to view available properties. He clicked open the latter, started scrolling through the alphabetical entries and came across Jeff's name filed under D, together with the address and phone number of Le Val, the details of the Manoir du Col and the date of their visit there.

Ben kept scrolling down the list until he found what he was hunting for. Filed under the letter H was one Bradley Hutchison who had likewise arranged to view the Manoir only the previous week, just as Sadler had told them.

'Hello, Mr Hutchison,' he said. Brad had registered in just his own name, with no mention of the female companion whom Sadler had taken to be Mrs Hutchison. There were two addresses on record, one in Carlsbad, California, and the other a place called Villa Blanche near the Languedoc village of Tarascon-sur-Ariège. Ben remembered Sadler telling them that the mysterious American couple had been renting locally during their house-hunting stay in the area.

Ben grabbed a pen and another Post-it note from the desk, scribbled down the address of the villa and folded the note into his wallet. Then, having got all he needed here, he closed down the terminal, wiped down all the surfaces he'd touched and left the office. Two minutes later he was back out in the street and walking towards the car.

During the time he'd been inside the building the night had grown even sultrier and the sense of an impending storm had intensified. He made it back to the car before the heavens could open, got in and entered the address he'd taken from the computer into the Alpina's sat nav. The map display told him that Villa Blanche lay just outside Tarascon-sur-Ariège and was just a forty-minute drive from Quillan.

It was after one a.m. by now, as good a time as any to pay an unexpected visit to the elusive Mr Hutchison. Perhaps then he'd find out what exactly Brad's involvement was in this. Predator or prey? Whatever the answer, it would bring Ben a big step closer to the truth.

Chapter 17

He was ten minutes out of Quillan, heading fast along a different route from the one that had led to the aqueduct the previous day, when the first lightning flash lit up the wooded hills along the horizon. Moments later came the long rolling rumble of thunder, and then the sky opened up. Storms in the French south could be violent, and this one was no exception. The rain came lashing down with ferocity, pounding on the car roof and quickly turning the road into a river.

Headlights carving twin beams through the rain, Ben threaded his way along the narrow, cobbled streets of Tarascon-sur-Ariège and followed the sat nav out of the village, where the road climbed and wound up a long hill flanked by woodland to one side and a steep rock-strewn downward slope to the other. His destination lay two kilometres beyond the village limits. When he'd covered half that distance he pulled the Alpina off the road into a layby overhung by thick oak trees and killed the lights and the motor, not wanting to be seen or heard by the occupants of Villa Blanche. He'd approach the house on foot.

Before he left the car he pondered for a moment what armament he should bring with him. Opting to leave behind the heavy artillery he inserted a loaded magazine into his Browning pistol, slipped another into his pocket, and stuck the sheathed commando dagger into the left side of his belt and the pistol into the right. Then he started walking through the rain, up the remainder of the long hill towards the villa. Water gurgled in rivulets along the sides of the road and dripped from the trees.

The thunderstorm had abated by the time he reached the house, and the clouds had scudded away to the east to reveal a bright moon. The grounds of the property were surrounded by a high stone wall with imposing pillars and a pair of wrought-iron gates. Standing some distance back from the road at the end of a long driveway, Villa Blanche looked more silvery-grey than white in the moonlight, its roofs and gables slicked by the rain and silhouetted against the night sky. It was a large, rambling property and must have been expensive to rent, Ben thought, remembering Sadler saying the American couple seemed to be well-heeled. That didn't necessarily mean anything in itself, although the worst kinds of people often had plenty of money. Ben had seldom dealt with a dirt-poor villain apart from the most desperate sort of kidnapper.

The gates were fastened with a padlock, but he wouldn't have gone in that way in any case. Further around the perimeter, a tree growing close to the wall enabled him to climb easily over. He dropped down the other side among the shadows and the wet foliage and spent a few moments observing the place. There were no visible vehicles parked by the house, but it was adjoined by a two-car garage with closed metal shutter doors. As was to be expected at this hour of the night, there were no lights in any windows and no sign of movement. The only sound was the patter of the dripping leaves and the soft hooting of an owl coming from somewhere in the darkness.

Ben emerged from the shadows and made his way across the garden towards the villa, staying low and out of sight. Automatic security floodlights and barking dogs were the double danger for the intruder looking to get inside a high-end property like this one, but he was happy to encounter neither as he crept right up to the house. Still nothing stirred within.

So far, so good. The front-door lock was less promising, an old-fashioned solid iron affair probably backed up with an internal deadbolt or two, which would be hard to get past. Deciding to check out the back, he skirted a side wall lined with terracotta flower pots, slipped around the corner of the house to the glass conservatory that served as a rear entrance. It was a more recent addition to the building with a modern lock that should be relatively easy to open.

He was about to take out his picks when he saw that someone else had been there before him. Except whoever that was hadn't been so subtle. The doorframe had been jemmied open and the aluminium housing of the lock was badly buckled, the door hanging loose.

He nudged it open an inch, but then before stepping inside he turned and examined the ground. There was a smear of earth on the paving stones by the conservatory that looked like the print of a shoe, partly washed away by the earlier rain. Another one nearby; and following their line in the pale moonlight he soon found a trail of footprints that some of the best manhunters in the business would have missed but which to him might as well have been marked by fluorescent yellow paint. Three sets of prints in the scrubby sunburnt grass, made by three people who certainly weren't the official tenants of Villa Blanche, or else they might have used a key instead of a crowbar. The trail led back across the rear lawn and to another section of the perimeter wall that had partially crumbled. This was where they'd got inside the grounds.

Three again. Funny how that number kept coming up.

Now Ben was ready to reconsider his hypothesis that Brad and the woman weren't the bad guys after all. And that would mean they really were in danger.

Or that they were already dead.

He stalked back to the house, drawing the Browning. He slipped inside the damaged door and through the conservatory to what had been the original rear entrance. Its lock had been forced as well, but it wouldn't open. Ben realised that was because someone had jammed the backrest of a chair tight up against the handle from within. He couldn't understand who might have done that, but it seemed to suggest that someone was still inside the house.

It took him just a few more seconds of effort to get past the braced back door. Then he was in, gun in hand, not knowing what he was going to find. The dead bodies of Brad and his wife, maybe. Or three killers lying in wait for their next victim.

The villa was as silent as a mausoleum. A back hallway led to a passage and from there to a series of open-plan rooms. Curtains were drawn, with just enough moonlight shining through the cracks to guide his way and show the rooms were all empty. The villa appeared luxuriously furnished, in a dated kind of way. Ben could see no signs of disturbance or a struggle having taken place. After he'd checked the entire ground floor – salon, dining room, library, kitchen and cloakroom – finding nothing he made his way to the staircase and padded silently up to a galleried landing. At its end was a floor-to-ceiling window, next to another flight of stairs continuing up to the second floor. Along the landing were five doors, which he checked one after the other, finding four of them opened into spacious bedrooms, decorated like the downstairs rooms in antique style, shabby but stylish and very French. And perfectly empty. The fifth door was another bathroom. Nobody was lying dead in there either, or waiting to attack him as he stepped through the door. Ben was beginning to get the feeling that there was nobody else here but him.

Or was there?

He was heading back out onto the landing when a sound suddenly caught his ear and he froze mid-step, listening hard. There it was again: a muffled thud, like someone moving around. The sound was coming from above, somewhere on the second floor.

He climbed the stairs, which were uncarpeted and creaky, forcing him to move very slowly. The second floor was the top of the house and it seemed to be little used, judging by the bare floorboards. It was much darker up here, with no windows or skylights to break the shadows all around him. His arm brushed a switch on the wall but he didn't risk turning it on. Barely breathing, he strained his ears for the sound he'd heard from downstairs. And then he heard it once more. Another soft *thump*, and what sounded like the scrape of a light footstep on bare wood. It had come from the other side of a door, just a few steps away. There was no wind outside. What he was hearing couldn't be the sound of a branch tapping against a window or the roof, or something flapping in the breeze. Someone was in there, for sure.

Ben moved cautiously towards the door. The landing was so dark that he could barely make out its rectangular shape in front of him. With the pistol in his right hand he reached tentatively out with his left and his fingers lightly touched the surface of the door. The paint felt cracked and peeling. He guessed the room beyond it might be an old servant's quarters, from back in the days when a well-to-do family living here might have employed a live-in maid or nanny. Empty and unused now, judging by the state of the door. Except as a hiding place for whoever was moving furtively about in there, apparently trying to remain unheard but not doing a very good job of it.

Pressing his ear to the door, once again Ben caught the same sound, another soft thump followed by a kind of scratchy scraping noise. He moved his hand down and gently, gently grasped the old wooden doorknob and turned it without making a noise. Then he took a deep breath, thought *fuck it* and threw the door open hard and fast and stepped through it with the gun pointing ahead, ready to shoot anything that came at him.

That was when Ben realised that he'd been wrong about the servant's quarters. Behind the door was an attic room that was used for storing junk. The moonlight from outside shone in through a single dusty window with one pane missing, casting its glow on the clutter of old chairs stacked on top of one another, boxes and crates, unmounted paintings and empty frames propped against one wall, a large broken mirror against another, an ancient bicycle turned upside down with no wheels, a gramophone, bits of discarded furniture covered in sheets, and all kinds of other bric-a-brac that had been dumped up here over many years.

Ben scanned the dark room finger on the trigger. There were all kinds of nooks and crannies among the junk where a person could be hiding, but whoever had been shifting about and making those noises had now stopped moving. Ben slipped quickly inside and moved into the shadows where the concealed occupant of the attic wouldn't be able to get a shot at him. His whole being was tense and on red alert, ready for anything.

Or he thought he was. Because what happened next took him completely by surprise. Something suddenly exploded out of the darkness and flew across the attic room. There was a tremendous beating of wings and an infuriated shrill raucous hooting and screeching as the barn owl that had made its nest up here and objected to being so rudely disturbed came bursting out of its refuge and went flapping in a furious panic around the room, cannoning off walls, knocking a candlestick off a shelf with a crash and making Ben duck. After three circuits of the room it disappeared behind a stack of boxes and went back to scraping about and squawking and hissing discontentedly to itself.

He let out a sigh. The owl must have been using the glassless window pane as its way in and out. The sounds he'd heard from downstairs had been its strutting about the attic, claws scratching against the bare floorboards. He clicked the gun back on safe. Feeling like an idiot for having been taken in by a damn bird, he retreated from the room and back out onto the landing, shutting the door behind him and leaving the silly thing in peace.

When he sensed the movement in the darkness behind him, it was too late to react or turn around. Then something very solid and heavy came down on his head. His vision exploded into a thousand starbursts and he blacked out.

He drifted. He floated, spinning blindly through a vortex of space and time. Only gradually did he begin to remember where he was. He sensed the hard wooden boards under him as he lay there sprawled out, smelled the dust on the floor. The pain from the blow kicked in next as his senses began to return, throbbing through the skull. There was a light shining on him. He could suddenly feel the presence of someone nearby, bending over him, and in a rush of alarmed realisation he understood it must be the same person who had hit him over the head. He groped around for his pistol that he remembered dropping to the floor, but it was gone. Then he went for the hilt of the knife tucked into his belt. That was gone, too.

The light shone in his eyes, dazzling him and making the pain stab through his head even more sharply. The person bending over him and holding the light now spoke. He heard the voice and was too stunned to make out the words, but they sounded soft and unthreatening. Which even in his dazed state struck him as very odd, if this same person had just tried to bash his brains out.

Now he heard the voice again. Speaking his name, sounding echoey and faraway in his ears. It wasn't a man's voice. It belonged to a woman. Ben blinked confusedly. *How does she know my name?*

Then as the fog slowly cleared from his mind, Ben sensed that the woman's voice was one that sounded strangely familiar to him.

'Ben? Are you okay? Talk to me.' She sounded anxious. Which only heightened his confusion. He tried to speak, but the words 'Who are you?' didn't seem able to form on his lips. He struggled to sit up, was forced down by a fresh jolt of pain in his head, tried again and managed it this time. He raised his hand to shield his eyes from the bright torch she was shining in his face. Behind it he could dimly see her outline, but he was too dazzled to make out her features.

Then that strangely familiar voice said, 'Hold on, there's a light switch.' She moved away from him for a moment and the torch beam stopped dazzling him. There was a click and the top-floor landing was suddenly illuminated by the glow of a dusty, moth-crusted bare bulb. And now, as he knelt there on the floor, slowly recovering from the knockout blow and gazing up at the woman standing over him with a look of concern and her long, thick curly red hair framing her face, his mind came into focus and he stared at her in disbelief.

'Roberta?!'

Chapter 18

'Yes, it's me,' she said, sounding no less astonished than he was at this meeting. 'Is that really you?'

He blinked. It couldn't be her. It seemed impossible. And yet it was true.

Roberta Ryder. The last person he'd expected to see again, least of all in this place and at this moment. Someone he'd known in the past. Known very well indeed and hadn't seen for a long time.

'You're supposed to be in Canada,' he said in a dazed voice.

'I don't teach at the university any more,' she explained quickly, as though brushing that aside. 'But never mind me. What the hell are you doing here?'

'Not looking for you, that's for sure,' he muttered in reply. He touched his fingers to the top of his head, winced, and was surprised not to see them red with blood. 'Jesus, what the hell did you clobber me with, a grand piano?'

'This,' she said, holding up a large cast-iron frying pan. 'I'm sorry I hit you so hard. I thought you were one of them. That's why I was hiding up here.'

His head might still be exploding with pain but his memory was returning clearly now. 'It was you who stuck the chair behind the back door.'

'In case they came back,' she replied in a fluster. 'I knew it wouldn't do much to stop anyone, but I didn't know what else to do.'

'When was this?'

She shrugged her shoulders. 'When did they break in? I've no idea, because I wasn't here at the time, thankfully. It happened sometime while I was away. I got home late tonight, after driving all the way back here from Paris.'

'What were you doing in Paris?'

'I had to go there to look into something, for our research.'

'Whose research?'

'Mine and Brad's. But that's not important right now. When I got home, that's when I found someone had forced their way through the back. They must have left when they found the place empty. I don't know who the hell they are or what they'd have done to me if I'd been here.'

All Ben could do in his confusion was to keep firing questions at her. 'So where's this Brad of yours gone to?'

'I wish I knew that. Last I heard from him was this strange message I got on my phone, and not a word since. I've been holed up in the dark all this time, terrified to turn a light on, trying to call him and getting no reply. I was thinking I should get out of here when I heard someone else come in, and I panicked and grabbed this from the kitchen' – waving the heavy frying pan in her hand – 'and ran up here. What else was I supposed to do?'

'I'm only glad it wasn't a carving knife,' he said.

'I really didn't mean to hurt you . . . I mean I did, sure. If some asshole was breaking into the house I wanted to beat his brains out before he could get me. But how could

I have known who it was? Anyway,' she added with a wry smile, 'I thought you Special Forces guys weren't supposed to be easy to sneak up on.'

When he'd first met her long ago, then a young independent scientist working in Paris, Roberta had already earned her black belt in karate. Apparently she'd become even handier at self-defence since then. 'We're not,' he said irritably. 'It was that bloody owl that distracted me.'

'Well, at least you haven't got brain damage. Memory seems to be working okay. Here's your gun,' she said, handing it back to him. 'And this cute little Arkansas toothpick you were carrying,' giving him the sheathed dagger she'd taken from his belt. 'You look like shit, Ben. Can I get you a glass of water? Do you actually drink water? I seem to remember the only liquid you used to consume was whisky.'

'I don't need water, thanks. What I need is for you to tell me what's going on. I came here looking for the wife of this American called Brad Hutchison who I don't know anything about. Instead I find you.'

She looked surprised. 'His wife? No way. We work together, that's all. Research partners.'

'You live in the same house.'

'It's just a base of operations. We're often not around at the same time.'

The ache in Ben's head seemed to be diminishing, from being cripplingly agonising to merely very painful. He used the landing railing to pull himself up to his feet, and leaned against it staring at her. She hadn't changed a bit from his memory of last time they'd met. Still the same long fiery red hair, more auburn than ginger. Still the same vivid green eyes and slender figure. She barely seemed to have aged at all, though it had been years. The only apparent change was her fashion sense, having ditched the tomboyish look for a slightly more feminine dress.

Maybe not enough had changed, he thought. Maybe some important lessons should have been learned, but never had been. He said to her, 'We have a lot to talk about. But first I think we need to get out of here. One thing you were right about, these people are going to come back.'

He'd have been happy to meet them, too. But not with Roberta here. His first priority had to be to get her away from danger.

She nodded. 'I think you're right. Can you walk? Do you have concussion?'

'Don't be silly. It was only a tap.'

'Ha. Says the guy who was out cold for a whole minute and a half. So where are we going?'

'Somewhere safe. Because, believe it or not, I worry about what happens to you.'

'I'm touched.'

'You won't be needing that any more.' He took the heavy pan from her hand, set it down and grasped her arm to lead her back down the stairs. 'Come on, let's go.'

They hurried down to the first-floor landing, still dark except for the moonlight shining in through the big window. He glanced out of it and could see only the empty grounds of the villa; but there was no telling who might have turned up while they were talking and be watching the house even at this very moment – or how soon they might be about to make another entry attempt.

'Ouch. You're hurting my arm,' she said, pulling back against his grip. 'You don't have to lead me along like I'm a horse.'

'Keep moving, Roberta. This isn't a game.'

She jerked her arm free and glowered at him. 'What is it with you? I get the feeling you don't seem all that happy to see me again.'

He turned to her, feeling a spike of anger rise up. This was hardly the time or place to have a conversation, but he couldn't help blurt out what he was thinking. 'Tell me why it is that every time I run into you, you've gone and landed yourself in another load of trouble.'

'Just a natural talent, I guess,' she replied.

'First time it was experimenting on cockroaches to see if you could make them live for ever, then you got yourself mixed up with that nutcase who wanted to find the elixir of life and people started getting killed.'

'Hey, you were mixed up with him first,' she reminded him. 'I was just a biologist carrying out perfectly legitimate and important experiments. And they were houseflies, not cockroaches.'

'Then it was all this stuff about manmade earthquakes—'

'That wasn't me,' she countered, getting defensive. 'That was my friend Claudine, remember? I only tried to come to her aid.'

An innocent episode that had seen them relentlessly pursued by ruthless killers, shot at, buried under rubble, almost killed in a plane crash and then half drowned by a giant tsunami in Indonesia. 'Come to her aid? I had to walk away from my own wedding to rush off to help *you*. Any idea what that cost me? You promised me you'd stay out of trouble after that, go back to teaching and act like a normal person. But oh no, of course, you could never do that, could you? And now here you are, back up to your old tricks again in the very same place we had all that fun and games the first time round. Why are you back in France? Who is this Brad, anyway? What the hell is the matter with you?'

She'd been looking at him blankly all through his tirade. 'So you never married her. What was her name again? Brooke, that was it. I remember now. What happened?'

'Never mind what happened with Brooke and me,' he snapped. 'You have no idea how serious this situation is, Roberta. People are dying and you want to ask me if I got bloody married. Come on, for Christ's sake. We're wasting time here.'

'Who's dying?' she asked, frowning. Then a look of alarm came over her face. 'Are you saying Brad's dead? How would you know that?'

'I have no way of knowing that,' he replied, trying to keep his voice calm. 'And to be quite honest with you, what may or may not have happened to Brad isn't very high on my list of concerns right now. I'm talking about my good friend, who happens to be lying in the morgue with a bullet in him. And I'm pretty damn sure he'd still be alive and well, if it hadn't been for whatever it is that you and your pal have stirred up.'

She looked stunned. 'I – I'd no idea.'

'Well, now you do. And so maybe you can understand if under the circumstances I'm not exactly overjoyed to see you again, Roberta.' He pointed towards the stairs at the far end of the landing. 'Shall we go, or do you want to continue this conversation with your friends here?'

She opened her mouth to reply. But the words didn't have time to come out, because in the next instant the tall landing window next to where they were standing exploded violently into a million fragments.

Chapter 19

In the same moment, the loud rattle of a machine gun sounded from somewhere outside in the grounds of the villa. Roberta barely had time to react before Ben had grabbed her and flung her down, pinning her to the floor and protecting her body with his. Broken glass and splinters of torn window frame showered over them as more gunfire hammered through the shattered window. A storm of bullets passed through the landing, tearing into the wall and blowing chunks out of the plasterwork right where they'd been standing instants ago.

The Browning was in Ben's hand but it was useless trying to return fire into the night. With his other hand he gripped her wrist and started dragging her bodily down the landing towards the head of the stairway. Another burst of automatic fire shattered the landing rail, punched a ragged string of holes in the bedroom doors and blasted a painting from its hook on the wall. But the angle of the window meant the shooters outside couldn't see them if they stayed low enough. Reaching the stairs they let themselves roll and slither down the steps until they were out of the field of fire. Then he took her by the hand and they bounded down to the ground-floor hallway.

'Looks like they're back,' he muttered.

'No kidding,' she managed to reply. 'Let me go. I can run on my own.'

Any second now the shooters would be invading the villa. Ben had no intention of making a stand here, as he might have done if not for the responsibility of protecting Roberta. Escape was the only option. If the enemy numbered only three like before, it seemed like a possibility. But if they'd come in greater force this time and were able to surround and attack from all sides at once . . . Ben was cursing himself for not having brought more of the armament that was sitting uselessly in the back of his car. But the old Browning had got him out of many a tight spot before now, and its cold hard steel in his hand brought at least some grim comfort to his mind.

With the back door already breached by the intruders' previous visit and likely to have been reused this time, Ben headed for the front. 'This way!' Roberta followed him as they sprinted up the long passage towards the main entrance. But it was too late to get away clean. Just as they were reaching the doorway, it burst open and there was one of the shooters standing there with a submachine gun pointed at them.

All the times Ben had encountered orchestrated attacks by multiple armed assailants like this, they'd often come equipped with full tactical gear – the masks, the gloves, the whole works. This time was different. The shooter was barefaced and he was dressed in regular clothes, just a bulky motorcycle jacket zipped to the neck. He was no amateur, though. Everything in his stance, his body language and the wild look in his eyes said to Ben that he wasn't here to take prisoners. That he wouldn't hesitate to open fire and gun them both down where they stood. But Ben's survival had depended many, many times on being the quicker shot, and in the split second before the man could fix his sights and squeeze the trigger, an ultrafast double-tap from the Browning had nailed him in the middle of the chest. The man's face contorted into a grimace of pain, he staggered back against the wall by the doorway, his legs crumpled under him and he slid down to the floor.

Witnessing Ben shoot people down in front of her wasn't a new thing for Roberta Ryder. If she was going to dissolve into a useless pile of mush at the shock of the gunshots, it would wait until later. In the meantime they were in too much of a hurry to stop and check if the guy was dead, let alone finish him off. They jumped over his fallen form and reached the doorway. 'Wait, my bag,' she yelled, pausing to snatch a small leather satchel from a coat stand by the entrance.

They burst outside into the night and found the gravelled courtyard in front of the villa empty. The rest of the attackers must have gone in the back way, unless they were skirting around the sides of the house and about to appear at any moment. Until that happened, though, there was a good chance of escape.

Just one problem.

'I left my car a way down the road,' Ben told her. 'We're going to have to make a run for it.'

'No need for that,' she replied breathlessly, pointing at the garage. 'I've got mine.'

'Okay, but hurry.'

Ben monitored the entrance with his pistol raised while she grabbed her keys from her bag, along with the electronic fob that activated the garage door. The whirring mechanism seemed to take for ever and seconds felt like minutes as he waited. The figure of a man appeared in the villa doorway, silhouetted in the light spilling from inside. Ben fired. The figure shot back an automatic burst that went wide and raked the garage wall, ricochets flying past Ben's ears. Ben fired again and the figure disappeared quickly back inside the house. He couldn't tell if he'd got him. He wasn't about to run inside and find out.

Roberta yelled, 'Come on!' The garage door was open and she was clambering behind the wheel of her car, signalling urgently for him to get in. He'd assumed her car would be one of the usual modern offerings from a rental company. His heart sank when he saw the old Citroen 2CV with its bicycle-thin tyres, antiquated front wings and headlights on stalks. Apart from its total uselessness as a getaway vehicle, the sight brought back some vividly unpleasant memories of his past adventures around France with Roberta.

'I don't believe this. Not again.'

'Ben! Move your ass!' she shouted from the car as she cranked its underpowered little engine into life. Its reedy, whining sound filled the garage.

Just then, all the lights simultaneously went out in the villa as if someone had flipped the main fusebox switch. Which, if they had, was a smart move because it meant Ben could no longer see any of the movements inside. But if it had also been intended to stop them from powering open the garage door, it had come moments too late. Muzzle flash flared white in the villa's doorway and bullets tore up the gravel at Ben's feet and spattered against the wall behind him, missing only narrowly and making him leap for the cover of the garage.

The third shooter had arrived. No time to argue. Ben sprayed a few wild, fast shots in the direction of the now unseen enemy, piled inside the open passenger door of the 2CV and threw himself into the seat. After the Alpina it felt like climbing into a child's pedal car, the front seats so close together that their elbows were touching. He yelled, 'Go, go!' as she crunched the car into gear and floored the accelerator.

The effect was undramatic. The 2CV rolled sedately out into the night and gently accelerated up the long driveway towards the road. Gunfire from the house hammered into them from behind. The back screen burst apart and a wing mirror exploded. Ben twisted around in the passenger seat and let off another five rapid shots through the shattered rear window, trying to chase the shooters back under cover long enough for them to reach the gates. 'Move! Drive faster!'

'I can't!' she yelled back.

But now at last the little car was reluctantly picking up speed as they hurried towards the mouth of the driveway. The headlights, little more than a candle glow in the darkness, picked out the gleaming wrought-iron bars of the closed gates ahead. 'Oh no,' she groaned. 'I forgot I locked them earlier!'

'Break them down!' Even as he said it, he wasn't sure if it was such a good idea. The gates probably weighed half as much as the car. Would they make it through? There was only one way to find out.

'Here goes,' she yelled over the straining warble of the 600cc engine as the gates came towards them. '*Shiiiiit!*'

The front of the 2CV slammed into the gates with a rending crunch of buckling metal, but it was the car that did all the buckling. The bonnet crumpled up to block their view, and then was torn away entirely as somehow, miraculously, the force of the impact ripped the gate hinges from the wall pillars and they went lurching on through, bouncing and gyrating all over the place. One headlight had gone dark and there was a terrible grinding rattle where the front wing had been crushed in to rub against the tyre.

'Keep moving! That way!' Ben shouted, pointing to the left, the direction of where he'd left the Alpina. No more gunfire was coming at them from the house but it wouldn't be long before the attackers gave chase. Roberta veered out into the road, twisting the steering so hard that the 2CV went up on two wheels and for an instant he thought they were going to roll right over. The single headlight barely illuminated the way ahead, but at least they were moving again. If all the little car could do was enable them to reach the Alpina in time, there might still be a chance.

'Let's hope they've come here in a donkey and cart,' he said acerbically. 'Then we might outrun them.'

'Don't be an asshole. I happen to like these. What else can you drive, in France?'

'Something that doesn't crumple like a beer can at the first bump in the road,' he said. 'I remember what happened last time you and I were in one of these tin boxes.'

'Yeah, what happened was that I saved your ass from getting squished on a railway line.'

'Are you going to sit there talking, or drive this bloody thing?'

'I'm going as fast as I can, goddamnit.'

The rattle from the damaged front wing was getting worse and the acrid stink of burning rubber was filling the cabin. Ben said, 'This is no good. Stop.' As she braked to a weaving halt he piled out of his door, and in three savage kicks had smashed the crumpled panel away from the car. Then he looked back to see the blaze of headlights on the road behind them, maybe sixty or seventy metres away but closing fast. His jaw tightened.

'Move over. I'll drive.'

Chapter 20

'Whatever you say, Mister Big Man.' She slid across into the passenger seat and he got in behind the wheel, stamped on the gas and they pulled away again with all the meagre acceleration the car could produce.

The headlights behind them were getting steadily closer. Ben tried to coax more power from the 2CV, but the car steadfastly refused to be rushed. The road ahead began to slope more steeply downwards as they descended the long hill towards Tarascon-sur-Ariège, with the dense forest to their left and to their right the barren slope, dotted with rocks and vegetation for the short distance their single dim headlight could shine, and beyond that nothing but darkness.

'Come on, come on,' Ben muttered, willing the car to go faster. As the descent grew steeper the force of gravity was beginning to allow it to pile on a little more speed. He wasn't sure if the feeble brakes would do much to slow them down when they reached the bottom. But in any case he was much less worried about that than he was about the headlights in the rear-view mirror, growing steadily closer and brighter. Just about any modern vehicle would have had a massive speed advantage over them, no matter how mercilessly Ben tortured the 2CV. This one more than most, since it was obviously a large, powerful SUV: from the shape of the headlights Ben was guessing a big Audi or a Porsche with three or more hundred horsepower compared to their twenty-nine, and it was gaining on them much too quickly for comfort.

The tree-screened layby where Ben had parked the Alpina was just a little further down the hill. The 2CV had been meant only to bring them that far, so they could transfer from one to the other. But as the car behind kept gaining ground, Ben realised with a sick feeling in his stomach that there would be no time for him and Roberta to stop and switch vehicles before their pursuers caught up with them. He pressed on, knowing they were going to have to find some other way out of this. The stand of trees flashed past, and the 2CV's candle glow headlight reflected momentarily on the Alpina's blue paintwork before it was gone again. So close and yet so far beyond his reach, along with most of his weaponry and ammunition.

Roberta looked anxiously back. 'Was that your car we just passed?'

'Can't stop, sorry.'

'What are we going to do?'

'The only thing we can do,' he said. 'Improvise.'

'I don't know if I like the sound of that.'

The lights behind them were right up close now, glaring through the 2CV's shattered rear window to light up the inside of the cab. If there was any shred of hope in Ben's heart that the car behind them constituted no kind of threat – that it was just another vehicle happening to be travelling along this road and was about to overtake them and roar harmlessly onwards into the night – then that hope was obliterated when the chasing SUV came surging up with a throaty roar and slammed into their rear.

The jarring impact whiplashed them back against their seats. Roberta let out a cry. The 2CV started like a spurred horse and then went into a wobble that Ben could barely contain. He stamped down as hard as he could on the accelerator pedal, wanting to drive it through the floor if that was what it took to get away. For a moment it seemed as if his prayers had been answered, as the engine managed to gather an extra little spurt of power from somewhere and they managed to widen the gap between themselves and their pursuers by a few metres. Then in the next instant he heard the sound he'd been anticipating with dread. The chatter of two submachine guns opening fire on them simultaneously from the rear, accompanied by the strobing white starbursts of muzzle flash in the mirror. Which told Ben that either it was more than three men who'd been sent after him this time, or that the one he'd shot had survived.

That was something else he could worry about later.

The 2CV was built to be light for the sake of economy and its tiny engine. That also made it less than bulletproof. The close-range gunfire chewed through the flimsy bodywork as if it had been paper. Ben ducked his head, reaching out to grab Roberta and haul her roughly down into the footwell as bullets passed between them and shattered the windscreen. The seats were only thinly padded canvas stretched over a frame like a deckchair. An unlucky shot could punch straight through, and it was going to happen any moment now if Ben didn't do something fast.

Sawing the wheel this way and that, he sent the little car into a wild slalom, in the hope that he could make it harder for the shooters to get a bead on him. The narrow tyres squealed and pattered on the road and the suspension creaked like a worn-out mattress. He knew he couldn't keep this up, and worried he was going to push the car so hard it would overturn.

He could see the village down below them at the bottom of the hill, just a few lights on here and there among the sleeping houses. Even if they could make it that far, the narrow, cobbled streets were going to force them to slow right down and their attackers would have no qualms about shooting them to pieces right there in the middle of the village. Ben's pistol had a few rounds left, but not enough to survive a fierce gun battle against determined opponents with automatic weapons.

In other words, there was no way Ben could stay on this road.

In which case, the best thing to do was to get off it.

'Here we go,' he warned her. 'Hold on to your hat.' As the 2CV slalomed from left to right he twisted the wheel even harder and sent them careering towards the edge of the road. Before Roberta had time to shriek, 'Are you nuts!?' they were dropping steeply down the rubble-strewn slope. They crashed over a large jagged rock that scraped down their underside and tore away the exhaust system, turning the engine note to a harsh reedy screech. No chance of stopping, or even slowing down, until they reached the bottom. Wherever the bottom was. Even if their headlight could shine that far, its single beam was bucking so wildly as they went juddering down the slope that it was impossible to see the way ahead. The wheels were crashing against their stops and the whole car felt as if it was about to shake itself to pieces.

Now she said it. 'What are you doing? You're crazy!'

And maybe he was, too. At least his decision had gained them some kind of advantage, as the powerful headlights behind them disappeared for a few moments. Then they returned, much further back, as the driver of the SUV followed suit and continued the chase. Its lights bounced wildly up and down as it crashed along in their wake. The guns opened fire again, but any kind of accuracy was impossible and the bullets missed, pinging harmlessly off rocks.

In any case, for the moment at least, the shooters were the least of their worries. In this deadly toboggan ride it was much more likely that Ben was going to lose control entirely and go smashing head-on into one of the huge rocks that came hurtling towards them. He saw one coming and managed to twist the wheel so that the 2CV's scrabbling tyres narrowly avoided the obstacle – but then another appeared so suddenly from their blind side that he couldn't react in time: a slab of rock that some ancient landslip had brought down the hillside, wedged up at an angle on top of another. Ben braced himself for an impact that didn't come, as the car instead hit the slab like a ramp and went airborne.

He was convinced that they were going to come down nose-first, hit and bounce and roll and go tumbling end-over-end all the way to certain destruction at the bottom of the slope. Maybe it was the car's light weight, or perhaps just pure luck, but somehow they landed on their wheels and survived to go careering wildly on down the slope.

To their rear, the SUV was having its own problems as its greater weight threatened to outdo its stability advantage. The driver was just able to scrape around the edge of the rock slab with inches to spare and keep up the pursuit while the shooters on board leaned out of the side windows and opened fire once more at their fleeing target, this time managing to get a few shots home. A bullet poked through Ben's flimsy seat, missing him by a whisker and cracking into the 2CV's dashboard.

They weren't out of the woods yet. In fact they were about to plunge deep into them – because as the sheer angle of the incline ahead of them began to level out a few degrees, Ben realised that the lower part of the hillside was thickly forested. An impenetrable barrier of trees and vegetation stretched far to both sides of them. With submachine-gun-toting pursuers right behind them they couldn't possibly slow down in time to avoid it, even if they'd wanted to.

More bullets slammed into the already heavily perforated rear of the car. The side window to Ben's left blew out and two fresh holes appeared in the windscreen, turning it into an opaque web of cracks. Driving blind for a few heartstopping moments he ripped out his pistol and used its muzzle to smash away the glass.

Now through the hole in the windscreen he could see the wall of forest flashing towards them in the dim glow of their headlight, and as he made out gaps between the massed trees he realised that the narrowness of the little car was going to work in their favour and enable him to steer between them. At this speed he was going to need reflexes like a fighter pilot to negotiate a safe path through, but it was the only chance he had and he was going to take it.

Roberta understood what he intended to do, and was too terrified even to scream at him. The first gap raced towards them. There was a whanging, crunching scrape as a tree trunk grazed their left flank and a rending clatter as they shed another body part, this time a rear wing. Ben twisted the wheel to aim at the next gap that was on them almost before he could react. Again they made it. And on, and on, half a heartbeat and a hair's breadth from one devastating, pulverising head-on collision and the next, and the next, weaving a crazy line through the obstacle course.

A crazy line that the much wider SUV behind them had no chance of being able to follow. But that realisation had come to its driver only at the last moment and a few seconds too late. He panic-braked, his wheels scrabbled for grip, gained it and then lost it, the vehicle skidded sideways and hit a thick trunk with a crunching impact that stopped it dead in its tracks.

Ben heard the dull CRUMP of the collision, risked a fast glance in his rear-view mirror and saw only darkness behind them. Twisting around in her seat Roberta yelled, 'I can't see the lights any more. I think they've crashed!'

'Fine by me,' he muttered. Another pair of knotty great trunks loomed suddenly in front of them. Once again they managed to scrape through the gap, bucking over tree roots, raked by low branches.

'We should go back and find out who they are!'

'And please tell me how I'm supposed to do that, Roberta.'

The slope was beginning to level out, but there was still no way he could stop without risking a skid that could see them piling to their deaths into a solid tree trunk. But then moments later, they were emerging from the lower edge of the forest. The wild ride carried them down another fifty metres before at last he dared to use the brakes and bring their descent a little more under control.

If anything the ground was even rougher at the foot of the hillside, ruts and boulders hiding in the long grass over which they went crashing and scraping. Then there was a stunning BANG as a large rock Ben hadn't even seen until too late ripped off their front wheel on Roberta's side, along with the remaining headlight and wing. The wheel went rolling and bouncing away into the darkness as the front of the car ploughed a furrow in the ground like the nose of a crash-landing aircraft. Its momentum carried it through a clump of thorn bushes, off a blind edge and abruptly downwards into a dry river bed that finally brought them to a halt. Ben and Roberta were thrown hard against their seatbelts.

Then, at last, all was quiet and still apart from the ticking of the stalled engine and the spinning of the remaining front wheel, which was stuck clear of the ground.

'Looks like this is where we get off,' Ben said, unclipping his seatbelt. 'Are you all right?'

'Me? Never felt more alive in my life,' she replied acidly. 'Considering I nearly just got killed a hundred times over. That sure was an interesting evasion strategy back there.'

'Are you complaining?'

'Hey, I'm still breathing, aren't I? And I'm back in company with the great Ben Hope, with whom life is never boring. Who'd ever complain about that?'

'Hm,' was all he replied, and tried opening the driver's door, which was so badly dented inwards from one of their collisions that it was pressing into his hip. He rammed his shoulder against the jammed mechanism, and the door burst open and fell off its hinges into the mud left from the rainstorm. 'These things are really built to take the knocks, aren't they?'

After he'd helped Roberta clamber out of her side, they stood there under the soft moonlight and gazed for a moment at what was left of the 2CV. The body panels that were still attached to the buckled chassis looked as though they'd been through a hydraulic crusher. A wisp of smoke was rising from the bared engine compartment.

'I really liked that car,' she said wistfully.

'That's what you said about the last tin can,' he replied. 'Come on, let's go.' He pointed towards the road.

'Shouldn't we double back up the hill to where they crashed?' she said, looking behind them towards the trees.

He shook his head. 'No chance, Roberta.'

'Why not? They're probably all dead. Or badly hurt, anyhow. Then we might be able to figure out who they are, or who sent them. It could help us learn what happened to Brad, if he's okay.'

Ben had already considered that possibility. If the men were all dead, there would be little to learn from examining the bodies. Professional gunmen like these wouldn't have been carrying any identification. And if they were alive, they were still potentially dangerous. Even a badly injured man could still pull a trigger, and Ben had known many a soldier who'd met his end going back to gather information out of a wounded enemy, only to collect a bullet instead.

'We'll have to figure those things out another way,' he said. 'Right now I have other priorities. You're one of them.'

'What's that supposed to mean?' she challenged him.

He could see this new partnership was going to be a lot of fun. 'Meaning I can't be responsible for anything bad happening to you. So I'm not taking any chances, you understand?'

'Hey, don't act like I'm holding you back,' she snapped. 'I'm in this too, you know.'

'Yes, you are,' he told her evenly. 'But only until we get you somewhere safe. After that, I'm going it alone like before.'

She rolled her eyes. 'Here we go again with the "I work alone" bullshit. And where exactly am I supposed to go while Chuck Norris takes on the bad guys single-handed?'

'How about back the other side of the Atlantic?'

'No way, Ben,' she said hotly, vehemently shaking her head. 'Without me, you have no idea what this is about.'

He looked at her. 'You're right. That's why you're going to tell me everything you know. But first, I suggest we get out of here, return to my car and find somewhere safe where we can talk.'

Chapter 21

They clambered out of the muddy river bed and hiked across the rough ground to the road. It was little more than a country lane, unlit except by the moonlight filtering through the trees. Getting his bearings Ben said, 'This will take us back to the main road through the village. Then we can loop around up the hill and get to my car.'

'What about them?' she asked, darting an anxious look back towards the trees.

'If you're right and they're all smashed up, we hopefully shouldn't have to worry about them.'

All the same, Ben kept his pistol to hand as they walked along the dark road. Four rounds left in the magazine, and once they were gone he'd only have his knife. The streets of Tarascon-sur-Ariège were silent and deserted this time of night, apart from the distant barking of a dog and an over-zealous cockerel's crowing at the moonlight. Leaving the last of the houses behind they continued up the long hill, walking in single file, keeping to the shadows at the side of the road and staying as silent as possible just in case any of their pursuers who might have survived the crash were lurking nearby. Ben was alert to any sign of movement among the trees and rocks, but the only other living thing they met on the road was a black cat that crossed their path, carrying the limp body of a mouse in his jaws. He hadn't been the only predator out hunting that night. He paused to eye them suspiciously, then slunk away into the undergrowth with his prize.

'Bad luck,' Roberta whispered.

'For the mouse,' Ben replied.

A little further up the road they found the skidmarks from the chase, fragments of broken windows and taillight lenses, and scattered 9mm shell casings. Picking one up to examine it, Ben saw without surprise that it was the same Serbian make of ammo that had been used in the motorcycle attack on the aqueduct. That made him think of Tuesday, and his jaw was tight as he walked on.

The green luminous hands of his watch were showing nearly three a.m. by the time he spotted the moon's reflection on steel and glass among the bushes. 'There it is,' he whispered. Rather than walk straight up to the car, he made Roberta crouch with him in the grass nearby for a full minute, watching for any signs of anyone lurking. The sudden sound of an approaching vehicle coming up the hill made them duck lower. Ben had his finger on the Browning's trigger as the headlights washed past them without slowing and disappeared down the hillside. He waited another thirty seconds, then only when he was satisfied they were completely alone again did they approach the Alpina and unlock the doors.

Before getting in, Ben first unzipped the holdall on the back seat and exchanged the depleted magazine in his Browning for a full one. Roberta's eyes widened at the sight of the armament inside the bag. 'Holy shit. You came ready for a war.'

'That's what they're going to get, just as soon as I catch up with them again.' He thrust the pistol back into its place behind his right hip, and zipped up the holdall. 'Now let's get moving.'

'Great. Where are we going, anyway?'

'As far away from here as possible,' he said. 'We can talk as we drive. Then we'll find some place we can hole up for the night. Unless you'd rather sleep in the car.'

'I've done that before. Can you take me back up to the villa first?'

He shook his head. 'You can't return to that house again. More of them could come back.'

'But I left a load of stuff there. Clothes, shoes, personal effects.'

'Do without. Anything you really need, we'll buy for you in the morning.'

'This is you taking charge, is it?' she asked, folding her arms.

'Looks like someone has to.'

Ben fired up the Alpina as she clambered irritably in next to him. The throaty roar of the eight-cylinder bi-turbo was a welcome sound after the warble of the late, lamented 2CV. He took off up the hill, and within moments they passed the entrance of Villa Blanche. He eased off the throttle to peer at the now quiet, empty house, then roared off again.

'Okay, wise guy,' Roberta said, pressed back into her seat by the acceleration. 'You want to talk, then let's talk. I still want to know what the hell you're doing here.'

'Likewise,' he replied. 'But before I tell you all about it, I need to make a call.'

More precisely, he had three of them to make. The first was to Jeff, who had been waiting anxiously at the hotel in Quillan to hear from him. 'Mate, what's up?' Jeff asked before Ben could say a word. He sounded morose and depressed.

'Been a couple of developments,' Ben told him. He gave Jeff a very concise account of the night's events, a military-sounding report that neither made any mention of Roberta nor conveyed much sense of the excitement and danger they'd just come through. But Jeff would get the picture clearly enough.

'Wish I'd been there with you,' he muttered. 'This sodding ankle's driving me round the twist. So what next?'

'I've shaken them off for now,' Ben said. 'But they'll try again. And while they won't find me, it's not safe to assume they won't know where to find you. So I need you to check out of that hotel as fast as you can, and book into another. Preferably some fleapit where you can pay cash and not use your real name. Sit tight and wait for me to call you again later.'

Jeff would have no problem staying in a fleapit. They'd both known plenty in their time.

'Hey, how come you never mentioned me?' Roberta asked indignantly as Ben ended the call. He ignored her and immediately moved on to the next, which was to Jimmy Moody at Le Val. Moody picked up on the second ring and it was clear from his sharp, alert tone that he hadn't been asleep.

'I had a feeling you might call, buddy. What's happening down there?'

'Enough to keep me busy for a little while,' Ben said. 'I could do with a few extra hands.'

'Whatever it is, Ben. You can count on me to get it done.'

Ben had known that, and he'd already worked out his requirements. 'I need you and five other guys to get down to the south of France as fast as you can. Bonnard and the others will have to stay behind to guard Le Val. Meantime three of you will hook up with Jeff in the town of Quillan and get him home safely. You've got his mobile number to call when you land.'

'Copy that,' said Moody. 'You do realise Jeff's not gonna take too kindly to being brought back here, don't you? But we'll handle it.'

'I know you will,' Ben said, with visions of bloody noses, black eyes and Jeff finally being persuaded with his arm twisted behind his back. 'As for the other three guys, their job will be to act as minders to a man called Matthew Sadler. He's currently recovering in the hospital in Quillan, and we need to make sure nothing else happens to him. But it's got to be discreet, because the less we're obliged to explain to the local police, the better.'

'No sweat. How long's this guy in the hospital for?'

'I can't say for sure. But the moment they're ready to discharge him, he's to be brought back to Le Val too. If he tries to protest, the guys can feel free to persuade him by whatever means necessary. As long as it doesn't put him back in the hospital.'

'Gotcha,' Moody said.

'I was thinking about Brett, Duke, Craig, Lockett and Rusk.' All five were as solid and dependable men as Jimmy Moody himself, former troopers Ben had served with and commanded in various theatres of war back in the day. A couple had done the odd spell as private military contractors after quitting the regiment, while the others had gone into the lucrative corporate security and close protection industries that were always clamouring for highly trained specialists. 'Rocket' Lockett had spent a few years in Saudi, consulting to their Special Forces.

'Mike Rusk I know is in London,' Ben said. 'Jack Brett was off to do a PMC stint in Ukraine last time I heard from him, but might be worth giving him a call. All the numbers are in my black book in the top drawer of the office desk.'

'No need to call them, buddy,' said Moody, and Ben could hear the dark smile in his tone of voice. 'They're already here. And more are on the way. There are hundreds of guys from back in the day who'd jump at the chance to help out. For Tuesday. And for you.'

Nothing was as heartwarming to Ben as the loyalty and friendship of these rugged, big-hearted veterans who would drop everything and fly into action for a former comrade at the drop of a hat. He knew that if he asked them to, they'd be at his side with guns in their hands and ready to do battle. 'I appreciate that, Jimmy. Take what you need from the armoury and stand by for the chopper.'

'Did you say cho—?' Roberta began asking as Ben got off the phone with Moody, but he was already dialling the third number and cut her off before she could finish her question. 'Valentina? It's me.'

The Valentina in question was Valentina Petrova, the teenage heiress to the business empire of Ben's old ally, the billionaire Auguste Kaprisky. Valentina and her 'Tonton' lived on a grand estate near Le Mans, and had a small private air force at their disposal twenty-four hours a day. This wouldn't be the first time Ben had relied on their help, as they had often called on his.

'Ben! It's so good to hear from you!'

'I'm sorry to phone so late, Valentina. I have to ask a favour.'

'Anything for my white knight. You know that.'

Ben hated flattery, and she always had a way to make him blush. He outlined what he needed and Valentina agreed without hesitation. With just two calls she would arrange for their helicopter to whisk his six-man team to an airfield near Le Mans, from where the Kaprisky jet could cover the eight hundred kilometres to Quillan in well under an hour. It was a huge weight off his shoulders to know that if nothing else, at least two of the key targets on the enemy's hit list would now be kept safe.

This time, as he got off the phone, Roberta was able to speak. 'Chopper?'

'It's the colloquial name we give to those flying machines without wings and a big spinny thing on top. You may have seen one before.'

'Don't be so facetious. Who's Valentina? Who are all these people?'

'Just friends.'

'You seem to have a lot more of those than I do.'

'One less than I did a couple of days ago,' he said.

'And what's this about Matthew Sadler? You mean the realtor guy in Quillan? I know him. I met him.'

'I know you did.'

'I don't understand. What's he doing in hospital?'

'Recovering from being beaten half to death by the same three men who tried to do for us tonight,' Ben replied.

'What? Why him?'

'Because he was with me and my friends Jeff and Tuesday when we happened to stumble across your man Brad sneaking around in the crypt below the Manoir du Col. Did you know he was there?'

Roberta only looked even more confused. 'Sure, I knew. But . . . why would *you* have gone to the Manoir du Col?'

'Small world, Roberta. There aren't many places for sale around here that would suit a business operation like ours. The three of us flew down here with a view to buying the place. Sadler just happened to be the local property agent we were dealing with. That's the only connection we had to any of it. And it all revolves around whatever Brad was looking for there.'

She reflected for a moment. 'Jeff and Tuesday. I've heard you mention Jeff before. But I never met them.'

'You won't be meeting Tuesday. Too late for that now.'

Roberta blanched. 'That was his name? The one who . . ?'

'The one they killed. His parents named him after the day he was born on. Turned out to be the same day he died on. He was one of the best people I've ever known. And now he's gone, for no reason other than that the same people who have it in for you and this Brad of yours seem to have convinced themselves that my friends and I are a problem, too.' He quickly ran through the events that had taken place on the aqueduct.

'I'm so sorry, Ben.'

'So am I,' Ben said. They fell silent for a few moments. The dark empty road sped towards them, trees and hills and the occasional lonely house flashing past. He fished out a Gauloise and his Zippo and lit up, cracking his window open a couple of inches for her benefit. Then he said, 'Now tell me about this Brad. Who he is, what he does, how you came to team up with him, and what's in that crypt that's so damn important people are losing their lives over it.'

Chapter 22

Things had not at all gone to plan for Jacques, Bertrand and Chrétien that night. Three consecutive unsuccessful attempts to locate and eliminate a solitary, defenceless female target at home at Villa Blanche; and now the fourth had ended in even worse failure. The sense of defeat had left Jacques and Chrétien stunned.

Meanwhile Bertrand had other things on his mind. He'd been the one unlucky enough to come face to face with the unexpected opponent in the house, who'd shot him twice in the chest before he could get a single round off. Only Bertrand's bulletproof vest had saved him from the knock-down impacts of the 9mm rounds. After managing to get back up on his feet he'd soldiered on as best he could and even managed to punch a few holes into the fleeing car, but now the numbness of the shock had worn off and the pain was crippling him. The bruise under the vest was a livid rainbow of red, purple and yellow and the flesh was agonisingly tender to the touch.

That was the only injury any of them had sustained in the course of their night's operations, other than to their pride, but their Audi Q7 had come off much worse. The solid tree trunk they'd rammed into had destroyed the radiator and fan, buckled the steering gear and generally ensured that their only way out of this place tonight would be on foot.

'We'll go this way,' Jacques said in his authoritative manner as their leader, pointing down the slope. 'There's got to be a road down below. Most likely it will lead to the village. We should be able to find a replacement vehicle there.'

'At this time of night?' Chrétien wondered.

'This time of night is the best for stealing cars,' Jacques replied. 'You leave that up to me, Brother.'

'I don't think I can make it,' groaned Bertrand, clutching at his chest and grimacing in pain. 'There are at least two ribs broken, maybe three. I can feel them cutting into me every time I breathe.'

'Stop moaning,' Jacques told him harshly. 'You'll survive. Just count your blessings that he didn't put those bullets in your stupid head instead.'

'She was supposed to have been alone,' Chrétien said. 'Who in the Lord's name was that man?'

'Someone we thought we'd seen the end of two days ago,' Jacques replied tersely. 'I caught a good look at his face. He's one of them. The one called Hope.'

'That's not possible,' Chrétien objected. 'We all saw the car sink. Nobody came back up. How could he have survived?'

Jacques had to admit he was at a loss to explain it either. 'Evidently, it would seem that we underestimated this man. Not only we ourselves, but our superiors too.' Except it wouldn't be seen that way, he thought. The three of them had been charged with responsibility for the mission. It was up to them to complete it. Failure would bring the inevitable repercussions. The rules of their order were strict.

'Then we have a problem,' said Chrétien.

'Yes, we do, Brother. Unless we can make this good. Let's go.'

They began the long march down the hillside, winding their way through the trees with their weapons at the ready. But it was slow progress, often having to stop to let the ailing Bertrand catch up. Jacques's hope of finding their targets mangled against a tree trunk diminished with every step. When at last they reached the bottom, they came across the river bed and the abandoned wreck of the 2CV lying in the mud.

'He's the luckiest man alive to have made it down that hill in one piece,' said Chrétien, gazing in amazement at the empty car.

'Or the most highly skilled,' Jacques replied. It was as he'd feared. This man Hope would be the hardest of their enemies to deal with. To make matters worse, now the woman had his protection.

Bertrand caught up with them again, head bowed in pain and still clutching at his bruised chest. The other two paid him little notice. One man's minor discomfort couldn't be allowed to distract them from their main focus. Jacques climbed up from the river bed to the rough ground between it and the road, and crouched to examine the tracks in the dirt, still moist from the earlier rain. He pointed left, along the road. 'They went that way.'

'Then we should hurry,' Chrétien said.

Jacques shook his head. 'No chance of catching up with them tonight, not with a wounded man in tow.'

'Then what do we do, Brother?'

'There's only one thing we can do. Return to base, contact headquarters and call in more of our Brothers to reinforce us.'

This was a hard blow to his two associates, since they knew this open admission of failure would be a dishonourable mark against their names. Shocked, Chrétien asked, 'How many more?'

'As many as the Grand Master is prepared to send us,' Jacques replied.

Chapter 23

As Ben and Roberta were speeding along the dark, empty backroads she replied to his question, 'What can I say about Brad? He's a rich guy from California.'

'Rich from doing what?' Ben asked.

'Oh, he doesn't have what *you'd* call a "proper" job. Never has had, as far as I know. The money comes from his family. They're loaded, from some patents that his father owns. He was an engineer. Brad was set to follow in his footsteps and did a year at college, then flipped out and went his own way. That was about fifteen years ago. These days he describes himself as an author, film maker and adventurer, but really he's a blogger and YouTuber.'

'And what the hell would that be?'

'Oh Ben, I know you live inside your own little bubble, but surely even you must have some awareness of the modern world out there.'

'I try not to get too involved.'

'Then you wouldn't know that there's this thing called the internet, and that on this internet are places called websites where people can upload their own videos. Millions of them, ranging from the silliest to the most professional, on every subject you can imagine. That's what Brad does. He has his own channel, where a whole army of followers flock to watch his video documentaries. You can make a lot of money from this stuff, if you have enough of an audience and know how to present your material well. Not that money matters much to Brad. He's spent the past fifteen years bumming about the world doing his own investigations. And of course, he has the funds to travel anywhere and delve into anything that takes his fancy.'

'Investigations into what?'

'His channel covers a lot of ground, but I guess you could say that the theme of his documentaries is mostly alternative history.'

'That's a nonsense term. History either happened the way it did, or not at all,' Ben said. Something about this Brad was putting him in a contradictory mood.

'But what if for some reason the version we're told is a lie, or a cover-up? That's Brad's take. He investigates the stuff we haven't been told about, the hidden secrets, unexplained enigmas. Everything from Egyptology to ancient lost civilisations, to what really happened to the *Titanic* to who shot JFK, to Bigfoot to UFOs and LGMs.'

'LGMs?'

'Little green men.'

Ben made a grunt. 'I see. In other words he's a raving lunatic.'

She shrugged. 'Maybe he is, in some ways. A fairly charismatic one, though. And actually quite an interesting and smart guy, when you get to know him. He's also a surprisingly good researcher, even if he does sometimes get carried away in his choice of subject matter.'

'And how the hell does someone like you get mixed up in that stuff? Last time you and I met, you were still teaching

Biology at Carleton University in Ottawa. You're a scientist. Or you used to be.'

'I *am* a scientist,' she countered. 'I always have been. But I'm also someone who takes an interest in certain subjects, certain mysteries and grey areas where not enough research has been done to reveal the truth. That's what science is, real science. All through history, the big advancements in learning were made by people who had the guts to raise their head above the parapet, challenge the consensus view and try to figure out what was really going on. And so I was getting bored teaching the same tired old lessons year after year. I had the urge to explore new directions.'

'The same directions as this Brad?'

'Most of the stuff he's into wouldn't interest me in the least. It's just too plain wacky for my tastes. But as you know, I always was drawn to areas of knowledge that some people might call esoteric.'

Ben certainly did know that. He remembered all too well the way her particular fascination with one of those areas of knowledge had landed her in a great deal of trouble, years back. Her research into the centuries-old and – according to her at least – much-misunderstood and misrepresented practice of alchemy had been the cause of their first meeting, when she'd been carrying out those rather unusual experimental biology studies of hers in an independent lab in Paris. Meanwhile in England, a wealthy tycoon called Sebastian Fairfax had hired Ben to find a fabled elixir that might save the life of a dying child. Ben had initially been reluctant to take on the mission, but had changed his mind and given it his all. Though he hadn't known it at the time, Fairfax was deceiving and using him, obsessed by the purported capability of that mysterious, ancient science to achieve his own immortality. That plan hadn't worked out too well in the end for Fairfax, who in fact hadn't lasted as long as his natural lifespan would have allowed. Ben's involvement in the situation had had something to do with his premature demise. But along the way, both Ben and Roberta had also come very close to meeting their own untimely ends.

'Here we go again,' he sighed. 'Didn't you get enough of all that back then? Have you forgotten our old friends Franco Bozza and his maniac archbishop boss Usberti, whom he used to carve people up for?'

'There's so much about the past that we don't fully understand, Ben. That's what drew me to try to figure out what was behind alchemy in the first place, but history is full of so many other riddles and puzzles, myths and legends. I'm fascinated by it all. And I'm not the only one.'

'So this is how you came into contact with this Brad character.'

She nodded. 'For a couple of years I'd been getting more and more back into reading and learning about esoteric and hermetic arts, the history of secret societies like the Freemasons and the Rosicrucians, things like that. I scoured the web for anything that could further my understanding. And then I discovered Brad's work. There were certain questions I had that I couldn't find answers to. I reached out to him, and he got back to me, and before too long we had an email correspondence going. Months went by. I felt like I was getting to the end of my tether as a university academic. And then one day Brad contacted me again, to tell me about the letter.'

'What letter?'

'It was part of a collection of very old manuscripts and documents from the thirteenth and fourteenth centuries, lost for all these years until they resurfaced in an old library and wound up going to private auction. As it happens, the person who bought them was a contact of Brad's.'

'Another rich lunatic?'

'His name's Corky. He's a millionaire, yeah, a conspiracy nut and a history buff who collects all kinds of crazy artefacts. Mostly junk. You should see his house. He even has what he claims is part of an ancient alien spacecraft. But sometimes, just sometimes, these crazy guys come across something of real value. The letter's written in medieval Latin, of course, and Corky had to hire a classics professor at UCLA to translate it for him.'

'Really? I'd have thought someone with a name like Corky must be a real scholar himself.'

Ignoring his sarcasm she went on, 'Now, a few months earlier, Brad had been telling him how he'd like to do a documentary about esoteric secrets from medieval times. He didn't really know what, at the time. But when Corky read the translated letter, he got all excited and called Brad to tell him he might have found a subject for his documentary.'

'And then you got involved.'

'Brad and I had been having similar conversations over email, and he knew about my interest in alchemy. When he told me about the letter, that was the trigger that finally convinced me to quit my job, sell my apartment in Ottawa and move to California. That's when Brad and I hooked up and started working together.'

'Hooked up,' he said, giving her a sideways look.

'What? No! Jesus, give me some credit. I didn't mean hooked up in any romantic kind of sense. Though,' she added after a pause, 'I get the impression he wouldn't have said no to that.'

'I'll bet he wouldn't.'

'Actually he can be a bit of an asshole. He did make one pass at me, before I warned him I'd put him on his ass if he ever tried it again.'

'Still keeping up with the karate, then,' Ben said.

'Got my first Dan last April. Explains how I was able to get the better of you, huh?'

'Go on with the story. So this letter is what brought you and your idiot friend to France.'

'Stop calling him names. I'm very worried about the guy. I have this feeling something terrible's happened to him. Before I tell you about the letter, let me show you something.' She reached into her bag and took out her phone, twiddled around with it for a few moments and then said, 'Look at this.'

He couldn't look at it while driving, so he pulled into a layby and turned off the engine thinking, *This had better be good*. Taking the phone from her, he peered at the lit-up screen in the darkness of the car. What she was showing him was an email message. A very short one, consisting of just one misspelt word.

DANGWER

Chapter 24

'I'm guessing that's how folks spell "danger" when they're in a real hurry,' she said. 'And scared as hell. Like when someone's coming after them and they're about to be caught.'

Ben thought she was probably right. 'You think they got to him?'

'Doesn't it look that way, after tonight? It's not every day you have people trying to kill you.'

'Happens to me fairly often,' he muttered, half to himself.

'And why won't he answer his phone any more? I'm telling you, something happened to him. First they got him, then they tried to get me. And I'm sure they must have been inside the house at least once while I was away in Paris.'

'Tell me again what was in Paris.'

'The Musée des Archives Nationale,' she said impatiently. 'Home to collections of some of the oldest documents of French and European history, dating back to the first century AD. That's what I was doing there, spending two entire days trawling through all these old historical papers that you can't find online. I needed to confirm a few details about our research.'

Ben was about to reply when he noticed another email on her phone. This one was also from Brad, and had pinged into her inbox just minutes before the alert message. The header was BINGO!!, and the short text of the email read

'*Who's your Daddy? Catch ya later. B.*' Judging by the casual, flippant tone, this had been written before whatever might have happened to send him into a panic.

Then Ben noticed that this earlier email also had a number of files attached to it. He tapped the screen and the first file opened. It was an image. A photo taken in a gloomy dark place, of a section of a rough stone wall. One that Ben had seen before. The wall of the crypt under the Manoir du Col.

'This is what he was doing when we found him down there,' Ben said. 'Taking pictures of the carved inscriptions on the wall. But why?'

'Because it's part of what we've been investigating.'

'To do with this letter you were telling me about?'

She nodded. 'Okay, so let me explain. It was written in June 1308, and it specifically mentions the very same house, and the crypt underneath. The place goes back to about 1250. Did Sadler tell you anything about its history?'

'Only what he knows,' Ben said. 'In any case we weren't interested in discussing its medieval past. That wasn't our reason for being there.'

'Well, it's actually a really important landmark for us. The letter was written by someone who took refuge there while on the run from the king's soldiers. Not just any someone. He was a knight. A Templar knight.'

Ben said nothing.

'You've heard of the Templars, right?' she asked.

'Of course I've heard of them. I just can't understand how this is connected to what's happening.'

'You will, if you let me tell you. Now, if you've heard of the Templars you know they were crusaders in the Holy Land, an order of warrior monks that was founded in the twelfth century, in Jerusalem. During the hundred years or so that the city belonged to Christendom after they'd captured it in the First Crusade.'

'Which was in 1099,' Ben said. 'And the Templar order was founded about twenty years after, starting with just a small group of poor knights who wanted to give safe escort to pilgrims travelling to visit the holy city. Yes, I did know that. But I'm surprised. *This* is the subject of your research? Why the Templars?'

'In a word? Because of alchemy,' she replied with a shrug.

That sounded completely unlike anything Ben had ever been taught about the Order of the Knights Templar. 'Alchemy? No. They were soldiers. Pure and simple. As they got more established they went from escorting pilgrims to becoming one of the first elite military orders, defending the Christian crusader states in the Holy Land from Saracen attack. They were fighting battles and protecting cities, not running around the desert turning lead into gold or whatever.'

'Oh, Ben, don't you remember anything from what we learned all those years ago? You of all people should know that alchemy was never really about that. Anyhow, you're wrong about the Templars. Because there's a lot of evidence that they were much more than just a bunch of guys with swords. They were into some very deep secrets.'

'According to flaky California rich kids like Brad and Corky, maybe. But you?' He shook his head. 'I can't believe you'd fall for this nonsense.'

'Yeah?' she countered. 'Then take another look at that image Brad took of the wall carving and tell me that isn't an alchemical symbol right there.'

Ben peered more closely at the image, then at each of the others Brad had sent her. All of them featured the same geometric symbol, one he'd never seen before. It was hard to make out in places, but clear enough overall to make out the lines carved in the stonework with a sharp steel tool or blade. The symbol consisted of several shapes, each within the other. A larger outer circle contained an equilateral triangle whose three corners touched its circumference. Fitted inside the triangle was a square, then inside the square was another, smaller, circle. Around the edges of the symbol were carved letters that he couldn't make out. 'Doesn't mean anything to me,' he said gruffly, handing her back the phone.

'Look, I don't blame you for being sceptical,' she said. 'For most people who've learned anything about history, they haven't gone any deeper into it and they just don't know this stuff. At the same time, it's true that the Templars are probably the medieval world's greatest gift to conspiracy theorists and internet crazies everywhere. Depending on what wacky websites you go to, they were either secret devil worshippers, or secret Muslims, teamed up with heretical Islamic sects they met up with in the Holy Land; or they were witches and sorcerers; or else they were guarding an ancient bloodline dating back to Jesus and Mary Magdalene; or any of the other stuff you'll read about them, some of it possibly accurate, other times ridiculous. So much rumour and legend surrounds the Templars that it's almost impossible to separate truth from fantasy. That's why most serious modern historians tend to shy away from investigating the more secretive parts of their history. It's become such a cliché that for academic researchers it's the kiss of death. The same way that no self-respecting scientist would dare go anywhere near the subject of alchemy, in case they'd be ridiculed by their peers and lose every shred of professional credibility. Just like happened to yours truly, back in the day. Tell me about it. I've been there.'

Ben remembered that Roberta's unusual interests in biology had once earned her a place on the cover of the magazine *Scientific American*, with the heading 'Unscientific American'. She'd been castigated for her claims by the whole mainstream establishment.

'And now you're going there again,' he said.

'Yes, I am, because I've got nothing left to lose, and because all these so-called experts who laugh and scoff at people like me are making the same mistake. You can't throw the baby out with the bathwater. Real scientists and historians are the ones who're prepared to get their hands dirty, to peel back the bullshit and find what's underneath. And when you start to drill deep into what the Templars were really about, you make some very interesting discoveries. To which the strange carvings on the crypt wall under the Manoir du Col are very much connected. After reading through everything I could find in the National Archives museum I'm more certain of it than ever.'

She paused. Then said in a different tone, 'Ben, I know what you're going through. Your friend is dead and all you want is to find out who did this terrible thing. You're hurt and you're angry, you're tired and you're confused. Why should you give a damn about all this other stuff? I can imagine how crazy and irrelevant it must all sound to you. But I'm begging you to be patient, and to trust me, because I believe if we work together we can get to the bottom of this. Not just for your friend's sake, but for all our sakes. Please.'

There was a long silence inside the dark, stationary car as Ben took in what she'd just told him. He truly, truly wished he wasn't here, wasn't hearing this, any of it. Wished that Roberta had stayed where she was in Canada, in her safe, cosy and well-paid little academic job. Wished that he could make all that was happening go away, press a reset button and bring back all that had been that was now lost for ever. He felt sick to the bottom of his heart.

Yet here they were, and this was all really happening. Night traffic flashed past outside, the glow of headlights illuminating her face, and he could see the look of absolute sincerity in her eyes. Whatever else she might be – headstrong, opinionated, just about the most stubborn person he'd ever known – Roberta Ryder was no fool.

'You're right,' he said. 'It does sound crazy to me, and my gut tells me that I shouldn't even be listening to it. But I also know that I doubted you in the past, and you proved me wrong. So however this might all be sounding to me right now, I have to trust you. And if whatever you have to tell me can help me to understand, then I'm all ears.'

Chapter 25

As they drove on through the night, Roberta explained that the name of the Templar knight who had taken refuge in the crypt, back in April 1308, was Thibault de Roucyboeuf.

'So he was the author of the letter,' Ben said.

'Right. Which he wrote a couple of months later to another knight, a Gerard de Vezelay. In it he talks about being on the run from the royal authorities, describes some of the tricks and ruses he'd used to evade capture, and warns his friend to do the same. You know about the persecution of the Templars?'

'A little. They'd been thriving and gaining wealth and power for the best part of two hundred years, when their leaders were suddenly arrested on charges of heresy.'

She nodded. 'That was what triggered their downfall. It all began in October 1307, on the orders of King Philip IV of France and Pope Clement V. Almost overnight, starting with the dawn raids that rounded up their Grand Master and his inner circle of knights, they went from being one of the mightiest and most venerable religious orders in Europe to being hunted outlaws. The heresy part, well, there's a lot more to that than meets the eye. They were accused of denying Christ, spitting on the cross, fraternising with enemy infidels, performing weird pagan rituals, worshipping mystical idols, and all manner of other alleged terrible sins against the faith they were sworn to uphold. As for the letter itself, what's most amazing about it, unlike so many other documents from medieval times, is that it's so well preserved. So well, in fact, that you could be forgiven for thinking it was a clever fake.'

'That crossed my mind.'

'Mine too. It's only good science to question everything, right? That's why I went to Paris, so that I could put aside any niggling doubts that the letter might not be genuine. The National Archives museum was the place to go for that. Only a fraction of documents that old have been digitised and made available online, and for the rest you need to delve physically into the period records. So that's what I did, leaving Brad to carry on his investigations here down south.'

'And?'

'I searched for hours and hours and almost gave up trying, but in the end I found the proof I was looking for. A royal court register of the time does indeed confirm that de Roucyboeuf and his correspondent Gerard de Vezelay were both among a group of fugitive Templars arrested in October of 1308. They'd been successfully evading capture for a year since the royal and papal decrees that denounced their order, but now their luck ran out. The king's soldiers finally caught up with them in Rouen, where they were imprisoned, tortured to extract their confessions of heresy, then executed by burning at the stake. Which tells us that the letter must be genuine, because who else could have known that de Roucyboeuf and de Vezelay had got in contact and been on the run together?'

'But before all that happened,' Ben said. 'Take me back to the crypt, when the letter's author was hiding there on his own.'

'Right. In his account he describes how he stayed there for nearly a month. How he survived, we don't know. It's possible that the owners of the Manoir du Col at the time were sympathisers of the Templars, which he wouldn't have mentioned in his letter so as not to incriminate them. Maybe he paid them for his lodging. Or else perhaps he was living down there without their knowledge, hunting and foraging for food and using the secret trapdoor to come and go.'

'That's how you knew about it,' Ben said, thinking back to the hidden hatchway through which Brad had entered the crypt and then made his escape.

'That's right. It's just the way Thibault described it to his correspondent. Anyway, however he managed to survive that month in hiding, it must have been a tough time. Never knowing when the soldiers might suddenly turn up, or for how long he'd be able to stay free once he moved on from there. The only thing he knew for sure was the fate the authorities would have in store for him if he was caught. And so that's why, in his desperation, he carved the inscriptions on the crypt wall. To leave a message that would outlast him, no matter what happened.'

'The wall carvings are a message?' Ben asked.

'In coded form. It's written in a combination of jumbled-up Latin phrases that don't mean anything when you try to look them up, and a bunch of alchemical symbols like the one you saw in Brad's photo, a circle within a square within a triangle within a circle. It's all got to mean something.'

'Please. Not another one of these puzzles,' he groaned.

The look on his face brought a faint smile to her lips. 'Codes and ciphers aren't your favourite thing, huh? I remember.'

'I was hoping I'd never have to see one again.'

'Just your luck. It so happens that this one's strikingly similar to other cryptic graffiti that captured Templars scratched onto the walls of their dungeon in Chinon castle, but better preserved and more complete, as far as we can tell. He carved it there in the hope that it might be found in the future by someone with the skill and wisdom to understand it. To Thibault and his fellow knights, whatever the code signified was too precious to allow it to be erased along with their order. As he said in his letter, it was a secret that the Templars had sworn to protect and uphold for all time.'

'A secret about what?'

She threw up her hands. 'I can't say. That's what Brad and I were hoping to figure out. From the photo it looks like some of the inscriptions have faded with time. Others seem to be encrusted with dirt and moss. If we'd had the chance to clean them up and get a better look at them—'

'You mean, if us lot hadn't barged in on him when we did.'

'It's too late now, in any case,' she said sullenly. 'I can't go back there because they could be watching the place. Nowhere's safe any more. And Brad . . . who knows what's happened to him?' She lowered her head and wiped a sudden tear from her eye. 'I know he's a jerk,' she said softly. 'But if they've *killed* him . . . oh, hell, he didn't deserve that.'

'Why all the sneaking around?' Ben asked. 'Why couldn't you just have told Sadler about the crypt, and said you wanted to see it? If this had been all out in the open, then everything might have been different.'

'Because we'd already had a warning before that,' Roberta said. 'Someone was onto us before we even got to France. We were scared they might be watching us, anticipating where we'd go. That's why we felt we couldn't be too open about what we were looking for.'

This sounded even crazier to Ben. 'What warning?'

'It was while we were still in California, scouring the internet for clues, emailing and phoning a lot of Brad's network of contacts who we hoped might have information about Thibault de Roucyboeuf or the secret he talked about needing to protect. We weren't getting much in the way of valuable feedback, so we decided to come to France and check things out in person, starting with the crypt. Then, a week before we were due to jump on a plane for Nice, he got an encrypted call on his cellphone, telling him to drop this line of research or face the consequences.'

'No idea who from?'

'None. They sounded pretty serious, though. And the consequences didn't sound too good either.'

Consequences that now included the bullet that had taken away the life of Tuesday Fletcher. Ben said, 'But you decided to ignore the warning all the same.'

'We spent an age mulling over what to do. I was convinced someone must be hacking our emails and phones, which scared me enough to want to cancel the France trip. Brad was pretty freaked out himself to begin with, but then he started coming round to the idea that the warning could just be some crank call and nothing to worry about. Maybe a rival YouTuber trying to put him off, he thought. You wouldn't believe some of the tricks people play.'

'It seems pretty real now, with hindsight,' Ben said.

'Anyway, I don't think Brad managed to reassure himself completely. That was why he decided to rent the villa instead of checking us into a hotel, which he worried was too easily traceable. He paid cash up front for a three-month lease on the house, and for our two cars.'

'Money to burn. Didn't do him any good, did it?'

'How were we to know, Ben? Warning or no warning, nobody could have predicted this mess we're in now. What the hell are we going to do?'

'No use crying about it,' he said. 'Just keep moving forward.'

'Okay,' she said. 'Then what's the first step?'

'To break down the facts we know so far, and see where that leads us. One, these people are out to get you, and by extension they're also out to get the rest of us. They're armed and they mean business. Which means they have, or think they have, a very pressing and important reason for wanting us out of the picture.'

'Sounds about right.'

'Two, this all started when you and Wonder Boy decided to start meddling in something that obviously matters a great deal to someone out there. Which tells us that, however strange it may seem, their motive has something to do with a closely protected secret dating back to medieval times. One that your research apparently threatened to uncover.'

'Which also says something about these people's influence and power,' Roberta added. 'How the hell did they know what we were doing? What does it matter to them so much for? How did they organise themselves so fast?'

'So we're not dealing with amateurs here. And it's clear there must be a lot more than just three of them involved. This level of systematic efficiency takes a whole network of people. An international organisation, with the means of mounting surveillance on anyone they suspect as a threat and the money and manpower to enforce it. Like an organised crime gang, but not just the run of the mill kind. You and I have seen something like it before.'

'Gladius Domini,' she said, referring to the deadly fundamentalist sect operated by the rogue archbishop Massimiliano Usberti, which had tried so hard to eliminate them both years ago in this same part of France. 'Are you saying *they*—?'

'I doubt it,' he said, answering the same question that had briefly been in his own mind. 'Usberti is dead and gone, a long time ago. His operation died with him. In any case, they'd have targeted us directly and I only got involved in this by chance. No, this is something else.'

'Okay, then what?'

'Let's go back to what we know. Whatever secret they're protecting, whatever knowledge or information they don't want anyone to discover, it's somehow connected with a coded message that someone inscribed on a crypt wall more than seven centuries ago. So it follows that if we knew what this secret was, it could lead us back to the people who're trying to cover it up.'

His mind was working hard as he turned to look at Roberta. 'Tell me more about these alchemical symbols. You've studied this subject in the past. You know a lot more about it than I do.'

She nodded. 'Glyphs, runes, whatever you want to call them. Sure, I'm reasonably familiar with some of the main symbols they used, but I'm no expert. Alchemy had a language all of its own. Some symbols represented the four elements of fire, air, earth and water. Others represented the seven planetary metals, lead, tin, iron, gold, copper, silver and quicksilver. Or mercury, as we'd call it. Others again symbolised other metals like antimony and nickel, and elements like phosphorus and sulphur. But there were also those alchemical symbols with much deeper meanings to do with magic and transformation, the dark arts that only the higher-up initiates would have been taught. Some had multiple meanings. Some, we can still only guess at to this day. The circular motif with the triangle and the square inside, I'm sure I've seen before, but I'm damned if I can remember where, or what it symbolised. It's been driving me nuts.'

'But do you think you'd be able to work it out? Did anything else you and Brad uncovered give you any ideas, any clues that could help us understand more?'

'Nothing,' she replied. 'Not yet, anyway, since we were only getting started. I could try, but the images don't give me a hell of a lot to go on. We'd have to go back to the crypt and see how much more of the message is still hidden under all the dirt and moss.'

'Which we've already dismissed as an option,' he said. Yet, as he drove on, it occurred to him that there might be a way to bypass having to decipher the damn thing.

'What if we could figure it out based on what we already know?' he suggested to her. 'Given that the code was apparently put there by a Templar knight, a member of a deeply devout brotherhood of Christian monks who lived pretty much entirely to serve God and fight infidels, it's reasonable to suppose that the secret's of a religious nature. Then again,' he added as another thought came to him, 'perhaps not. The Templars were a wealthy order. We might be looking at something a lot more straightforward.'

'Ah,' she said. 'Sounds like you're thinking along the same lines that Brad was, right back at the start of this. That's what got him so excited about it all in the first place. And it's probably what kept him on the hook, even after that first warning to drop the investigation. See, the Templars weren't just wealthy. They were *fabulously* wealthy beyond anything anyone could imagine. After the Church granted them official status as a religious order in 1129, these once dirt-poor knights who'd started out as a group of just nine men only eleven years earlier suddenly drew in a flood of new members and a lot of rich patrons who were only too happy to donate land and property in return for their protection. Over time those donations added up to over nine thousand grants of land, estates, castles and fortresses, stretching from England and France all across Europe to Portugal in the west, to Poland in the north, and to the Holy Land in the east. They got so rich themselves that they could build their own churches and cathedrals. More than that, they became the first international bankers, and created one of the earliest forms of credit so that travellers didn't need to risk carrying large amounts of gold through dangerous lands full of bandits.'

Ben hadn't realised their wealth had grown quite that much, but now he could see where this was leading. 'And Brad was thinking about their money.'

'You can see why. The sheer amount of capital the order had amassed was enough to bankroll entire military campaigns, which made them a useful source of ready cash for Christian rulers looking to expand their empires. By 1307, King Philippe of France himself was deep in their pocket after all the fortunes in loans he'd borrowed from them. Even the Vatican owed them a ton of money. And it's been said that one of the reasons both the king and the pope turned against them when they did was so they wouldn't have to repay their debts. But being the kind and generous soul he was, King Philippe went further, because after he'd arranged for them all to be rounded up and executed his next plan was to get his hands on the enormous sums in gold that the Templars were reputed to have stashed away.'

'And did he?'

'Nope, and neither has anyone else who went hunting for the Templars' legendary loot, right up until the present day. But, in Brad's way of thinking, we had something that nobody else had ever had: the coded message, connected to a letter written by an actual Templar knight.'

Ben could see it now. 'So Brad got the idea—'

'That Thibault de Roucyboeuf's letter and the markings in the crypt under the Manoir du Col might have set us on the trail of the Templars' lost treasure.'

Chapter 26

Ben asked, 'So the code is what, a treasure map of some kind? A set of directions to where X marks the spot? The medieval equivalent of GPS coordinates?' If that was the answer to the mystery, he could understand the motivation behind wanting to prevent others from finding it out. And understanding the criminal's motive was half the job of catching him. This felt like a breakthrough.

'That's if you go with Brad's way of thinking.'

'You don't?'

'It's an interesting theory,' she replied. 'Plausible in a lot of ways, given what we know from history. And very tempting to believe you might be able to follow a bunch of clues that'll lead you to unearthing vast amounts of gold. But personally, I was never convinced Brad was on the right track with it.'

It suddenly felt to Ben as though they were right back at square one again. 'But for you to have stuck around, you must have some other ideas of your own.'

'I have. But they're vague, Ben. I can't be at all sure that I'm on the right track either. Brad certainly doesn't agree with me.' She frowned and looked down. 'That is to say, he *didn't* agree with me,' she corrected herself in a sad tone.

'I need to know,' he said. 'Whatever you can tell me, no matter how tenuous it is.'

'Then I'd have to take you through the whole hidden story of the Templars.'

'So be it. We have time.'

Or did they? Ben was acutely aware of every minute that ticked by while they remained in the dark like this, searching desperately for understanding. He was tired, too. Dawn wasn't far away, and after the running chase and their escape through the night he could feel his energy draining out of him like blood from a wound. Just then the Alpina's bright headlights flashed on a road sign for a motel ahead.

When they came to it soon afterwards, the place looked more like a giant concrete bunker than a motel. But a flickering neon sign above the lobby doorway said CHAMBRES LIBRES, and the thought of a coffee and a quiet room was deeply welcome. Ben pulled into the forecourt. Only a couple of other cars were parked outside. Through the glass door they could see the reception desk was unattended.

'It's a pretty lugubrious-looking joint,' Roberta commented. 'Of all the beautiful places in the historic heart of the Languedoc, we manage to find the Bates Motel.'

'I did say we could sleep in the car,' he replied, holding the door for her. He rang the bell on the desk, and a sleepy fat guy with a walrus moustache and his shirt hanging out of his trousers appeared from a staff doorway. Ben asked him in French if they had two adjoining rooms free. Which they did, and Ben shelled out the money and signed the register for both of them, as Monsieur and Madame Harris. The fat guy didn't seem to care one way or the other.

'Remember the last hotel you and I stayed in, near Montpellier?' Roberta said as they headed along a walkway to their adjacent doors on the ground floor. 'It was just a little bit more upmarket than this. And all they could give us was the bridal suite, with a four-poster the size of a Buick and complimentary champagne. We even checked in using the same fake names. I taught you to dance to an old Edith Piaf song on the radio. Years ago, but it seems like only yesterday.'

'Yeah, and it ended with you getting kidnapped and me having to give the slip to a tactical police team with dogs,' he reminded her. 'But we didn't come here to reminisce about our romantic past, did we?'

The rooms were in keeping with the motel's exterior, basic and utilitarian. 'Take your pick,' he said. 'For what it's worth.'

'They're both so charming and quaint I can barely make up my mind. I'll have room eight.'

'Then I'm in seven. We'll rest here for a few hours before we move on.'

The best of the motel's amenities was the strong black coffee from the vending machine in the lobby. With a tall Styrofoam cup each they perched on the edge of Roberta's bed. She took her phone from her bag and tried again to call Brad. 'Still no reply,' she said, biting her lip.

'I'm sorry, Roberta.'

'There's not much hope we're going to find him alive, is there?' she asked. A tear welled in her eye and she wiped it away.

'How can I answer that?'

'Don't bullshit me, Ben. You know there isn't. I can see it in your face.'

'All right, then. No, I seriously doubt we'll be seeing him again.'

She heaved a sad sigh. 'At least you and I are safe for the moment. That's what matters, I guess.'

‘If Brad’s dead,’ Ben said, ‘then maybe he didn’t die in vain. Now let’s talk this through. Everything you can tell me.’

She paused a moment to collect her thoughts. ‘So much has been written about the Templars and their exploits, but the really interesting stuff is much less well known about. Be warned, though. Some of this might sound pretty weird to you.’

‘I would have expected no less,’ he told her. ‘It is you, after all.’

She gave him the finger. ‘Ha ha. So we know that the Order of the Knights Templar had its very humble origins way back in the early twelfth century. Jerusalem had been the holiest centre of Christendom since Biblical times, until the new religion of Islam burst onto the scene hotter than a chilli pepper, intent on conquering as many territories as they could. The city was captured into Muslim possession in around 637 A.D., five years after the death of the Prophet Muhammad. They held it until 1099, when it was reclaimed in the First Crusade, by Christian forces led by the French knight Godfrey de Bouillon. Godfrey became the effective king of Jerusalem, succeeded by his brother Baldwin. This is all basic history, straight out of the mainstream account.’

‘Okay, go on.’

‘For the next eighty-eight years the city was peacefully occupied by its crusader liberators, including a small group of knights who came together in 1118 to act as escorts for Christian pilgrims, who were often attacked and massacred or enslaved by Muslim raiding parties on the long and dangerous road to the Holy City. Not to mention the dangers of lions and bears, starvation and thirst, and losing their way in the wilderness. The leader of this group of knights was a man called Hugues de Payens. He'd been born in Troyes in northern France in 1070 and probably first arrived in the Holy Land as a pilgrim himself in around 1104. How he and his little band came to be called the Knights Templar was that the new King of Jerusalem, Baldwin II, granted them quarters in a part of the city that stood on the Temple Mount, on top of the much older ruins of Solomon's Temple, which had been destroyed long ago by the Babylonians.'

'Or maybe by the Edomites,' Ben said. 'Depending on which version you side with.'

'Ah, of course, you studied theology,' she remembered. 'Back in your Ivy League days. Or should I say "the dreaming spires"?'

'That was another life,' he said, wishing he'd kept his mouth shut.

'What's interesting is that during the time the knights were based in Jerusalem, they did a lot of excavating around the old ruins. Were they creating cellars for underground storage? Or were they looking for something? Some people, including Brad, have believed they were searching for the Holy Grail, or maybe for the Ark of the Covenant, which the Books of Kings and Chronicles tell us had been brought from the City of David and placed in the Holy of Holies of the old temple.'

'The Holy Grail,' Ben groaned. 'Give me a break.'

'Yeah, this is the stuff that gets parodied around so much that it's become a joke, and the only people who'll even entertain those ideas are the usual bunch of crackpots who've been watching too many Indiana Jones movies.' She paused. 'Anyhow, what we do know is that this tiny band of knights rose up amazingly fast in size and power, soon becoming one of the most influential military powers in all of Christendom. I've already told you how after being nominated a fully-fledged religious order at the Council of Troyes in 1129 they were able to start collecting huge areas of property all over Europe and the Holy Land. They were the original warrior monks, partly soldiers charged with the defence of Christendom against all enemies, and partly a monastic order taking vows of poverty, chastity and silence. By papal decree they were answerable only to the Vatican, and no secular ruler, not even a king, had authority over them.'

'In theory,' Ben said. 'That didn't work out too well in the end.'

'Right. Who can trust kings and popes to keep their word?' She smiled. 'At their peak they had about twenty thousand members, of which only a minority were fully ordained Brother Knights, and the rest were their co-brothers or *confrères*. They played an administrative support role as scribes, servants, cooks, squires and a small army of accountants to keep tabs on all the order's financial dealings. Additionally they needed members to help build and maintain their many castles, fortresses and cathedrals. Those were the Mason Brothers, who some believe were the origin of the later freemasons. It's often been thought that the freemasons became the guardians of many secret traditions of the Templars, and still are to this day.'

'I've heard all that stuff,' Ben said dismissively.

'And so much of it is a bunch of hooey,' Roberta agreed, 'that it's easy to disparage everything you hear. Once you start separating the wheat from the chaff, though, you begin to realise that some of the weirder claims and rumours that have been repeated through the centuries might actually have a basis in truth.'

'Like what?' he asked her. 'What do you believe?'

'I'll tell you what I *don't* believe,' she said. 'That at the end of this trail is a hidden cache of treasure sitting waiting for some smart or lucky fortune seeker to discover it. The golden chalice that Christ drank from at the last supper, or a mountain of the Templars' alchemical gold, or any of the other schoolboy fantasy tales that resonate all around the online wacko community. People like Brad and a thousand others have been following the Grail trail for centuries and never found a damn thing. None of the old historical accounts can even agree on what the "Holy Grail" was. In early Welsh chronicles, the "dish of Rhydderch" is described as one of their ancient royal treasures, but it was just a plain common platter. In total contrast, according to the Vatican, the Grail is a magnificent gold cup housed in the cathedral of Valencia, in Spain. Then there are all these other accounts of what it could have been. A mysterious vessel hidden in Rosslyn Chapel in Scotland. Or else it's the green glass chalice that was brought back to Genoa in 1102 and later taken to Paris by Napoleon before it got smashed to pieces, one fragment of which is in the Louvre. Or maybe the Grail is some kind of crystal ball that can kindle fire from sunlight, like the mystical Urim and Thummim from the Hebrew Bible.' Roberta waved her hands in the air. 'Frankly, as far as I'm concerned, anyone who gets pulled into all that wild goose chase might as well go looking for the pot of gold at the end of the rainbow, guarded by leprechauns.'

'So much for the cup of Christ, then,' Ben said.

'You ask me what I *do* believe, based on a ton of research I've done into this, I'd have to say that the so-called treasure of the Templars wasn't any kind of material treasure at all. I think that its value is of a different kind. And that whoever finds it won't enrich themselves with gold or money, but philosophically, intellectually, perhaps even spiritually.'

He looked at her. 'Yeah? And how are they going to do that?'

'How else? By gaining special knowledge or wisdom. Learning the truth of an esoteric secret that's been kept wrapped up in mystery for centuries. And that's why I came into this.'

Chapter 27

'All right,' Ben said. 'So just what *is* this secret knowledge you were so keen to learn?'

'That's the question, isn't it?' she replied with a dark chuckle. 'Wouldn't be much of a secret if it was that simple to pin down. Again, a lot of people have tried to figure it out, and sometimes their ideas are almost as wacky as those of the golden Grail hunters. A couple of centuries ago there was an Austrian oriental expert called Joseph von Hammer-Purgstall who collected a large body of research on ancient Masonic lore and believed in a strong connection with the Knights Templar. He proposed that the old word GRAL is an acronym for the Latin "Gnosis Retribuit Animi Laborem", which translates roughly as—'

'*Knowledge rewards the labour of the soul*,' Ben said.

'Thank you, Mister Classics Scholar. Suggesting that what we call "the Grail" was really the quest for true understanding. But of what? According to Hammer-Purgstall, the Templars were the guardians of a mythic secret. Another historian who took an interest in the same subject was the British author Nesta Helen Webster in the nineteenth and twentieth centuries. She believed that the Templars imported a secret form of religion from the east, which they'd learned about and become initiated into during their time in the Holy Land.

'Now, you've got to be a bit careful with old Nesta,' Roberta went on, 'because she might have been a little loony herself, with all her theories about Illuminati and globalist Jewish conspiracies. But again there's got to be a core of truth there. Because there's no doubt that on their travels in foreign lands the Templars did come into contact with what would have been very new, radical ideas to them.'

'From who?' Ben asked.

'You were a soldier yourself, right? You don't need me to tell you how modern Special Forces troops deployed into war zones overseas often need to learn to mingle with the local populations. It's the reason you learned to speak Arabic and other languages.'

'That's true enough.'

'So think of the Templars as the original crack troops, the forerunners of today's SAS or Navy SEALs, who spent years in the Holy Land often rubbing shoulders with people they'd never encounter back home in Europe. They sometimes had to deal with enemy spies and informants, communicate with local tribespeople and go deep undercover on reconnaissance missions, wearing Saracen garb. That's how they came to mix and form alliances, sometimes mysterious alliances, with Muslim sects like the Assassins and the Druze. Those were Shia Muslims, rivals of the Sunni majority just like today, over the same old dispute about what was the legitimate succession of the Prophet Muhammad. And because the two opposing Islamic factions were always at each other's throats and sometimes found it hard to unite against the Christian crusaders, the Shias weren't necessarily above the occasional collaboration with the enemy as a way to strike against the other guys.'

'You said the Templars were later accused of secretly following pagan religious ideas.'

'Which in the eyes of the Catholic Church would certainly have included any titbits of "infidel" Islamic doctrine they might have picked up on their travels. Likewise, it's easy to understand how the knights in the Holy Land could also have come into contact with much older, pre-Christian religious ideas belonging to Jewish mystics, which had come down the line all the way back from the ancient Israelites and old Egypt, and were very much still in circulation in the near East during medieval times. I'm talking about schools of religious doctrine like Kabbalah, preaching what they held to be deeper mystical truths behind the teachings of the Torah and the Hebrew Bible.

'Now,' Roberta went on, 'it's almost certain that a lot of the heresy charges against the Templars in 1307 were a load of bullshit trumped up by the Church and the monarchy. Like I said earlier, it was in the financial interests of certain extremely important people to see the order taken down for good, and so they threw anything at them they could think of, including the customary accusations of corruption, practising sodomy and other "dubious activities". But at the same time, *some* of the accusations might not have been completely unwarranted. Meaning that they were distortions, perhaps deliberate distortions, of the truth. Because even though I think the knights were basically innocent of the charges brought against them, and certainly weren't enemies of the Church or of the Christian faith as their accusers were making them out to be – and let's face it, how many people found guilty of so-called "heresy" throughout history weren't just simply victims of someone who wanted them conveniently gone? – nonetheless, the evidence does suggest that the Templars were into some rather strange things.'

'Let me guess. This is where we get to the alchemical stuff,' Ben said.

'They might have dabbled in that practice, who knows? But that's far from all of it. And where the story seems to go next is even weirder than alchemy.'

Ben couldn't wait to hear it. He lit a Gauloise in anticipation. 'Go on, then. Then we might actually learn something useful from all this.'

Roberta asked, 'What do you know about the cult of Baphomet?'

He thought for a moment as he clanged his lighter shut and sucked in the welcome Gauloise smoke. 'I've heard the name. In connection with devil worship, as I recall.'

'That's right. Or at least, that's what's commonly supposed,' she said. 'Sure, Google the word "Baphomet" and the first thing you'll come across is that image straight out of creaky old Hammer horror movies, this evil-looking monster with an androgynous human body, wings like a bird of prey and the head of a goat, with long horns and a pentacle symbol on its brow. It's become our modern image of Satan, and it was even used as a model for the eight-foot bronze statue commissioned in 2015 by the Satanic Temple and put on display in parts of the US. Which didn't win much favour with American Christian groups. Sign of the times, I guess. But forget all that baloney, because that familiar image of the Devil was only invented in the nineteenth century and has no relation to anything from medieval times, let alone anything to do with the Templars. And yet one of the central accusations made against them at their heresy trial was that during their secret, closed rituals they worshipped this thing called "Baphomet".'

'So what was it?'

'Sources of the time are pretty conflicting. Some thought it might have been a cat, or a mysterious idol that was said to have great powers. Some said it was a bearded man, others said a woman. It was sometimes imagined as having two or more faces. Depending on the source it might be made of gold, or glass, or wood. And these great powers included the ability to make land fertile, trees grow, and more importantly to give its worshipper the key to great riches. You might speculate that was something else of the Templars' that King Philippe was keen to grab for himself.'

'In other words, it's anyone's guess what this thing is,' Ben muttered.

'It's all very confused, I'll admit. But among the raft of charges brought against the Templars, it was explicitly stated that "they venerate an idol, a bearded male head", which also apparently had great powers the court didn't elaborate on. They were said to each wear a cord around their waist that had been wound around the head, perhaps as a way of passing these strange powers to the wearer.'

The more Ben listened to this stuff, the more he began to frown. 'This all sounds completely mad.'

'I told you it was weird, didn't I? In fact it's so weird, and so much more unusual and specific than those other trite and unimaginative accusations of corrupt dealings and homosexuality, that it seems pretty probable that they really did have such an idol at their ceremonies.'

'You're talking about a head,' he said, giving her a heavy stare. 'An actual *head*. What did they do, dance around it? Grovel and pray to it? What kind of head was it anyway?'

'I guess it would have to have been a human one,' Roberta mused. 'Severed, obviously, which wouldn't have seemed so freaky to people in those times as it does to us. It was very common in war back then to cut off the heads of the vanquished, stick them up on posts or fling them over castle walls with catapults. Both Christians and Muslims did it to one another as a matter of course.'

Ben said nothing, but he could have told her that those kinds of practices weren't restricted to wars of bygone centuries. He'd seen it for himself, back in his military days when his unit had come across the grisly results of tribal warfare and raiding parties, entire villages massacred and the heads of the men, women and children stacked into pyramids taller than he was.

Roberta went on, 'But this must have been a special sort of head. One could speculate it had been mummified in order to preserve it. It could have been very ancient, and perhaps belonged to someone very venerable and wise. A holy man, maybe. Or a saint from earlier in history, which would explain why they attributed special powers to it. Or very possibly it wasn't a Christian idol at all. Which rules out its being an Islamic one, as their religion strictly prohibits idols of any kind and especially ones that represent a deity. By contrast, magic heads were very much a part of the esoteric rituals of Kabbalistic and other ancient pre-Christian religions.'

Ben's frown was beginning to turn into a scowl. He'd mostly been listening patiently to her talk, but now he felt his frustration welling up. 'So you're saying that's what this is about? A bunch of people protecting the secret of this chopped-off head, which for some reason is so important that they'll kill to stop anyone learning about it. Are you serious, Roberta? You actually expect me to swallow this rubbish?'

She shrugged. 'I know how it sounds. I can't help thinking that there's something deeper to it, but who knows? Maybe there was no head at all. Maybe it's all symbolic, a representation of great learning and wisdom. Or then again, I could be totally wrong about all of this, and the bearded head was just another phony charge that the Templars' prosecutors dreamed up. I've a feeling it wasn't, though. Anyway,' she said, raising her hands in a gesture of helplessness. 'These are the ideas I've been working on. I really want to know what this Baphomet thing is. I'm convinced I'm close to figuring it out, Ben. Or I was, before all this happened.'

'In other words,' Ben said, containing his annoyance, 'this is about as far as your research goes to date, and beyond some vague and absurd notion about a severed head, you basically haven't the faintest idea what any of this is about.'

Roberta's cheeks flushed as she became defensive. 'We have a lot to go on,' she countered. 'Now you're here, you and I can work out the rest together. Like we did before. We're a pretty good team, the two of us.'

He got up from the bed and started pacing the floor. 'Really? And what if we're just wasting our time with all this nutty Templar crap? Meanwhile, these bastards are getting away.'

'Damn right it's nutty,' she said, getting to her feet and facing him angrily. 'It seems that way even to me, and that's saying something. But it doesn't matter what you or I believe. What matters is that *they* do.' She pointed towards the window, as though their enemies were standing right outside looking in. 'And they'll kill us over it, like they'll kill anyone who tries to poke their nose into whatever this thing is they're trying to protect.'

'It doesn't make sense,' Ben said, shaking his head as he tried to form some kind of order out of all his jumbled thoughts. 'We're getting nowhere like this. There' got to be another way.'

'They're a secret society, Ben. And that's what they do to stay that way: protect their secrets, or else they'd stop existing. Which means that the closer we are to the truth, the more of a threat we'll be to them and the harder they'll try to stop us. Maybe that's how we get to the truth, because sooner or later they have to reveal themselves.'

Ben stopped pacing and looked at her. He was about to reply when his phone suddenly started burring in his pocket. He pulled it out.

'Not sleeping?' Jeff said. 'Me neither.'

Chapter 28

The sound of his friend's voice was a welcome respite and filled Ben with relief. Or it would have, except for one thing that he couldn't fail to notice immediately: the slurred tones that told him Jeff had been at the booze, and obviously hitting it pretty hard.

Ben couldn't blame him. Left to his own devices, hampered by an injury and stuck helpless in a room somewhere, he'd probably have been drowning his sorrows in just the same way. Maybe even more so. 'Where are you?'

Jeff laughed, but there was no humour in it. 'Don't you worry about me, mate,' he drawled. 'Everything's taken care of, strictly according to instructions.' Some of those two-and three-syllable words were having trouble finding their way past his thick tongue.

'You checked out of the hotel?'

'Yup, and now I'm booked into this other joint across town. You're talking to Mr Walsh. Can't remember the name of the place. Got a card here. Hold on.' There were some fumbling sounds on the line, and then Jeff read out the name and address of the hotel. His French pronunciation was so bad that Ben made him repeat it twice. 'Any trouble?' Ben asked.

'Nah, mate. Life's fucking perfect. Only problem I've got is that my second bottle's run empty and I can't get any more until the hotel bar opens again.'

'Take it easy, Jeff.'

'I am taking it easy,' Jeff said bitterly. 'What other choice do I have? But to hell with all that shit. How's things for you?'

'We're fine,' Ben replied, and instantly regretted his words.

Even half drunk, Jeff's wits were still sharper than most and he instantly picked up on Ben's slip. 'Eh? Who's "we?"'

'Forgot to mention,' Ben said, not wanting to get into a lengthy explanation. 'I ran into an old friend tonight. You remember Roberta?'

There was a momentary pause on the line as Jeff's clouded memory cranked into action. 'The American chick? What the fuck's *she* doing there?'

'Helping us,' Ben replied, glancing at Roberta, who was listening intently and trying to glean all she could from the one-sided conversation. He was only glad she hadn't been able to hear Jeff's 'chick' reference, or there'd have been hell to pay. Before Jeff could start firing off more questions he changed the subject. 'Never mind that for now. Heard from Moody yet?'

'Matter of fact I have,' Jeff slurred. 'Couple of minutes ago. That's what I was calling about. Six of the guys just landed outside Quillan and they've phoned to tell me they're on their way here right now. What's that about, mate?'

So Valentina had come through, Ben thought with a smile. 'To get you home safe, Jeff,' he replied. 'Things are going to start hotting up and I need you out of there.'

'Home is the last sodding place I want to be right now,' Jeff objected, predictably enough. 'I'm in this too, busted ankle or no busted ankle. And nothing you can say or do is going to get me to change my fucking mind, all right?'

'Don't argue with me, Jeff. Please. And don't give Jimmy and the boys a hard time, now will you?'

Jeff gave another harsh laugh. 'Who, me? No worries. I'll be as docile as a fucking little lamb, mate.' He fell into a simmering silence as Ben explained the rest of the plan. When he spoke again, he sounded resigned and suddenly very dopey. 'Okay, I get it,' he muttered. 'What about you?'

'Everything's under control,' Ben told him. 'We're going to try and grab some kip. I suggest you do the same.' The best thing for Jeff would be to pass out in an alcoholic stupor until Jimmy Moody and the guys came to collect him. Ben added confidently, 'Then we'll move to the next phase.'

Jeff sighed. 'All right. Well, you take care, mate. I'm only sorry I can't be . . .' Then his slurring words trailed off to nothing, and Ben heard the inebriated snore on the line. He shook his head and ended the call.

'I think I got most of that,' Roberta said. 'Your friend didn't sound very pleased that I was with you, did he? Probably sees me as a troublemaker.'

'Where did you get that idea? Anyway, he's too drunk to think straight.'

'And the next phase?' she asked, raising an eyebrow. 'Care to enlighten me what that is?'

Ben was too weary to try to pretend. 'Roberta, right now I haven't the faintest clue where we're going from here. I was only telling him that to sound positive. He needs it.'

For the moment, though, what mattered was that things were in hand back in Quillan and they were safe here at the motel. All Ben wanted was to rest a while, in the hope that some inspired new idea, if not a fully-formed strategy then at least the germ of one, would come to him when he felt fresher. 'Nobody's going to find us in this place,' he told her, pulling the Browning from his belt and offering it to her. 'But take this just in case. You've used it before. Do you remember how?'

She pushed the gun away. 'Thanks, but no thanks. You're just next door. If the bad guys come in the night I'll thump on the wall for Superman to come rescue me, okay?'

'Good night, then. Don't forget to lock yourself in.'

'Good night, Ben.'

He left her room feeling a little dazed, not just with the extreme fatigue that was dragging him down, but with the strangest impression of how completely natural and familiar it felt to be so close to Roberta Ryder again. However unexpected and bewildering their sudden reunion and despite everything that was happening, he was acutely aware of being as comfortable in her presence as if they'd never been apart these last few years.

He'd loved other women since, and thought about them often. There had been Leigh Llewellyn, the deepest heartbreak of his life. Brooke Marcel, whom he'd come so close to marrying. Abbie Logan, the one thing he'd regretted about leaving Australia. Most recently, there had been his short-lived relationship with a Chinese police detective called Shi Yun Lin.

But Ben would have been deceiving himself not to admit that it was his memories of his and Roberta's time together in France, then in Canada, that had most often haunted his dreams on and off over the years. And now here she was, this fiery-headed will-o'-the-wisp, this untamed spirit, every bit as independent and irrepressible and mysteriously alluring as he remembered her. Even those traits of her character that were perhaps somewhat less cosy and heart-warming – the ever-ready sharp tongue, the barbed comments she could pull out and fire off faster than a gun, that acerbic look that came into her eye when she became defensive, as she frequently did – were like an old pair of shoes that he could slip into with ease.

'I must be crazy,' he murmured to himself as he paused for a moment on the walkway outside their rooms. He heard the reassuring click of her lock, and the sounds of her moving about inside. Maybe he should have stayed in there with her, he thought. Sleeping on the floor while she took the bed. Or maybe that wouldn't have been a good idea, for either of them.

He looked at his watch, then up at the sky. The deep reds and purples of dawn were beginning to lighten, shot through with threads of glimmering gold as the sun began its rise behind the hills and mountains to the east. If things stayed true to plan, Jeff would be back at Le Val not long after daybreak and Ben would be able to stop worrying about him. Their home base was fast becoming an impregnable armed camp as more of the faithful turned up in support of their comrades. Then as soon as Sadler could leave the hospital, it would be his turn to be taken there for safekeeping, too, until this was over. Something else less to stress over.

But then there was the other concern, the acute constant pressure that couldn't be pushed to the back of Ben's mind and threatened to steal away any hopes of rest if he allowed himself to dwell on it too much. Nothing could make him forget the constant ache he felt for Tuesday. He knew that Jeff was feeling it too. Soon it would be time to make the necessary arrangements for transporting the body to Jamaica for the funeral, and the worst part of that dreaded occasion would be meeting the distraught family. It occurred to him that if things went badly here down south in the meantime and he didn't make it out of this situation alive, then he'd at least be spared that ordeal. Jeff would be left having to make the arrangements for both of them.

So be it, if necessary. He didn't fear death, not his own. But now that Roberta was in this too, the responsibility for her safety changed everything. It wouldn't be easy to convince her to stay safely in the background.

He stood for a few minutes watching the sunrise and pensively smoking a Gauloise to try to calm his mind. Then he flicked away the glowing stub and retreated to his own room. It was a mirror image of Roberta's, basic and utilitarian and stuffy from the heat of the previous day. He was so tired that he didn't bother to use the bathroom or undress, but instead fell straight into the lumpy single bed, closed his eyes and let the welcome darkness close over him like a blanket. In just a few heartbeats he began to drift off to a place where at least some of his troubles were far behind him. He could see Roberta's face in his mind, hear the sound of her voice and feel that tangible, strangely comforting presence of her close by.

But Ben didn't drift very far, or for very long. He couldn't have been dreaming for more than a few short minutes before he was jolted suddenly wide awake again by the vibration of his phone in his pocket. He snapped upright and swung his legs over the edge of the bed to answer the call.

This time, it was from Jimmy Moody. And Ben knew from the moment he heard his voice that something had gone wrong.

'Ben? Ah, listen, buddy. We have a problem.'

Chapter 29

Sometime before dawn Jimmy Moody, Mike Rusk, Jack Brett, 'Rocket' Lockett, Nobby Duke and Mel Craig had disembarked from the Kaprisky corporate jet at a private airfield half an hour's drive from Quillan. Each of the six carried a concealed weapon borrowed from the Le Val armoury and wore a steely expression that said 'don't mess with me'. They were all seasoned experts in their trade, and they were only too ready and willing to encounter trouble.

As they stepped down onto the tarmac, a black mini-van appeared and took them into the town. They spoke little, partly because of their sombre mood, and partly because each man was already thoroughly familiar with his role. As arranged, the mini-van stopped first at the Centre Hospitalier de Quillan in Rue du Dr Roueylou, where Lockett, Duke and Craig were dropped off. They parted from the rest of the team with barely a nod, and started making their way towards the hospital buildings.

From there the van continued across town to the address they'd been given, a hotel on the outskirts called Le Petit Moulin. The van driver was a lowly employee of the Kaprisky empire and had no idea of the purpose of the men's mission, only that his passengers were here to pick up someone else who would be flying back with them that morning. He parked in a narrow side street near the hotel, with instructions to wait until his passengers returned. Moody, Rusk and Brett got out and walked to the hotel.

None of the three paid any attention to the innocuous silver Peugeot 308 parked across the street. Nor did any of them notice that behind its tinted windows were two men, who watched them closely as they approached the hotel and disappeared inside the reception lobby. The two men exchanged glances. 'What now?' one of them asked. 'We keep waiting,' replied the other. They both spoke Italian, though for the second man it wasn't his native language.

Unaware that their movements were being observed, Moody, Rusk and Brett strode into the small front office and rang the service bell on the reception desk. The night manager was nearing the end of his shift. He'd been notified in advance that their somewhat disreputable British guest Monsieur Walsh, who'd only checked in hours before, was due to receive three visitors. The hotel disapproved of these early morning comings and goings, but thankfully it looked as though Monsieur Walsh wouldn't be staying long. In any case, the manager wasn't about to complain to these rather intimidating and taciturn foreigners, whom he duly showed up to Room 11.

They knocked, the door opened after a pause, and the manager caught the smell of spirits wafting from inside the room. Monsieur Walsh was dressed but rather the worse for wear, thanks no doubt to the bottles of spirits he'd been clutching when he'd limped into their establishment earlier that night. Shaking his head and muttering something under his breath about these *connards de rosbifs*, he left them to it and returned downstairs.

What happened next came as a total surprise to Jimmy Moody and his companions.

'What do you mean, you're not coming?' Moody said, stunned.

'You heard me,' Jeff answered, slurry but quite resolute. 'Changed my mind, so fuck off and leave me alone 'cause I'm not going anywhere.'

'But we've come all this way specially,' Moody said, lamely.

'I never asked you to, did I?'

Moody put on a smile, trying to be conciliatory. 'Come on, buddy. You're pissed as a fart and you can hardly stand on that ankle. Let's go.' He gently reached out to take Jeff's arm. But Jeff jerked his arm away, clenched his fist tight and rammed it into Moody's chin. Moody fell back and collapsed on the floor.

'I said leave me alone!' Jeff yelled incoherently. Next to make a grab for him was Mike Rusk, but he should have moved faster because even full of booze, Jeff Dekker was no slouch when it came to hand-to-hand fighting. Before Rusk knew what hit him, he was joining Moody on the carpet with a smear of blood under his nose. Jeff backed away, staggering on his bad ankle but fists raised and a ferocious gleam in his eyes.

His blows had been delivered hard, but only hard enough to fend off his friends, battle-hardened professionals that they were, without doing any critical damage. Moody and Rusk sprang back up to their feet, and Jack Brett joined them as they closed in on Jeff shoulder to shoulder and forced him back into the corner of the room. A side table toppled over, and with it a lamp and the two empty vodka bottles whose contents Jeff had poured down his throat.

'Come on, Jeff. Don't be stupid! We're your mates!'

'If you were, you wouldn't be doing this,' Jeff drawled, pointing an accusing finger at them. 'Now get out of here, or you'll wish you had.'

This time it was Brett's turn to make a determined lunge at Jeff. He managed to get a hold of his collar and then let out a yell as his fingers were bent back and his wrist folded at an angle that caused a jab of excruciating pain. Jeff kept hold of his arm and used the leverage to dump him on the floor like a sack of potatoes. But Jeff's reflexes were impaired and he'd taken his eyes off the other two for a split second too long; seeing his opportunity, Moody launched himself back into the fray, dodged a vicious punch that would have knocked him unconscious if it had landed, and after a brief struggle somehow managed to pin Jeff's arms behind his back. By this time Brett was upright again, and he and Rusk helped Moody manhandle the wildly resisting Jeff over to the bed, where they got him face down. Brett did what he could to control his arms while Rusk lay across both of his legs to stop him thrashing out with his feet.

'Cut it out, Jeff mate!'

'Go fuck yourselves!' came the muffled yell from underneath.

'This is no bloody good,' Moody said breathlessly. A trickle of blood ran from the corner of his mouth. It was like trying to handle a wild animal, and a wounded and enraged one at that. How the hell they were going to get him out of the hotel and into the van without it looking like the world's most inept kidnapping and bringing down every cop in Quillan on their heads, was anyone's guess.

'We need help,' Rusk panted, barely able to keep their prisoner from wriggling out of his grip.

Moody nodded. There was only one person alive who could persuade Jeff to cooperate. He reluctantly took out his phone and started dialling the number.

Chapter 30

It was on the outskirts of the sleeping village of Tarascon-sur-Ariège that Jacques, Bertrand and Chrétien had been able to steal a car with which to limp back to base. Dawn wasn't far off by the time the three defeated men ditched the vehicle in a thorny hollow in the wilderness of the garrigue and made the rest of the way to the fortress on foot with the ailing Bertrand lagging badly behind.

Once back at their refuge they put away their weapons and stripped off their dirty, sweaty clothes, together with the bulletproof vests that in Bertrand's case had been a life-saver. In their place they donned their loose-fitting long robes, and though they were all desperately hungry and thirsty they went straight to their prayer altar to kneel in penitence to God for their failure that night and beg for His Divine mercy.

After the solemn prayers were done, it fell on Jacques as their leader to make the call to the Grand Master. This time they couldn't expect much in the way of forgiveness for their lack of success.

Far away, the Grand Master was sitting in the private haven of his castle turret when the phone rang. It was a place in which he spent a great deal of his time bent over the old volumes from his extensive library: he was often deeply immersed in the same leather-bound Bible he had been reading all his life, or else poring over rare works of ancient philosophy or history. He was a highly-learned man who had spent most of his adult years in deep, solitary reflection. He lived alone and had never married nor ever been close to a woman, having sworn his vow of chastity and celibacy before God as a young man and adhered to it as strictly as a monk ever since. As a solitary lifelong bachelor he was free to keep his own hours, enjoying the stillness of the night and often not retiring to bed until later in the morning. He'd been wide awake when he'd received the call.

He listened quietly as Jacques gave him the bad news. On the stone wall behind where he sat hung the great emblem of their order, gleaming in the early morning light from the tower's east-facing window, a priceless and ancient relic that he honoured greatly. The view from the high windows gave a view of part of the château's grounds and the dawn-lit contours of the vast hedge maze that dominated the formal garden below.

'So you failed,' he replied. His voice was as cold and unemotional as the punishment he was liable to dish out in retribution. 'And what exactly seems to be the problem?'

'The problem is this man Hope, Master,' Jacques explained, anxious not to sound as though he was making excuses. 'He's proving to be harder to eliminate than we anticipated. It's going to take more men to complete the task.'

'I see,' said the Grand Master. 'That sounds suspiciously like you telling me how to run my operation.'

'Master, I beg you to believe that wasn't my intention! I only meant—'

'But let's suppose for a moment,' the Grand Master went on, cutting him off, 'that your assessment is correct. Certainly, everything we have learned about this man would indicate that he is extremely difficult to kill. One can only suppose that many others must have tried and failed to do so before now. It was the nature of his profession. And so perhaps it's simply the case that I overestimated your ability to handle the task. There's also the other matter of Sadler, the English property agent. That was a job half-finished that I might have expected to have been completed by now.'

'He is still in the hospital, Master.'

'And I suppose you're going to tell me that you can't get to him, with only three men at your disposal.'

Jacques made no reply. There was little point in reminding the Master of the two targets they'd successfully eliminated so far, a poor excuse for failing to get the others.

'As I thought. Now, as to your request for reinforcements. Perhaps I need only provide one extra man, to take over from you personally. A replacement leader more capable of satisfying my instructions.'

Jacques felt a chill go down his spine. And rightly so, because if the Grand Master ordered his execution it could be carried out immediately by the others. Death was almost preferable to the eternal shame of being banished from the order.

The Grand Master paused thoughtfully for a moment. 'That said, I'm prepared to be lenient with you, Jacques. You have always been loyal to me. And I always repay loyalty. I will provide you with the extra resources you require to swiftly and comprehensively stamp out this threat to our order. It's imperative that both Hope and the woman be eliminated, and as soon as possible.'

'Thank you, Master.'

'And on further reflection,' the Grand Master added, 'it occurs to me that we possess other assets to be deployed in addition, to help ensure our success in this matter.'

Jacques couldn't ask what those assets might be, and needless to say the Grand Master wasn't compelled to reveal his thoughts while speaking to an underling so far below his own station. But his superior had a particular individual in mind.

That was because the Grand Master of the order was much more than just the all-powerful head of a secret society that had survived and protected its interests for the better part of a thousand years. He was also a political figure in his own right, a skilled businessman and a wily tactician who understood better than most the art of wielding control over others. That control was often simply bought for cash, but on other occasions it could be obtained by means of fear, manipulation and blackmail. During his long tenure as Grand Master he had greatly extended the network of connections inherited from his predecessor. It ranged all across Europe and included some very lofty names indeed.

As the Grand Master was well aware, the higher one climbs the tree, the riper the fruits for those looking to gain the advantage of entrapment. He regarded his victims simply as investments for the future, which could be cashed in at opportune moments.

But it wasn't only the rich and powerful who could be made to pay dividends with a metaphorical gun to their head. Over the years, thanks to his small army of spies, loyal informants and private detectives, the Grand Master had also garnered a surprising amount of dirt on even some of the lowlier names on his list. One of those individuals over whom he'd gained a hold was a particular state employee within the Languedoc region. The Grand Master was in possession of certain information which, if ever made known to the authorities for whom this individual worked, would bring their career to a very sudden and dramatic close. It might very possibly also land them in prison for a long, long time.

Once the Grand Master had you in his clutches he would never let you go. Like a virtuoso chess player weaving a multi-dimensional web of potential strategies across the board, he'd been holding on to this information for years, allowing it to rest in a dormant state quite unknown to the hapless stooge, who was now shortly to discover to their horror that they'd become a useful pawn in his game.

'Leave it with me,' the Grand Master told Jacques. 'I will make the appropriate calls and set things in motion. In the meantime, do nothing until your reinforcements join you at your base. Then we'll strike hard and fast at each of our targets simultaneously. There'll be no possible chance of escaping us this time.'

Chapter 31

While their associates were being kept busy at the Hotel Petit Moulin, Lockett, Duke and Craig had begun attending to their protection duties at the Centre Hospitalier across town. As expected, the local police had made no effort to post anyone on watch at the hospital for the safety of the injured man they were here to safeguard. So much the better, for their purposes.

It had been a sultry night, and having just flown in from England they were still acclimatising to the heat. All three had removed their jackets and were wearing short-sleeved shirts underneath, from which the muscles of their arms bulged like strings of sausages. Craig had a faded regimental insignia tattooed on one of his, and Duke wore the ugly scar of a machine gun bullet that had ploughed a furrow from wrist to elbow. Their compact concealed weapons were strapped into inside-the-waistband holsters nestled invisibly into the smalls of their backs.

In the passable French that Lockett had taught himself while working as a private military security adviser in Gabon and Burundi, he introduced himself and his companions to the receptionist as friends of Mr Sadler, and asked about visiting hours. They were told that the patient was still in a weakened state, and although he'd had a few visitors already he could only see people for a short while as he was apt to tire very quickly. Nobody would be allowed in until a few hours' time, later that morning.

No matter. They had no real intention of seeing him anyway and the less Sadler knew of their presence here the better, in case he blabbed it to anyone and blew their cover. The three men repaired to a public waiting area and sat patiently, browsing through some magazines which, being all in French, only Lockett could make any sense of but had enough pictures of tanned, toned young female celebrities to at least pretend to pass the time with. Like all former combat soldiers they were well schooled in the art of sitting around on standby for long periods, silent and outwardly relaxed but primed to go into action at a second's notice. They were quite prepared to remain tacitly on guard duty for days if necessary, taking alternate watches, moving position around the buildings and grounds and remaining highly discreet while closely monitoring the comings and goings at the hospital for any sign of a threat against their VIP principal. Each of them was highly skilled at spotting a covert operator, whether it was an undercover terrorist or an infiltrating assassin, and they had the training to deal with any such threat in the most efficient way.

But on this occasion their skills had let them down, because no sooner had they arrived than someone else in the hospital was aware of their presence, and its reason for being.

The elderly man was sitting at the far side of the waiting area, where he'd apparently been for some time before the men appeared. He was slightly built and in his late seventies with thinning white hair, very neatly dressed in a dark suit and gleaming patent leather shoes, a Burberry trench coat carefully folded on the plastic seat next to his, and a small leather satchel at his feet. Unusually in the age when everyone was constantly glued to some digital device or other he was engrossed in a real, actual book, a hardback edition of a political memoir, which he was reading attentively through an old-fashioned pair of half-moon spectacles.

Lockett, Duke and Craig had had a good look at the old geezer as they'd walked into the waiting area and immediately dismissed him as harmless. Just some relative of a patient at the hospital, no doubt. Perhaps waiting, as they ostensibly were themselves, for visiting hours to come around. He seemed too engrossed in his reading to have noticed their arrival.

But in fact, from the moment the three of them strolled casually by and took their seats on the far side of the waiting area, the well-dressed old gent had been observing them with a penetrating and thoughtful eye; and if they'd really been paying attention they would have noticed that he'd stopped turning the pages of his book so often. After a few more minutes of this, he smiled knowingly to himself, quietly closed the book and laid it down beside him on his coat, then stood up and walked over to them. They looked up, taken aback, as he approached.

'Excuse me, Messieurs,' he said, bending down to speak softly to them in English. 'I wondered if I might have a moment of your time?'

'Who're you?' Lockett asked fairly gruffly, eyeing him with some suspicion. 'How'd you know we're British?'

'Do please forgive me for eavesdropping,' the old man said, 'but I couldn't help overhearing your conversation with the receptionist when you arrived. Your accent is, shall we say, not native to this country.' His own was very much so, though his spoken English, while rather formal and a little archaic, was perfectly fluent.

'So what can we do for you?' muttered Duke, scowling up at him.

'May I sit?' the old man asked politely, motioning to an empty chair nearby. 'My knees are a little weak in my old age.' Making himself comfortable, he said, 'Allow me to introduce myself. My name is Jean-Rafael Silvestre. I gather that we have a mutual friend in your fellow countryman, Mathieu Sadler.' He pronounced it the French way. 'Then, sadly, you have come here for the same reason as me.'

This was a potential problem for the three, because they hadn't reckoned on meeting anyone who knew Sadler personally and weren't sufficiently well briefed to be in any way convincing. 'That's right,' Lockett said with an awkward smile that looked more like a leer.

The old man was peering so intently at them that his pale grey eyes, magnified in the half-moon lenses, seemed to bore unsettlingly right into theirs. 'Please correct me if I'm wrong,' he said with that knowing smile, 'but I form the general impression that you three gentlemen are not exactly relatives of his, and I don't believe I have ever seen you around. This is a rather small town, where people tend to know one another at least by sight. Therefore I would conclude that, in the light of my friend's reasons for requiring treatment at this hospital, you must be here for a particular purpose. Namely, to help protect him from any further harm. Yet it appears to me that you are not police officers. Am I correct?'

Lockett, Duke and Craig all frowned at the old man and said nothing. In a matter of just minutes, their cover had been blown wide open. How could he have seen through them so easily?

Jean-Rafael Silvestre said, 'I understand your mistrust, which is highly justifiable under the circumstances. For all you know, my own intentions towards Monsieur Sadler are not benevolent. And yet, please be assured this is anything but the case. He and I have known one another for many years, since he was a child. And I'm only too pleased to know that someone is looking out for his wellbeing.'

Nobody spoke. Duke's jaw had dropped. Craig was staring wide-eyed. Lockett's expression was surly and hostile.

The old man paused, still peering at them with a strange kind of intensity. 'You may ask, how can I be sure of your good intentions and that you are not, yourselves, a group of sinister miscreants come to murder my poor friend in his hospital bed?' He pointed at their bare arms. 'That is because, if you were, you would be wearing the mark. And I can see that you are not; therefore I am confident that you represent no threat either to him, or to me. Please tell me, am I correct in my assessment?'

'Yes,' was all Lockett could say. Duke and Craig just nodded dumbly. All three were utterly confused.

The old man's smile widened. 'Good. I believe I have some idea who might have sent you, for which I am extremely grateful.' Taking an elegant calf-skin wallet from his inner suit pocket he produced a card, which he held out to them. 'Please let Mathieu's benefactor know that I would be interested in speaking with him, as I have information that may be of the utmost importance to him. He should not hesitate to call, day or night.'

Lockett took the card and gazed at it. It bore only the name the old man had given them, along with a phone number. 'I'll pass the message on,' he muttered.

'Thank you so much,' the old man said. He looked suddenly tired. 'And now you are here, I believe I can end my own vigil over my poor friend and return home to get some much-needed rest. Your presence is a great relief to me, gentlemen. Goodbye, and God bless you.'

With that, he stood up, returned to the seat where he'd left his coat and satchel, picked them up and left the waiting room.

Lockett, Craig and Duke exchanged baffled looks, all with the same question. 'Who the hell was *that* guy?'

Chapter 32

The instant he got off the phone with Moody, Ben was racing from his room and thumping on Roberta's door. After a few moments she answered the door in her underwear, making him instinctively avert his eyes. Her hair was tousled and she looked as if she'd been fast asleep.

'What's up?' she asked, alarmed.

'Get dressed. We have to leave here right away.'

'Give me a minute,' she said, and closed the door in his face. He hovered impatiently outside for less than forty-five seconds before it opened again and she reappeared, fully dressed and ready and saying, 'Let's go.' Roberta Ryder wasn't one to spend long on hair and makeup, bless her. Ben quickly explained why he needed to hurry back to Quillan.

'Reminds me of the time you got drunk as a skunk in that village, Saint Jean, after we'd hit a dead end,' she commented as they headed for the car.

'That was different,' he said. 'And it's my fault. He's not himself. I should have seen it and taken better care of him.'

'There you go again,' she sighed. 'Always wanting to take the blame. You don't change a whole lot, do you?' But Ben wasn't listening as he jumped behind the wheel. His face was severe and he didn't say another word until they reached Quillan. The Alpina screeched to a halt at the kerb outside the Petit Moulin, where Jimmy Moody would have been waiting to greet him if he hadn't had his hands full upstairs.

'Christ knows how many speed limits we just busted,' Roberta said. 'But here we are still in one piece, and now I'm about to meet the famous Jeff Dekker.'

'Not at his best,' Ben warned her. 'Might want to stay back. This could get a little rough.'

But that at least was one needless concern, because as Moody showed Ben and Roberta into Room 11 a minute later, they found that the litre and a half of vodka Jeff had consumed had finally knocked him out and he was lying semi-comatose on the bed. One look at the wreckage of the room and the bruised, bloodied state of the three men was enough to give Ben a pretty good picture of the spirited resistance his friend had put up, sprained ankle or not.

'I'm afraid to wake him in case he kicks off again,' Moody said apologetically. 'Not that I can blame the poor guy for taking it so badly. We're all feeling like dogshit after what's happened.'

'Leave him to me,' Ben said. 'Brew up some coffee.' When it came, hot and black, he sat on the edge of the bed and gently prodded Jeff awake. 'Easy, easy,' he said as his friend reared up with his eyes blazing and fists clenched. Coming to his senses, Jeff softened and fell back with a groan. 'Fuck, my head! Feels like someone jammed a phosphorus grenade in my skull.'

'Get this down you,' Ben said. 'And then let's see if we can't behave ourselves, eh? Honestly, what a state. Your eyes look like two burnt holes in a blanket.'

'Seen yourself in the mirror, mate?' Jeff countered. 'You don't look so great either.' And Ben would have to admit Jeff was probably right about that.

It took a few minutes for even Ben to persuade the badly hung-over but still resistant Jeff to cooperate and let himself be taken home to Le Val. Finally, with a more subdued and contrite Jeff in tow, they stepped out into the morning sunshine. The mini-van was still waiting nearby to take them to the airfield. Ben shook hands with Moody, Rusk and Brett. Then turned to Jeff and gave him a tight hug. 'Take care, Jeff. Be good.'

'Call me,' Jeff muttered. 'And watch your back, all right?'

Ben nodded. He watched as Jeff reluctantly boarded the van, followed by Rusk and Brett. Moody paused before getting in, and turned to Ben. 'Who are these bastards, Ben?'

'We're working on that,' Ben said.

'Let us know if you need us. I mean that.'

'Just get him home,' Ben said. 'And don't let him leave.'

He raised his hand in a wave as the van drove away. In just a few minutes they'd be boarding the Kaprisky jet, and they'd be back at the safety of Le Val long before midday. He kept watching it until it was gone. Then he and Roberta were alone again.

But they were about to discover that they weren't as alone as they thought.

'You look upset,' she said, tenderly reaching for his hand.

He said nothing, but as her warm fingers intertwined with his he felt a surge of sadness from deep inside him. He covered his emotions hoping she wouldn't notice, but Roberta didn't miss much.

'We passed a café back there down the street,' she said. 'Want some breakfast?'

Before he could reply, the doors of a silver Peugeot parked opposite the hotel opened and two men got out. Ben's spider sense made him turn to look at them. He caught their eye. They were looking straight back.

'What's this?' Roberta asked, suddenly anxious. 'Ben?'

The two men stepped away from the silver car and began crossing the street. One was tall and thin with fair hair turning grey at the edges, the other shorter and stockier, dark with a grizzled beard. In casual clothes, open-neck shirts and loose jackets, they could have been anybody. But Ben knew instantly they were here for a special reason – and that it concerned him.

He let go of Roberta's hand, and his own went quickly and quietly around his right hip to where the butt of his pistol was hidden under his jacket. He didn't pull the weapon out from his waistband, but his thumb was riding the safety catch ready to draw and fire if he needed to.

The two men kept advancing across the street. They paused in their step to let a car go by, then came closer. They walked with their hands in plain view and made no threatening moves, or else Ben would have had the pistol out and pointing at them.

'Ben?' Roberta said again. Her eyes were full of trepidation. 'Who are they?'

Ben didn't know the answer to that, but he sensed they were about to find out.

The two men finished crossing the street and stepped right up to where Ben and Roberta were standing warily waiting for them. Nobody spoke for a moment. Then the short, dark one of the two men said, 'Signore Hope?'

Signore. Whoever they were, they weren't from around here.

Ben relaxed his gun hand, but he didn't let go of the pistol butt. He looked the two men in the eye, first the tall one and then the short one, and replied, 'I'm Ben Hope.' And waited for them to say more.

The taller man spoke next. Unlike his colleague he wasn't Italian, but to Ben's surprise spoke with the accent of someone born and raised in Dublin. Ben had lived long enough in Ireland himself to recognise it right away.

The Irishman said, 'Mr Hope, we know who's threatening you. We know why they're doing it. And we would like to help you.'

Chapter 33

'Is there somewhere we can talk?' the Irishman asked.

Roberta looked uncertainly at Ben, waiting for his lead. Ben considered for a moment. He thought about that café down the street that Roberta had just mentioned, then decided a less public place might be better suited. 'Fine,' he replied. 'But not here. Let's go upstairs to my office.'

Ben hadn't yet settled Jeff's hotel bill, so for the moment Room 11 was still technically theirs to use. He showed the two men inside the lobby, past the frowning manager and up the stairs. As they headed towards the room Roberta was giving him looks as if to say, 'Are you sure about this?'

When the door was closed, Ben drew the pistol from his belt and pointed it loosely at the strangers. 'Stand there and don't move,' he ordered them. 'Hold your arms out to the sides. Hands where I can see them.'

They seemed to have anticipated it, and obeyed willingly enough. Ben passed the pistol to Roberta for her to train on them while he patted down each man in turn for weapons. They had none. When he was finished, he picked up a couple of chairs overturned in the struggle earlier, and made the two men sit with their backs to the wall where he could watch both them and the door. Roberta gave him back the Browning and he replaced it in his belt.

'You take no chances,' observed the Irishman.

'It's why I'm still here,' Ben said. 'All right. You have something to say, let's hear it. Starting with who you are. You can leave out the preferred pronouns bit.'

'My name is Father Dominic Sheehan,' the Irishman said. 'This is my associate, Father Claudio Bertolli.'

'You're priests?'

Both men nodded. 'We are on special detachment from the Vatican,' said the one called Bertolli, in his thick Italian accent.

Roberta stared at them in astonishment, but Ben's expression remained hard. 'You have some form of ID to verify that?'

The Irish one, Sheehan, shook his head and replied, 'Under the circumstances, it wouldn't be wise for us to openly reveal our identities to too many people. That's also the reason we're travelling in plain clothes. I can show you my driving licence, if you like.'

Ben examined the photo card licence, which seemed real enough but you never could tell. He'd had plenty of fake documents made for himself in the past. Returning it to Sheehan he said, 'Then for the moment I'll have to take your word for the rest of it. Now let's get to the part where you managed to find us. I'm not too amenable to having a couple of strangers shadowing me around, and it usually doesn't work out well for them.'

Sheehan seemed to want to do most of the talking. 'A lucky coincidence,' he explained. 'We've been sitting outside this hotel, watching and waiting in the hopes that we might be able to meet and talk to you personally.'

'And why would you be watching the hotel?'

Sheehan replied, 'We weren't there long. Only since your friend Mr Dekker checked in here last night. We'd followed him from the other hotel, the one you both were staying in before, along with the late and I'm sure much lamented Mr Fletcher. It was easy enough to find you there.'

'Our condolences for your sad loss,' Bertolli said. 'Eternal rest grant unto him, O Lord, and let perpetual light shine upon him.' He bowed his head and made the sign of the cross over his heart.

'Thanks for the sentiment,' Ben said. 'And I see you've been doing your homework about us. But you're going to have to work a little harder to make me understand why two Vatican priests would be sneaking about watching our movements.'

'All will become clear if you allow us to explain,' said Sheehan. 'You see, Mr Hope – or should I call you Major Hope? – we, or should I say our superiors, became interested in this situation after hearing the news of what happened. The terrible incident that tragically claimed the life of your friend has been reported to a limited extent in the media, but only a small few people privy to certain inside knowledge understand what it really was about.'

'And I'm not one of them,' Ben said. 'Not yet.'

'Then it will interest you to know that we have a shared enemy,' Sheehan replied. 'The same men who murdered your friend Tuesday Fletcher are members of a secret organisation that has been waging war against the Vatican for decades, centuries in fact. A war that is still very much in progress. Our mutual foes are a group calling themselves the Custodes Sacri Secreti.'

'"The Guardians of the Holy Secret,"' Ben translated from the Latin. 'But who are they?'

Bertolli looked grave. 'In a nutshell, Signore Hope, they are the modern-day descendants of a heretical cult whose sworn goal for the last seven hundred or more years has been to destroy the Catholic Church by any means possible. Today, I very much regret to admit, their hateful mission has never been closer to achieving its purpose.'

Ben smiled. 'Put that way, now I'm in danger of beginning to sympathise with them. So tell me, just how do these "heretics" intend to pull off this amazing feat?'

If either priest was offended by his sarcasm, they didn't show it. 'Though their order exists in almost total secrecy,' Sheehan explained, 'the Custodes are a large organisation possessing considerable wealth and resources. We have reason to believe that their current plan is an assassination attempt on the Holy Father. A monstrous act that, as you can imagine, would send shockwaves through the entire establishment, rocking it to its very foundations.'

There was a moment of silence in the room as the enormity of Sheehan's words sank in. Ben raised an eyebrow.

'Kill the pope?' Roberta burst out. 'But I don't understand. What's it got to do with us?'

'It has absolutely nothing to do with us,' Ben told her, without taking his dubious eye off the two priests. 'Our two friends here are either totally insane or they're just talking shit.'

This time, Ben's words had their effect, because Bertolli's face darkened at the insult. 'I assure you, we are perfectly serious.'

'And there's a good reason for telling you,' Sheehan insisted, remaining calmer than his associate.

'I have no interest in your pope,' Ben said. 'But even if what you say is right, aren't they a little off the mark? Tuesday Fletcher was a good man, the best. Even so I can't see anyone mistaking him for the Holy Father of the Catholic Church. My friends and I were the targets, not your boss in Rome.'

'Not to mention me and Brad,' Roberta added.

'There are deeper goings on,' Sheehan told them, 'of which you are even less aware. It goes without saying that the Vatican will do anything in its considerable means to prevent this threat which, were it to succeed, would be a calamity of unimaginable proportions. However, being brutally realistic, even in the worst possible case scenario an assassinated pope can be replaced. The Church itself cannot. Whatever their short-term murderous aims, the more fundamental threat that the Custodes hold against us is a piece of secret information. One that has been kept concealed from the world throughout much of history, and which they claim has the power to bring the whole edifice of the Church to its knees.'

'So that's what they're guarding,' Ben said. He was suddenly thinking back to the mystery of the coded message carved on the crypt wall by Thibault de Roucyboeuf way back in the fourteenth century. But how could it be connected to what these two priests were telling them?

Bertolli nodded solemnly. 'This threat has been hanging like a sword of Damocles over the Vatican for a very long time. But we believe that the day is coming soon when they plan to release their secret. If their claims are true, it could do untold damage.'

'But until the moment they choose to reveal it,' Sheehan said, leaning forward in his chair with an earnest look of appeal in his eyes, 'these bad, bad people will kill anyone who gets too close to finding it out. And that's why we're here. We believe that whatever it is you've uncovered, you've become a very real danger to them. And so they've mobilised their forces against you. Thus it became necessary for us to find you before it was too late.'

'To learn what we know?' Ben asked. 'Then I'm sorry to disappoint you. We can't help you there. As you seem to be such experts on the matter, perhaps you'd share your information with us?'

Sheehan smiled slyly, fixing Ben with a knowing eye. 'Are you saying you do know, but you don't want to tell?'

'I'm saying I'd like to hear it from you first,' Ben said.

It was a stalemate, neither side wanting to make a move. Bertolli broke the tense silence. 'Let us be honest with you. The fact is that we, neither, have any clear idea of just what this deadly secret information consists. Nonetheless we would be very interested in learning more for ourselves in order to establish the nature of the threat and, if genuine, to neutralise it.'

'If you don't know what it is, why would you take it this seriously?' Ben asked.

'Given the nature of their organisation,' Sheehan said, 'we have little choice but to assume it's every bit as real and dangerous as they claim.'

'But apparently you have come much closer to discovering the real truth,' said Bertolli. 'If so, why not tell us what you know?'

Ben looked at the two men and said nothing. He didn't trust them for an instant, and sensed they were playing games with him. This whole thing could be lies and bluff. The tempting thought occurred to him to stick his gun in their faces and force some truth out of them. Instead he opted for leaving the weapon where it was, and said, 'Even if I could answer that, the Vatican's squabble against a rogue religious organisation is none of our affair.'

'It's unfortunate that you should think that way,' Sheehan replied, looking disappointed. 'If you'd been amenable to cooperating with us, we might have been able to help you. By combining our efforts we'd have a much better chance of foiling the Custodes' plans.'

'Combining our efforts in what way?' Ben asked.

Bertolli said, 'At the moment it seems you are the main focus of their attention. They are very intent on eliminating you, that much is clear. And they will not stop trying until either they succeed or you defeat them. The latter option being highly unlikely, I am sorry to say. Whereas we, by contrast, have the resources to deal with them, if only they can be drawn out into the open.'

'With us as the two wriggling little worms that bait your hook,' Ben said.

'That is a crude way of putting it,' Bertolli replied. 'But in effect, yes.'

'You would be well protected from harm,' Sheehan said. 'Working with us would bring the full might and authority of the Vatican to back you up, ready to pounce on them the moment they show themselves. And you'd be handsomely rewarded for your role, not least because the threat against you would be gone for ever. Plus the fact that you would be bringing your friend's murderers to justice. On top of all that, we would of course be looking to show our appreciation in other ways.'

'Ah,' Ben said. 'Good old money. Can't leave that bit out.'

'And all you have to do, Signore Hope,' Bertolli said, 'is share whatever information you have with us and agree to join forces.'

Ben looked at Roberta and could see the doubt in her eyes. She gave a small, almost imperceptible shake of the head. That would have been enough to decide him, if he hadn't been already.

'Well, gentlemen,' he told them, 'that all makes for a very interesting proposition.'

Both priests' eyes gleamed, as if they were confident of having won him over. 'If you would like to take some time to think about it,' Bertolli said, 'that would be acceptable to us.'

'There's no need for that,' Ben replied. 'You can have our answer right now.'

'So what do you think?' Sheehan asked eagerly.

'I think that whatever you're trying to sell us,' Ben told them, 'we're not buying. I'm also thinking that the pair of you had better piss off back to Rome, pronto, or you won't like what happens next. And don't ever show your ugly faces here again.'

Bertolli had turned purple with indignation. Sheehan shrugged resignedly. 'Then there's nothing more to be said.' Slowly, reluctantly, they got up to leave.

But Ben hadn't quite finished with them yet. 'Before you go,' he said when they were halfway to the door.

They froze and turned in unison to gaze back at him.

'Listen very carefully to what I'm about to tell you,' Ben said. 'Because you'll only hear it once. The reason I'm letting you walk away is that I don't really believe a word of what you say and frankly, I'm too tired to give a shit. But if you ever give me cause to regret that decision, I will hunt you down and leave you where I found you. Am I making myself perfectly clear?'

The two men stared boggle-eyed in mute acquiescence for a moment and then shuffled from the room.

'Well, I think they got the point,' Roberta said when they were gone.

'To hell with them,' Ben said. 'Let's go and grab a bite to eat.'

Chapter 34

By the time they'd settled the hotel bill and stepped back outside into the rising heat, the silver Peugeot had disappeared from across the street and the two supposed priests with it. Ben and Roberta left the Alpina where it was in front of the Petit Moulin and walked down to the café she'd noticed on their way here earlier. Roberta checked her phone as they went, then put it away without a word.

'Still nothing from him?' Ben asked.

She shook her head. 'Not a peep. He's gone. Might as well get used to it.'

Ben couldn't think of anything to reassure her otherwise, so he made no reply.

Quillan was in full swing by now as the townsfolk went about their morning routines ahead of another long, warm day. Life going on as it always did, except for some people. Not too many of the locals would be walking around with a pistol hidden on their person, and on the lookout for armed killers who might appear out of nowhere at any moment. There were still a couple of tables free in the busy little café, and Ben and Roberta sat down to order coffees – *noir* for him, *au lait* for her – and a couple of tartines, grilled quarter baguettes sliced lengthwise, which Ben had plain and slathered with a little butter and Roberta, to his surprise, greedily covered with Nutella chocolate spread. 'It's comfort food,' she explained. 'I need comforting.'

'You carry on like that, you'll soon look like your mother.'

'You've never seen my mother.'

'Hold on, you have a bit of chocolate there.' He reached out and gently wiped it from the corner of her lip with his finger, then licked his finger clean. 'Too sweet.' It was an intimate moment that happened so naturally he didn't even realise until he'd done it. For her part, Roberta barely seemed to even notice as she nibbled on a corner of her tartine, looking pensive. 'Think we'll ever see those assholes again?'

'Not if they know what's good for them,' he replied. 'There's something phony about those two. The way they were holding back makes me think they were just fishing. And I don't like being strong-armed into working with a bunch of shady strangers who follow you around like spies and may or may not even be who they say they are.'

'If they're not priests then what are they?'

'I've no idea.'

'You reckon they might have told us more? If we'd put a bit of pressure on them?'

'Like a gun to their heads? The thought did occur to me.' Ben broke off another piece of bread and dunked it in his coffee. Good and strong, the way he liked it, helping to take the edge off his fatigue. 'I don't know, Roberta. Maybe it was a mistake to send them packing so soon. But then how could you trust they were telling the truth, whatever they might have told us?'

'Well, at least we learned something this morning,' Roberta sighed, gazing into her cup. 'Didn't we?'

Ben gave a bitter laugh. 'Yeah, sure. Which is that now apparently we've got the bloody Vatican mixed up in this thing, and all of a sudden you and I are their only hope of preventing a papal assassination. Give me a break. Meanwhile, back on planet Earth, we're back at square one here in Quillan, with precious little to show for our efforts, your buddy Brad still missing, and a bunch of murderers on the loose looking for us. I'd say we're making great progress.'

'The Guardians,' she said thoughtfully. 'Guardians of what, though? If only we could go back to the crypt and work out that damn code.'

He shook his head. 'I told you, that option doesn't work for us. There's got to be a better way of moving forwards.'

'And besides which, you can't stand codes and riddles.'

He was about to reply when his phone went off. As he made a grab for it he expected the call to be from Jimmy Moody or Jeff, but the caller ID told him it was Rocket Lockett phoning him from the hospital. He felt a stab of anxiety.

'No problems this end,' Lockett reassured him. 'Patient seems to be doing okay, except he's sleeping most of the time so they don't want him disturbed. Spoke to a nurse who says they should be able to let him go home in a couple of days.'

Which was all good news to Ben. 'So you've seen nothing suspicious, nobody hanging around the place?'

'Not a soul,' Lockett replied. 'Nobody you'd call suspicious, anyhow. There was just this one funny old geezer we met in the waiting area. Actually that's what I was calling about as well.'

'What funny old geezer?'

'Said he was a friend of Sadler's, come to visit him. Harmless enough, but he freaked us out a bit 'cause he seemed to have figured out exactly who we were. It was like he could read our bloody thoughts. Told us he wanted to talk to you.'

'To me? What about?'

'He wouldn't tell us any more, only that he had important information and you needed to call him. He gave us his card. Hold on a mo . . . Yeah, here it is. Name's Silvestre, Jean-Rafael Silvestre. Want the number?'

'Fire away.' Lockett read it out, and Ben instantly committed it to memory. He'd been looking for a better way forward. Maybe fate had just thrown them a lifeline.

He thanked Lockett for the call, told him to stay in contact, and ended the call quickly so he could punch in the number of this Jean-Rafael Silvestre. As the dial tone sounded in his ear Ben wondered who on earth he might be.

The voice that answered sounded old and crackly. '*Allo? Qui est-ce?*'

'My name is Ben Hope,' Ben said in French. 'Am I speaking to Monsieur Silvestre?'

'This is he. I had been hoping I would hear from you.' The old man paused. 'I suppose you must be wondering who I am.'

'I'm told you're a friend of Matthew Sadler's?'

'Oh yes, for many years. It was he who gave me your name. I also have followed the news story of what happened on the Pont de Clothilde. A terrible business. Terrible!'

Before he'd have to listen to yet more condolences, Ben replied, 'Yes, it was. Monsieur Silvestre, I understand that you had some important information for me.'

'Indeed I have,' Silvestre said. 'However, I think it would be best if you heard it from me face to face. It is really not a conversation to be had over the telephone, for reasons you'll understand.'

'Then we should meet,' Ben said. 'Name the time and place. I'll be there.'

'The best would be for you to come and see me here at my home. It's quite secluded and very private, and only an hour's drive or so from Quillan.' Silvestre read out an address.

'I'll find it,' Ben said. 'When?'

'I would think it in both our interests to meet at your earliest possible convenience,' the old man replied. Then he added cryptically, 'I'm afraid we may not have much time.'

'I'll be on my way,' Ben said.

'Then I will see you soon. *À bientôt*, Monsieur Hope.'

'So what's *this* about?' Roberta asked, perplexed, as Ben got off the phone. 'Another dodgy character says he wants to team up with us?'

'No, this one sounds as if he really does have some information to share,' Ben said. 'Right now that's good enough for me.'

'Except it could be a trap, Ben.'

He nodded. 'Of course it could. Then we either take the risk, or we pass up the opportunity and spend the rest of forever wondering what we might have learned. I'll go alone, if you prefer.'

'While I sit twiddling my thumbs back at the motel waiting to hear what happened? No chance. If you're going, I'm going with you.'

Funny how he'd known she would say that. 'Fine,' he said. 'Then let's finish up here and make a move.'

'Shouldn't you write that address down that he gave you?'

'Why would I need to?' he replied.

'I forgot. You're Ben Hope.'

They quickly polished off their coffees, paid for their breakfast, left the café and started walking back down the street towards the Petit Moulin and Ben's Alpina parked outside.

But they never got that far, because someone was lying in wait for them.

They were just twenty paces from the hotel when there was a burst of a police siren from the side street where the van had been earlier. A patrol car skidded out and screeched to a halt, blocking the pavement behind them. Then a second police car appeared from the opposite direction and pulled up sharply in front of them, blue lights flashing. The doors flew open and armed cops spilled out onto the pavement, yelling at Ben and Roberta to put their hands up and get down on their knees.

In the next instant an unmarked car came speeding up the street and halted at the kerbside behind the Alpina. Ben had seen it before, the morning when the recovery crew had been pulling the sunken, bullet-riddled Renault Espace from the river with Tuesday's body inside. Now as then, the unmarked car's occupant was Gardien-brigadier Pierre Grosjean of the Police Municipale.

Grosjean got out and stepped importantly between the uniformed cops who were pointing their weapons at Ben and Roberta. He seemed to be radiating joy from every pore of his being at this marvellous moment.

'Monsieur Benedict 'Ope, Mademoiselle Roberta Ryder? You are both under arrest.'

Chapter 35

With half a dozen police service automatics pointing at him, Ben could either whip out his Browning and get into a suicidal firefight right here in the middle of the street, or he could surrender to them. In which case he and Roberta wouldn't end up aboard a coroner's meat wagon riddled with holes.

It wasn't much of a choice. He slowly got down to his knees, raised his arms and laced his fingers together over his head. Roberta, at his side, did the same. At an order from Grosjean the officers rushed in to secure their prisoners. It took two cops to secure Ben's wrists behind his back, while a third removed the pistol from his belt and a fourth held out a plastic evidence bag to put it in.

'You might want to make that safe first,' Ben said to them. They awkwardly removed the magazine and emptied the loaded chamber, in the process smearing the weapon all over with their own prints, then sealed it inside the bag and handed it to Grosjean who clutched it as though he'd found the lost treasure of the Templars.

While Ben was being dealt with, two more of the cops were doing the same with Roberta. One of them was a big, broad-shouldered guy with gingery hair and dead eyes, wearing a vacuous, toothy grin on his face as he roughly jerked her arms up behind her back and tightened the plastic tie around her wrists. In any other situation, with her black belt in Shotokan Roberta could have turned this idiot upside down and dumped him to the pavement head-first, wiping the grin off his face before he knew what hit him. But now the tables were turned, and she let out a stifled cry of pain as he levered her trapped arms up to haul her to her feet and propel her towards one of the waiting patrol cars.

Ben made a mental note of the guy's face, in the event that they should ever meet again under different circumstances. 'Hurt her again and you'll regret it,' he warned him. The cop just flashed the grin at him and went on roughly shoving her to the back of the car.

'I think you have already done enough harm, Monsieur 'Ope,' gloated Grosjean.

'I must teach you how to pronounce my name properly, Grosjean,' Ben replied. 'In the meantime perhaps you'd care to tell us on what charges you're arresting us?'

'Attempted murder,' Grosjean declared with a beaming smile. He motioned to the officers surrounding Ben. 'He can ride in the other car.'

'I'll see you soon,' Ben called to Roberta as the cops put her into the back of their vehicle. He caught her anxious look; then they slammed the car door and it took off with a squeal of tyres. In the next moment he was being manhandled into the other patrol car. They made him sit in the centre of the back seat, leaning uncomfortably forward with his arms behind him and sandwiched between two of the uniforms. Nobody spoke. Ben watched through the window as Grosjean climbed back into his own car. Then they were pulling away and accelerating off down the street.

Quillan wasn't a big town and it was a short ride to the same shabby and unostentatious backstreet headquarters where Ben and Jeff had endured Grosjean's interrogation the day of the attack. Around the back of the Police Municipale HQ was an adjoining building that looked something like a military command bunker, but which Ben knew was the station's 'maison d'arrêt', France's answer to the town jail, where suspects and newly convicted prisoners were temporarily housed before being transferred to one of the main prisons dotted around the country. The patrol car that had been carrying Roberta was already parked outside the building, now empty. The cops unloaded Ben from the second patrol car and marched him towards a back entrance with a heavy steel door. Inside, they were met by two more cops with automatic weapons that they trained on Ben as though he was Carlos the Jackal or one of the Red Brigade. 'What do you think I'm going to do?' he asked them. There was no reply. 'You never know,' he added with a menacing smile. 'Maybe I will.'

His taciturn escorts guided him through a maze of dingy corridors to the same interview room where he'd previously sat with Jeff. After being made to sit for forty minutes at the empty table under the watchful eyes of the armed guards, the door opened and Grosjean walked in, accompanied by two more plainclothes detectives.

'Where's Miss Ryder?' Ben demanded. But Grosjean and his colleagues seemed not to have heard him as they seated themselves across the table, opened various files and produced a flurry of paperwork. In the next few minutes Ben was formally charged with attempted murder and a whole laundry list of associated crimes that had taken place at Villa Blanche near the village of Tarascon-sur-Ariège the previous night. He listened to Grosjean's confident-sounding declaration that the forensic evidence gathered at the scene matched unequivocally with the firearm recovered from his person during arrest, making this formally a slam-dunk case.

'Who's the victim?' Ben asked them. 'You can't have a murder, or even an attempted one, without a named victim. I'd be interested in knowing who I tried to kill.'

'So you admit that you tried to kill someone,' said Grosjean. 'Sounds like a confession to me.'

'I thought you already knew that,' Ben said. 'Or are you just blowing smoke?'

'I can assure you that we are not, Monsieur 'Ope.'

'Actually I'm impressed,' Ben told him. 'Especially with the way you managed to link the evidence to me, even before you had my gun to examine. To nail the right man first time without needing to eliminate any other suspects, that's really efficient work. And you must have the fastest forensic lab of all time, to be able to carry out all those tests within just a few minutes. You've far exceeded my expectations. I take back all I said before about you being a crappy detective.'

'You may be as facetious as you wish,' Grosjean said, peering at him sternly across the table. 'But let me tell you this is no laughing matter. You're facing many years in prison, perhaps even a life sentence. There isn't a lawyer in France who could disprove your guilt in this matter. And of course there is no possibility of parole.'

'Well, that's unfortunate,' Ben replied. 'And what about Miss Ryder? Did she try to kill some anonymous victim, too?'

'Your lady friend is being charged with conspiracy to commit murder,' Grosjean said officiously. 'It's a lesser charge but if found guilty she will be repatriated to the United States to face sentencing.' He shuffled some more paperwork, replaced it in its file, and got up from his chair. 'This concludes the formal charging procedure. You will be detained here in the custody of the Police Municipale until your first trial hearing, after which you'll be transferred to the Penitentiary Centre of Béziers.' He added with a smile, 'I think you'll find the conditions there rather less comfortable than those on offer here, so I'd encourage you to enjoy the comparative luxury of our accommodation while you can. That is all. Officers, please escort the prisoner to his cell.'

Ben was led to a processing room where he was photographed and fingerprinted. When they'd finished with the administrative formalities they marched him back through the maze of neon-lit corridors to a cell block that was like something from the 1940s and didn't appear to have been cleaned too often since then. There were just two cells, little more than cages with thick steel bars and bare concrete floors sloping down to a drain hole where rats could get in, judging by the droppings scattered about.

'Welcome to presidential suite, moron,' said one of his escorts. 'Enjoy your stay.' Then the iron-barred door slammed shut with a resounding clang, and they walked away laughing.

From the interview room Grosjean walked back to his office in a different part of the building. Long before he reached his door, the confident smile had faded from his face and his step had lost its spring. He slumped behind his desk, spent a moment with his hands over his eyes, then sighed. 'Agathe,' he said wearily into his intercom console, 'please hold my calls for the next half-hour. I'm not to be disturbed.' Then with another heavy sigh he took out his personal mobile phone and dialled a number.

The voice at the other end belonged to the same unidentified representative of the group of people who had contacted him only hours before, just after dawn that morning, to tell him that his life was no longer his own and to give him very specific instructions to follow if he didn't want his whole world to be blown to pieces. Grosjean was still reeling from the call, numb with shock, and could hardly believe the sudden turnaround in his fortunes.

'I trust that you have some good news to tell me?' said the voice.

'Everything went according to plan,' Grosjean said, closing his eyes and pinching the bridge of his nose. He had a headache coming on. 'Hope and the Ryder woman are now in custody here at the maison d'arrêt in Quillan, as you instructed. Both have been formally charged and the legal machinery is in motion.'

'Excellent,' said the voice.

'But let me warn you that these charges are extremely tenuous, especially considering the speed it all happened, and the highly circumstantial nature of the evidence. When the lawyers get involved the whole case stands to fall apart very quickly. I'm not sure we can hold them for long.'

'That need be no concern of yours,' said the voice. 'You have played your part in this, now all you have to do is stand back and let us take over.'

'No concern of mine?' Grosjean snapped back, unable to stop his frustration from overflowing. 'Are you insane? I couldn't be more involved in this. You people have got me in so deep I can't ever get out again. You're destroying everything, making me do this! Do you understand? My career, my whole life, will be ruined!'

'You already put those at risk when you committed your own, shall we say, *indiscretions*,' the voice smoothly replied. 'Did you really believe you could get away with it for ever? I'm afraid you only have yourself to blame for this situation.'

'All right, all right. You don't have to remind me. But I can't let you kill them inside my maison d'arrêt,' Grosjean objected, less for the sake of the intended victims than as a desperate last-ditch plea to save his own neck.

'Again,' said the voice, 'thanks to your past transgressions you're in no position to dictate terms. We can do whatever we wish. However, if your concern is that we're intending to send assassins to your jail facility to murder two prisoners right under your nose, you can rest assured that isn't what we have in mind.'

'Then what are you going to do with them?' Grosjean asked, only slightly relieved and steeling himself for what was coming.

'We have our own ways of dealing with problems like Hope and Ryder,' said the voice. 'Which require more time and privacy than your prison would permit. You will therefore personally see to it that they are delivered into our hands, so that we can extract the information we require before disposing of whatever remains of them.'

Grosjean swallowed. Behind the man's calm, delicately worded phrasing was a chilling meaning. 'In other words, you're going to torture them to death?'

'I expect Hope to be somewhat more resistant to our techniques than the woman,' the voice said. 'One of my men in particular is a specialist at loosening even the most stubborn of tongues, however, and I'm confident Hope will soon break. Especially when we force him to witness what we do to her.' A chuckle. 'Don't worry, you won't be required to watch. Unless of course it would give you pleasure to do so. Once the handover is complete, you'll be free to leave. Your service to us will be fulfilled and you won't hear from us again.'

All Grosjean wanted was to be let off the awful hook from which these people were dangling him. He wiped the sweat from his brow and cheeks, and nodded. 'Fine. Fine. Whatever you say. I'll do it.'

'Then we'll be expecting your call very soon, and will make the necessary arrangements,' said the voice.

Chapter 36

Some kinds of luxury were more comparative the occasion when than others. Ben was sure he'd spent time in worse cells than this, but he couldn't remember any since he'd been briefly incarcerated in a military prison in Indonesia. The toilet in the corner was no more than a stinking hole, in plain view of anyone passing by the barred walls of his cell. The thin blanket that was his only bedding smelled of someone's stale urine – maybe that of multiple someones – and his mattress was a rather unyielding concrete slab. They'd taken his watch, along with his boot laces and belt to ensure he didn't hang himself, and everything else; so with no external windows to the block he had only his instinctive sense of what time it was.

Everything about his predicament screamed 'set-up' and there was only one possible explanation of how they'd done it. All but one of his questions kept leading back to dear old Gardien-brigadier Pierre Grosjean, who was clearly being used as a cat's paw by someone on the outside, someone with a great deal of power and influence.

Which left just one remaining question: how to get out of this. He could find no ready answer to that one.

Ben sat on the bunk with his head in his hands, trying to still his thoughts and ignore the loud, incoherent ravings of the drunken hobo next door, his only fellow prisoner in the cell block. In addition to the incessant noise were the interesting aromas that were coming from his cell. Ben slowed his breathing, tuned out and lapsed into the totally still, almost trancelike state in which he could remain for hours on mental standby, his body loose and relaxed, detached from all distractions but fully awake, alert and ready to spring into explosive action in an instant. He'd spent countless hours in that state, whether it was hunkered down behind a sniper rifle totally concealed among rocks or bushes, a lurking lone predator waiting to strike; whether it had been huddled with his men in a droning troop plane about to be airdropped into some enemy hotspot; whether it was sitting out the calm before the storm of impending battle, or crouched on a remote hilltop watching for signs of movement in a kidnappers' lair.

His inner clock told him that one hundred and thirty minutes had gone by before the rattle of keys, followed by a creak of hinges and the clash of steel as the barred outer door of the cell block was unlocked and swung open, announced the arrival of three uniformed cops on jailhouse duty. This wasn't their favourite part of their job, judging from their sour expressions. One was carrying two jugs of water, another held a tray with two plastic containers presumably filled with something that passed as food, and the third had the job of standing guard with a pistol and make sure that their dangerous prisoner didn't get up to any tricks. A big, broad-shouldered ox with gingery hair and dead-looking eyes that went with his vacuous grin. There was no mistaking him as the same idiot who'd handled Roberta roughly during their arrest that morning. His belt holster had its retaining strap unsnapped, the sidearm loose and ready for what he probably fancied was a quick draw. These guys didn't know the meaning of quick.

The one with the tray had the ring of jail keys clipped on a chain from his belt. 'Wakey wakey, boys,' he called out. 'It's feeding time at the zoo. Ladies first, now it's your turn.'

That told Ben that Roberta was being kept in the same building, in a separate female section. He stayed where he was on the bunk as they shoved his food and water through a serving hatch in the barred door and then quickly bolted it shut again. 'What, you don't have a nice canteen serving a choice of delicacies?' he asked them.

'Wait till you get to Béziers, dickhead,' said the cop with the gun. 'You'll love it there. All the amenities on offer, especially for scum like you.'

Next they went to feed the hobo next door. Ben had pretty much got used to the smell by now. 'Oh *fuck*,' moaned the cop with the tray, wrinkling his nose in disgust as he peered through the guy's bars. 'The filthy bastard's done it again. Hey, prick, what do you think toilets are for?'

'He'll be out of here tomorrow, thank Christ,' said the cop with the water jug. 'Come on, Barthélemy, let's get you cleaned up for dinner.'

'Hey, with any luck you and he will be cellmates in your new home,' laughed the cop with the gun, turning to make a wolfish grin at Ben. They set the food and water aside and unwound a length of fire hose from a reel on the wall. Before they could open up the jet on him, the hobo rushed at the bars with something in his hand, screaming, 'I got something for you fuckers too! Ha ha!' and flung a sloppy turd straight into the face of the cop with the gun, who recoiled from the cell braying like a bull and wiping the excrement from his eyes. Half blinded for a moment, he staggered a couple of steps too close to the bars of Ben's cage.

Which was all the opportunity Ben needed. Before anyone knew what was happening, he'd launched himself off his bunk and shot his arms out either side of the big guy. His left arm locked around his thick, muscular neck and pulled him in with his back pressed hard against the bars. The other hand stunned him with an expert blow just below his right ear, then flashed down to rip the pistol from his unsnapped holster. Still pinning the struggling cop against the bars, Ben pointed the gun at the other two. They froze still, wide-eyed and speechless.

In a hard, clear voice he ordered them, 'You, back up into that corner, hands on your head and don't move. You' – to the one with the keys – 'get your arse over here and open this cell. Move it, or I'll blow your bollocks off.'

With very little hesitation the officer shuffled quickly over to Ben's cage door, fiddled with trembling fingers for the right key and unlocked it.

Ben instantly let go of the big guy and surged out of the cell, grabbed the keys from him and whacked the butt of the pistol into his head, a single vicious blow that knocked him unconscious. The big guy collapsed to the floor without a sound and Ben stepped over him towards the one who was backed cowering into the corner, still with his hands over his head. Ben pistol-whipped him a couple of times, battered him to the concrete and put him out of action with a savage kick to the temple. Nothing he wouldn't recover from fully in a few months. Then he wheeled back towards the big gingery-haired one he'd taken the gun from, who was struggling up to his feet and opening his mouth to yell out and raise the alarm.

Ben had no personal animus against the first two, but this was the guy who'd mishandled Roberta and he wasn't going to be quite so easy on him. He rammed him violently back against the wall of the cell and used a fistful of his gingery hair to crack his skull into the bars a few times until the resistance went out of him. Then he stamped him to the floor and added a few more blows for good measure. In a few seconds he was nicely unconscious with a broken nose and a few loose teeth into the bargain, blood seeping through the human faeces smeared over his face.

'I told you you'd regret it,' Ben said to him.

He listened for the sound of more officers outside the cell block, and heard nothing. A provincial little police station like this probably wasn't too heavily manned, but even so Ben couldn't afford to hang about in case someone came. Working fast, he dragged all three of the unconscious cops into his opened cell, dumped them in a heap by his bunk and tethered them together with their own cuffs, hands behind their backs. He ripped lengths of the thin, piss-smelling blanket, gagged them so they couldn't cry out when they woke up in a few minutes' time, and locked the cell door shut.

'Hey, dude, what about me?' the hobo asked, clutching his bars.

Ben stepped over to his cell and held up the ring of keys. 'You want me to let you out? That depends on what they banged you up for. I wouldn't want to free a rapist or anything.'

'I never raped nobody,' the hobo protested. 'Just beat up a magistrate, that's all! Wish I could've hit him half as hard as you clobbered these bastards.'

'Good enough for me,' Ben told him. 'I'll get you out of here. Just sit tight and stay quiet until I come back. There's something I have to take care of first.'

He moved on quickly. The little foyer outside the cell block had a fire door that opened into the maze of corridors he'd been led through earlier. He kept a lookout for more cops as he went; and moments later he very nearly ran into two of them as they appeared at the top of the corridor. Ben ducked through a side door into what turned out to be a file storage room. He waited for them to walk by, then stepped out behind them and banged their heads together. Moments later he was dragging the limp bodies into the room and closing them in. Five down. Only one more significant one left to deal with.

The significant one was sitting at his office desk, halfway through dialling a number on his phone when his door burst spectacularly open and he almost lost control of his bowels as he looked up to see the last person in the world he'd expected to pay him a visit. Ben was on him in two strides, dashed the phone out of his hand, grabbed him by the neck and hauled him out of his desk chair.

'You!' Grosjean managed to squawk as Ben jammed him hard against the wall. A framed photo of the Gardien-brigadier posing for a cheesy grip-and-grin with the current president of France fell off its hook and smashed on the floor.

'I got bored sitting in that cell with so little to do,' Ben said. 'Thought it was time to liven things up a bit. Let's you and I have a chat, shall we?'

'Argh! You're choking me!'

'You can still breathe,' Ben told him, not relaxing the pincer grip he had around Grosjean's flabby throat. 'Which is more than you'll be able to do in about ten seconds from now if you don't behave yourself. Where is she?'

Grosjean flapped one arm. 'I-in the women's cells,' he croaked.

'Good. Then you're going to take me to her. But first you're going to fill in a few blanks for me. Starting with who got to you, and why.'

Grosjean seemed about to clam up, but then his sheer terror got the better of him and he blurted, 'I don't know who they are! I swear! I know nothing about them. They just contacted me out of the blue and told me what to do. I don't even know how they found out!'

Ben shook him. 'Found out what?' Grosjean closed his eyes and wouldn't answer. Evidently not scared enough yet to reply to that one. Ben shook him again, much more roughly. 'Found out what, Grosjean?'

And the confession came gushing out, like a lanced boil. 'I was a police chief in Marseilles before I came here. For years I was in with the organised crime gangs, the drug racketeers, everything. I took bribes to look the other way. But then that wasn't enough, so I helped convict innocent people to exonerate murderers. When the money started pouring in, I paid off prosecutors to let criminals go free. I tampered with witnesses. Threatened their families, wives, children. I obtained false confessions by blackmail. There were suspicions. Rumours. But nothing was ever proved. I thought I'd covered my tracks, been too clever to ever get discovered. But I was wrong. I was wrong!' Grosjean's face was flushed and contorted and tears ran down his cheeks. 'I'm so sorry!'

Ben couldn't give a damn for his sorry. 'Sheehan and Bertolli. Are they part of this? Tell me!'

Grosjean opened his eyes wide in confusion and shook his head. 'I don't know anything about them. I never heard those names. Please believe me!'

'How did you find us?'

'Y-your car registration was picked up by three speed cameras heading towards Quillan this morning. I had officers out searching for it. We only found it by chance, parked outside the hotel.'

Ben let go and Grosjean slumped to the floor, looking piteously up at him. 'Are you going to kill me?'

'I'd snuff your miserable life out in a heartbeat and forget in the next that you ever existed,' Ben told him. 'But lucky for you, at this moment you're marginally more useful to me alive. So here's what's going to happen. First you're going to sign a release order dropping all charges against me and Miss Ryder. Oh, and while you're at it, you can free Barthélemy in the next cell too. He's harmless. Just a bit smelly, is all.'

'I don't have the power to do th—'

'Yes, you do,' Ben said. 'And you'd better make the best of it, to cover your arse for what happens next.'

Grosjean turned pale. 'What happens next?'

'That's the fun part,' Ben said. 'You're going to call your handlers. I'm sure they've already instructed you to hand us over to them, once we were in custody. And that's exactly what you're going to do. You'll arrange a nice private, secluded rendezvous point in the middle of nowhere. Then later today you're going to deliver us there in person.'

Grosjean gulped. His eyes glittered as the wheels whirled in his head and he began to realise that maybe this wasn't going to work out so badly for him after all. 'But if I hand you over to them—'

'They'll kill us,' Ben said. 'Probably very slowly and nastily, drawing things out as much as possible so that they can find out everything we know and who else we might have told. After which, in theory, having done everything they asked of you, you might think you were free to go. That's probably what they promised you, didn't they? But think again, Grosjean. The reality is they'll slice your ugly little head off, to make sure you stay quiet. You'll wish you were back with your cosy gangster buddies in Marseilles.'

Grosjean groaned in dread. His face had gone from pallid to corpse-white.

'Unless,' Ben said, 'we can think of a way that works out better for the three of us. What do you reckon?'

Chapter 37

The road that had climbed up and up into the garrigue, far from sight of the nearest village or farmhouse, was no more than a rocky track over which the tyres of the heavy, lurching truck pattered and slithered for grip, loose stones crunching and pinging under their treads. It was late in the afternoon and the worst of the sun's heat was over for the day, but it would go on baking down over the rugged, empty landscape for hours yet. The smells of the garrigue hung in the still, heavy air, rich with the mingled scents of wild thyme and lavender and rosemary. White limestone crags appeared here and there among the greenery of dense, impenetrable forest and scrubland on the high ground.

The truck that Gardien-brigadier Grosjean had borrowed from the Police Municipale's small fleet was the one they used for transporting prisoners, a modified panel van with beefed-up suspension to deal with the weight of the heavy-duty cage in the back and its armoured bodywork, someone's brilliant idea to prevent high-profile criminals from being assassinated while in transit between prisons and court-rooms. Not that the Languedoc justice system ever dealt with too many prisoners of that sort, but the truck was built to cope with any eventuality. The rear doors were solid steel and would take a bomb to blow open. Normally the vehicle would be carrying at least a couple of armed guards to escort their often dangerous cargo, but Grosjean had clear reasons for wanting none of his subordinate officers present that afternoon.

As he drove, he checked his sat nav for the hundredth time since leaving Quillan. The way was unfamiliar to him as he seldom ever ventured out into the wilderness, and certainly never under the circumstances in which he was doing so today. He was sweating profusely, and not only from the brutal heat. He didn't like being away from the comfort of his office. Hated driving this lumbering big truck over roads it was never meant for. Resented being made to do any of this, being used like a servant. Most of all, he loathed the feeling of absolute helplessness as these people he'd allowed to get a hold over him now dictated his every move.

Never had Grosjean rued his past misdeeds more than today. Especially now that the fortunes of dirty money were long gone, the last of his ill-gotten gains squandered and frittered away years ago. All he wanted was to get this whole dreadful business over and done with and go back to whatever miserable tatters would be left of his life. That was, if he lived to see the sundown.

This was the spot he'd been looking for, a flat expanse on the high rock-strewn plateau with a sweeping view for miles all around. Grosjean let the truck roll to a halt and killed the engine, then climbed down from the cab and looked around him at the empty ruggedness of the garrigue, shielding his eyes from the flat white glare that reverberated off the rocks. In the sudden silence all that was to be heard was the ticking of the engine as it cooled, the constant grinding chirp of the cicadas unseen in the sparse and sun-yellowed grass, and the pair of tawny buzzards circling high over the hills, calling back and forth to one another with their high-pitched *keee . . . keee* as they scouted the landscape below for any unsuspecting prey.

Grosjean was an urban creature at heart and felt uneasy being in nature. There were snakes everywhere in the countryside, some of them poisonous. Not to mention the deeply worrying presence of things like wild boar, roaming packs of wolves and even brown bears, for heaven's sake. It was like nothing had changed since way back before the age of civilisation, when sudden violent death was an omnipresent reality of people's lives. But even worse dangers than the wild beasts of the Languedoc haunted his mind. And if he was getting the uncomfortable feeling that he was being watched, that was because he was.

From some distant vantage point overlooking the rendezvous spot, hidden observers had seen the truck arrive and were already mobilising to meet it. It wasn't long before Grosjean, anxiously scanning the hillsides around him, caught sight of a glint of metal under the sun. Then another. Two vehicles approaching from the east – no, three of them, he realised, winding their way single-file towards him along another track. The small convoy consisted of a mini-van between two large SUVs to the front and rear. Dust clouds rose up in its wake, blowing like smoke in the wind and sometimes obscuring the vehicles from view as Grosjean watched them come closer with a sense of growing apprehension.

At last the vehicles pulled up on the plateau a short distance from Grosjean's truck. He fought to contain his panic. There was no going back now, even if he'd wanted to. The two SUVs spread out into a V-shaped formation to the rear of the mini-van in the middle. Doors opened and several men stepped out into the settling dust. All of them were armed, carrying an assortment of automatic weaponry that hung from tactical slings or rode in shoulder holsters. With a shiver of fear, Grosjean was reminded of those times in his crooked past when he'd had to be present at illicit gatherings of the rival drug gangs, meetings arranged to exchange cash and merchandise or negotiate business agreements, but which all too often ended in violence. He'd always somehow managed to escape without a scratch from the scene of the trouble. Would he be so lucky today?

A group of three men who'd got out of the mini-van began walking towards him while their associates from the SUVs hung back near their vehicles, cradling their weapons. Nobody spoke. The three were brawny, severe, tough-looking individuals, black pistols dangling from meaty fists. The one on the left was moving a little stiffly, as though he was recovering from a recent injury and it hurt him to walk. In the warmth of the afternoon he and one of his companions were clad in T-shirts while the third had rolled up his sleeves, all showing the same distinctive tattoo each man had inked in bright red on his right forearm. To Grosjean's surprise the tattoo was the familiar Christian cruciform symbol, except for its square dimensions with the vertical and horizontal bars the same length and the four ends flared out like a Maltese cross. It looked like some kind of badge they were wearing, an identifying mark. Who were these men? he wondered. What could they want with Hope and the Ryder woman? But it was only a fleeting concern to him, as long as he himself wasn't harmed.

They stepped close and gathered round him, all much taller than he was and peering down at him with forbidding expressions, despite the prize he'd brought them. The man in the middle pointed at the rear of the prison truck. 'Is he in there?' he asked in an abrupt tone.

Grosjean nodded sheepishly. 'As arranged,' he replied. 'The woman too. They won't give you any trouble. They're both handcuffed and locked inside the cage.'

The man nodded. 'Good. Give me the keys and step aside. We'll take it from here.'

'Then I can go?' Grosjean hardly dared to ask.

The man eyed him coldly. 'It's them we want, not you.'

Grosjean wanted to weep with relief. He handed over the set of keys for the rear doors and the inner cage, and then scampered out of their way as the three men stepped up to the back of the truck. The man in the middle inserted the key into the rear door lock.

If anyone had been watching Grosjean as he hastily retreated along the length of the van and ducked around its front with a wide-eyed look of terror, they might have guessed from his furtive behaviour that something was up. But at this point all eyes were fixed on the rear doors. The man in the middle finished unlocking them and stepped back while the other two grabbed a handle each and yanked them open. All three, and their associates watching from a distance, looked pleased at the prospect of seeing the two prisoners inside, cuffed and helpless. Once the inner cage was unlocked they would be hauled out and frogmarched over to the waiting SUVs. The male prisoner would be stuffed into one car, the female into the other. Then the convoy would speed off, whisking their captives to their remote fortress stronghold less than forty minutes' drive from here.

There the prisoners would meet their painful and grisly fate. Neither would be leaving the place alive, and their bodies would be disposed of in the same efficient manner as that of the first American. Everything had been made ready for them: the two robust chairs fitted with leather restraining straps, gags to stifle their screams, the instruments of torture laid out on a table and freshly honed to a shaving-sharp edge, the sawdust thickly scattered over the flagstone floor to soak up the blood. Not to mention the picks and shovels needed to dig a double grave in the rocky soil of the Languedoc hills, and the sacks of quicklime that would be poured into the hole with the corpses to ensure they could never be found.

That was the plan, at any rate. And until this moment it seemed to be going as arranged. But the men yanking the back doors open were about to get a surprise. It wasn't the sight of two cowed and miserable captives locked in a cage and about to meet a horrible, lingering death that greeted them. Instead it was the muzzle and black steel flash hider of a loaded AR-15 rifle pointing right at them.

And on the other end of it was Ben Hope, alone, uncuffed, and ready to say hello.

Chapter 38

Prison vans weren't designed for the sake of passenger comfort and it had been a bumpy, jarring ride for Ben inside the unlocked inner cage. He'd spent it mentally preparing himself for what would happen the instant the back doors were opened, and the explosive events of the following few seconds.

Now that moment was here he didn't hesitate, because he knew they wouldn't. But surprise was on his side, and surprise along with aggression and speed were the hallmarks of the military unit that had trained him to make the fullest use of them. As the doors were yanked open and the bright sunlight flooded into the darkness of the truck his first split-second impression was of three armed hostiles standing there, and he pulled the trigger before they had time to realise what was happening. The AR-15 was the one he'd brought from the Le Val armoury and it was set to spew out the contents of its thirty-round magazine on fully-automatic fire. The noise inside the truck was eardrum-burstingly loud. The weapon juddered like a live thing in his grip as a golden stream of empty shell cases poured from its receiver, catching the sunlight.

The three men outside the back doors raised their pistols to return fire, but nobody could have reacted fast enough and they didn't stand a chance. Worse for them, because they'd been expecting a pair of defenceless captives they hadn't strapped on their bulletproof vests. The storm of military-grade .223 full metal jacket projectiles from Ben's rifle ripped into their chests at point-blank range and hammered them backwards off their feet, sending them sprawling and kicking and flailing in the dust, fingers clawed, teeth bared, blood flying.

It was a stunning moment, but it didn't take long for the rest of the men gathered outside to recover from the initial shock, bring their weapons to bear and start shooting back. Ben couldn't have known in advance how many he might find himself up against. It could have been three like before, or it could have been fifty. Now he could see that the small number of opponents he and Roberta had faced at the villa had been reinforced by another eight men, maybe more. They'd been standing next to the two big SUVs, a Volvo on the right and a Toyota on the left, that were parked at an outward V-angle either side of the mini-van from which he supposed the three dead guys had come. Now the others were scattering in alarm, ducking for cover behind their vehicles, shooting as they went, firing over the roofs and bonnets, their combined noise shattering the silence of the garrigue.

As Ben retreated momentarily back inside the truck a storm of bullets raked its sides, shattered its rear lights, blew out the tyres and ricocheted off its chassis. The ballistic armour built into its bodywork kept them from penetrating the prisoner compartment, but that didn't make it a safe space for Ben to shelter in. He was very aware that he risked closing himself into a dead end from which there would be no escape if the enemy mounted a direct attack on the rear doors, directing their concentrated gunfire inside. He angled his weapon left and right, firing off a burst to each side, peppering their vehicles with bullets, shattering windows; then in the split second while the shooters ducked their heads down behind cover he threw himself out of the back of the truck and rolled down between its flattened rear wheels and underneath. The exhaust system was still hot from the drive and only a few inches above his head, but from beneath the truck he had a better field of view while the chassis members and double-wide wheels gave him protection from their angle of fire.

The AR had eaten most of its thirty-round magazine, but he had two more in the back pockets of his jeans and another in his jacket. He ejected the spent mag, loaded in another and kept firing, now switching the weapon to single shots and directing his aim smoothly from one target to another. His fullbore rifle packed far heavier punch than the pistol-calibre submachine carbines the enemy had brought to the gunfight. Its conical bullets, burning through the air at three thousand feet per second, could blow straight through both sides of a car and destroy anything that was behind it. The men fell back, driven down behind cover where he couldn't find them in his sights. But they weren't reckoning on his low-down angle of fire, which allowed him to see beneath the skirts of the SUVs. His rounds could penetrate boot leather even more easily than sheet steel.

Two quick shots, two howls of pain and shock, and a couple of men who an instant earlier had thought they were safe now toppled over, dropping their weapons and clutching at their perforated ankles. Once they were down they made easy targets. Ben shot one in the chest and the other in the head, and they sprawled out flat on the ground with their arms outflung and didn't move again.

Five down: and so far, so good. Ben's surprise resistance had caught the enemy badly off balance but he knew it was only a matter of time before they started mounting a determined counter-attack. And now here it came, as two of them broke out from behind cover and made a wild sprint for the truck, one on each side so that Ben couldn't track them both at once in his sights. He snapped off a round at the runner on the right but his shot missed its target and blew apart a car headlight instead.

Now the two breakaways had managed to reach the truck and were working their parallel way along each side. Ben saw their ruse, and it was a smart one that he might have used himself, in their shoes. They were going to drop belly-down to the ground, playing him at his own game and giving themselves a clear shot under the truck from opposite angles at once, so that he couldn't defend himself simultaneously against both. If he couldn't shoot back in two directions at the same time, at least one of them would hit his mark and Ben would be a dead man.

But two-handed shooting at multiple targets was just one of the many life-saving close-quarter battle drills Ben had long ago been taught by his grizzled, wily SAS instructors and still passed on to his trainees at Le Val. With lightning reflexes he switched the rifle to his left hand, clutching it just by its pistol grip, then yanked the Browning Hi-Power from his belt with his right.

Only a chameleon can swivel its eyes in opposite directions to look two ways at once. Ben's answer to that human physical impossibility was to keep his gaze fixed on the centre and use his peripheral vision to track both his running targets together. A fraction of a second before the two men dropped flat on their bellies in the dust and stones and scrubby grass he had both weapons ready to meet them.

His trigger fingers twitched fast, hammering out shots left and right, aiming by pure instinct. It was a less than perfectly accurate technique but at this extreme close range, in the hands of a naturally gifted warrior with as many thousands of hours of combat training under their belt as Ben had, it was damn well good enough to get the job done. The guy on the left managed to squeeze off just a single shot that clanged violently off a chassis member a few inches from Ben's head, but that was the closest they got to nailing him before Ben's own bullets found their targets. To his left, the AR-15 caught his opponent in the throat and almost decapitated him with its high-velocity power, instantly snatching the life out of him. To Ben's right, the less powerful but still very deadly 9mm Parabellum round from his Browning punched into his enemy's shoulder blade and tore through muscle and flesh to travel down the length of his body, destroying every organ it pierced. The man let out a scream, writhed and tried to scramble away, then his lights went out and he face-planted in the dirt, twitched and became inert.

Now enough was enough, and Ben had no intention of remaining under the truck waiting for the next strategic attack to get the better of him. He thrust the pistol back in his belt, and grabbing the rifle with both hands made use of its underbarrel grenade launcher to lob a 40mm explosive charge at the Toyota SUV to the left of the truck. He hadn't brought these toys all the way from Le Val not to play with them.

The grenade pumped out of the fat launcher tube, sailed out from under the truck and hit the Toyota amidships. Ben pressed his face to the ground as the shockwave and scorching flames rolled outwards from the explosion that ripped the car apart and hurled its flaming wreck over sideways. One of the three remaining men who'd been sheltering behind it was crushed as it rolled on top of him. Another had been blown into the air by the blast and sprawled lifeless and broken among the rocks. The third staggered from the leaping curtain of flames, his whole body from the waist upwards violently ablaze and his arms flailing desperately to beat out the fire. To burn like that was no way to die. Ben put him out of his misery with a shot to the heart, and he crumpled and fell back into the flames.

Ben wasn't sure how many opponents were still left alive, but it wasn't many. He rolled out from under the truck and jumped to his feet, switching his rifle back to full-auto to sweep arcs of rattling fire left and right to clear up any survivors behind the Toyota. His second magazine was running empty now; in the moment it took him to dump it out and snick in a third, he heard the engine of the Volvo SUV roar into life. The wind was blowing thick dark smoke across from the burning vehicle, and had prevented him from spotting the three remaining men as they leaped into their car. He ran through the smoke and saw it taking off, wheels crashing over the rocks as the panicked driver floored the gas in his haste to escape.

Ben would have destroyed the fleeing vehicle with another grenade if he'd had time to load it onto the launcher tube. Instead he brought the rifle back up to his shoulder and chased the Volvo with a long stream of gunfire that shredded the rear end and shattered the back window, perhaps killing one or more of its occupants – although he'd never know. The Volvo swerved and for a moment looked about to smash headlong into a big limestone rock to the left of the track; but then it righted its skid, somehow managed to stay on course and went tearing away over the rough ground. He fired off a few more bursts but then it was gone, dropping out of sight down the hillside.

Then all was silent, apart from the familiar post-battle ringing in Ben's ears and the muffled crackle of the flames. He lowered the rifle and took his finger out of the trigger guard, looking around him at the devastation. The overturned Toyota was still burning fiercely and the column of black smoke rising from the plateau would be visible for miles across the garrigue. The flames from the blazing wreck had spread to the bushes, but the rocky ground would block it from turning into a full-on wildfire. Veiled in the drifting smoke were bodies strewn about, their fallen weapons lying scattered. None of those left behind were still alive.

He stood for a moment, catching his breath and letting his system shrug off the tension of the fight. He checked himself for injuries: he sensed no pain but he'd seen men come out of less nasty little skirmishes than this one with no idea until afterwards that they'd lost a finger, a thumb, an ear. But apart from a torn knee from scrambling under the truck, he hadn't taken a scratch. Still, he felt the same as he always had in the aftermath of battle, sick and weary not from the effort but from the depression that came over him as he asked himself, yet again, why men had to do these things to one another. Now he had a few extra deaths on his account, adding to the cumulative burden he'd accrued over so many years.

He sat on a rock with his rifle across his knees, lit a Gauloise and took out his phone. She'd have seen the smoke from afar, and would be anxious to know what had happened.

Roberta picked up his call instantly, as if she'd been waiting for the phone to ring – which in fact she had. 'Ben? Are you okay? How did it go?'

'Not so well for them,' he replied, talking unnaturally loudly because of his muffled hearing. It hadn't gone quite as well as he'd have liked it to go for him, either. He knew the survivors would try again, and that next time they'd bring greater forces against him. 'They'll be back. But the coast's clear for now.'

'On my way,' she said.

It was only after Ben had ended the call and gone on quietly smoking his cigarette that he remembered he wasn't alone up here on the plateau. Grosjean had spent the firefight cowering for cover behind the front of the prison van. Now he tentatively poked his head out, his face as pale as a sheet. 'Is it over?' he croaked.

Ben's first instinct, out of pure dislike of the man, was to raise his rifle and add one more to the pile of bodies on the plateau. But there'd been enough death for one day.

'Yes, you can come out now, you little creep,' Ben called over to him.

Grosjean got shakily to his feet, stared in horror at the bullet-holed truck and then gulped at the sight of the corpses. 'What am I going to do?' he bleated. 'I can't return the truck in this state. How am I supposed to explain any of this to my superiors?'

Of course, the Gardien-brigadier would be thinking only of himself in a situation like this. 'I'm sure you'll be able to come up with some implausible story,' Ben told him. 'And you'll have to think fast. Because if you tell them what really happened here today, I'll come back and find you, and this time I *will* kill you.'

Grosjean pointed a trembling finger at the bodies on the ground. 'You might as well. When those people hear that I betrayed them . . . My life will be worth nothing after today.'

'It wasn't worth much to begin with. Now get the fuck out of here before you really begin to annoy me. And don't ever let me see your face again.'

Ben lit another Gauloise and sat ignoring Grosjean while the police chief gave up on the prison truck and managed to start the mini-van, slightly less riddled with holes. By the time Grosjean at last was hurrying away from the scene, babbling and weeping over his misfortunes, Ben's Alpina with Roberta at the wheel was making its way up the rocky track. She pulled up on the plateau a few metres from where Ben sat, got out and came over to hug him.

'I was so worried about you.'

Ben shrugged. 'Day in the life.'

'You okay?'

'Yeah, I'm okay.'

'I just passed Grosjean back there on the track. I was surprised you let him go.'

He nodded and puffed some more smoke. 'I couldn't bring myself to shoot him. Must be getting soft-hearted in my old age.'

Roberta gazed around at the battlefield of littered corpses, the wrecked truck, the burning SUV and the cartridge cases strewn everywhere. 'Yup, this has definitely got soft-hearted written all over it. I thought you said you were going to get tough with the sons of bitches. What's the matter with you, Hope?'

Ben flicked away his cigarette. 'Now let's see if we can't figure out who these people are.' He got to his feet, propped his rifle against the rock and walked over to the three men lying dead behind the truck, the first ones he'd shot. He stood for a moment looking down at them. Even the toughest men looked so sad and pitiful in death. One of them had had his shirt ripped wide open by the flurry of gunfire he'd taken in the chest. Under all the blood was a great purple and blue welt that Ben at first thought was a birthmark, but then realised was a bruise.

'Gross,' said Roberta, come to stand at Ben's side.

'This one's been shot before, and recently. See the bruise? He was wearing a bulletproof vest when he took a couple of hits dead centre of mass. And I'm wondering who put them there.'

She looked at him. 'The one you shot at the villa?'

Ben nodded. 'I didn't have much time to think about it before now,' he said, pointing at the bruised corpse and its two companions. 'But I reckon these were the same three shooters who hit us on the bridge. When they tried a second time at your place and failed, that's when all these other guys were sent in to reinforce them.'

'Didn't do them a whole lot of good, did it?'

'This isn't over yet,' he replied.

It suddenly occurred to Ben that if his theory was right, it meant he was likely looking at the three men who had killed Tuesday. Whichever one had actually fired the fatal shot, he'd never know and he didn't really care. All that mattered was that today, here, he'd gone some way to avenging his friend. It was a grim satisfaction, but a short-lived one. Because the real targets were the people who'd employed these hired guns to carry out the job. The same people who wouldn't stop trying until they got what they wanted, or were wiped out to the last man.

Ben searched all the bodies, the ones that hadn't been burned up, for any form of identification. It was no surprise to him to find none. The men were all white, all in their thirties and forties, in good physical condition other than that they were dead, and generally pretty nondescript. The only distinguishing mark they had was the bright red tattoo that each one wore on his right forearm, in the shape of a cross.

'There it is again,' Ben said, rolling up the bloody sleeve of the last corpse he checked. 'The same tattoo. It's like they were all wearing a membership insignia. But membership of what?'

'Remember what Bertolli and Sheehan told us?' Roberta reminded him. 'About the modern-day heretical group calling themselves the Guardians or Custodians?'

'What kind of heretics are still devout enough to get themselves tattooed with Christian crosses?' Ben asked.

'Not just any old Christian crosses,' Roberta pointed out. 'These are Templar crosses. No question about it. See the shape of them?'

'Then maybe Sheehan and Bertolli were telling us the truth,' Ben said, regretting even more that he hadn't tried to press them harder.

'Never mind them,' Roberta said. 'Maybe there's someone else who can answer that for us. Matthew Sadler's friend

Silvestre, the old guy from the hospital. You still got his address?'

Ben tapped his head. 'In here. It's time we went to speak to him.'

'Unless, like I said, it turns out to be another trap.'

'I doubt it,' he replied. 'But if it is, then we'll be ready. Help me gather up all these weapons.'

'What should we do about them?' Roberta asked, pointing around at the scattered bodies.

Ben looked down at the dead. Then glanced up at the sky, where the hunting birds of prey were still lazily circling over the hills, calling to one another. They were a little closer now that they'd most likely spotted the fresh meat lying on the ground far below, and were just waiting for the living humans to clear the scene before coming in for their ripe pickings.

'Forget about them,' Ben said. 'The buzzards and vultures need to eat, same as everyone else.'

Chapter 39

The address that Jean-Rafael Silvestre had given them was in the countryside a few kilometres south of the ancient walled city of Carcassonne. Ben and Roberta had travelled these same roads together before, in their escapades around southern France years earlier. To reach their destination on this late afternoon they would have to pass close by the tiny Languedoc hamlet of Saint-Jean, a place with a lot of memories for them, and especially for Ben. That was where he'd met Father Pascal Cambriel, the kindly old priest who'd tended to him after he was injured in a gun battle not unlike the one he'd just come out of unscathed. Ben hadn't been quite so lucky on that earlier occasion. If Roberta hadn't been there to get him to safety, he might not have made it.

'I remember that time so clearly,' she said as the Alpina rocketed along the winding country road. 'Like it happened yesterday. Father Pascal's little house in the village, where we stayed while you were recuperating. His housekeeper, Marie-Claire. I even remember the goat they had, Arabelle. He was a sweet old guy. I wonder what became of him. You think he still lives there?'

'He died,' Ben said, with a twinge of deep sadness for the man who'd become his friend, almost like a surrogate father to him. Ben had opened his soul to very few people in his life, but Pascal was someone he'd been able to trust and confide in with all his heart.

'Damn. I'm sorry to hear it. I suppose he was pretty old, even then.'

'He'd have lived longer than he did,' Ben replied. 'It wasn't old age that killed him. It was bad people.' He didn't want to say any more about it. Roberta saw the dark look that had come over his face and understood.

'Will it ever end, Ben?' she asked sadly. 'Sometimes it seems like all we humans can do is hurt and kill one another. It happened all through our history and it's not about to change anytime soon. Like our species is just doomed to wipe itself out and there'll never be peace on earth until we're gone.'

'That's why we need to look after the good people,' Ben said. He paused a moment before he added, 'If we can. Sometimes it's too late to do anything to help them. Too damn often.'

She reached a hand across the car's centre console and gently touched his arm. 'You're one of the good people.'

'Pascal was,' he replied. 'And Tuesday. Not me. If I was, then I might have prevented what happened to them.'

'You can't save everyone, you know that.'

'But I have to keep trying.'

'Is that going to be your whole life?' she asked.

'Do I have any other choice?' he replied.

'Yes, you do. You've paid your dues, Ben.'

'When we're done here, when it's over, then I'll have paid my dues. Not before.'

'And then?' she asked. 'What happens after?'

'You mean, if I'm alive?'

'You will be alive,' she said firmly.

'Maybe I will, and maybe I won't.' He shook his head. 'As for what comes next, I'm not thinking that far ahead.'

'You must have some idea of what the future holds.'

'One thing I do know,' he replied. 'I'm not sure I can go back to the old life at Le Val. Not now.'

'What will you do?'

'I might travel. Move around. The way I did years ago, before I put down roots here in France. Maybe I never was the settling kind. Been in one place too long.'

She smiled sadly. 'Sounds like me. I can't go back either. Guess people like you and me are destined to be wandering spirits.'

Her words echoed for a moment in his mind. *Wandering spirits.* Where the journey might go from here was anyone's guess. He said nothing.

There was a long silence between them. Then Roberta said in a soft voice, 'Of course we could always wander together. For a while. I'd like that.'

It had been a long and busy day, but evening was beginning to fall at last by the time they reached Silvestre's secluded home in the hills. Carcassonne's castle battlements and cathedral spire could be seen far off in the distance. Silvestre's elegant *maison de campagne* wasn't quite a manor house, but with its ivied stone walls and traditional shuttered windows, the round tower attached to the east wing and the indoor pool extension at the other end, it was the kind of place that its owner's property-agent friend would have loved to get his hands on. The grounds were encircled by a high wall, within which peacocks strutted about and an ornamental fountain sparkled in the last golden rays of sunlight. Innumerable white doves roosted on the chimney stacks, cooed from the trees and fluttered in and out of their dovecots.

For all his home's old-world grandeur, though, there was nothing ostentatious about Silvestre himself. His car parked in front of the house was an ancient Peugeot 404 that was covered in pigeon droppings and rust; and he appeared from a doorway to greet them clutching a wooden spoon and wearing a sauce-stained apron.

Ben and Roberta stepped out of the Alpina and introduced themselves. 'I was beginning to think you must have had second thoughts about my invitation,' Silvestre said. His smile was sincere, but up close it was apparent that he wasn't a well man. He looked thin and gaunt, somewhat shrunken inside clothes that seemed a size too large for him.

'We were waylaid,' Ben replied.

'Still, better late than never. It's a pleasure to meet you. Please come inside. Excuse my appearance. I was just finishing cooking dinner. Perhaps you'd care to join me?'

'We wouldn't want to intrude,' Roberta said. For Ben, the mention of food made him suddenly acutely conscious of how hungry he was.

'Not at all, not at all,' Silvestre replied. 'I eat like a sparrow these days and have prepared far too much food for one. It would be a pleasure for me to share my table with guests again. And of course you must stay the night. This old house has far too many empty bedrooms.' An afterthought came to him and he added, 'Dear me, I do hope you're not vegetarian, or anything like that.'

'Not in this life,' Ben said.

'Thank goodness. There's so much of it around these days, even in France.'

Ben carried his green bag and the heavy holdall from the car, which Silvestre had insisted on his parking inside the converted stable block garage across from the house. 'Otherwise the doves will do to your paintwork what they have already done to mine.' He brought them into the coolness of the house and urged them to make themselves comfortable. 'I'm so glad you're here,' he kept saying. 'I have such a great deal to tell you.'

'You have a beautiful home,' Roberta said. 'I love that pool.'

'It's rather superfluous to my needs,' Silvestre laughed. 'I don't even swim. But I have a grandniece who visits from time to time with her children, and it's a joy to see the youngsters splashing about.'

The house's interior was very much in the French *style ancien*, with a lot of heavy Louis XV furniture, half-panelled walls and threadbare rugs on the floor. As well as several chess sets laid out in various stages of different games, Ben noticed the large and very opulent gilt crucifix on prominent display above a marble fireplace.

'That?' Silvestre said, catching him looking at it. 'A memento of my past life. I was in Rome for over forty years.'

'You were with the Church?'

Silvestre nodded, his old eyes full of wistful memory. 'For a long time I was archpriest of the Basilica di San Giovanni in Laterano, the first Frenchman to hold that post since 1428. Later I had the great honour of being appointed to the Vatican as a cardinal by the Holy Father himself.'

'I've never met a cardinal before,' Roberta said. 'What should we call you?'

The old man laughed, then his laughter dissolved into a fit of coughing which spluttered on for some time. 'Do excuse me. You can call me Jean-Rafael. Or simply Jean. Come, please take an apéritif and then let's eat.'

Chapter 40

Their gracious host led them into a large, tasteful dining room, set about laying out two extra places at the table and brought them some pre-dinner drinks. Roberta was happy with a small glass of Muscat to start, while Ben quickly developed a taste for the ex-cardinal's own home-made pear brandy. 'It's too overpowering for me these days,' Silvestre said. 'A drop of wine is my only remaining vice in my old age.'

Dinner was a hearty chicken casserole prepared with tomatoes and olives from Silvestre's own kitchen garden. He confessed that he did employ a cook and a gardener, but only for a couple of days a week as he liked to do as much as possible for himself. Today was one of those days when he had the whole place to himself.

'It's important at my age to try to maintain one's independence,' he explained. 'Of course you're both far too young to understand. In any case I quite enjoy my solitude out here. Now please, tell me what you think of this Syrah. It's from a mountain vineyard near Peyrepertuse, a little to the south of here. Good? I'm so pleased. I can only have a tiny glass, I'm afraid. I mainly stick to water.' He motioned at the large carafe of it that sat by his end of the table, embellished with thin lemon slices. 'But please help yourselves to as much as you want. There are plenty more bottles in the cellar.'

'Why did you say we may not have much time to talk?' Ben asked him.

Silvestre coughed again, and wiped his mouth with a napkin before replying, 'Because, *mon jeune ami*, despite my outwardly deceptive show of radiant health it so happens I am not long for this world. Congestive heart failure is not something I would particularly recommend to anyone, and nor is the medical procedure I underwent some time ago, supposedly for my benefit, that seems to have aggravated the condition. My doctors don't seem able to agree on the duration of the time that remains to me. One says months, another says weeks, while yet another declares that I should already be dead by now. Some days are better than others, but each new dawn could be my last. Only God knows when that will be, and he'll take me when he's ready. But for the sake of prudence, I thought the sooner we talked, the better.'

'I'm very sorry to hear that,' Ben said.

'Bah. It's no great matter. I have lived long enough. The material joys of this world have largely ceased to tempt me to want to stay, and I look forward to being with my Lord very soon.' Silvestre smiled. 'I only hope that they play chess in Heaven. That's one thing I will certainly regret leaving behind.'

Ben asked, 'Is that how you know Matthew Sadler?'

'Yes, it was thanks to the glorious game of chess that we became friends, many years ago, when he was already a child prodigy at the tender age of seven. I had the good fortune to have risen to a decent standard myself as a young priest, and we played a well-publicised game in which he thrashed me quite thoroughly in fewer moves than I care to recall.' He chuckled. 'But I forgave him for it; how could I not?'

He described how Sadler had gone on to become a great champion while he himself pursued his own career. 'We kept in touch all those years, playing the occasional correspondence game. Then when I retired from the Church and returned here to my homeland, I devoted myself quite intensively to studying the medieval past of this area of the Languedoc. It is very rich in history, as I'm sure you know. Then some years later, Mathieu gave up competitive chess and relocated to France in order to start up his agency. We see one another now and then.'

The delicious casserole was disappearing fast as they talked, and the first bottle of Syrah wasn't going to last long either. Silvestre offered to fetch more, but Ben insisted on doing it himself, and followed his directions through the labyrinthine house to the wine cellar. He managed to lose his way, ended up in the indoor pool room, then retraced his steps back to the dining room with two bottles.

While he'd been gone the conversation had drifted to the subject of Rome, a city Roberta had never visited and about which Silvestre talked with nostalgia. Ben was beginning to wonder if they'd made a mistake coming here. Did Silvestre really have something to tell them, or were they wasting time?

Silvestre seemed to have read his thoughts. 'But you didn't travel all the way out here to sit listening to an old man's sentimental reminiscences. I have yet to mention my reasons for retiring from the Church. I believe that they concern you directly.'

'I'd be interested in hearing,' Ben said.

'And I trust you won't be disappointed. But first let me tell you about the last time Mathieu contacted me. It was the same day that you and he, together with your friends, happened upon the hidden crypt below the Manoir du Col. He told me you were interested in buying the place.'

Ben leaned forward in his chair. 'You're familiar with what's down there?'

'I am now, thanks to him,' said Silvestre. Turning to Roberta he added, 'I understand, my dear, that it was your American colleague whom they came across examining the wall carving that day.'

'Brad,' she said softly, and looked down for a moment. 'I don't know where he is now. He just disappeared.'

'I pray for him, the poor soul,' Silvestre said sadly. 'As for Mathieu, he was so intrigued by the discovery that he returned there that same day for another look, after you had gone. Like our friend Brad he took photographs of the carvings, not because he understood their meaning or significance, but because it had occurred to him that their presence could potentially enhance the historical value of the property, and hence its asking price for future buyers, should you and your associates ultimately decide not to proceed with the purchase.'

'That was astute of him,' Ben said.

'He didn't become a chess champion for nothing,' Silvestre replied with a brief smile that faded as he replayed the memory. 'But though he may be a genius in other ways, he would make no claims to being a historical expert. Knowing about my particular interest, you might say obsession, with this region's past, he telephoned me in his excitement that evening to tell me all about your tour of the Manoir du Col that morning, the strange presence of an intruder inside the crypt, and the even more bewildering discovery that had been made, on which he was curious to know my thoughts. This was only hours before the attackers broke into his home and tried to murder him, though at that stage I had no idea there was any danger. How naive I was.'

Silvestre shook his head ruefully. 'I was intrigued to know more, and asked Mathieu to email me the images he had taken, which he promptly did. When I saw them, to my astonishment I realised at once what I was looking at. To an amateur local historian like myself they seemed to confirm the centuries-old legend of the fugitive Templar knight who took refuge there from the king's soldiers.'

'Then you know about Thibault de Roucyboeuf,' Roberta said. 'His letter to Gerard de Vezelay.'

'You're evidently something of a keen historian yourself. Yes, I know the story well, though of course I was unaware until then of the markings de Roucyboeuf had inscribed on the crypt wall. As I'm sure you have concluded yourself, it's clear they were intended as a coded message for posterity.'

'You've figured it out?' Roberta asked, full of anticipation.

'There I must disappoint you,' Silvestre replied. 'Even the simplest code requires a key to make sense of it, and though I am no cryptologist this one appears to be anything but simple. I doubt even the most expert Latin scholar could make sense of these baffling words and phrases. Then when one factors in the ravages of time that have made so many of the markings impossible to make out, I regret to say that the code as it stands may be undecipherable.'

'I was afraid you might say that,' she replied, deflated.

'However, its significance goes further than merely understanding the message,' Silvestre said. 'I didn't realise that at first, not until what happened to poor Mathieu shortly afterwards, followed by the attack that claimed the life of your poor friend. That was when I understood that these terrible incidents were strangely connected to my own reasons for having left the Church.'

Ben stared at the old man and wondered if he'd heard right. 'How could that be?'

'All will be explained,' Silvestre replied. 'And then you'll understand why I wanted us to meet. People are dying and I believe I know who is responsible. You deserve to know the truth.'

Chapter 41

When the fading late afternoon sunlight hit the castle turret's windows from just the right angle and the multi-hued illumination from the stained glass shone over the golden crest on his wall, it seemed to glitter and gleam as though animated by a life of its own. This must be how it had looked nine hundred years ago, the Grand Master thought as he tenderly stroked the priceless object, when the desert sun scorching down on the crusader kingdoms had bathed it in God's holy fire. He could almost hear the thud of the destriers' hooves on the sand as they rode into glorious battle amid the heat and the dust, the crackling flutter of the red-crossed banners, the massed footsteps of the Christian soldiers advancing in their thousands over the arid plains, the clink of chain mail and steel weapons as . . .

His vision was suddenly punctured by the ringing of his phone. With a mutter of discontent, the Grand Master hurried over to his desk. He'd been expecting this call for some hours, and he expected the news to be good. By any rights, Hope and the Ryder woman should by now be securely in the hands of his men, and the worthless existence of their stooge, that low-down cockroach of a local police chief, would have been snuffed out as arranged. He felt he'd played his cards faultlessly this time.

'Well?' he snapped, snatching up the receiver. 'Did you get them?'

But once again, the Grand Master was about to be badly let down.

'We went to the pick-up,' said the Brother initiate. 'Everything was going according to plan. Grosjean, the cop, said he had them locked up in the back of the prison van. All we had to do was bring them in. But . . .'

The Grand Master's eyes narrowed to slits and his grip tightened on the phone. 'But?'

'But it was a trick. Grosjean betrayed us.'

'What happened?'

'I didn't want to have to be the one to tell you, Grand Master—'

'JUST TELL ME WHAT HAPPENED!' the Grand Master screamed at him down the phone. Then, appalled at his own loss of control, he added in a quieter voice, 'Are you saying that Hope and the woman are still free? That they weren't even there? How can that be?'

'It's worse than that, Grand Master. Hope was there. But he was ready for us. He . . . he killed everybody.'

'What do you mean, everybody? Then how can you be talking to me? Are you a ghost?'

'Only two of us got away. Everyone else died. Jacques, Chrétien and Bertrand. All of them.'

'Two survivors, out of all I sent. He must have had help. He surely cannot have done this alone.'

'It was just him, Grand Master. It was as if he was everywhere, all at once. You couldn't pin him down. He just kept firing, our Brothers dropping dead all around me.'

'Well, well,' the Grand Master said, cooling down a little as he slowly began to accept the reality. 'This Hope is truly exceeding all expectations. And what about the police chief? I suppose he perished as well?'

'I . . . I don't know what happened to him. We were gone by then.'

'So you ran away before it was even over.' The Grand Master was about to launch into a fresh tirade, but then he stopped himself. 'Very well,' he sighed. 'What's done is done. You say there are just two of you remaining? Then listen to me carefully, because my next instructions to you require only a pair of men to carry out.'

'Anything, Grand Master, if it's in our power to do.'

'Your loyalty is appreciated. Here are my orders. If Grosjean, the policeman, is still alive, then he must die. We know where he lives. One of you will pay him a visit tonight and ensure he doesn't see the morning. Meanwhile the other of you will find a means to get inside the hospital in Quillan and eliminate Sadler.'

The Brother initiate gave a solemn nod. 'It will be done.'

'As for our friend Benedict Hope,' the Grand Master mused, 'what a shame he doesn't work for us. I cannot expect two men to tackle a problem like him, when so many have already died in the attempt. It appears I'm going to have to take charge of this personally, deploying all the resources I have at my disposal. Are you at the fortress?'

'Yes, Grand Master.'

'Then stand by. I'm coming to France myself.'

Chapter 42

Jean-Rafael Silvestre poured more wine for his guests. 'You see,' he continued his account, 'when I speak of my having "left the Church", I'm being a little euphemistic. The unfortunate fact is that I resigned from my post at the Vatican, which I had considered the greatest honour of my life and the sum total of all my worldly ambitions, under a dark cloud. It was inevitable, however. For a long time I had been suspicious that things weren't what they seemed.'

'What things?' Ben asked. His doubts about the value of their visit here were quickly melting away.

'I could come straight out with the shocking reality that underlies all this,' Silvestre replied, 'and tell you about the radical, clandestine counter-church that lies hidden at the heart of Christianity. About the secret war that has been raging within the hallowed corridors of the Vatican for centuries, completely unbeknownst to the outside world. But it would only confuse you, because to understand how this is connected to your situation one has to go back to the beginning of a long, complex story whose origins date from the time of the Templars. Are you ready to hear it?'

'It's what we came here for,' Ben said.

Silvestre reached for the carafe of lemoned water and poured himself another glass, drank it slowly and cleared his throat. 'It's generally believed,' he explained, 'and has been for centuries, that the Order of the Knights of the Holy Temple ceased to exist when it was disbanded, outlawed and destroyed in the early fourteenth century by royal and papal decree. I'm sure I needn't remind you of the sequence of events that led to their doom. As the familiar old story goes, while other military-religious orders remained in existence for long afterwards – such as the Knights Hospitaller, who, following the collapse of the crusader states in the Holy Land, moved their headquarters to Cyprus, later to Rhodes and thence to Malta where they stayed for over two and a half centuries – the Templars were stamped out and eradicated for ever following the execution of their grand master Jacques de Molay and his immediate circle of knights.'

'That's what we know,' Roberta said.

'Or think you know,' replied Silvestre. 'In fact, nothing could be further from the truth. Because what very few people realise is that the Templar Knights still exist to this day, and in a form not so very changed from what they were in medieval times. Now tell me, my dear,' he said, turning to Roberta, 'as you've obviously studied the history very closely: has your research led you to learn of the exploits of one Bernard-Raymond Fabré-Palaprat?'

She looked blank, and gave a little shake of her head. 'I've never heard of him. Who was he? Or is he?'

'He was born in 1773 and died at the age of sixty-four in the southern French city of Pau, some way to the west of here. During his lifetime he was a priest and mystic, who had the distinction of claiming to be the head of an organisation calling itself "l'Ordre du Temple". Which in itself is nothing remarkable, considering the vast proliferation of such self-styled orders throughout the years, many of them little more than fringe cults. But what sets Fabré-Palaprat apart is that, in November 1804, he revealed the existence of an ancient document called the Larmenius Charter.'

'I never heard of that either,' Roberta admitted. 'Or Brad.'

'It isn't well known,' Silvestre said. 'It was written in an obscure code based on ecclesiastical Latin and is supposed to trace an unbroken line of Knights Templar Grand Masters all the way from 1324 to 1804, with Fabré-Palaprat's name last on the list.'

Yet more codes, Ben thought. 'So they continued all that time.'

'Hold on. Why from 1324?' Roberta asked. 'The order was officially dissolved years earlier. If they'd carried on undercover after Jacques de Molay's death in 1312, wouldn't someone else have taken over as Grand Master?'

'An excellent question,' Silvestre replied. 'Let me explain. The charter was named after a Johannes Marcus Larmenius, who was secretly named Grand Master by Jacques de Molay before his execution. De Molay was passing on his title in the hope that the order could quietly survive the attempt to wipe it out, and continue into the future. That may be why Larmenius chose to keep his position secret, and his own name does not appear on the charter that he created. The first Grand Master to appear there was Larmenius' successor, Thomas Theobaldus Alexandrinus, in 1324, marking the official start of the order, though of course it remained strictly secret. That practice continued for five centuries, all the way to the time of Fabré-Palaprat.'

Ben asked, 'So where is this document now, assuming it ever existed?'

'Oh, it exists,' said Silvestre. 'The Larmenius Charter ended up in Masonic possession and today is kept at the Mark Masons Hall in London. But even though the final entry dates to 1804, the Order of the Temple itself continued long afterwards. They claimed to be in possession of important relics, such as the sword of Jacques de Molay and the helmet of Guy Dauphin d'Auvergne, a fellow knight who was arrested with the other leading Templars and may or may not have been burned at the stake next to his beloved Grand Master. The relics also included a collection of burnt bone fragments claimed to be the remnants of the executed Templars, gathered from the foot of the pyre on which they met their fiery end. These were actually put on display in March 1808, the anniversary of the execution, at a public requiem ceremony held in honour of the martyred knights at the church of St Paul in Paris.'

'This is all totally new to me,' Roberta said in wonder. 'And I thought I knew something about the subject.'

'I don't blame you,' Silvestre said. 'I have had many years to accrue all this information. Now, it was around that same time, during the imperial reign of Napoleon Bonaparte, that the order sought to reconcile themselves with the Vatican. Not surprisingly, considering they had been condemned by papal authority in the first place, they were met with a frosty reception. Over the following years they moved their base of operations from place to place around Europe. By the time of the outbreak of World War II they were headquartered in Brussels. After the Nazis invaded there, they relocated once again, this time to Portugal, that country having remained neutral in the war. As they had always done, whenever they moved their base they brought with them all their valuable assets.'

'As in money, gold, treasure?' Ben asked.

'They were still extremely wealthy, of that there's no doubt,' replied Silvestre. 'But their greatest treasure, prized most highly of all, was the store of ancient archives dating back to the dawn of the Templar order. At that time the man responsible for preserving these priceless manuscripts was Antonio Campello Pinto de Sousa Fontes, who declared himself the next in the line of Grand Masters. Then in 1948 came the great watershed moment in their modern history, when all hell broke loose.'

'What happened?'

'De Sousa Fontes rather impetuously broke the long-standing traditions of the Templar order by announcing that his son, Fernando, was to inherit the position of Grand Master on his death, which happened in 1960. This was a dramatic development for the Templars, as they had never before conferred their leadership by heredity, only by democratic vote. The resulting dispute led to a major schism within their ranks. The order would never be the same again. Eventually it fragmented into various splinter groups, some of them more moderate, others more radical and fundamentalist. The most extreme of these was a group calling itself the Custodes Sanctorum Secretorum Templi, or CSST for short.'

'The Guardians of the Holy Secret of the Temple.' Ben was instantly reminded of what the two men claiming to be Vatican priests, Sheehan and Bertolli, had told them in the hotel room in Quillan. He could see Roberta was thinking the same. Except that Sheehan and Bertolli had called the group by a slightly different title, the 'Custodes Sacri Secreti', without any mention of the temple. Why would they have changed it? he wondered.

'The order still exists today,' Silvestre went on. 'Their sign is the same red Templar cross that the original knights wore as military insignia on their white surcoat or, in the case of their non-combatant *confrères*, on a black tunic or robe, as only the initiated knights were considered pure enough, close enough to God, to wear white. In modern times, the fully-fledged sworn initiates or so-called Brothers wear the red cross as a tattoo upon their right forearm as a mark of their loyalty and a symbol of their strength.'

Ben wanted to say, 'We know. We've seen it.' But that would have entailed telling Silvestre the whole story of their encounter earlier that day, and he didn't want to interrupt the flow, any more than he wanted to incriminate himself or terrify the old guy that he was dealing with an armed maniac. He shot Roberta a glance to tell her to stay quiet for the moment. Instead he asked, 'How many still exist?'

'That's uncertain,' Silvestre said. 'Though I have spent a long time studying them, I have managed to learn relatively little about the present-day extent of the order, their structure and organisation. All I can really tell you is that they are an extremist religious group sworn to protect a secret, or secrets, that they claim has been handed down the centuries from its original guardians.'

At last, they were getting closer to unravelling the mystery. Ben asked, 'And what are these secrets?'

Chapter 43

The old man smiled. 'I was coming to that. I think you'll find it very interesting. But before I do, first it's necessary for us to backtrack for a moment to our old friend Bernard-Raymond Fabré-Palaprat, the one-time Grand Master of the Order of the Temple. Few people know that he also founded something called the Johannite Church of Primitive Christianity, as a rival to its mainstream counterpart. Or should we say *revived* it, for in fact it had already existed for a very long time, dating back a thousand years before the time of the Templars.'

'Johannite,' Roberta said, thinking hard. 'As in Johannes Marcus Larmenius, the Templar Grand Master who took over from Jacques de Molay?'

'Johan is an old form of the Christian name John,' Ben said.

'John,' she echoed. 'Then was the Johannite Church named after John the Apostle?'

Silvestre shook his head. 'You have an enquiring mind, my dear, and you're on the right track. Saint John the Apostle, or John the Beloved, one of Christ's twelve disciples, did become a member of the Johannite Church and he will be coming back into our story. However its name originates from a different, and equally important, John from the Bible.'

‘There’s only one other who could compare with John the Apostle,’ Ben said. ‘That would be John the Baptist.’

‘Correct,’ Silvestre said. ‘The son of Mary’s sister Elizabeth, making him a slightly elder cousin of our Lord Jesus Christ. It was he who gave Jesus his baptism, from which he earned his title. Later he became Jesus’ teacher, as well as the founder of the Johannite Church. That’s why it became known as the church of *primitive* Christianity, in the sense of it being the very earliest and oldest. Now flash forward over a thousand years to when the original Knights Templar learned of its existence in the Holy Land, soon after the formation of their order in 1118. As devout Christians raised in the traditional doctrine, they would never have heard of such a thing. However it wasn’t long before they became assimilated into the new denomination.’

‘How did they find out about it?’ Roberta asked.

‘The ruling patriarch of the Johannite Church at that time was a man called Theoclete,’ Silvestre replied. ‘He personally met the founding Templar Grand Master Hughes de Payens and not only passed on its secrets to him, but made him his successor upon his death. Inheriting the title of Grand Pontiff, de Payens then became in effect John the Seventieth in a long line of Johannites, the Gnostic “Johns”, that had begun with John the Baptist and included John the Apostle, as well as, according to some, Jesus himself.’

‘How could Jesus be a John?’ Roberta asked, puzzled.

‘The name John was more than just a given name,’ Silvestre explained. ‘It was also an honorific title derived from the Sanskrit word *Jnana*’ – he pronounced it ‘Yana’ – ‘and translated as “He of Gnostic Power and Wisdom”.’

'How do we know for sure that the Templars actually inherited this church?' Ben asked.

Silvestre said, 'It was alluded to by Pope Pius IX in his papal allocution against the freemasons on April 20th, 1849, proof that the Vatican had known about these events for many centuries. In his speech the Holy Father acknowledged that Hughes de Payens had been initiated into the mysteries of the Johannite sect. Needless to say the pope and the Church took a very dim view of this. However the evidence shows that Johannism was the unofficial doctrine of the Templars almost from the beginning of their order. And they would have been aware that the Holy Land, as elsewhere, was full of Vatican spies whose job was to detect and report the merest hint of heresy to their superiors. The Catholic Inquisition had been in existence since the twelfth century and was as powerful as it was ruthless in its quest to police the faith and root out blasphemers, apostates and anyone else deviating from the correct path. If the Templars had been found out to be practising this very unorthodox form of religion they would have suffered the harshest punishments imaginable. As a result they had to keep the veil of secrecy tightly drawn. Only the innermost circle of initiates could be introduced to their true beliefs.'

'I *knew* they were into something,' Roberta said. 'I just didn't know what.'

'Now,' Silvestre continued, 'on inheriting the position of Grand Pontiff of the Johannite order Hughes de Payens allegedly received a large quantity of scrolls and manuscripts. These were said to date back to the time of the Essenes, an ancient sect from the east that included the Nazarenes for whom John the Baptist had been a great prophet. As we know, he was also Jesus' teacher. And so the story goes that Jesus, having been initiated by his master into the ancient mysteries of Egypt and Greece, then passed this wisdom on to his favourite disciple, "the one whom Jesus loved".'

'The other John,' Roberta said.

'John the Apostle. He is generally considered to be the author of five books of the New Testament of the Bible. Those are the Gospel of John, the three volumes of the Epistles of John or Johannine Epistles, and the Book of Revelation. However,' Silvestre said enigmatically, 'there is another work of which John the Apostle was the author, according to Palaprat. The latter claimed to have discovered a second Gospel of John, an alternative version and perhaps the true and correct version, of the one that appears in the traditional bible. And you may be quite surprised at how much it differs from the scripture we all know so well.'

'You're talking about the Apocryphon of John,' Ben says. 'The so-called secret book of John, found among the Nag Hammadi scrolls in 1945.'

Silvestre raised his bushy white eyebrows. 'Ah, I see you are well educated in theology.'

'He's a bit of a dark horse,' Roberta said.

Silvestre smiled and went on, 'But in fact we're talking here about another book entirely, one that's almost completely unknown to mainstream theology. Only two written copies are believed to exist.'

'If it's so unknown, how do we know it exists at all?' Ben asked.

'Because I have seen one of them,' Silvestre replied. 'It was rediscovered quite by chance in 2004 in one of the more ancient and little-used sections of the Vatican library, completely forgotten and unread since the earliest days of Christianity. What scholars call the Apocryphon of John is only a fragment with many missing pages. By contrast, this is a complete and intact version of an even earlier Gnostic text translated into Greek sometime during the second century AD. And it is one of the most heretical scriptures of all.'

Chapter 44

'Every Christian believer on the planet is familiar with the teachings of the Gospel of John, as recounted in the New Testament,' Silvestre went on. 'At its very heart is the idea that Jesus Christ was endowed with the Divine spirit and nature of God, that he was in essence a manifestation of God, having existed through all time before the Universe was created. This is one of the most essential tenets of the Christian faith as we know it.'

'That's what I was taught in school,' Roberta said.

'You and every child in the Christian world,' Silvestre replied. 'All the more shocking then, that the rediscovered "secret" Gospel of John should teach such a radically different view of Jesus. In this version, he is portrayed as a simple holy man who, in common with the various other mortal prophets, had received a revelation from God and was inspired to preach the message to his fellow men. According to what we're told here, he was no more divine than you or I. Not only that, when his time came he died the same mortal death as lies in store for all of us. This version completely does away with the idea of his being resurrected.'

'Even a low-down agnostic like me can see how that could cause a stir in religious circles,' Roberta said. Ben went on listening and made no comment.

'There's more,' Silvestre said. 'According to traditional Catholic teaching, out of his apostles it was to Saint Peter that Jesus promised a special position in the future Church. Thus Peter went on to become the first bishop of Rome – that is to say the first pope – and the first bishop of Antioch in the Holy Land. This leading role Peter played among the apostles is called the Petrine Primacy, and it's a central tenet of Catholic tradition. But according to the Johannite version of the story, Christ's successor isn't Saint Peter but rather John himself. In other words, this alternative gospel is describing the founding of a completely new and different religious establishment.'

'And that's what the Templars believed?' Ben said.

'It certainly seems so,' Silvestre replied. 'Jean-Marie Ragon, the nineteenth-century freemason and member of Palaprat's Order of the Temple, echoed the same view that the Templars had rejected and renounced the conventional Christianity of Saint Peter in favour of a rival doctrine.'

'Easy to see why the Vatican wouldn't approve of that one,' Roberta said.

Silvestre nodded. 'To say the very least, my dear. Such a message was, and is, considered an abominable heresy. Of course this was nothing new, in itself. Many heretical schools of thought had existed within the early Church, like the so-called Adoptionists who denied the deity of Christ although accepting the Resurrection. By contrast, the believers of Docetism held the view that Jesus was entirely divine and his fleshly incarnation was just an illusion. Then there was so-called Arianism, which regards Jesus as a superhuman creature, something like an angel, midway between man and God. And the Ebionites, who, somewhat akin to the Johannites, claimed he was not divine in any way, but merely a holy man and a prophet. Needless to say, all these differences had been ironed out and dissenters suppressed at the Council of Nicaea in 325 AD, when the early Catholic Church consolidated its power and the official doctrine was decided upon. From that moment forward, any teaching that contradicted that agreed narrative was ruled as a heresy to be stamped out by any means necessary.'

Roberta said, 'But for something as radical and contradictory as this Johannite stuff to come from the pen of the author of one of the traditional gospels would be a much tougher problem for them.'

'It certainly was,' Silvestre agreed. 'And not only thanks to its illustrious authorship, but also due to having so much in common with the key principles of the Christian Church's great enemy, Islam. It's not at all difficult to see elements of Islamic thought in the Johannite doctrine. As we know, Jesus is venerated by Muslims as a prophet, albeit a far lesser one than the religion's founding father Muhammad. But where Islam has always violently disagreed with Christianity is over the notion that a man could be the son of God, or the personification of God on earth, or in any way personally divine. Those are simply unthinkable concepts to a Muslim. One of the very ignorant misconceptions about Islam in medieval Europe was the idea that Muslims worshipped the Prophet Muhammad as a god. I should add that the Christian west held many other erroneous views on their rival religion. Such as the notion, circulated for a time in Europe, that Muhammad had been eaten by a herd of pigs while unconscious from a drunken stupor. This was some medieval Christians' way of explaining why Islam banned the consumption of pork or alcohol. But I digress.'

'So,' Roberta said, 'if the Johannite Gospel sided with the Islamic view of Jesus as just an ordinary mortal man who happened to receive a revelation from God and become a prophet, you can see why some folks might have thought the Templars were guilty of practising the religion of their Saracen enemies. Which was one of the things they were accused of at their trial.'

'Very true,' Silvestre said. 'Along with spitting on the cross, which was a common ritual practised by Muslims who had conquered Christian cities. Having slaughtered and enslaved their populations and raped all the nuns, the victors would then break all the crosses off the churches and defile them by dragging them through manure heaps while spitting on them to express their contempt for the infidels. However it wasn't only the obvious comparisons with Islam that their accusers seized upon to vilify the accused Templars. Remember that Islam itself was a much younger religion, having been founded only in the seventh century. Muslim scripture borrowed significant chunks from the Bible; perhaps more importantly it also incorporated elements of far older pre-Christian and Judaic creeds that had already been around for thousands of years. The ancient wisdom that had filtered through from the east over the centuries had given rise to a bewildering variety of schools of thought, including the hermetic traditions that had long been preached by Jewish mystics and found their way into the doctrine of Johannism. There's plenty of evidence to suggest that the Templars' religious ceremonies involved the use of strange idols that would be strictly forbidden in Islamic tradition. That in itself should have been sufficient evidence to disprove the accusation that they were somehow secret Muslims. But it would have been much more in line with certain forms of eastern mysticism considered no less heretical in the eyes of the medieval Church. Éliphas Levi, a Jewish mystic himself much later on, in the nineteenth century, was convinced that the Templars were secret initiates of the Kabbalah.'

'Yes!' Roberta exclaimed with a fist-pump and a gleam of triumph in her eyes. 'That's exactly what I told you, remember, Ben? I knew it!' Turning back to Silvestre she said, 'When you mention these "strange idols", are you talking about Baphomet? I could never figure out what that was, except that it had something to do with a magic head of some sort.'

Ben groaned. 'Oh, please. Not the thing with the head again. We've been through this nonsense before.'

'No, no,' Silvestre assured him. 'What the dear lady is saying actually makes a great deal of sense, and she's to be congratulated for her excellent research.' Smiling at Roberta, he went on, 'Indeed, in addition to the litany of their other heinous crimes, it was alleged the knights had been worshipping this entity that may or may not have taken the form of an enigmatic head. I'm not surprised that you were confused about it. Baphomet, like so many other things about the Templars, has been shrouded in mystery and secrecy for many centuries.'

'So what was it?' she asked.

'Oh, there are so many strange tales. For some, this thing called Baphomet represents a horned, androgynous pagan god, the Goat of Mendes, our traditional image of the Devil.

For others it takes on a much more esoteric symbolism. But in the light of what we've been discussing, there may be a simpler explanation. Think back to the original founder of the Johannite Church, and let's see how well you remember your Bible history.'

Chapter 45

'Tell me now,' Silvestre said, 'what was the fate of Jesus' cousin and teacher, John the Baptist?'

Roberta thought for a moment. 'Nothing good, if I recall. Wasn't he executed by King Herod?'

'Well done. But that King Herod isn't to be confused with his namesake who is said to have infamously ordered the Massacre of the Innocents at the time of Christ's birth. Saint John's nemesis was Herod Antipas, one of his sons. The gospels differ slightly on why he had John imprisoned, and the non-Biblical Jewish sources may be closer to the mark when they claim John's popularity with the people was a threat to the king. But whatever the reason, do you remember specifically *how* John was executed?'

She looked blank. 'I don't think it was crucifixion. Did they hang folks in those days?'

'They chopped off his head,' Ben replied for her, making a slash gesture across his throat. 'Please don't tell me that the Templars somehow managed to get hold of the head of John the Baptist,' he said to Silvestre.

'I'm afraid that's exactly what I'm going to tell you,' replied Silvestre. 'To you, perhaps it is just a head, which may seem somewhat farcical. But we're talking here about one of the most important and revered icons of the early Christian Church. The severed head of the Baptist has even been depicted in classical art, such as the famous painting by Caravaggio that hangs in the National Gallery in London, showing the freshly severed bearded head on a platter. Then in the Musée d'Orsay in Paris is the 1876 watercolour by Gustave Moreau, titled *The Apparition*, in which the Baptist's head appears like a mystical vision floating in mid-air, surrounded by a halo of light.' He turned back to Roberta. 'Now, here's another question for you: what might have happened to the Saint's head afterwards?'

'I have absolutely no idea,' she replied.

'You see, it was quite common in history for the various body parts of deceased prophets and saints to be preserved as sacred items. In fact one of the roles of the Templars was to provide protection for important relics when they were taken on tour from city to city for public view around Europe. To this day many people believe that just touching a holy relic could bring one closer to God or even bring about a miracle.

'As for the head of John the Baptist,' Silvestre went on, 'there are various versions of where it might have ended up, depending on which you believe. According to Islamic tradition it was interred in Damascus, in a basilica where the Umayyad Mosque now stands. A skull claimed to be that of the Saint is on display at the Church of San Silvestro in Capite, in Rome. I've been to see it many times, although I could never be sure of its authenticity. Meanwhile the thirteenth-century cathedral of Amiens was specifically built to contain the head. It has also been claimed to belong to the Residenz Museum in Bavaria, among a number of other holy relics. But for our purposes, the most interesting story of its fate is the rumour that circulated at the time of the

Fourth Crusade: namely, that the mummified head was found by a Templar knight during the sacking of Constantinople in April 1204, and retained for their own private purposes.'

'What purposes?' she asked.

'Remember that in keeping with their Johannite beliefs the Templars would have venerated John far more highly than Jesus, whom they regarded as the latter's junior and subordinate. This extremely important relic reportedly then became a central part of their secret initiation rite. It is said they believed a form of mystical energy to emanate from the head. This energy, or perhaps we might say this spirit of wisdom, would supposedly pass into the body of the initiate by means of some kind of alchemical transference, allowing them to experience the same enlightenment that God had bestowed upon the founder of their church. Indeed, some scholars believe that the word "Baphomet" is a corruption of the Greek term meaning "Baptism of Wisdom".'

Roberta's eyes had begun to glow as he talked. 'Then I was right again,' she said excitedly. 'It's like I told you, Ben. That's what they were after all along. They were alchemists, except not the kind who were trying to create gold. Their treasure was spiritual enlightenment.'

Silvestre nodded. 'Yes, and further proof of that can be gleaned from the coded markings on the crypt wall.'

'I thought you said they were undecipherable,' Ben said.

'Certainly, the parts of it that consist of these scrambled, meaningless Latin phrases that are far beyond my ability to understand,' Silvestre replied. 'But then there are the symbols, which may reveal much more to the enlightened few.'

'Like this one?' Roberta asked, taking out her phone and bringing up the images Brad had taken. She showed Silvestre the symbol of the circle-within-a-square-within-a-triangle-within-a-circle. 'I was sure I'd seen it somewhere before, but I couldn't remember where.'

'Well now, that I can tell you is the alchemical symbol for the Philosopher's Stone,' Silvestre said, peering at the image. 'It was the first thing I recognised from Mathieu's own photographs.'

Roberta clapped her hand to her head. 'Of course! What a dumbass I am, not to have remembered it.'

'The Philosopher's Stone?' Ben said dubiously.

'The Holy Grail of the alchemists,' Silvestre replied. 'Said to hold the power to transmute base metals into gold and the key to everlasting life.'

Here we go again, Ben thought, but kept it to himself.

'But that doesn't mean every alchemist was literally trying to create gold,' Roberta said. 'Because as we know, those concepts are symbols in their own right. The idea of transmuting base metals was a metaphor for inner transformation, attaining perfection and finding . . . I don't know what exactly. Revelation. Enlightenment. God, even.'

'And so the presence of this symbol within the Templar knights' code tells us that theirs was a quest of the soul,' Silvestre said. 'The urge towards a spiritual epiphany not so different from the search for the Divine upon which every true believer is embarked. We need to remember that for all their esoteric ideas, the Templars were essentially Christian monks, sworn to the same vows of poverty and chastity as their non-combatant brothers in the Church. These sacred traditions were at the heart of everything they had held most holy since the founding of their order almost two centuries earlier. Now this once mighty organisation found itself on the brink of extinction, a whisker away from being stamped out once and for all by their persecutors. Imagine that was you, sheltering in the crypt knowing that the king's men were scouring the countryside for you, and that if you were caught, not only would they torture and burn you at the stake, there would be nobody left to pass the secret on for future seekers, and prevent it from falling into the wrong hands. What if the holy relic of John the Baptist still existed? Who would protect and honour it once you and all your fellow knights were gone?'

'Fine,' Ben said. 'Tell me one thing, supposing for one moment that any of this is true. These Custodians, the nutters with the red crosses on their arms, they must have known about the message on the crypt wall or else they wouldn't have been able to tell who was down there looking at it. So if this secret of theirs is so damned important, why didn't they just take a hammer and chisel and erase the clue that might have led someone else to find it?'

'Because that would constitute an act of desecration in its own right,' Silvestre replied, 'no different from defacing any other holy monument or artifact. The carving made by Thibault de Roucyboeuf is no less sacred to them than the secret itself.'

'Which would imply they were on permanent guard duty watching the Manoir du Col around the clock, just on the off chance someone might come looking for it one day,' Ben said. 'That's not possible.'

'Or else they were there because they'd been watching me and Brad,' Roberta reasoned. 'Monitoring every move we made, everyone we were in contact with, like Corky and others. Maybe that was the trigger for everything, because they'd got wind of what we were searching for. Then it all started happening in quick succession, one thing after another. First they got Brad, then they tried to get Sadler, and next they came for you.'

'I believe she's right,' Silvestre said to Ben. 'This is the only way it makes sense.'

Ben made no reply. Silvestre peered closely at his face, reading his expression. 'Are you still not convinced of what I've been telling you, my young friend?'

'It's a hell of a story,' Ben said. 'Some solid, tangible evidence would be useful. Starting with this scroll, or manuscript, or whatever it is, claiming to be a secret Gospel of John. You said you'd seen it. Where is it?'

'It was in the possession of a very good friend of mine, when I lived in Rome. His name was Alessandro Lambertini. You would know him by his official title, Pope Clement XV.'

Chapter 46

The two men who had been watching the house from their car were now joined by the others they'd called to report the arrival of the visitors.

'It's them,' had said the one making the call. He spoke in Italian.

'You're sure?'

'A tall male with blond hair accompanied by a woman in her thirties. *Una testa rossa.* They arrived in a blue BMW.'

'Stay put and make no moves until we get there,' had said his superior on the other end. 'We're on our way.'

The two obeyed their orders and waited patiently. As evening fell, they peered over the wall and were able to see the lights in the windows of what they knew to be the dining room. The shutters were open, and they could make out the figure of the red-haired Ryder woman sitting at the table facing the window. There were dishes and glasses and bottles on the table around her, so it was clear they were having dinner. But there seemed to be more talking than eating going on. The woman was sitting forward in her chair, only occasionally reaching for her wine glass to take a sip between bouts of animated discussion. Because of the angle of the window the two watchers were unable to make out who she was talking with, but it was an academic point in any case as only Hope and their host, Silvestre, were there in the house with her.

Over thirty long and suspenseful minutes dragged by before the watchers' associates arrived, in two vehicles. They switched off their lights as they approached the property, so as not to be spotted from the window. The two vehicles pulled up silently next to the watchers' own, and six men got out. Inside the lead car were the two men in charge of the operation, the tall Irishman and his shorter, swarthier companion, who had previously approached Hope and Ryder using the aliases of 'Sheehan' and 'Bertolli'.

'They've been talking a long time,' said one of the watchers to the man whose real name wasn't Bertolli. 'He could be telling them everything. We have to stop him.'

The man who wasn't Bertolli knew this was bad. He, like the others in his organisation, had long suspected that it was only a matter of time and opportunity before the ex-Cardinal turned into a much bigger problem for them. He knew far too much, and should never have been allowed to leave Rome alive. Now the old man was digging himself into a hole from which he'd never get out – and potentially digging them in with him.

The man not called Bertolli exchanged nods with his associate not called Sheehan. The time for monitoring and surveillance was over. The time for action had arrived.

And they'd come equipped to make sure it was completely effective.

'Let's do it.'

Chapter 47

Ben was struck into silence for a moment, at the reminder that this somewhat eccentric old man with whom they were talking had once been a close aide of the most exalted and powerful figure in the Catholic Church. Reflecting on what Silvestre had just told him, he cast his mind back and said, 'Clement XV. That was the pope who only held his position for a few days before he died, twenty years or so ago.'

Silvestre nodded solemnly. 'Your memory serves you well. He was elected in April 2005 and his Pontificate lasted only three weeks and a day. Had he survived, he would have been one of the worthiest of his line.'

Roberta said, 'So you're saying that he knew about the secret gospel?'

'He most certainly did. It had been discovered languishing in the most ancient, least frequented part of the Vatican archives only the year before Cardinal Alessandro Lambertini became Pope Clement XV. He was as fascinated as he was deeply perplexed by it, and often used to pore over its pages in the privacy of his rooms. Now, as we know, such so-called "heretical" ideas were nothing new to theology. But this particular scripture was the most troubling to the Holy Father, because if it were authentically penned by one of Christ's own disciples, it seemed to confirm those unsettling myths and legends that haunted the Christian orthodoxy and suggested that the divine and later resurrected Jesus of the traditional Gospels might in fact just be a second-century invention. Could such a thing be true? The possibility shook him to the core of his faith.'

'Wow,' Roberta said. 'The pope had doubts?'

'How it came about that he should regard me as worthy of his confidences, I can't begin to explain. Our friendship started as a close rapport between a senior cardinal and a lowly archpriest, and our theological conversations used to last late into the night. Later, when he became pope, he used to invite me into his private chambers in the Vatican and we would talk as openly as we always had.'

'Did he believe it?' Ben asked. 'In the Johannite Gospel?'

'He took it seriously enough to read it many times, both before and after he was pope. What he truly believed in his heart at the time of his death, nobody will never know. But of one thing I am certain. You see, the Vatican, whatever else it may be, is a political organisation, and an immensely powerful one at that. When certain people within those corridors of power discovered his interest in the Johannite text, they became terrified that he might reveal its existence to the wider world – worse still, that he might embrace it as a legitimate scripture. Twice they called for its destruction, claiming that a heretical work of that nature had no place in the Vatican library. Twice he used his influence over the Cardinals to have that request quashed. Then when his ascension to the papacy was confirmed, those forces who would have sought to suppress the Johannite Gospel became even more anxious.'

'And then he died,' Roberta said.

Silvestre was looking tired and grey from so much talking. He averted his face and coughed again into his napkin. 'Yes, he died. A man in his early seventies, with no pre-existing health conditions, who kept himself fit, ate a superbly healthy diet and was in better physical condition than many men half his age. To find *me* dead in my bed, that would be no great surprise to anyone, especially at this late stage. But for it to happen to him when and as it did, discovered on the floor of his chambers by an assistant, was a strange thing indeed.'

'What are you saying?' she asked with a growing frown on her face. 'That it was suspicious? They *killed* him?'

'That's quite a statement,' Ben said. 'How can you be so sure?'

'Because nobody was closer to the Holy Father than I was at the end of his life, and I knew what was troubling him. When he became gravely ill soon after his promotion, he told me that he believed he was being slowly poisoned. Who but someone inside the Vatican's own administration could have had access to his meals and beverages? A week later, after only twenty-two days as pope, he was gone. And the autopsy revealed nothing, or so we were told.'

Ben said, 'So we're supposed to believe that agents within the Church murdered the pope to stop him talking.'

'Perhaps to your ears it sounds absurd and fantastical,' Silvestre said. 'But you must believe it, for your own sakes. You have already seen what lengths your opponents are prepared to go to. But this is no longer just about them. You're caught in the crossfire of a deadly conflict between opposing forces that will stop at nothing to protect their own interests. On one side is the secret Order of the Custodes Sanctorum Secretorum Templi, sworn to keep the oath of silence from centuries ago. On the other is the

Vatican itself, ready to deploy all its power to suppress the hidden gospel that could undermine the authority of the Church. Either opposing side, for its own separate reasons, is prepared to eliminate anyone who poses a threat to its agenda. Even if that person just happened to accidentally witness the discovery of a clue that could potentially lead them to the truth. For the Holy Father it was because his scholarly curiosity as a theologian led him into dark and dangerous waters. In the case of your unfortunate associate,' he said, turning earnestly to Roberta, 'whether or not either of you were aware of it, your investigation was getting too close for their liking. And in the case of your late friend Monsieur Fletcher,' he finished, turning back to Ben, 'it was very simply a case of being in the wrong place at the wrong time.'

Ben was silent.

'Now you know the secret,' Silvestre said. 'And you understand why I could no longer remain in the Church after that. Of course they tried to talk me out of resigning my Cardinalship. Interestingly it was some of those of whom my suspicions were strongest that tried the hardest to make me stay. I believed then, and believe now, that it was so they could keep an eye on me. To abdicate from such a high position without a scandal hanging over one's head was unheard of, they said. We were all grieving, they said. I would feel better in time, they said. Take six months off, I was advised. Go and float around the Mediterranean on a yacht and come back whenever you're ready. But no. My faith was broken, not in God but in the Church that men built in His name. My doubts were simply too much to bear. Not to mention the sorrow of losing one of the closest friends I have ever known. He was truly a kind and wise man. Twenty years on, my heart still aches for him.'

'We should tell him about those two guys,' Roberta said, throwing a look at Ben.

Silvestre listened gravely as Ben explained how they'd been approached by a pair calling themselves Father Sheehan and Father Bertolli, claiming to be special envoys from Rome. 'They said they wanted our help, in return for their helping us. Talked about a secret that could bring down the Church.'

'And about an assassination plot against the pope,' Roberta added. 'Which from what you say, is something the Vatican already knows something about.'

'Then it is as I feared,' Silvestre said, looking grim. 'This can be no coincidence. And that they should approach you so openly must mean that they are onto you, and me as well.'

Ben said, 'Explain.'

The old man's energy was flagging and he sounded suddenly exhausted. 'I told you how Mathieu called me that evening, before he was attacked, to tell me of the incident in the crypt and describe what had been found there. I realise now that there's only one way these men Sheehan and Bertolli – I doubt those are their real names – could have known so much about your involvement. They must have been tapping my telephone.'

'But why would they tap your phone?' Roberta asked.

'The cloud under which I left the Church was one of deepest suspicion,' Silvestre replied. 'The sinister forces within the Vatican knew how close I was to the Holy Father, and especially at the end. They could only speculate on the nature and extent of our discussions about the Johannite

Gospel, and what I might intend to do with that knowledge after I left Rome and returned here to France. For years afterwards I was convinced they were there in the shadows, watching my every move. And though I eventually relaxed and told myself I was being foolish, now it seems as though I was right after all. The evil that has infiltrated the house of God never rests, and it never forgets.'

The double game that 'Sheehan' and 'Bertolli' had been playing was becoming more apparent to Ben. It wasn't impossible that they were genuine priests, or at any rate genuine agents of the Church – but that was about as far as the truth went. By tricking Ben and Roberta into luring the Custodians out into the open they'd have had the combined opportunity of killing the two of them while putting the blame on the enemy, covering their own tracks in the process. He understood now, too, why the pair had given them a different name for the Custodians, rehashing the Latin to omit any reference to the Temple, in case they figured out too much.

Tricky bastards, those Vatican guys. If they really were Vatican guys.

Either way, Ben could see that Silvestre was right. Just as they'd thought they only had one powerful enemy to deal with, it now turned out they were caught in a war between two opposing factions that were equally cunning, powerful and dedicated to destroying each other and anyone who stood in their way.

'But what can we do?' Roberta asked.

'You cannot hope to fight them and win,' Silvestre replied. 'They are too many and too powerful, and even if you were to evade them at first they will keep coming until they succeed. As will their enemies the Order of the Temple, who are just as dedicated to crushing all opposition.'

'Then we're screwed,' Roberta said. 'It's like we walked into a turf war between rival mafia families.'

Silvestre went into a coughing fit, more violent than before, and it was a few moments before he regained control of himself. He closed his eyes, seemed to be asleep; then he opened them again and looked across the room at one of the chessboards set up with a game in progress. The tactical wheels in his head were turning. He said, 'There is one strategy that may serve you against both sides at once. You will recall that I mentioned a second existing copy of the Johannite Gospel. You must obtain it and use it as a bargaining tool to protect yourselves.'

'Blackmail?' Ben said. 'Anything happens to us, we show the secret gospel to the world? That's a good one. As if anybody would care, nowadays.'

'You're right. Our modern secular society thinks it has more important things to worry about. But believe me, *they* care, and deeply. It would be your only chance.'

'If we knew where to find it,' Ben said.

Silvestre smiled a dark smile. 'That might not be as difficult as you think.'

Ben looked at him. 'You know where it is?'

'I told you there was much that is unknown about the modern-day Order of the Temple,' replied Silvestre. 'But one piece of information I do possess is the whereabouts of their current headquarters. They're based at the residence of its Grand Master, a castle in—'

'Wait,' Ben said. He'd heard something from outside. Only a faint sound, but it had set his alarm bells jangling. And when it came to danger, his instinct had never been wrong. He got up from his chair and stepped quickly over to the window. Night had fallen fully while they'd been talking. He peered out into the night and could see nothing, but his senses were jangling with alarm. Was he just being paranoid? His instinct was suddenly telling him otherwise.

'Ben?' Roberta asked. 'What's wrong?'

'Someone's out there,' he said. 'Don't ask me how I know. I can feel it.'

'Then it would seem I may have inadvertently led you into a trap,' Silvestre said. 'I'm so sorry, my friends. But perhaps it was inevitable.'

Ben closed the window blind, then strode out of the dining room and retrieved the heavy holdall from where he'd left it at the foot of the stairs. Bringing it back into the room he cleared dishes aside, dumped the bag on the table and zippered it open. 'You know how to use a gun?' he asked Silvestre.

The old man seemed unperturbed by the sight of the weapons in the holdall. 'I'm a man of peace, not of war,' he replied calmly. 'My Lord Jesus taught that I should turn the other cheek.'

'He tried to teach me that too,' Ben said. 'It didn't stick.'

Roberta was on her feet. Ben passed her the MP-5, slipped his Browning into its familiar, comfortable old place behind his right hip, then selected the sheathed commando dagger from the holdall and thrust it through the other side of his belt, crossways like a pirate. He felt much more fully dressed now, more complete somehow. 'How secure is that tower at the side of the house?' he asked Silvestre.

'The walls are solid stone and impenetrably thick. There are no windows lower than twenty feet from the ground and those that exist are barred and inaccessible from outside, while the only external door is made of riveted iron, heavily bolted shut from within and as far as I know has not been opened for centuries. Does that meet your definition of secure?'

'Well enough,' Ben said. 'Then that's where we'll go, and make our stand if need be. Now let's move.'

And then the dining-room window shattered and a projectile tore through the blind and cannoned off the tabletop in a shower of broken glass.

Chapter 48

Most people's first instinct might be that someone had put a brick through the window, which would be shocking enough to the average citizen. In the world Ben Hope inhabited, such a projectile would be more likely to be a bomb or a grenade, and his reaction was to grab whoever was within arm's reach and pull them out of the blast radius before the explosion killed everyone in range.

But Ben was wrong, because it wasn't a bomb. It was something else, just as bad.

The incendiary device hit the floor and erupted into a huge sheet of flame that was instantly pouring a river of fire up to the ceiling. In a matter of seconds it would engulf the entire room. Ben knew that because he'd seen what these devices could do and how fast they could totally overwhelm an entire building. Once they got going nothing could put them out. All you could hope to do was escape, and you'd better move fast. As quick as a snake he snatched the carafe of water from in front of Silvestre, upended its contents over the tablecloth and then jerked the cloth away, spilling plates and cutlery and glassware everywhere as the fire hungrily spread over the wall, engulfing everything with a whooshing crackling roar.

Roberta was already braced for action, recoiling from the flames with the MP-5 in her hands, but Silvestre was still sitting there as though transfixed in shock and horror by the surreal spectacle of his dining room on fire. Ben grabbed the old man's arm, jerked him out of his chair and propelled him towards the door with Roberta, draping the wet cloth around the two of them like a fire blanket to protect them from the flames that were already leaping up on both sides of the doorway and singed his hands and face as they raced from the room. Thick black smoke was rapidly filling the air, acrid and choking.

'The tower!' Ben yelled over the roar of the blaze. Too horrified to speak, Silvestre just pointed up the passage to their right, flanked by broad windows. But even as he was motioning in that direction, the windows burst inwards and two more incendiary devices sailed into the house, hammered off the passage wall and erupted into roiling flame that completely blocked off the way ahead.

Whoever was out there had encircled the property and was systematically pumping the firebombs in from all directions. Total destruction was their aim and they were certainly going the right way about it. There was no longer any chance of taking refuge in the tower, and in any case with no means of ground-floor escape, it could soon have become a death trap for them all.

But that meant they had to make another plan, and it looked as though their options were running out fast. Over the roar of the spreading inferno came the sound of another crash and tinkle of breaking glass, followed by yet another as the unseen enemy outside launched more of their projectiles at the house. These two had smashed through the tall windows of Silvestre's salon, filling the room with a rolling fireball that devoured everything in its path.

'The kitchen!' Silvestre spluttered, pointing a shaky finger in the only direction that wasn't rapidly being engulfed in wall-to-wall flames and billowing smoke. Ben led the way, the others following with the wet cloth swaddled around them. The kitchen was smoky but as yet still untouched by the blaze. Its other door led to a scullery, from which there was an exit to the rear of the house. But as Ben tore the door open and the freshness of the night air poured in, a blast of gunfire from outside drove him back. He rattled three rapid pistol shots into the darkness, but the shooters out there were too well hidden and he was firing blind. More bullets thudded into the door and Ben retreated quickly. For the three of them to try to escape that way would be suicide – though to remain inside was to invite certain death of a different sort. Their assailants were clearly intent on pinning them within the house until the whole thing collapsed about their ears. The thought occurred to Ben that Silvestre's old enemies within the Vatican were set on doing to them what the Church had done to the Templars centuries ago: roast them alive. In the aftermath it would look like an accident. The same way a poisoned pope could be made to look like he'd died of natural causes.

With no other option, Ben urged Roberta and Silvestre back inside the burning house. The multiple fires that had broken out in different rooms were combining into one and fast gaining an unstoppable foothold all around them. What little air was still breathable was so hot that it scorched their lungs. Drapes, paintings, furnishings were all violently ablaze. Ben's eyes were streaming tears and he could barely see, except to keep pressing forwards towards where there were no leaping flames. 'Cover your noses and mouths,' he yelled at the others. 'Follow me!'

He suddenly knew where he was going, to the one location inside what remained of the house that could allow them to survive, if only they could get to it in time. He'd managed to stumble on the adjoining pool house by accident on his return from the wine cellar earlier, and he remembered the way but the route was becoming less accessible with every passing moment as they battled through the flames. Silvestre was stumbling and wheezing and Roberta was having to clutch him tightly to keep him from falling. Any hesitation, any delay, their last chance would be gone and they would be trapped inside their fiery tomb.

If ever there was a time to pray to God for a miracle, this was it. God hadn't listened to the prayers of the Templars condemned to the flames, but maybe he was listening now – because as Ben wiped the streaming tears from his eyes he saw the heavy double doors of the pool house ahead of him through the smoke, and, barely able to draw breath, he surged towards them in desperation. And then they were inside the dark glass-covered building and shutting out the smoke and flames behind them. The doors might hold back the blaze for now, but not for very long. The pool itself had to be their only salvation.

Through the glass walls and roof of the pool house they could see the flames belching from the windows of Silvestre's home. The sky above was lit orange, burning embers soaring up into the darkness like swarms of fireflies. It would be only a few short minutes before the out-of-control blaze gained the roof, and soon after that the entire building would be a shell. Meanwhile the unknown number of attackers surrounding the grounds would be watching for any sign of their targets trying to escape, so they could force them back inside or maybe just gun them down in their tracks.

Ben didn't think they could be seen in here, not yet. That would change when the fire breached the doors and lit up the interior of the pool house. Glancing back, he saw with dismay that the first tongues of flame were already curling around the edges of the doors, much sooner than he could have wished.

'Into the water,' he told Roberta and Silvestre.

'But I can't swim!' the old man protested hoarsely. He doubled up coughing again, clutching at his chest. Ben wanted to yell, 'What fucking choice do you think you have, pal?' But maybe a softer option was called for. He glanced around him and saw that, piled in one corner of the tiled floor, close to the window where the firelight from outside was flickering dully over them, was a collection of children's pool toys that he guessed was used by Silvestre's grandniece's kids on their visits here. He ran over to them and picked up an inflated rubber flotation ring, then hurried back over to the old man and looped it over his head and shoulders. 'This will keep you from sinking. We'll keep you safe. Now jump.'

He laid his pistol down on the tiled edge of the pool and Roberta did the same with the weapon he'd given her. Then he grabbed Silvestre's arm and launched himself into the water, taking the old man with him. The pool was warm and smelled of chlorine. Ben kept hold of Silvestre's arm as they paddled closer to the edge of the shallow side.

They hadn't jumped a moment too soon, because only seconds later the fire in the main part of the house touched off the main gas pipe and a huge explosion ripped through the interior and the pressure wave blasted open the pool house doors. Ben yelled, 'Under!' and they sucked deep breaths and ducked their heads below the water just in time before the volcanic breath belched from the doors and flames seared the surface of the pool just inches above them. Ben could feel Silvestre beginning to panic, and clamped him tight in case he tried to break the surface too soon and got his head burned off. Then as the fireball receded, they came up for air and began to paddle quickly towards the far side of the pool where the flames would be last to reach. Silvestre was spluttering and coughing so hard he seemed barely able to breathe.

Ben needed an alternative plan, but the fire from the main building was gaining a hold of the pool house faster than he could come up with one. Everything was happening too fast. And then something else happened.

Roberta let out a cry as a secondary gas explosion lit the sky in a flash above them. Ben whipped his head around in the water and saw part of the house roof blown clear off, sections of tiles and entire timbers and chunks of solid oak A-frame spinning upwards into the air as if in slow motion, silhouetted against the flames, before they began to fall earthwards. Heading straight down to the glass roof of the pool house.

There wasn't time even to yell 'Look out!' Ben seized hold of Silvestre's collar and ducked his head and shoulders violently back under the surface, plunging down with him, closely followed by Roberta. In the next instant it seemed as if the whole building was falling on top of them. Shattered glass and bits of crumpled aluminium roof frame and scorched beams and tiles and the brickwork from a shattered chimney stack all came crashing down at once. A large piece of oak timber hit Ben across the shoulder and might have smashed his collarbone if the impact with the water hadn't absorbed a lot of its momentum. As it was it only knocked the wind out of him and dashed his body to the bottom of the pool. A torrent of bubbles erupted from his mouth and for a few terrible moments of total disorientation he couldn't tell which way was up, which way the surface was. Then he felt something strong and lithe grasp his wrist, and realised it was Roberta's hand trying to heave him back up.

He battled to the surface and sucked in the air – the same air that was now rushing into the shattered pool house and fuelling the fire into even more of a raging inferno. They had to dive down a third time as a curtain of flame descended over the water, narrowly missing incinerating them. From below the surface it looked as if the entire pool was a lake of fire.

This wasn't going to work. He might have managed to delay the inevitable by bringing them in here, but the reality was they were all going to die.

Chapter 49

Or maybe not. Because in a flash of realisation Ben saw that the collapse of the roof had brought them an unexpected advantage. A triangular section of the metal pool house structure that had fallen in was resting partly across the tiled floor and partly submerged in the water, jutting upwards like a tent; and its angle would give Roberta and the old man a place to shelter from the flames and keep their heads above the surface to breathe.

As for Ben, he was seeing the opportunity to even the odds a little, and maybe even get them out of here alive. 'Look after him,' he told Roberta.

'Where are you going? Stay with me!' Her hair was slicked across her face and there was a small cut on her brow where a piece of broken glass had hit her.

'I'll be right back.' *I hope*, he added mentally. Leaving the two of them huddled under their shelter he reached up and hauled himself out of the water. His pistol and the MP-5 were still where they'd left them, part buried under glass and broken tiles, the steel hot to the touch. He slung the submachine gun over his shoulder and jammed the pistol into the waistline of his wet jeans. The commando dagger in its steel scabbard was still in his belt. His Arkansas toothpick, as Roberta had called it. Useful for those times when you might have to take out some murdering piece of trash without making a sound.

The burning wreckage around the edges of the pool hid him from the view of anyone outside and his soaking clothes protected him from getting burnt as he pushed through the flames and made it to the shattered glass wall of the pool house. He slipped through one of the broken panes. The night air was suddenly chill against his skin, though the heat from the still burning house was strong on his back. He ran for the shadows of the bushes, ducked low to the ground and looked around him, letting his eyes adjust to the relative darkness. Somewhere out here, the men who'd surrounded the property would be waiting for the inferno to finish its work. They'd be too busy gazing at the blaze to see him coming.

Ben started creeping through the bushes, moving like a panther with the pistol in his hand and the submachine gun slung over his shoulder. Then he froze as he made out the shapes of two men among the dancing firelight shadows. He could just about discern enough of their features to tell that one of them he'd never seen before; but there was no doubt in Ben's mind that the taller, leaner man standing next to him was Sheehan. Both were armed with pistols, and the stranger had a grenade launcher hanging from his shoulder that he'd used to pump incendiary projectiles at the house. Neither was speaking as they intently watched the burning building for any sign of survivors trying to escape.

Ben was close enough to smell them by the time he moved into the attack. The one with the launcher let out a stifled cry as the steel of the Fairbairn-Sykes dagger plunged into his heart. Ben let the dead man slump to the ground and then turned his attentions on Sheehan. The Irishman was too terrified to shout or scream. He aimed his trembling pistol, but Ben savagely knocked it aside and in a single upward sweep buried the seven-inch double-edged blade up to its hilt under Sheehan's chin. With the razor-sharp leaf tip embedded in the base of his brain, it was lights out instantly for him. Which Ben felt was maybe a little too quick and humane, under the circumstances, and he'd have liked to take the opportunity to make the guy talk. But you couldn't have everything.

Ben moved on, circling the house. In the next eight minutes he encountered six more men. The first four met their sudden bloody death on the end of his blade. The fifth man saw him approach, purely by chance, and his mouth opened in shock at the sight of the dripping wet, wild-eyed and bloodied hunter stalking towards him out of the flickering shadows like some primal apparition. The man aimed his pistol but Ben drew his first and fired a single shot that caught him exactly between the eyes and felled him like a tree. The sixth man was only just nearby, and on hearing the report he whirled around to open fire. Ben put a double-tap into his chest and he toppled backwards with a grunt.

Ben stepped over to the fallen enemy, peered down and recognised the dark features and grizzled beard of the man who'd introduced himself to him and Roberta in the hotel room in Quillan as Father Bertolli. He was still alive, stirring in the dirt, gazing up with bulging eyes and trying to raise his hand clutching the pistol. Ben kicked it from his limp fingers, then crouched beside the dying man and said, 'Tell me who you are, who sent you, and I'll try to help you live.'

But it was too late for Bertolli. His mouth opened and closed, a wheezing hiss came from his lips with a bubble of blood, and then his head lolled sideways and he was on his way to whatever fate his Maker had in store for him.

Ben frisked Bertolli and found a phone, which he took. As he stood up he heard the sound of a car accelerating fast away from the scene. However many were still left, they must have fled at the sound of the shots. 'Cowardly bastards,' he muttered, then turned and started running back towards the fire. He was halfway back across the grounds when he heard and felt the earth-shaking crash, saw the flames leap higher and realised that more of the roof had collapsed, bringing down the remaining chimney stack that had pulverised whatever was left of the pool house.

His blood froze and he quickened his run to a sprint. He couldn't see anything except fire and wreckage. He didn't care about getting scorched as he reached the pool house and tore through a gap in the flames to see the rubble scattered everywhere, the burning timbers now lying across the pool, the mass of debris floating on the water and the huge blackened piece of chimney stack that had totally crushed the aluminium framework under which Roberta and Silvestre had been sheltering. He raced to the edge of the pool, dived back into the water and looked around him, near to panic.

'Ben! Over here!'

He turned and saw her through the smoke. She and Silvestre were huddled by the side of the pool, half-hidden behind rubble and wreckage. She'd managed to haul him clear of the water. The rubber flotation ring he'd been wearing hung loose and punctured around his narrow shoulders. He wasn't moving. There was blood on his face and neck. Blood all over him. Blood all over the tiles around him, red rivulets running down the edge of the pool and clouding the water. Ben splashed over to join them. Tears were running down Roberta's cheeks as she held the old man. His eyes were shut and in the firelight his face looked chalky and lifeless. 'He's hurt bad, Ben. We have to get him out of here and to a hospital.'

Ben clambered out of the water and saw the long, wicked spike of glass that was jutting from the base of Silvestre's throat. And knew that the old man wasn't going anywhere from here, except maybe to a better place. He'd be there soon. The blood was bright and arterial and it was flowing too fast for there to be any chance of saving him.

The old man's eyes fluttered open, tried to focus on Ben and then closed again. Ben gripped his shoulder and shook him back awake. He spoke calmly but urgently. 'Jean-Rafael, you need to finish telling us what you were saying. Where's the castle? Where are the Custodians' headquarters?'

The old man's lips moved but no sound came out, only a trickle of blood.

'Jean-Rafael! Focus. Talk to us.'

Silvestre's eyes opened to hazy slits. He tried again to speak. 'Por . . .'

'Jean-Rafael, Por—what?' The name he was trying to tell them could be so many places. Port-Brillet. Porspoder. Porte-Joie. And scores of others.

'Por . . .' the old man croaked again. '. . . tug . . .'

'Portugal?' Ben now remembered that he'd said the order had shifted its headquarters there after the war. 'Where in Portugal?'

'The Alen . . . Alentejo region. Near . . . Évo—' Silvestre had spent all his energy getting the words out, and those would be his last. His eyes closed, a long breath hissed from his mouth and he lay still in Roberta's arms. He looked as peaceful as though he were sleeping.

'God bless you, Jean-Rafael,' Ben said quietly.

'I tried to help him, Ben,' Roberta wept. 'I tried so hard.'

'There was nothing you could have done,' he said. 'It's over now. Bertolli and Sheehan are dead. And it's time to go to Portugal.'

Chapter 50

'Get away. He never said such a thing!'

'He did. I'm not kidding.'

'But that's just awful. I can't believe he would have said that.'

'It's the truth. Just ask Marthe. She was as shocked as I was.'

'Huh. I certainly won't be voting for *him* again. And he always seemed like such a nice man.'

'They're all the same, you can't trust any of them. I mean, even I had high hopes for the last one, and look how he turned out.'

This conversation had been nattering on for several minutes as the two nurses, Jeanne and Simone, working the evening shift, were preparing to go up to attend to Monsieur Sadler in Room 7. Jeanne was the junior of the two, younger and thinner than her colleague. 'You go ahead, Jeanne,' Simone said, placing the patient's night medications on a tray. They were mostly to manage his pain levels, along with some antibiotics for the minor infection he'd developed and some sedatives to help him sleep. 'I just need to confirm this new dosage level with Doctor Lerouge, and then I'll be along in a few moments.'

'Okay. See you in a minute.'

Everyone was pleased with the patient's progress. A couple of the hospital staff had gone through his property agency in the past, and he was a well-respected figure in the Quillan community. It was generally agreed how shocking it was that such a thing could happen to such a lovely, charming gentleman. What was the world coming to? But thankfully he'd been responding very well to his treatment, and Doctor Lerouge had said he could leave them in two or three days' time. Pity, thought Jeanne as she trotted up the stairs. Most of their inpatients were such bores, and all the nurses adored him. Technically, it didn't require two of them to administer his meds. It had to be said that a few eyebrows had been raised at the presence of Monsieur Sadler's three friends who seemed to have taken up permanent residence in the waiting area downstairs – but despite their slightly intimidating looks, they'd been courteous and polite with the hospital staff.

Reaching his door she opened it quietly, closed it behind her and padded into the silence of the dimly-lit room. She regretted having to wake her favourite patient at this time of the evening, but the doctor insisted that he be given his treatment at strict intervals. Without a glance at the still, prone figure beneath the sheets she stepped over to adjust the side lamp and give herself a little more light.

Once that was done, she turned back towards the bed with a smile and was about to greet him with a cheery '*Bonsoir*, Monsieur Sadler' when she froze in her tracks and let out a cry.

The man standing in the shadows over the patient's bed was wearing a doctor's long white coat and a stethoscope around his neck, but even in the semi-darkness of the room

Jeanne was certain she'd never seen him before during the three years she'd worked at this hospital. He was much taller and more heavily built than Doctor Lerouge, with broad shoulders and short black hair and a look of impassive cruelty in his eyes that terrified the life out of her. As did the fact that he was clutching a pillow in his surgically gloved hands, which he had pressed down over the patient's face in a fairly obvious attempt to smother him.

'What on earth are you doing?' Jeanne demanded, stunned almost speechless and pointing accusingly at him. 'Who are you? Stop that at once, do you hear me?! STOP IT!'

The man said nothing. His expression didn't change as he dropped the pillow and strode rapidly around the side of the bed towards her. He reached Jeanne in three long strides, drew back his fist and punched her hard in the face. She crumpled to the floor without another sound, unconscious and bleeding. The man peered down at her for a moment as though contemplating whether to finish her off with another blow. Then he walked calmly back to the bed, picked up the pillow and resumed what he'd been doing. This wouldn't take long. The patient had been fast asleep but now woke with a start and began to struggle, legs kicking, trying to claw away the pillow that was suffocating the life out of him. But the killer in the white coat was too strong to resist.

Just then the door opened again and Jeanne's more senior colleague, Simone, entered the room carrying the tray with the medications. She halted after two steps, gaped down in horror at the sight of the younger nurse sprawled on the floor, then looked up at the stranger in the doctor's coat, realised what he was doing and instantly reacted by flinging the tray at him. Its metal corner caught him in the eye, and with a grunt of pain he staggered away from the bed. Half-blinded and furious, he came charging towards her with his gloved hands raised to grab her by the throat and throttle her.

Simone was just a couple of steps from the door. She made a dash towards it, simultaneously activating the emergency alarm button on her pager device. As she reached the door she managed to get partially through, yelling blue murder for security to come quick, before the man grabbed her from behind and dragged her back inside the room. He was large and powerful and intent on beating her to death with his bare hands; but Simone was a burly woman, stronger than she looked, and eight years of her nursing career back in the day had been spent working at a mental health clinic where violent schizophrenic patients had sometimes had to be restrained. She put up a spirited resistance, flailing her chubby fists against his chest, lashing out at his shins and biting the hands that tried to strangle her. The man threw her to the floor and went to stamp on her neck, but she managed to wriggle out of the way of the blow, picked up a chair and hurled it at him. He ducked and the chair crashed against the window blinds.

The struggle had been going on for nearly half a minute when the door burst open once more, and this time it was a pair of armed security guards who came piling into the room, yelling loudly and reaching for their pistols. Neither man had drawn his service weapon a single time during the combined forty-plus years of their security guard careers. The intruder, however, had had plenty of experience – even if his marksmanship was affected by his damaged eye. He reached inside his white coat for the concealed handgun that he'd brought as a last-ditch measure, drew it out in a smooth movement and fired twice.

The loud snapping gunshots were a startling, shocking contrast to the tranquillity of a small, quiet hospital. One security guard was hit in the chest and the other in the forehead. They dropped to the floor dead beside the unconscious Jeanne.

Then the intruder coldly directed the weapon towards Simone and fired a third bullet that cut her straight down. As her knees buckled under her he turned his sights towards the half-smothered patient, squeezed off another two hurried shots and then bolted for the door, jumping over the bodies. He burst out into the corridor still clutching the pistol. A foolishly brave orderly with a trolley tried to block his path and was shot in the thigh. The intruder turned towards a fire exit staircase and kept running.

Rocket Lockett and Mel Craig were downstairs in their usual seats in the waiting area when they heard the commotion above. 'Something's happening.' At the sound of the gunshots they threw down their magazines, sprang to their feet and raced for the stairs.

Chapter 51

Ben was sorry to have to leave Silvestre here like this, just another body in the burnt-out killing ground that had been his cherished home. But it was only a matter of time before one of his rural neighbours saw the fire glow in the sky and called the emergency services. Ben had no intention of being anywhere near the place when they turned up and found his signature dead men lying everywhere.

He and Roberta escaped from the wreck of the pool house before the flames from the rest of the building could devour it completely. They'd lost nearly everything in the fire – her leather satchel with all her stuff in it, Ben's haversack and the holdall with most of the weapons. But they still had the Alpina, protected from more than just the pigeons by having been stored in the converted stable block garage across from the house, where the blaze had yet to reach but soon would. Ben bundled her quickly into the car, jumped behind the wheel and they roared out towards the gates.

Roberta was distraught and crying as they sped away into the night. 'If only we could have done something for him,' she sniffed, wiping her eyes.

'We'll be doing something for him,' Ben replied, 'when we get the people who did this. All of them. I don't care who's on what side, and I don't care why. They made a big mistake when they got us into the middle of their little war. Now they're all going down together.'

She looked at him. 'If this is the part where you say to me that you're going it alone from here, you can save yourself the trouble. I'm sticking right by you, whatever happens.'

He took his hand from the wheel, reached out to her and their fingers clasped together in the darkness. He said, 'Thanks for pulling me out of the water. I'd have drowned.'

'You're the one who saved us. You always do.'

'We'll need to see to that cut on your brow. I'm pretty good at stitching wounds. Had a lot of practice, usually on myself.'

She touched her fingers to it, as though she'd forgotten it was there. 'Bah. It's only a scratch. And don't you even think about coming anywhere near me with a needle.'

That sounded like the kind of thing he'd have said, too.

But the last thing she was thinking of was her injury. 'If we're headed for Portugal, I don't know how I'm going to get on a plane with no papers. My passport was in my bag along with everything else.'

He shook his head. 'We're not going by plane. It's only half a day's drive from here, depending on where that castle is Silvestre told us about. But we're not going anywhere until we've got ourselves cleaned up, rested up and resupplied.'

'Back to the motel?'

They'd never checked out of there, and Ben still had their room keys in his pocket. It was only a little after midnight now. So much had happened since they'd left there – getting themselves arrested, escaping from jail, the gun battle in the garrigue, the visit to Silvestre and the events that had unfolded afterwards – that it was easy to forget it had all taken place within such a short time.

He replied, 'Just for a couple of hours or so. Then we'll go shopping for some new clothes and a few other things before we hit the road.' He pulled his phone from his jacket pocket, tried to turn it on and wasn't surprised to find it as waterlogged as his clothes. It had been a while since he'd talked to the teams at Le Val and Quillan, and he was anxious for updates on both fronts.

Back at the motel, Ben dug out the room keys and was about to unlock hers when she said in a low voice, 'I don't want to be on my own, Ben. Is that okay with you?'

'That's fine by me,' he said, showing her inside his own room. While she was getting cleaned up he stripped off his wet, dirty clothes, wrapped himself in one of the pair of fluffy bathrobes that came with the room and lay back on the bed with his eyes closed, listening to the patter of the shower and the sounds of her moving about. She was in there for long enough for the bathroom to be steamed up like a jungle by the time she emerged, wearing the other bathrobe. His turn in the shower was the opposite of hers, short and cool, but when he came back out he found that she'd crawled into bed and fallen asleep. He was badly in need of rest, too, and wondered whether he should grab a few hours in the armchair instead.

'What the hell,' he muttered, deciding, and slipped under the sheets next to her. Last time they'd shared a bed had been a somewhat different matter, and it was the oddest feeling to be so close to her again. But Ben had little time to reflect on it, because he was asleep within three minutes.

When his eyes blinked open in the darkness two hours later she was lying with her face nuzzled into his shoulder and her arm draped across his chest. He gently lifted it away, got up with care not to wake her, and went over to the window. Dawn was still hours away. Come first light, they'd be on their way to Portugal. What awaited them there, he could only guess.

Roberta slept on for another hour, and he used that time to hand-wash their clothes in the bathroom sink as best he could with soap and hot water, wring them out and dry them with a hairdryer. Then he headed over to the lobby to get them a couple of coffees from the vending machine.

'Morning,' he said, nudging her awake. 'Got breakfast for you. Get it down you while it's hot and then we're out of here. We have a long day ahead of us.'

As the spectacular colours of dawn bathed the eastern horizon they were already far away, shopping around a 24-hour hypermarché outside Toulouse for fresh clothes. Ben had never deviated much from his standard uniform, maybe because of the institutional behaviour drilled into him by his military past. He exchanged his wrinkled, hand-washed black jeans, black T-shirt and pale blue denim shirt for the nearest equivalents possible, and even found a pair of olive-green socks not too different from his old ones. He regretted the loss of his faithful haversack, an obsolete military pattern that was probably irreplaceable.

'I suppose you'll be hanging on to that old leather jacket,' she said, eyeing it with something less than approval.

'This? I'd never replace it. We've been through a lot together.'

'Yeah. It shows.'

Ben's final supermarket purchases were a brick of Gauloises, a bottle of Laphroaig, some antiseptic lotion and sticking plasters for Roberta, and a pair of prepaid mobiles, one for each of them. His waterlogged phone might recover or it might not, but he couldn't do with waiting for it to dry out before making the two calls he wanted to make. Back in the car park, he sat on the Alpina's bonnet in the rapidly warming sunshine waiting for Roberta to finish in the ladies' room and ripped his new acquisition out of its packaging, fitted the SIM card and wondered whom to call first. After a moment's hesitation he decided it was more pressing to talk to Rocket Lockett before checking in with Le Val.

And the instant he heard Lockett's voice, he knew something serious had happened there, too.

Chapter 52

'Mate, where've you been?' Lockett's agitated voice said on the line. 'We've been trying to call you all night. Left a dozen messages. Thought something must've happened. We called Le Val to ask them if they knew anything. Jeff and the others are going nuts.'

'I lost my phone,' Ben replied. 'What's up? Is something wrong?'

Locket sighed. 'I'm sorry, mate, we did our best.'

Ben felt his blood run suddenly cold despite the warmth of the morning. 'What's happened?'

'It was never going to be possible to guard him,' Lockett said. 'Not properly, I mean. All we could do was watch the entrance. We couldn't be in the room with him. But the bastards managed it, by dressing their guy up as a doctor.'

Ben's heart sank as he pictured the worst happening. He couldn't blame Lockett and the guys. It was true that they'd been limited from the start in their ability to guard poor Sadler, and that was his fault, not theirs.

'If it hadn't been for them two nurses,' Lockett went on, 'he'd have done the job right under our bloody noses. Couple of heroes, they are.'

'You mean Sadler's not dead?' Ben asked, brightening.

'Nah, mate, but it was a close one. They caught him in the act, raised the alarm and he shot one of them. Then he popped off two more rounds at Sadler, but one of the nurses had whacked him in the eye and his aim was off. Both bullets missed. Next thing the guy legged it down the fire escape.'

Ben listened as Lockett recounted the rest of the story. 'Nobby was having a kip back at the boarding house at the time, but me and Mel were downstairs when we heard the shots. We was heading for the stairs when we see this bastard in a white doctor's coat come down the fire escape like a bat out of hell with a pistol in his hand and go running across the car park for his mate who was waiting for him. But we managed to head him off before he got there. Next thing the car's taking off without him, and the guy jumps a fence and is hammering down the bloody street waving the gun at people and screaming to get out of the way. Then he takes a bad turning down this dead-end alleyway. When he saw we was going to catch him, he fired a couple more shots at us and then saved the last one for himself.'

'He shot himself rather than be caught?' Ben asked. It sounded more like the behaviour of a fanatical cult member than a religious order. 'Did he have a tattoo on his arm, a red cross?'

'Couldn't tell you, mate. Mel and me had to scarper before the police started swarming all over the place. We made it back to the hospital without getting collared, but that was a close one too.'

'What about the nurse who got shot?'

'Poor cow's in a bad way. They reckon she'll survive, but you know how it is.'

'They'll try again,' Ben said, thinking out loud. 'We've got to get him out of there.'

'That's not all that's been happening here,' Locket told him. 'Like I said, we've been trying to call you all night.'

'Tell me.'

'The police chief, what's-his-name.'

'Grosjean,' Ben said.

'Yeah. He was found dead last night in his home. Neighbours reported a scream. Cops got there to find blood all over the floor and up the wall, the body lying on one side of the room and the head on the other. Someone'd hacked it off with a sword or a machete, they reckon.'

It had been a busy night in Quillan, by all accounts. Sadler had had a very lucky escape. Ben wasn't too surprised to hear about Grosjean's less fortunate outcome, and he couldn't say he was heartbroken either. But he felt bad about the nurse. After he'd thanked Lockett for what they'd done and ended the call, he was about to dial Le Val when he changed his mind again and called a different number instead.

'This is absolutely the last favour I'm ever going to ask of you,' was his opening line.

Valentina laughed. 'Am I complaining? You know I'll do anything for you. As long as you promise to marry me.'

'You're not serious,' Ben said after a beat. He might have actually flinched.

'What if I was?' she fired back, undeterred.

'You're just a kid.'

'I'm eighteen.'

'I don't think your granduncle Auguste would approve,' Ben said. 'In fact he'd probably hire a hitman team to shoot me.' And I've got enough of those kinds of troubles already, he added silently to himself.

'Nonsense. He thinks the world of you.'

'Anyway, it's the worst idea I've ever heard.'

'I knew it,' she said. 'There's someone else. And there was me thinking you were an eligible bachelor, footloose and fancy free.'

'I am.'

'I don't believe you,' Valentina chuckled. 'So who is she? When do I get to meet her?'

Ben had the distinct impression that she was teasing him. 'Do you want to hear this favour or not?' he asked, a little tersely.

'All right, all right. I must have touched a nerve there. So what is it? Another jet plane ride? A yacht, like that other time? And don't forget you're still entitled to that billion euros I offered you for saving Tonton.'

'None of those things,' he replied.

'Then what?'

'I wouldn't even ask. Only I don't know anyone else who owns their own private hospital, right in the grounds of their home estate.'

By the time they'd finished talking five minutes later, the wheels were already in motion for the Kaprisky Clinic to wield its authority as one of Europe's pre-eminent state-of-the-art medical facilities to have the patient transferred from the Centre Hospitalier de Quillan into their capable hands. For the remainder of his recovery period Sadler would receive the very best care, safely surrounded by an impregnable ring of security. Ben blamed himself for not having thought of it sooner.

'Stop worrying,' Valentina told him. 'I'll take care of everything, trust me.'

From Toulouse the boundary line between France and Spain was just a seventy-five-mile blast. With no ID Roberta was concerned about border controls, but Ben assured her that they were unlikely to be manned. That was, unless the Spanish authorities were especially on the alert for organised crime gangs, terrorists, or the kind of people who might be inclined to smuggle automatic arms and ammunition across two countries in order to effect a small massacre against a nefarious secret society. It wasn't the first time Ben had stashed illicit hardware in those hidden nooks and crannies of his car where none but the canniest customs officials would think to search. But as he'd anticipated, it turned out to have been an unnecessary precaution and they flew through the border controls unimpeded.

The route Ben had chosen was the most direct diagonal slash across the country that connected Zaragoza and Madrid all the way to Badajoz right by the border, and from there into Portugal and their destination in the deep south. The Languedoc had been hot enough, but as midday approached the Alpina's air conditioning was working hard to cool the soaring Spanish temperatures. 'This is worse than Arizona in August,' Roberta complained. 'If I take off any more clothes I'll get us arrested again.'

'That's the last thing we need,' he replied.

They stopped for fuel, a light lunch and cool drinks at a roadside eatery near the sun-scorched municipality of Almudévar, where even the locals looked worn down by the heat. Under the shade of a parasol they took out their new burner phones and consulted the oracles of Google Maps and the wider internet to try to figure out exactly where their journey was taking them.

'Here's our problem,' Ben said. 'All we know from Silvestre, assuming that his information was good, is that the Order of the Temple has its headquarters at a castle in the Alentejo, somewhere near a place called Év—something, which I'm guessing must be the city of Évora, in the centre of the region. That's fine as it goes, but it's one of the largest, most spread-out and underpopulated regions in southern Portugal and there are dozens of castles scattered all over the place. Évoramonte, Estremoz, Veiros, Terena, Monsaraz and a load more; take your pick. Finding the right one could take weeks.'

Roberta, who'd been trawling through all she could find on the historic Templar sites of southern Portugal, had to reluctantly agree. 'I knew they'd been active in those parts but they built so many bases there that it's making my head spin. I just wish we knew more.'

Ben sighed, put away his phone and took another sip of his ice-cold beer. 'To hell with it. We're committed now. And it's not as if we can go back to ask Silvestre for more specific directions. I say we proceed to the Alentejo region as planned, and worry about it when we get there. Something will come up.'

Back in the car, they continued the high-speed journey south-westwards. Roberta spent time dozing on the back seat and keeping cool as best she could in the blast of air from the open windows while Ben worked his way through his brick of Gauloises and stayed alert by listening to a modern jazz station he'd tuned into. He kept his foot down with little regard for speed limits, and one eye on the rear-view mirror in case he triggered the attentions of the Spanish traffic police. The scenery became gradually more arid and yellowed the further they blasted south and one region after another passed into their wake: Aragon and its capital city of Zaragoza, where he'd once cracked an international kidnapping ring and liberated more than twenty kids stolen from their families; the urban sprawl of Madrid; Castilla-la-Mancha and Toledo, land of Quixotic windmills and vineyards and mountains, here and there a lonely castle dotted over the landscape beneath the sinking late afternoon sun. As dusk fell they crossed into the western region of Extremadura and made their last fuel stop before they'd finally hit the Portuguese border.

'You should rest,' she told him. 'You look beat.'

'Just a few more hours,' he protested. 'We're nearly there.'

'All the more reason to give yourself a break. Wherever the hell it is we're headed for, it's been there for centuries and it'll still be there in the morning, when we're fresh.'

Ben didn't like interrupting their progress when they were so close, but by the time they reached Badajoz, last stop on their route through Spain, the tiredness was weighing heavily on him and he finally relented. Locating their destination would be a lot easier in daylight.

The Hotel Cervantes was an old building untouched by time, on Plaza San Andres in the middle of the old city and just a short walk to the Catedral Metropolitana de San Juan Bautista, the Cathedral of Saint John the Baptist. The Johannites would have approved, Ben thought – though he couldn't have cared less about the historic sights, and would just as happily have slept in the car somewhere secluded outside the town. They checked in as Mr and Mrs Harris again, as they'd done at the motel back in France, and a taciturn young girl showed them up to their room. If the hotel staff were surprised at the new guests' total lack of luggage, they didn't show it. When nobody was looking Ben retrieved their weapons from the car, wrapped in his leather jacket.

The room was simple but comfortable, with a cool stone-tiled floor and a tall window with a balcony. Ben stepped out to lean on the wrought-iron railing, light a Gauloise and gaze uninterestedly at the evening view of the city. The nearby cathedral had a square tower for a spire, silhouetted against the dark sky; and in the distance beyond he could make out the walls of the older Moorish citadel, dating back to Spain's many centuries under Islamic rule.

Sensing a movement behind him, he turned to see Roberta's smile. 'I know you're itching to move on,' she said, touching his arm. Her fingers felt warm and pleasant.

'This was a good call,' he replied. 'We'll get to the Alentejo in the morning and see what we can see.'

After all the rush of their journey, time seemed to have slowed down. At eight-thirty they ventured out into the quiet streets and followed the hotel owner's directions to the restaurant he'd most recommended. The night was balmy and the stars twinkled in their billions. Ben could feel his restlessness beginning to subside. Roberta's presence here with him was soothing. Maybe it was only the lull before the storm, he told himself, but he let himself relax into the mood and shut out his troubled thoughts.

After their late dinner they wandered back through the streets. As they walked, he felt her fingers intertwine with his again. 'I'm glad you're here with me, Ben,' she said.

He smiled back and squeezed her hand. 'I'm glad you're here with me, too.'

'I wish it could have been different, though,' she said. 'Without all these things happening. Just normal. Peaceful.'

'I know. Me too.'

She slowed her step to glance up at him, and as her eyes caught the starlight it hit him for a moment that she looked startlingly beautiful. 'We never have had much of a chance, have we, you and I?' she asked. 'Let alone any kind of a normal, peaceful time together.'

'Things will be different,' he replied, and it was only after a few moments had gone by that he realised what he'd said.

They walked on in silence until they reached the hotel. Neither of them spoke as they climbed the creaky wooden stairs to their room. 'It's late,' she said, taking off her jacket and draping it over a chair.

'I'll go out on the balcony for a smoke while you get ready for bed,' he told her. 'Then I'll sleep on the sofa. Looks comfortable enough.'

She stepped closer to him, reached for his hands and raised herself up on tiptoe to kiss him softly on the lips.

'No, you won't,' she said.

Chapter 53

When Ben drew open the blinds the next morning, the sun was already up and climbing over the red-tiled roofs, towers and battlements of the old town. Everything felt different, and not just because of the bright daylight.

'Let's not be in a hurry to leave just yet,' Roberta said when she emerged from the bedroom, smiling and tousled. 'Please?'

'After breakfast,' he replied gently but firmly.

Once they'd showered and dressed they headed back out into the town, and found a bustling little café a few blocks away serving tasty breakfast tortillas, empanadas and *pan con tomate*, which was fried bread with tomatoes and olive oil. They washed it down with coffee, black as usual for him, *con leche* for her. 'No buttery rolls and chocolate spread for her ladyship this morning?' he observed.

'Uh-uh. That's because she doesn't need comforting,' she replied with a twinkle. 'Not now. She's got all she could ask for.' She reached out and they clasped hands across the table.

'I know you don't want to hear this,' he said after a beat. 'You've heard it before, and I don't expect you to feel differently now. But I'm going to say it anyway, one last time.'

'I think I know what you're going to say.'

'This is a nice city. You like it here.'

'I like it because I'm here with you.'

'All the same,' he said. 'I'm asking you to stay and wait while I finish this. Alone.'

'Two of us haven't managed to figure out yet where to go. What chance does one person have on their own?'

'I'll work it out,' he replied.

'I thought we were together now,' she said, raising an eyebrow. 'Didn't we just make that official, so to speak?'

'All the more reason.'

'Don't get mushy on me, Ben.'

'What happened before, like in the garrigue,' he said, 'that was bad. But things could get a lot nastier. I might have to do things that I wouldn't want you to see. Go into places and situations where I wouldn't want you following.'

She sighed. 'You're right, Ben. I don't want to hear it. But thanks for saying it. The answer is still no.'

'I had to ask.'

'You know I'm a stubborn bitch,' she said with a disarming smile.

'The worst.'

It was hot by the time they left the café. Ben looked at his watch. They'd already spent much longer than planned in Badajoz. Some of the reason for that, he wasn't going to complain about. But the urge to move on was coming back – along with the same nagging sense of uncertainty about what they were going to do when they reached the Alentejo. This wasn't over yet, by a long shot. And he hated not having a plan.

'I was looking up the history of this city this morning,' Roberta said as they walked. 'You know it's changed hands so many times. First the Romans came here in about 200 BC. Then later the Moors had it, up until 1230 when it was recaptured by King Alfonso of Léon. After the Reconquista the Spanish and the Portuguese kept fighting over who should control it because it was so close to the border.'

'All I know about Spanish medieval history was from the movie *El Cid*,' he admitted.

She snorted. 'The one with Charlton Heston? That's a crock of shit. The final scene when they strapped his dead body into the saddle and he rode out and scared all the Turks away because they thought he was immortal? Never happened.'

Her mention of history was still in his ears moments later, and had triggered off a thought association in his mind, when they passed an antiquarian bookshop. He paused outside the shop window, which was filled with old books of all shapes and sizes. 'Let's take a look inside,' he said.

'For what, a little light reading for the rest of our vacation?'

'Not exactly. A thought came to me just now, after what you were saying. Then that got me thinking about the name of the cathedral here in Badajoz.'

'Saint John the Baptist? But I don't understand what—'

'It's just a hunch,' Ben said. But his instinct was telling him it was a good one.

The bookshop looked the same inside as it did on the outside, pleasingly dusty and anachronistic, the kind of place you could browse in all day long and find all kinds of material that had been out of print since before you were born. Shelves everywhere, from floor to ceiling, were crammed with volumes some of which were almost falling apart with age. The shop owner looked just as old as his stock, a tiny little man with white hair and a droopy moustache. Ben asked him in Spanish if he had any historical maps or atlases of southern Spain and Portugal. The old guy thought for a moment, then led them between the cluttered aisles and pointed to a section. 'Dating from what year?' he asked in a raspy voice.

'Not too recent and not too ancient,' Ben said. 'Say, within the last century or so?'

'How about this one?' The bookseller pulled down a thick, battered volume filled with period maps, the pages yellowed and frayed around the edges. 'Or else there's this other one here,' he said, producing another that was even tattier. 'It's a little older. Might be what you're looking for?'

'Mind if I have a quick look through both of them?' Ben asked him.

'Help yourselves. What is time in a place of forgotten old books and bygone history?' the old guy rasped with a grin, and returned to his desk at the front of the shop.

Any hint of a secret code or cipher might have been enough to send him running for the hills, but when it came to maps and charts Ben was perfectly at home. He carried the two collections over to a table and laid them side by side. He started with the slightly more recent volume first, bent over it to studiously leaf through the pages. Map after map of every region in that whole area. He ignored the Spanish ones and focused on the Portuguese, narrowing down his search page by page.

'What *are* we looking for?' Roberta asked him, frowning.

'Hold on,' he muttered distractedly. 'Like I said, it's just a hunch. I might be right or I might be wrong. Just let me check . . .' He'd been through nearly the entire book before he found what his instinct had told him to look for. He traced his finger back and forth, up and down, over the grainy paper, stopped and peered down closely at the tiny print. 'Ah. Yes. Here's something. Now let me see . . .'

'Ben?' she said impatiently, but he ignored her as if he hadn't heard. He left that book open at the page he'd found, and moved over to the older, tattier, book, leafing carefully through its frayed pages. The colour images had faded with age but were still perfectly legible. 'Here we go,' he said at last. 'This is it.'

'What is?' she asked. 'What have you found?'

Ben pointed to the second book. 'This is a small-scale survey map of the area of the central Alentejo region around Évora, drawn in 1928,' he told her. 'See, it shows all the castles, churches and old monuments in the region.'

'Okay, I'm looking,' she said. 'But what am I looking for?'

'This,' he replied, pointing. 'Tell me what you see.'

Roberta peered closely at the faded page. 'It's a castle. I vaguely remember having seen it on Google Maps when we searched before.'

'Located about nine kilometres south of the town of Vila Nova da Baronia. And what's the name of the castle?'

'Castelo de Cristo Salvador,' she read from the page.

'Which means?'

'My Portuguese isn't the best,' she said. 'But I'd say it translates as "Castle of Christ the Saviour".'

Ben nodded. 'Okay. Now take a look at the other book. Same region, different map. This one was printed a few years later, in 1951. And here's the castle again.' He pointed. 'But do you notice anything different about it?'

Roberta moved over to the more recent map, brushed a lock of red hair away from her face and examined the spot where he was pointing. 'It's the same location, all right,' she said after a moment. 'A few kilometres south of Vila Nova da Baronia. But . . . looks like the name has been changed.'

'To "Castelo São João Salvador",' Ben said. 'The castle of Saint John the Saviour. Not the most conventionally Catholic title, wouldn't you say? Sounds a little odd. Unless of course you were of the Johannite persuasion. In which case you would regard Saint John as much more of a saviour than Jesus, even if that seemed somewhat heretical to your regular Christian peers. And what if you had arrived in Portugal after the war looking for a new base for yourself and your followers, and had the money and influence to buy a castle of your own, and rename it to suit your religious beliefs?'

Roberta looked up from the book with wide eyes. 'It must mean—'

'Two things,' Ben said. 'Firstly, that the more conventional name was used in compiling the data for the modern satellite map online. Depends what source they were using, maybe. Perhaps that's how it still appears on most official records. Secondly, that if we were to check a local register of property transactions between 1928 and 1951, we'd almost certainly find that the castle changed hands between those dates. I'm guessing sometime after 1946, tallying with what Silvestre told us. But I'd also bet that the real name of the new owner doesn't appear there. These people are too careful for that.'

'The castle of Saint John the Saviour,' she murmured, shaking her head in amazement. 'This is it. You found it. This is where those sons of bitches have been hiding for the last seventy years.'

'And now all we have to do is get over the border and find the damn place on the ground,' he replied. 'And if we're right, they'll be in for a surprise.'

Chapter 54

Deep in the heart of the sweeping barren plains and olive groves of the Alentejo, where little whitewashed hamlets, walled medieval villages and Roman ruins nestled among the endless rolling hills, the sun beat down on the grey stone turrets and battlements of the Castelo São João Salvador. The castle dominated a craggy escarpment that loomed high above a cork forest, with a single narrow road that snaked through the trees and up the hillside towards it.

And it was on that road that the solitary white van was making its way towards the arched castle gates, throwing up a tail of dust cloud in its wake. The lone driver was a local, in his forties, with silvering black hair and a deep leathery tan. Despite having the windows cranked down for the breeze, runnels of sweat were pouring off his brow and his shirt was sticking to him. His hands were clasped tightly on the steering wheel and he sat unusually upright and rigid in his seat. The anxiety he was displaying wasn't due to being nervous of driving, or having to concentrate especially hard on negotiating the uneven rural road. He was more worried about the loaded, cocked nine-millimetre pistol whose muzzle was pointed at where it would hurt the most.

'Keep driving, Tonio,' Ben said, behind him. 'Just remember what I told you.'

They'd spotted the white Fiat panel van from afar as it climbed the little road that had nowhere to go except up the hill to the castle. Through the binoculars he'd bought before leaving Badajoz, Ben had been able to see that the driver was alone.

'Let's take him,' Roberta said. They'd hurried from the scrub-covered ledge that had been their hidden observation platform, back to the dusty Alpina, and gone bumping over the rough ground to rejoin the road and intercept the van before it cleared the forest and came within sight of the castle battlements. Ben cut sharply across the van's path, forcing it to a halt. The driver reached for the long-range walkie talkie radio on the dash, but dropped it and quickly put his hands up when he saw the pistol pointing his way.

Ben kept the gun on the driver as he stepped up to the van. He reached inside the window, turned off the engine and plucked the key from the ignition. 'What's your name?' he asked the driver. Ben's spoken Portuguese wasn't as fluent as his Spanish, but he'd done some courses in the language back in his days as an international kidnap and ransom specialist and could get by well enough.

'T-Tonio.'

'Okay, Tonio, take it easy, cooperate with us and you'll be fine. Get out of the van. Nice and slow, hands where I can see them.'

Tonio climbed out and kept his arms raised as Ben gave him a pat-down. He was clean, and a quick check of the vehicle glove box revealed no hidden weapons. Which raised a momentary doubt in Ben's mind: what if this man was completely innocent and they'd picked the wrong castle?

'What do you want with me?' Tonio quavered, staring at the gun. He wasn't acting much like a hardened member of a violent cult, either.

'It's simple. You're going to take us in there and lead us to your boss. We'd like to meet him.'

Tonio's reply assuaged Ben's doubts that they'd come to the wrong place. 'He's not there. He left, along with most of them. There's only a few Brothers left behind to guard the place.'

That sounded good to Ben. The fewer, the better. 'And you?'

'I'm nobody,' Tonio said, shaking his head and looking earnest. 'Only a *confrère*, a servant. My job's just to bring in supplies, run errands and stuff.'

'Prove it. Roll up your sleeves.'

Which Tonio obligingly did without hesitation, and Ben saw there were no red crosses inked on his skin. 'See?' Tonio said. 'I'm not one of the soldiers. Look in the van. I was out getting sacks of onions and potatoes, olive oil, fish, some chorizos and a few fresh herbs and stuff for the kitchens.'

While they were talking, Roberta had hopped behind the wheel of the Alpina and was pulling off the road to hide the car back behind the trees. Ben checked inside the van and saw that Tonio wasn't lying about the food supplies, at least. 'Where did the boss and his men go?'

Tonio managed a thin smile and replied, 'Looking for you.'

'To France?'

Tonio nodded. 'That's what I heard. Some of the Brothers were talking about this man who was causing trouble for the order and hurt some of our people there. That's all I know.'

'But you do know who I am,' Ben said. 'That means you also know what I'm capable of doing to you if I find out you're bullshitting me.'

'I'm telling the truth, I swear it!'

'Swear it on the Johannite Gospel?'

Tonio's eyes bulged. How could an outsider possibly have learned these protected secrets of the Order of the Temple? 'Yes! I swear! Just please don't shoot me.'

'I believe you,' Ben told him. 'A real initiated Brother would have shown a bit more grit.'

By now Roberta had locked up the car and was running over, carrying the MP-5. Ben tossed the ignition keys back to Tonio and commanded him to get back in behind the wheel. Then he opened the sliding side door and he and Roberta clambered into the cargo area among the onion and potato sacks and crates of other produce. The smell of fresh fish was salty and pungent, mixed with the aromatic scents of spicy sausage and cut rosemary and basil. Ben crouched behind the driver's seat as Tonio restarted the engine. 'Whose job is it to unload all this stuff, you or the guards?'

Tonio shook his head as if Ben had said something scandalous. 'The Brothers don't do menial work like that, only the *confrères*. Nobody's going to look twice inside the van.'

'Good. When we reach the gates, you're going to act like this is any other delivery, drive on through and straight to the kitchens. I'll be watching you, Tonio. One look, one word amiss, and when I'm finished dealing with your buddies I'll make a gelding out of you in the most painful way possible. Understood?'

Tonio seemed to get the message. The van continued along the winding road up to the castle gates, where once there might have been a great iron portcullis, now replaced by a pair of huge wooden doors. Up close, the grey stone battlements loomed high overhead. Tonio honked his horn; a few moments later the doors opened and the van was met by a couple of guards. One was wearing a plain green military T-shirt that showed off the vivid red cross tattoo on his right forearm. Both had Beretta assault weapons hanging casually from slings over their shoulders. The latest model, well-oiled and shiny in the sunlight and tooled up with optical sights and high-capacity magazines. Ben and Roberta shrank back among the food supplies in the rear. The sight of the guards was the last proof, if any more had been needed, that they'd come to the right place.

The guards ambled up to the van and unsmilingly greeted Tonio, who played his part well enough and didn't give any cause for suspicion as they waved the van through the gateway without a second glance. Amazing how effectively the threat of violent castration can guarantee best behaviour from a man.

Ben and Roberta exchanged glances as the van rumbled onwards under the arch, wheels bumping over the cobbles of the courtyard within as it delivered them inside the enemy stronghold. The doors closed behind them. No going back now. The grey stone walls seemed to close in all around. Roberta swallowed. From this moment onwards, if anything went wrong they were either going to have to find some other means of escape or they'd leave here in bodybags. Ben emerged from behind the crates and boxes and laid a hand on Tonio's shoulder. He could feel the guy's bunched muscles through the dampness of his shirt. 'You're doing well. Keep rolling.'

Tonio drove on through a smaller archway at the far side of the courtyard, then another, and after what seemed like a long time the van finally pulled up in a garage block outside a long, low building that was a modern addition to the castle. Tonio parked in a row of other vehicles that Ben thought must belong to the supporting staff needed to maintain the daily needs of an operation this size. He wondered how many fully-fledged initiates lived within the castle walls on a normal day, when their Grand Master hadn't taken them off hunting for the likes of him. It made him smile to think he'd managed to stir the bastards up so much. But the best was yet to come, if the two of them could pull this off today.

'What do you want me to do now?' Tonio asked, not daring to turn around.

'Turn off the motor,' Ben told him.

Tonio did as he was told. If he'd been about to ask 'What next?' he never had the chance to get the words out, because Ben brought the hard steel of the Browning down against his skull and knocked him out. Tonio went limp without another sound.

'Help me get him back here,' he said to Roberta, and the two of them heaved the unconscious body out of the driver's seat, let him flop to the floor of the van and dragged him into the back. Then it was time to make use of some of the other purchases they'd made in Badajoz. By the time Tonio regained consciousness he'd find himself securely trussed up with cable ties and duct tape over his mouth.

After a check from the window to ensure nobody was around, they slipped out of the side door, ducking behind a wall as a couple of unarmed staff emerged from the low building, walked straight past the van without a glance and disappeared around the corner.

'Only question now,' Ben muttered when they were gone, 'is where the hell we go to start looking for what we came for.'

Roberta gazed at the massive stonework that stood around them. Her eyes followed the height of the walls, all the way up beyond the battlements that loomed against the background of the clear blue sky. Then she pointed upwards.

'There,' she said.

Chapter 55

Ben craned his neck upwards to see what she was pointing at. At the same moment a gust of wind blew over the escarpment and caught the object that she'd spotted up there, far above them on the highest of the round turrets that dominated an entire corner of the castle walls. The flag fluttered with a crackle in the breeze: a snow-white banner with the same vivid red cross of the Templars emblazoned at its centre.

'If you were Grand Master,' Roberta said, 'you'd put yourself up above everyone else at the highest point. That's where we need to go.'

Ben could see the glow of absolute self-confidence in her eyes, and he sensed she could very well be right. 'It's as good a place as any. Let's do it.'

They glanced right, then left, then broke from their hiding place and started making their way for the turret. But out in the open like this, they were too exposed and it was just a matter of time before they were seen. Spying a small doorway recessed into the thick wall to their right, Ben tried the iron ring handle and it swung inward with a groan. Behind the door was a narrow stone passage leading to an upward stairway. It might not take them where they wanted to go, but it had to be a start.

‘If we run into trouble in here,’ he warned her, ‘stay behind me. Anything happens to me, get the hell out as best you can.’

‘Don’t worry about me,’ she replied. But he did, and that was the whole problem.

The bright sunshine couldn’t penetrate the castle’s tiny slit windows and it was dark and shadowy inside. At the top of the steps was another murky, narrow passage. *If in doubt, turn left* had always been Ben’s mantra – and that direction seemed to lead towards the high turret. That passage in turn led to another climbing stairway, and from there another passage. ‘This place is a goddamn labyrinth,’ Roberta’s whisper echoed behind him as they kept moving. ‘We’re going to end up wandering about for hours.’

‘First chance we get,’ Ben told her, ‘we’ll stop and ask for directions.’

He’d been half-joking, but that chance came sooner than expected. As they cautiously emerged through another arched stone doorway, found themselves in yet another passageway and were deciding which way to go, Ben tensed at a sudden sound from around the corner up ahead. He quickly shoved Roberta back into the doorway as the footsteps ringing off the stonework came closer. Shrank into the shadows and held his breath.

The echoing footsteps belonged to a pair of Brother initiates who came into view a few moments later. In the dim light Ben could make out the crosses on their arms, and also the fact that neither man was carrying an assault weapon like those outside. The only firearm visible was a holstered pistol on the hip of the smaller of the two men, who would be closer to Ben as they passed by the dark doorway.

He could so easily have killed them both before they ever got there, but he couldn't risk a gunshot for fear of raising a general alarm. The men were talking in low voices. Coming closer. Closer. Ben waited until they were reaching the doorway. And then he pounced.

The one with the pistol was too slow to react and Ben took him out quickly and silently with a killer blow to the side of the neck. His companion was faster and wilier, a skilled fighter and light on his feet despite his larger build. As the first hit the floor the second was skipping back out of reach, then gathering his strength and charging at their attacker. His first strike was a lucky one and caught Ben below the right cheekbone. The power of the blow knocked Ben off balance and there was nothing he could do to stop himself from going down, half aware of Roberta yelling his name somewhere in the background. Sensing victory his opponent waded aggressively in, reaching behind his back to draw out a long double-edged dagger to slit his throat. But Ben wasn't alone. Roberta burst out of her hiding place with a yell and threw herself at him fearlessly. He slashed the blade towards her, she ducked and he sliced only the air above her head before he came at her again and this time grabbed her by the hair. She let out a scream as he went to draw the knife across her neck.

The steel never made contact, because in the next instant the man's legs were swept violently out from under him by the kick that Ben, still on the floor, had lashed his way. The man's knife clattered to the flagstones and he fell, but landed on his elbow and managed to scrabble furiously back upright as Ben sprang to his own feet. Snarling in rage the man charged like a bull, forcing Ben back against the wall as he swung a face-crushing punch at him. Ben dodged the blow and the man's big fist smacked all his force into the stonework. He let out a grunt of pain, and then another as Ben's counter-strike hit him full in the mouth and split his lips open.

And now the tide of the fight was turning, and, fuelled by all his pent-up anger at what this man had tried to do to Roberta and what his associates had done to Tuesday, Ben launched in hard and fast with blow after pummelling blow, not letting up until the man staggered and dropped to his knees. Ben floored him with a side-kick to the chest, grabbed him by the ears and brutally dashed his head against the ground, three, four times, until all the resistance had gone out of him and the blood on the stones was redder than the cross tattoo on his forearm.

'Are you all right?' Ben asked Roberta, who was leaning against the wall and breathing hard.

'I'm fine. I think.'

The blade of the fallen dagger scraped the stone floor as Ben snatched it up.

'Don't kill him!' Roberta cried out, thinking he was about to slice the guy's head off in his rage.

'No, I want him alive,' Ben said. 'For now. He's going to talk to us. Aren't you, my knightly friend?' He pressed the tip of the blade against the side of the man's neck, a millimetre from his pulsing carotid artery and ready to sink into the flesh if he'd applied any more pressure.

The man didn't seem to understand English. Ben held the pressure of the blade steady and asked him, 'Onde está seu chefe?' *Where's your boss?*

'Não está aqui,' the man groaned. Echoing what Tonio had said. *The boss isn't here.*

'Then take me to where he would be,' Ben told him.

Even with a knife to his throat, the man spat defiantly at this foreigner who thought he could make him betray his master. Ben's bluff had been called. So instead of cutting him, he used the skull-crusher steel pommel of the dagger to shatter the guy's left collarbone., Then the right. He was conscious of Roberta behind him, seeing everything. This was the kind of unpleasantness he'd have preferred her not to witness. He'd warned her. But this guy was a tough customer and uncompromising treatment was the only way to get through to him.

'Next it's your eyes,' Ben told him, bringing the tip of the blade back up his face so he could see it up close. 'Which first?'

The man wasn't calling Ben's bluff any longer. Gasping in pain and fear he relented and said, 'Okay, okay. Eu me rendo.' *I surrender!*

'That's what we like to hear.' Ben's cheek was hot and throbbing from where he'd taken the punch. He dragged their hostage roughly to his feet. With two smashed collarbones he wasn't going to put up any more of a fight. 'Lead on, Macduff.'

Bent over in pain, the limping, bleeding Brother initiate led them deeper inside the castle until they came to a door that opened onto a broad spiral staircase. Looking up it seemed to go on for ever – and Ben realised they'd reached the high turret from which the Templar banner was flying. 'O Grande Mestre?' he asked the prisoner, and the man nodded wearily.

It could be a trap, but there was only one way to find out. Ben used a nerve point below the man's ear to render him instantly unconscious and he flopped to the stone floor, hitting his head with a crunch. At least he wouldn't be feeling the pain of the broken collarbones for a while.

'Relax,' he said to Roberta. 'He's not dead. Just looks it.'

'That's a neat trick with the nerve points,' she said, looking down at the inert body.

'A little old Chinese guy taught it to me. It's called Dim Mak.'

'It seems to work pretty good, whatever it is. Will you teach me? Every girl should know these things.'

'We should get rid of him in case anyone comes,' Ben said. They bundled the comatose Brother initiate into a shadowy alcove and began the long climb up the spiral staircase.

Chapter 56

Up and up, round and round, until they were clutching at the iron rail for support and their calves were burning. Ben looked down at the dizzying spiral drop down the centre shaft of the staircase and saw how far they'd climbed. If a person were to slip and lose their footing, it would be like falling off a cliff. 'I think I'd get an elevator fitted,' Roberta panted. 'This grand master must be a helluva fit guy, to hoof it all the way up here every day.'

Some minutes later, they finally reached the top of the steps and found themselves in a large circular chamber the entire width of the turret. 'Looks like nobody's at home,' she said, her voice echoing up to the ceiling. 'Just like they told us.'

'I'm only sorry I missed him,' Ben replied. But something told him he'd have that pleasure sooner or later.

The enormous space had been made into a study and library rolled into one. A well-worn leather chair sat behind an antique desk whose surface was bare except for an old-fashioned telephone and a personal diary and address book. Around the walls stood three tiers of bookcases, and tall stained-glass gothic windows between them looked out over the castle grounds and far beyond. But it wasn't the sweeping views from up here that caught their attention, nor was it the Grand Master's impressive book collection.

‘If these are original Templar artifacts,’ Roberta said, gazing around her in amazement, ‘they must be absolutely priceless.’ Among the treasures was a full hauberk of chain-mail with a snow-white robed surcoat bearing the iconic crusader cross, draped over a mannequin and topped with a gleaming steel helm bearing the scars and dents of ferocious combat.

‘Who do you suppose this might have belonged to?’ she wondered aloud, fingering the cloth of the surcoat. ‘Hugues de Payens? Jacques de Molay? It’s incredible. The Louvre and the British Museum would kill to have exhibits like these.’ Nearby stood a display case filled with medieval weaponry, an arrangement of maces and battleaxes, encircling a great sword with a jewelled hilt and a long, broad double-edged blade inscribed with the Latin words *Non Nobis, Domine, Non Nobis, Sed Nomini Tuo Da Gloriam*. ‘Not unto us, Lord, not unto us, but to Thy Name give the glory.’

‘Some glory,’ Ben muttered under his breath. Tuesday’s face had appeared in his mind, as clearly as if he’d been there in the chamber with them.

Roberta had already moved on and was gaping at the other Templar relics like a kid in a toyshop. ‘Ben, you need to check this out.’

He turned away from the sword to see her looking up at the wall, where more of the order’s precious artefacts hung in the spaces between windows and bookcases. One of them he recognised as the traditional emblem of the Templars, an image of two mail-clad warriors riding together on a single horse to represent their original status as poor monk-knights, emblazoned on a large circular gold crest the size of a dinner plate, which would once have topped the flagstaff bearing their battle banner. He hadn't known that any original examples of the venerable Templar crest still existed, but here it was, gleaming in the coloured light streaming through the turret's windows.

Next to the golden crest hung the object that Roberta had wanted to show him. 'Look,' she said, pointing. It was a large and magnificently ornate medieval tapestry, suspended by loops from an iron pole mounted horizontally on the wall. Its central motif was an octagonal design of a labyrinth or maze, similar to the image he'd seen depicted on the floor of Chartres cathedral, where pilgrims come to worship would traditionally walk the complex path in search of Divine grace. Where this one differed was the inclusion of another symbol at the labyrinth's centre: one that Ben had also seen before, and much more recently.

'Look familiar?' Roberta said. 'It's the same alchemical symbol of the Philosopher's Stone that Thibault de Roucyboeuf carved on the crypt wall under the Manoir du Col.'

Ben stepped closer to the tapestry and spent a few moments studying it as Roberta moved away towards a window. 'It's a symbol within a symbol,' he said. 'The twists and turns of the labyrinth represent the journey of the seeker in search of truth. If they manage to find their way to the centre, they get rewarded with wisdom and illumination. The path to God, to righteousness and eternal happiness. Or something like that.'

'I guess so. But what if it wasn't just a symbolic labyrinth?' Roberta asked.

He turned to look at her, unsure what she meant. 'What makes you think it isn't?'

'Because I'm looking at the real thing,' she replied, pointing out of the window.

Ben stepped over to join her and peered through the stained glass. 'Well, I'll be damned.'

The east-facing window of the turret overlooked a large walled garden within the castle grounds. And the Order of the Custodes Sanctorum Secretorum Templi had evidently been tending to it very assiduously over the years since making this quiet corner of Portugal their base. Or their gardener-confrères had, at any rate, by creating an enormous hedge maze identical to the one in the tapestry. In a landscape parched and baked by some of the hottest and driest summers in Europe they'd managed to keep it thick and verdant and leafy, while whoever had the job of maintaining its complex contours had been busily trimming away for many years. The huge green circle was at least a hundred metres in diameter and over two metres high, its many convoluted internal pathways laid with ornamental gravel. At its middle the concentric walls converged so closely that even from their high-up vantage point it was impossible to make out what a person might find there.

'Makes the one at Hampton Court look like someone's back garden topiary,' Roberta marvelled.

'But why?' Ben asked. 'What would make them go to all the trouble of planting something like that? It can't just be cosmetic. There's got to be a better reason.'

They both looked back at the tapestry and the Philosopher's Stone symbol at its centre. And both had the same idea at once. 'Holy crap,' Roberta said, her eyes lighting up. 'You don't think—?'

Ben was already nodding his agreement. 'Follow the path and reach the centre, and the seeker can find enlightenment there. Yes, I do think.'

Roberta could hardly contain her excitement. 'I was right. It's not symbolic at all. There really is something in the middle of that thing.'

'And we're going to go down there and find out what,' Ben said.

Chapter 57

Finding their way out to the inner walled garden proved to be like negotiating a maze in its own right. At the bottom of the spiral staircase, close to the alcove where the still unconscious body of their captive lay limp in the shadows, they came across another doorway leading deeper into the labyrinthine passages of the castle. Now Ben was thankful for the absence of the order's Grand Master and the bulk of his men, because otherwise this whole place could have been teeming with armed guards and their search would have turned into a suicide mission. As things were, he was relieved to encounter no one else in the confusion of passages. At last, coming to what looked like an external door, Ben tentatively turned the ring handle and pulled it open a crack to peer through. 'Bingo.'

It was a short dash from there across the open ground to the entrance to the maze. Nobody had seen them. Nobody followed. Ben grabbed Roberta's hand and said, 'Come on. We may not have a lot of time.'

But finding their way through wasn't going to be as quick or easy as they might have hoped. As they soon discovered, the maze's designer had created a puzzle to test even the sharpest mind. Time and again they found themselves either going around in circles or coming up against a dead end and having to turn back and retrace their steps in search of another route. Ben's attempted trick of keeping one hand constantly in contact with the leafy wall, which he'd hoped would lead them through, was defeated by the fiendishly deceptive layout.

'A trail of breadcrumbs would come in useful about now,' Roberta groaned in confusion. 'I'm getting snow-blind where there isn't any snow.'

Refusing to admit defeat, Ben racked his brain for a half-remembered version of what he'd long ago read about as the so-called Tremaux's Rule for scientifically breaking down even the most bewildering of mazes. That system, of course, had been devised without factoring in the added stress of being potentially confronted by armed hostiles at any given turn – but he bore that possibility in mind while keeping his pistol to hand. At each new junction, he relied on his 'if in doubt, turn left' habit and only backtracked if it led to a dead end or a junction they'd already visited. Then they'd scuff a line in the gravel to show they'd been there before, and move on. Whenever they came to an old junction by a path taken before, they switched to a different path if one was available, or else one used no more than once previously.

Bit by bit, they worked their way deeper into the green circle. The narrowing contours around him told Ben he was getting closer to its heart, but he was starting to get bamboozled by his own system of marks in the gravel and wishing he could have just been given a nice code to decipher instead. He was deep in trying to work out his bearings when Roberta, a few metres ahead, rounded the next corner and let out a discreet whoop of elation. 'We made it!'

Running around the corner after her, filled with relief and anticipation, Ben saw that the dead centre of the maze was encircled by a screen of sculpted greenery into which a single arched doorway had been neatly cut. Something was there, all right. But at that moment he could have had no idea what they were about to find.

A twinge of caution made him call out, 'Roberta, wait,' as she raced on in front of him. She reluctantly let him pass through the cutaway doorway first. Ben had to blink at what he saw in front of him, which had every appearance of being a concrete bomb shelter dating back to around the time of the Second World War, buried deep with only its pitted, moss-covered entrance protruding above ground and worn steps leading downwards.

After the confines of the medieval castle, even a utilitarian and comparatively worn construction from the first half of the twentieth century seemed strangely modern. The electrics added long after the building's installation were much more recent still, and as they descended the steps Ben found a switch for an LED lighting system that illuminated every cranny of the underground space around them like day.

'What the hell is this place?' Roberta breathed.

'It's a store,' he replied. But he was wrong. Because as they arrived at more steps and descended another level deeper below ground, they now found themselves in a subterranean chamber that could better have been described as a latter-day sacred shrine.

This was where the present-day Templar knights kept the real treasures of their historic past. On a plain wooden altar lay fragments of blackened objects that mystified Ben until he realised with a shock that they were pieces of burnt human bone, perhaps even the relics of the execution of Jacques de Molay and his fellow martyrs. Then, on a bible stand above the altar, Ben and Roberta discovered the ancient, hand-illuminated bound manuscript that they'd come all the way from France to find: the sole known copy outside the Vatican library of the heretical Johannite Gospel.

Up until this moment, a part of Ben had found it hard to believe that such a book truly existed. Now he was actually holding it in his hands, turning its pages with infinite care in case the ancient binding fell to pieces, staring in fascination at the faded writing. 'So everything poor Jean-Rafael told us really was true,' Roberta said in an awed hush. 'And this is what it's all about. The secret they've been protecting for so many centuries. How many people have been killed over it?'

But as they discovered when they started exploring more deeply, the priceless Johannite Gospel was only one small part of the vast Templar archives contained inside the shrine. The underground space extended from room to room, like the enormous book repository stored beneath the Bodleian Library in Oxford. There was so much that it couldn't have been loaded aboard fewer than three large trucks.

'Now we have what we came for,' Ben said, 'let's get out of here before our luck runs out.'

'And leave all this other stuff behind?'

'Are you nuts? We couldn't carry a fraction of it. Not that we need it anyway.'

'Okay, but I say we keep searching. There might be something else of value to us.'

'We've already been here too long.'

'Trust me, okay? Woman's intuition.'

And moments later, she turned out to be right. Finding a locked wooden chest marked with the seal of the order, she used the butt end of the MP-5 to hammer open the padlock and opened the lid. Inside was a large and antiquated leather-bound volume that at first glance resembled an old-fashioned register, like the kind used for entering the names of hotel guests. It wasn't until they looked inside that they realised what it really was.

'Oh, Jesus, I think we just found the Mother Lode,' she breathed.

Chapter 58

The book that Roberta had broken out of its chest was indeed a register containing page after page of names, but it wasn't a record of visitors who might have enjoyed the hospitality of the Castelo São João Salvador over the years.

'They're members,' Ben said, realising. 'Secret initiates of the Johannite religion, going all the way back.' He flipped forwards through the pages until he came to the most recent entry, dated only a few years ago. 'And all the way up to the present day.'

'A lot of these names I've never heard of before,' Roberta said, pressed close to Ben's side and peering intently at the entries. 'But oh my God, look at some of these others. Who *hasn't* heard of them?' She was right. The list included numerous names of religious figures, high-level public figures from all across Europe, well-known business tycoons, world leaders and even royalty.

'Everyone might have heard of them,' Ben replied, 'but I suspect nobody would have a clue that these people belonged to something like this.'

'It's sensational,' she breathed. 'It's mind-blowing.'

Ben was no less dumbstruck than Roberta was. This wasn't just another obscure religious cult living on the fringes. He suddenly understood that the Order of the Custodians, the keepers of the secret, had been a major, if shadowy and highly clandestine, flipside to the whole traditional Christian doctrine all along. The implications of this radical counter-theology would subvert everything the mainstream Church had been preaching since the beginnings of Christendom.

And if it were true? Not just for the monolithic institution of Roman Catholicism but for every Christian creed and denomination out there, from the Anglicans to the Anabaptists to the Eastern Orthodox, the Methodists and the Lutherans and the Evangelists, all the way down to the Plymouth Brethren and the Latter Day Saints and the Swedenborgians, it would be a disaster of unimaginable proportions. A virtual extinction event. The whole concept of the Holy Trinity, wiped away at a stroke. The Resurrection, unthinkably reduced to no more than a magical fantasy. The cross itself, the quintessential symbol of the Christian faith since its inception, rendered meaningless. The authority of the mainstream Church all across the world totally undermined. Only Islam and the eastern religions would come out of the train wreck undamaged, and most likely laughing their socks off.

'No wonder the order is so well funded,' Roberta said. 'And it's even less of a surprise that they'd have done anything to keep this under wraps through the centuries. All these important and powerful people were protecting themselves too, in case the truth ever came out.'

'I don't care what they were protecting,' Ben answered. 'This is what my friend lost his life for.'

'The members who are still alive today,' she wondered, 'you think they know their names are listed on a register?

You think maybe the Grand Masters have been covering their asses by keeping records on them like this?'

'Whether they knew or not, it's all going to come out now.'

'We need to keep looking,' she insisted.

He wasn't happy with the idea. 'It's not safe here. Believe me, an underground bunker with only one way in or out is no place to get cornered by a bunch of armed guards.'

'Just a few minutes, Ben,' she pleaded. 'What we've found so far is just incredible, but there could be even more.'

And there was.

As Ben went to shove the opened wooden chest out of his way to investigate more of the archive, he felt a lateral movement inside the box, something sliding as it moved. 'Wait a minute. There's something else in here.'

'Can't be,' she said. 'The register was all there was.'

Ben tilted the chest this way and that, and felt it again. 'It's got a false bottom.'

It didn't take long to hack and splinter away the wood to reveal the hidden compartment underneath. It was only after he'd ripped out the false bottom that he realised that there was a tiny hidden release catch on the underside of the chest that would have made the task far easier. Someone had designed it that way to enable easy and regular access to the secret compartment. But why?

The answer soon became clear as Ben pushed his hand into the splintered cavity and his fingers closed on a thick, heavy envelope. He pulled it out and his heart began to thump faster as he sifted through its contents. There were copies of documents, letters, photographs, lists of transactions. A whole file.

'What is it?' she asked, itching to see.

'You were right again,' he said, examining it with a quickening heart rate. 'The Grand Masters have been covering themselves with their members. And that's not all they've been up to, seemingly.'

'Let me see!' She snatched the envelope from him, tore through the contents and her mouth dropped open. 'I can't believe it. This is a shakedown file. They've got enough dirt on some of these people to put them away for ever.'

Some of the photographs were hard to look at, and to possess material like them, still less to have participated in the activities they depicted, was beyond illegal. One or two of the people in the pictures were very well-known indeed. 'Is that—?' Roberta began, pointing at the glossy photo print she was holding, her face twisted in disgust.

'Unless it's his identical twin,' Ben said. 'And if those two girls with him are anywhere near old enough to be legal tender, I'm a monkey's uncle.'

Also inside the envelope was hard evidence of financial fraud and other shady dealings, all neatly documented and ready to be made public, along with copies of the letters making that threat known to the perpetrators. And somewhere among the rest of the papers, Ben already knew, would be the sordid details of the tight hold the order had had on a certain late Languedoc police chief called Grosjean.

But it wasn't just the blackmail racket that the current Grand Master and his predecessors had been running at the expense of the famous and wealthy. Other photographs, letters and details of illicit payments made it clear that the crimes of the order included the murders and assassinations of a number of high-profile people throughout the years. Some of those images weren't pretty to look at, either, though not for the same reason as the others.

'Old man Silvestre reckoned we might be able to gain ourselves a bargaining chip,' Ben said. 'I wonder if he had any idea how right he was. This stuff will do very nicely indeed.' He replaced everything back inside the bulging envelope and stuffed it inside the register, then took off his leather jacket and rolled them up in it along with the ancient Johannite Gospel.

'Careful with that,' Roberta urged him.

'Oh, I'll be careful, don't worry. This is our lifeline. And now, if you don't mind, I'd suggest that it really is time to get out of here.'

'I think you're right,' she said.

They set off on their return journey through the maze, and this time their progress was smooth and uneventful as Ben's improvised system of scuffing signpost markers in the gravel came back to reward them. In well under half the time it had taken them to penetrate to the centre they were reaching the outer concentric circle and the exit that now led them across the open ground to the castle wall from which they'd come. Energised by their discovery they worked their way through the cool, shadowy passages and arches, retracing their steps in the hopes of a clean escape by whatever means they could devise.

But something was wrong. The further they went, the more obvious it was becoming that the place had suddenly gone into a state of high alert. Every few yards Ben and

Roberta found themselves having to retreat hurriedly into doorways or hide in the shadows as armed guards came running past in twos and threes, weapons drawn and ready. It was obvious that they were hunting for someone – and even more obvious who that someone might be.

'We're in trouble,' Roberta whispered.

Chapter 59

It was a kitchen staff member called Estêvão, having run out of onions to prepare the big cauldron of *caldo verde* they were planning for tonight's dinner and wondering what had happened to those supplies Tonio was supposed to have been bringing in, who'd gone out and discovered the white delivery van parked in its usual place, but no sign of Tonio himself. Where could the silly bastard have gone? The answer be came clear a moment later when Estêvão opened the van and saw his fellow *confrère* lying bound and gagged among the sacks and crates.

From that moment, it was action stations throughout the stronghold as word spread that they'd been infiltrated. The skeleton crew of Brother initiates remaining in the castle were galvanised into searching high and low for the intruders whose description, according to the breathless and apologetic account the freed Tonio gave to the captain of the guards, beyond any doubt matched those of the individuals the Grand Master and the rest of the Brothers had gone off to search for in France.

'They're bound to be here somewhere,' the captain of the guards snapped at his men. 'Find them and bring them to me alive if you can. You and you, stay here and watch over the vehicles in case they try to escape that way.'

The two guards were still posted dutifully by the van, clutching their weapons and poised for action when, unknown to them, the pair of fugitives crept around a corner and ducked out of sight behind a low wall just fifteen metres away.

'Shit,' Roberta whispered, crestfallen at the sight of their blocked escape route. 'What do we do now?'

Ben briefly considered the simple option of shooting the two guards, but changed his mind. The sound of gunfire would bring the others down on them in seconds, and there were too many to fight all at once. Thinking fast, he decided on another plan. The kitchen building was just a short run across the courtyard and the two guards by the van had their backs turned for the moment. He pointed and hissed in Roberta's ear, 'That way. Go.'

They broke from cover and raced across to the kitchen building unnoticed, slipped through the door and inside. With the general alarm going on throughout the castle, whatever servants or junior *confrères* would normally have been manning the kitchen seemed to have abandoned their posts and found a hiding place from the dangerous armed intruders. Which suited Ben fine, because he'd had no desire to have to deal with a bunch of panic-stricken menial staff.

'What are we doing in the kitchens?' Roberta said, looking at him urgently. 'Making lunch?'

'Not exactly what I had in mind,' he replied. A diversion was what they needed, and in his experience kitchens were good places for creating them. This one was even better than most.

A medieval castle in the middle of the remote Portugal countryside was unlikely to have a mains gas supply. With satisfaction Ben spotted the row of five tall red Butane cylinders standing against one wall of the kitchen. Two of the bottles were attached to regulators to feed the big range stoves. The other three were spares. He rocked them on their metal bases. They were heavy, which meant they were full of extremely flammable liquid gas. And that suited him perfectly, too.

Next he ran his eyes along the kitchen worktops adjacent to the range cookers, which were cluttered with all the usual culinary appliances and utensils. He snatched a pair of heavy-duty scissors from a knife block and used them to shear through the thick rubber pipes connecting the first two bottles to the cookers. Then turned on the valve taps, and the gas began to hiss. He did the same with the three spare bottles.

'You're crazy,' Roberta said as she realised what his plan was. 'You'll blow this whole place to smithereens and us with it.'

'Mad, bad and dangerous to know,' he replied. 'I'm the guy your mother warned you about.'

The gas was hissing loudly from the severed pipes, spewing out like vapour and its fumes already making their eyes sting. Working fast, he grabbed a twin-pack of kitchen paper rolls and a five-litre flagon of olive oil from a shelf. Olive oil was his favourite thing for frying steaks and making salad dressings. It was also pretty good stuff for lighting fires with, more combustible than kerosene. He tore the plastic wrapping off the kitchen rolls and set them on top of an electric toaster, then dumped half of the olive oil over them, soaking the paper and running thickly all over the worktop in yellow rivulets.

Then he pushed down the slider of the toaster. Sending a surge of electricity to the thin wire elements, which immediately began to glow red and then to smoke as the oil started to burn. In moments the paper rolls on top would begin to smoulder, and then they'd burst into flames. The rest of the chain reaction would follow suit as the gas bottles ignited one by one. It wasn't the most sophisticated bomb he'd ever improvised, but its effects should be quite spectacular.

'Let's move,' he said to Roberta.

A back door of the kitchen building led out to a narrow alleyway lined with old crates and wheelie bins. At its end was another gated entrance that opened out onto the courtyard near the staff vehicles. Ben and Roberta hurried through the alley, crouched low behind the wall by the gateway and waited.

They didn't have to wait long.

With a flat, percussive BOOM a ground-shaking explosion rocked the building, blowing off part of its roof and showering the courtyard with debris. Liquid fire rolled from the shattered doorway and windows, followed by a thick outpouring of black smoke through which yellow flames darted like snakes. The two guards who'd been standing by Tonio's van were blown off their feet by the force of the blast and lay still. Then within moments, shouts and cries of alarm sounded from all over the castle and the Brother initiates who'd been scattered here and there in search of the intruders now all came sprinting to the scene of the inferno, armed with fire extinguishers, buckets of water, anything they could find to help douse the blaze. A second explosion ripped through the building, then a third as the spare gas cylinders started popping off in the heat. Flames shot fifty feet into the air and the crowd were driven back by the heat. The impenetrable pall of smoke drifted over the courtyard, swallowing the vehicles, the men lying on the ground, obscuring everything.

And in the midst of the total chaos as the panicked initiates and *confrères* desperately fought to put out the fire before it spread, everyone was too distracted to notice the two figures that flitted from the half-crumbled gateway to the side of the stricken building and ran through the smoke towards the parked vehicles. Seconds later the general mayhem of crackling flames and chorus of raised voices all but drowned out the rasp of the diesel engine bursting into life and Tonio's van, slightly battered and scorched by raining debris, screeching out of its parking space and veering crazily away across the courtyard. At the same moment, the last of the spare Butane bottles inside what was left of the kitchen building went off in a huge blasting fireball and the rest of the roof collapsed inwards, bringing most of the walls down with it and spewing burning wreckage in all directions.

'Did they see us?' Roberta yelled, trying to look back in the wing mirror as Ben sped towards the gates.

'We'll find out soon enough.'

Under the archways; and then the closed gates loomed up ahead. This was the moment Ben had feared the most, because a pitched close-quarter battle with the gate guards was something he and Roberta were unlikely both to survive unscathed, if at all. But he saw now with a surge of intense relief that the sentries had left their post, either scrambled for the search or to run to assist with putting out the fire.

Ben skidded the van to a squealing halt a few yards short of the gates and jumped out while it was still moving. Roberta clambered into his place at the wheel while he ran to haul open the first of the heavy gates. He grabbed the massive iron handle and yanked hard, and the gate slowly began to swing open. Nobody was following, but they could appear at any instant and his heart was in his mouth.

The second gate was opening; Roberta slammed the van back into gear, gunned the throttle and shot through, battering against the gate in her impatience. Still nobody had appeared. Ben heaved the gates shut one by one, then signalled for her to drive on. As the van started to accelerate he ran alongside it, unlatched the sliding side door and piled in among Tonio's still undelivered food supplies.

Now the van was gaining speed down the winding little hill road away from the castle. Ben glanced behind them at the gates, still shut. He could see the thick, dark pall of smoke rising above the battlements. The precious loot they'd taken from the Grand Master's archives was safely wrapped up in his jacket on the passenger seat. And it was only then that Ben allowed himself the thought: *we made it.* It had been the neatest little raiding operation, and it had paid off far beyond their expectations.

Roberta was so pumped full of adrenalin that she was shaking and unable to talk, and she was driving so fast that when they reached the forest, they almost sped right by the spot among the trees where they'd hidden the Alpina. Pulling off the road they jumped out with their weapons and the rolled-up jacket, and ran to the car where Ben dived behind the wheel. Then the turbocharged V8 was blasting its note through the twin exhausts and they were spinning their wheels over the rough ground to rejoin the road and make their escape.

Neither of them dared to speak until they'd put ten blisteringly fast miles between themselves and Castelo São João Salvador, Ben as concentrated as a fighter pilot at the wheel. At last he eased off the gas and let their speed drop to eighty, and turned to see that Roberta was grinning from ear to ear, clutching the rolled-up jacket on her lap.

'I have to hand it to you, Ben Hope,' she said, shaking her head. 'Nobody's got a gift for mayhem and destruction like you do.'

'It was always my best feature. You didn't do too badly yourself.'

She laughed. 'Oh boy, are those bastards gonna be pissed as hell when they find out what we took from them.'

'And they'll never stop coming after us,' he replied. 'Not until we put an end to this whole thing once and for all.'

Chapter 60

Ben was almost getting to like the ropey motel near Quillan, enough to have returned there to use as their ongoing base of operations. The only difference was that now they only required one room. Roberta might have preferred something a little more comfortable, but they wouldn't be staying here long.

On their return from Portugal Ben had slept for nine straight hours and awoken refreshed, clear-headed and knowing exactly what he needed to do next. He was going to be busy on the phone for quite a while, with several points of business to take care of. The first one was to let himself be berated by a raging Jeff Dekker, who had been frustrated almost to the point of insanity all this time at Le Val with nothing to do except recuperate from his injury and no news of what was happening, and erupted with a mixture of relief and annoyance at the sound of Ben's voice.

'Where the sodding hell have you been? I've been chewing the fucking carpets and climbing the walls here, mate, never knowing what was going on.'

'I'll make it up to you,' Ben said. 'I promise.'

'By the way, we have a visitor here at the compound. Flew in from Italy the day before yesterday, and he's not too pleased with you either, so get set for a right proper arse-kicking.'

It took a while to talk Jeff down from his state of irritability, but between friends so closely bonded resentments never lasted long and they ended the call as amicable as they'd ever been. 'That Jeff,' Ben muttered to himself, smiling and shaking his head. He lit a Gauloise, drank a slurp of coffee and spent a few moments gathering his thoughts for the next call he needed to make. 'Fuck it, let's do it,' he said out loud.

The number he dialled had been lifted from the desk diary they'd found in the Grand Master's turret at the Castelo São João Salvador. Amazing, what kind of personal information people left lying around when they weren't expecting their most dangerous enemy to call by unannounced.

The phone rang eight times before someone answered. It was a man's voice on the line, deep and smooth and remaining unruffled even when he realised who was calling him.

'So you're back home,' Ben said. 'Shame about the wasted trip. And I'm sorry we missed each other.'

'So am I,' said the voice. 'It would have been an interesting meeting.'

'Almost as interesting as some of the reading I've been doing. It makes me wish I could have stayed longer and delved some more into those archives of yours. What should I call you, by the way? Do you prefer to be addressed as "Grand Master" or by your real name, Hercule de Scorbiac?'

'I prefer not to be addressed at all by a man who would break into my home, ransack my personal property and steal valuables of inestimable worth.'

'And after all, you have such scruples,' Ben replied.

'These items of mine you have in your possession,' the Grand Master said, 'I would like to have returned.'

'I'll bet you would, Hercule. The thing you took from me, though, there's no getting that back, is there? I'm talking about the life of my friend.'

'Highly regrettable. But he shouldn't have involved himself in our affairs. Neither should Monsieur Hutchison. These things inevitably carry a penalty.'

'And you should have stayed out of mine,' Ben said. 'Too late now. You want your things back?'

'I'm sure you appreciate their value to me. And needless to say I expect you would wish to be financially rewarded for their safe return.'

'Handsomely,' Ben replied. 'Either that, or else I was thinking some of the people you've got over a barrel might be only too eager to take them off my hands, for a fee. Or maybe I should go straight to the newspapers. Or the cops. What do you think, Hercule?'

'You don't strike me as a man who would go running to the authorities,' the Grand Master said. 'If it's money you want, I think I can make you a better offer than anyone else.'

Ben smiled. 'I daresay you can. Given how much you stand to lose over this. Now as to a figure, I think we should discuss the matter face to face, don't you? Not really a conversation to be had over the phone.'

'Very well,' said the Grand Master, and Ben could hear the wheels turning in his head. 'Of course you will agree to bring the items in question, so that I can verify everything is there before I make my offer?'

'And of course, I have your word that you wouldn't resort to anything unchivalrous, like have your religious maniacs try to kill me again?'

'It seems to me that option has been tried and failed enough times,' the Grand Master answered smoothly. 'I suggest we move on to more civilised means.'

'Then maybe we can do business. I'll call you again to arrange a meeting. My choice of time and place.'

'As you wish. I will look forward to hearing from you soon.'

What a charmer, Ben thought as he ended the call and started dialling the next number. This one was the most recent to have been called from the phone he'd lifted from the corpse of the man calling himself Father Bertolli.

Like before, after a few rings the call was answered by the deep tones of a man's voice. '*Pronto.*' The Italian sounded older, gruffer and less polished than Hercule de Scorbiac.

'Hi there,' Ben said in Italian, which he spoke pretty well. 'I'd ask to speak to Father Bertolli, but I happen to know that he's no longer with us. So maybe you can help me instead.'

'Signor Hope?' said the gruff voice after a long pause.

'In person. I'm so pleased you already know who I am. Saves a lot of complicated explanations. Shall we cut to the chase? I have something here you might be interested in. It's an item my recently departed friend Jean-Rafael Silvestre brought to my attention. A certain gospel by . . . let's see, what was the guy's name again? John someone. I gather you're keen to add it to your collection.'

Another long pause, filled with shock and surprise. 'Where did you get it?' the Italian asked, his voice so eager he could barely talk straight.

'Never mind that,' Ben replied breezily. 'What matters is I'm looking to sell. And right away I thought of you folks.'

'That's interesting to hear,' said the Italian.

'I'm glad you feel that way. How about I call you back tomorrow, and we can discuss particulars?'

'I will be here,' the Italian replied.

And Ben had every confidence that the guy meant it.

The phone session wasn't quite done yet. Ben lit another Gauloise and dialled the fourth number on his list. In his limited experience, teenage billionaire heiresses could always be relied on to pick up quickly.

'How's our friend Mr Sadler doing?' he asked her.

'Recovering very well. In fact I can see him from my window even as we speak, sitting out in the garden with Tonton. Playing chess, of course. The two of them have hit it off amazingly.'

'That's good to hear. I'd like to talk to him about buying some property in the Languedoc.'

'You're still thinking of moving there?' Valentina asked.

'It's not so much for myself. I was thinking if I found the right place, I'd like to let some friends make use of it. Something historic and interesting. My friends have a penchant for nice old houses.'

'That's very generous of you. I should imagine it'll cost a lot, though.' Coming from the girl who'd one day inherit one of the biggest fortunes in Europe.

'There's some loose cash in the kitty,' Ben said. 'And maybe Matthew can do me a good price.'

'Why don't I take the phone out to the garden, and you can ask him yourself?'

Minutes later, Ben was deep in conversation with Sadler, who had just checkmated Auguste Kaprisky for the fourth time in a row that day and was in good spirits. 'I'm happy to hear you sounding so much better, Matthew.'

'Oh, I feel like a different person. They've been so kind to me here. And it's all thanks to you.'

'Don't thank me,' Ben says. 'Just find me what I'm looking for.'

'I take it the Manoir is no longer on your wish list,' Sadler said ruefully. 'However it just so happens that there's another available property on my books that sounds like it could suit your new requirements quite nicely. The current owners have been looking to offload the place for some time.'

'Describe it to me,' Ben said.

Chapter 61

The nineteenth-century folly stood perched high on the flat top of a hill, overlooking from a distance the small medieval village of Lagrasse in the Corbières region. From the top of the tower could be seen Lagrasse's ancient stone bridge over the River Orbieu, and the fourteenth-century Benedictine abbey of Sainte-Marie. The sun beat down over the rugged, unspoilt landscape, buzzards and eagles wheeled and screeched in the perfect blueness of the sky and the incessant chirruping of the cicadas sounded from the wild lavender and purple-flowered thyme that carpeted the hillside. Life here went on as quietly and peacefully as it had for over a thousand years. But all that was about to change, in the flash of an instant.

Modelled after a complete fantasist's whimsical storybook vision of the kind of medieval tower from whose upper window Rapunzel might suddenly appear, the solitary and somewhat odd-looking construction had been the brainchild of an eccentric Victorian Englishman named Sir Leopold Butler Soames. Back in his heyday, Sir Leopold had built a fortune in silk and opium from his mercantile dealings in the East India Company. Later in life the colourful gentleman had fallen in love with the south of France and lived there for several years prior to his eventual demise from syphilis, his fortune squandered away to the last penny, in a Grenoble madhouse in 1874.

Locally dubbed 'la Tour du Fou', Sir Leopold's tower had been sitting idle on the Languedoc real estate market for the last twelve years or more, unsold partly because it had never been of much practical use to anyone as a residential property, and also as a result of the damage caused to its roof by a particularly violent lightning storm back in 2012, which would cost a considerable sum to repair. The general state of the building had been declining steadily over the years, along with its value.

To its new owner, though, the tower's condition was of little concern. And in any case, thanks to Matthew Sadler's expert wheeling and dealing, the sellers had been convinced to reduce the price tag to a minimum, a fraction of the cost of more usable properties like the Manoir du Col. It was the best money Ben had ever spent.

That afternoon, just hours after closing the deal on his new acquisition, Ben and Roberta drove along the narrow road from the village that led through a farmyard and up the hill to the fenced half acre of land in which the folly stood.

'So that's the Madman's Tower,' she said, getting out of the car and frowning up at it with her head cocked and arms folded. 'Well named. You'd have to be nuts to buy it.'

'It doesn't look too bad from a distance,' he said, squinting to improve its appearance a little more. 'Anyhow, I'm not going to live in it.'

Ben looked at his watch. Any time now, they were going to have company. 'There they are,' Roberta said, pointing towards the horizon.

The little red speck in the sky grew bigger and bigger and the clatter of the rotors built up to a whistling roar as the Bell Jet Ranger came in to land, its downdraught flattening a wide circle of grass and wild herbs. The side hatch opened, steps folded out, and down them limped Jeff Dekker with one foot in plaster and supporting his weight on a crutch. His pained expression lit up into a smile as he saw Ben walking up to the chopper. Moving away from the wind blast, the two friends embraced each other as if they hadn't met in years.

'Still got that Yank chick in tow, I see,' Jeff said, nodding over towards where Roberta stood by the car. Some things about Jeff Dekker you couldn't change even if you shot him.

Jeff hadn't flown out from Le Val alone. Next to climb out of the idling chopper, a warm affectionate grin splitting his whiskery face, was the visitor Jeff had mentioned on the phone. Feeling all kinds of emotions welling up, Ben shook hands with his older comrade, the veteran SAS sergeant who'd trained him as an elite soldier back in the day and stood by his side in many a tight scrape.

'It's been a while, Boonzie. How the devil are you?'

'Och, never better. It's guid tae see ye again, laddie.' Years of retirement in Campo Basso, Italy, had done nothing to soften the grizzled old Scotsman's accent. Once a proud and fearless warrior, now he spent his days tending to his greenhouses and enjoying his autumn years with the love of his life, his Neapolitan wife Mirella. Ben thought Boonzie had lost a little weight since they'd last seen one another, and his bristly crew-cut hair and beard were purer white than before. The heart condition that had almost laid him low a few years back was slowly, imperceptibly taking its toll on him. But he was still Boonzie, with the resolve and attitude of an ox if no longer quite the strength.

Boonzie had never known Tuesday Fletcher personally, but the moment he'd heard the news he'd come rushing straight to Le Val to offer support to his friends. Though death had always been an ever-present reality in the lives of men who'd made the art of war their profession, the loss of a comrade was a deep and too-familiar sorrow shared by all.

'It was good of you to come, Boonzie,' Ben said, clapping him on the shoulder. 'And for agreeing to come out of retirement like this. Strictly as a one-off thing, of course.'

'Och, ye know me, laddie. Always game tae lend a haund, if I can. Besides, I could dae wi' a wee bit o' excitement in ma life.' Boonzie gave a dangerous smile that made him look momentarily like a hungry shark, and cast an eye over the two cases he'd brought with him off the helicopter. The materials they contained had been supplied at very short notice by one of their various contacts. Such things might have seemed a little out of place for a retired ex pat tomato gardener. But then, Boonzie had always liked to keep his old skills sharp, because however unlikely it seemed, you never knew when they might come in handy again one day. And Ben and Jeff had never known anyone else with his degree of expertise.

'Then let's get to work,' Ben said.

Chapter 62

Two days later

The location for the meeting hadn't struck Hercule de Scorbiac as particularly unusual, on the face of it. It seemed only logical that Ben Hope would have chosen a place far from the public eye, where sensitive and important matters could be settled undisturbed. It also suited the Grand Master very well that he would be free to deal with Hope as he wished, once the stolen items were safely back in his possession. The man would shortly rue the day he had ever dared to cross swords with the Order of the Custodes Sanctorum Secretorum Templi. Who did he think he was messing with?

And so without hesitation, the moment Hope had contacted him with the details of where the meeting was to take place, de Scorbiac had gathered together five of his best remaining men, the same men he'd already taken with him to France for their failed attempt to catch Hope on his home ground. One of them was known among the Brother initiates simply as Le Marteau, 'the Hammer', and he would play the dual role of chief bodyguard to his Grand Master as well as executioner, once they had Hope finally in their clutches.

The eight-hundred-mile flight from the Alentejo to the Languedoc was just four hours in de Scorbiac's chartered jet, with a chopper to meet them at the airport for the final leg of the trip. The Hammer and his men had brought with them all that was necessary to finish off their enemy once and for all. At precisely two-thirty that afternoon, their helicopter thudded over the hills and vineyards of the Corbières region and the village of Lagrasse came into view below, bathed in hazy sunshine. And there on the high ground beyond the village, standing alone against the sky, was the tower where the first and last meeting between Hercule de Scorbiac and his enemy was about to take place.

As the chopper came in to land, it did cross the Grand Master's mind that Hope had chosen a rather odd location. But he soon dismissed that idea, in his eagerness to recover what had been taken from him and exact the punishment this man deserved.

De Scorbiac, the Hammer and the other four men descended from the aircraft and made their way towards the single arched doorway at the foot of the tall round tower. The Brother initiates' weapons were all carefully concealed for the moment. De Scorbiac noticed the blue BMW Alpina parked by the side of the building, which he knew from previous reports belonged to Ben Hope. He'd expected the man to appear to greet them personally, but there was no sign of him yet.

That was when the Grand Master's phone rang. He fished it from his suit pocket. 'This is de Scorbiac.'

'Glad you could make it, Hercule,' said Hope's voice on the line, sounding very close by. The Grand Master strongly disliked being addressed by his first name, but he tolerated it for the moment. He'd soon have the last laugh. 'Please come inside,' Hope told him. 'The meeting will take place in the room right at the top of the tower. You'll like it. It's got an even better view than your castle turret.'

Swallowing his hatred of the man and composing himself to appear polite and congenial – for the moment, at least – de Scorbiac led the way inside and up the spiral stairs, not unlike the ones he climbed each day inside his own domain. They arrived at the top of the tower, a white-walled circular room with a plain wooden floor coated in dust, a plain table surrounded by a few chairs. And no Hope.

'Where in God's name is he?' de Scorbiac muttered to himself. He sat at the table and looked at his watch. He loathed to be kept waiting. The impudence of the man!

The Grand Master didn't have to wait long. But things weren't quite as he'd expected.

The small procession of vehicles that wound up the track to the foot of the tower was led by a black Mercedes saloon, dusty from the drive. Riding in the back of the car was a man called Dante Lorenzo Esposito, who had flown from Rome that same day. He had never visited this region of France before, but had little curiosity about seeing the part of the world in which his former colleague, the late ex-Cardinal Jean-Rafael Silvestre, had chosen to retire to. Esposito was here for one thing, and one thing only. His business would be conducted quickly, efficiently and with his customary ruthlessness.

'What kind of place is this for a rendezvous?' he muttered disgustedly as the cars pulled up outside the very peculiar building. They clearly weren't the first to arrive. The expected blue BMW was parked nearby, as well as a helicopter. Esposito thought nothing of it, though, as he stepped from the Mercedes and his half-dozen associates got out of their vehicles.

Esposito wore a black Fedora hat and a long black coat, despite the heat. He'd walked a few steps from his car when he felt his mobile vibrate in the coat pocket. He reached inside and pulled it out. '*Pronto*.'

'Good afternoon, Your Excellency,' said the voice on the line. 'Welcome to my humble home. Please forgive me if I don't come out to meet you personally.'

Boiling with resentment at being treated with such flagrant disrespect, Esposito trudged up the tower steps with his six associates following in single file. A couple of the men did a last press-check of their pistols on the way up. 'Keep those out of sight,' Esposito scolded them.

At last, the Vatican contingent reached the white round room at the top of the tower. Esposito walked inside with his associates close behind him. Then halted in his tracks and stood speechless. Hope wasn't there. But the room was far from empty.

The assembled thirteen men all stared at one another. Nobody spoke for several seconds.

Hercule de Scorbiac was the first to break the silence. 'Who in God's name are you people?' he demanded in French, standing up from his chair and pointing.

Dante Lorenzo Esposito turned to the closest of his associates. 'Chi sono questi idioti?' he grated. The man shrugged, clueless. The others were ready to pull out their pistols. So were the Hammer and the rest of de Scorbiac's men. The tension was rising by the quarter-second. It would take only the tiniest of sparks to ignite the tinderbox.

'Where is Hope?' de Scorbiac said angrily.

And in reply to his question, another voice came through the audio speakers hidden around the room.

It said, 'I'm right here, gentlemen.'

Chapter 63

It was true that poor mad Sir Leopold's folly looked much better from a distance. Standing on a rock ledge at the summit of a neighbouring hill some two hundred yards away, Ben, Roberta, Jeff and Boonzie had patiently awaited the arrival of their visitors and watched them enter the tower one group after the other. They'd been listening to every word spoken inside the round room at the top.

Now Ben spoke again into his phone:

'I'd like to thank you all for coming. Unfortunately, I won't be joining you in person after all. That's because I have something special arranged for the occasion. A kind of going away party, you might call it. Except that you're the ones who are going away.'

Total stunned silence for a moment; then the simultaneous uproar of rage and panic sounded through Ben's phone speaker as the tower's thirteen occupants all started yelling at once.

'I know what you're thinking,' Ben told them. 'And you're absolutely right. But there's no use in trying to escape. Even if you could make it down the steps in time, I've remotely locked the exit door and there's no other way out. But in any case you wouldn't get halfway to the bottom, because eighty pounds of C4 high explosive, the kind that my former SAS demolitions specialist friend has rigged the entire tower with, goes up awfully fast. It'll shoot off like a firework and collapse the building in its own footprint, you along with it. Nothing lasts for ever.'

Hercule de Scorbiac's enraged voice could be heard screaming even more loudly than the rest of them. 'Hope!'

'I only wish I could have arranged something a little more drawn-out for you all,' Ben said. 'It's what you deserve. But some compromises are worth making, don't you think?'

'HOPE!' de Scorbiac screamed again. 'You'll regret this!'

'Nice doing business with you,' Ben replied. He ended the call.

'Here ye go, laddie,' said Boonzie, handing Ben the remote control, a plain device with an arming toggle switch and a red detonator button. Ben clicked the switch to its armed position. He stood gazing at the remote for a moment, then at the tower. Then he turned to Jeff, standing at his shoulder.

'All yours, Jeff,' he said, and held the remote out to him.

Jeff took it. He looked at Ben and nodded his thanks.

'For Tuesday,' Ben said.

'For Tuesday,' Jeff replied, and pressed the red button.

EPILOGUE

Long before the ruins of the building had stopped burning and the sirens of the fire engines could be heard in the distance, Ben and his companions had disappeared. The inquiry that would take place over the coming months would ultimately conclude little, with such scanty evidence and insufficient data to go on. When the rubber stamp of officialdom finally came down, its ruling would be that the incident had just been some kind of inexplicable freak accident.

But all that was still a long way off and furthest from their minds as Ben, Jeff and Roberta waved goodbye to Boonzie at the airport in Perpignan and watched his plane depart for home. Then it was the long, mostly silent, drive northwards through France in their hired Kia, rented in Jeff's name, Ben's Alpina having been destroyed in the demolition of Sir Leopold's tower.

Before heading towards Normandy and Le Val, the three stopped off at the Kaprisky estate near Le Mans. There Ben found the recuperating Matthew Sadler engaged in some intense chess warfare with old Auguste, sitting at a parasol-shaded garden table with the elderly billionaire's most cherished board and pieces, having once belonged to Napoleon Bonaparte, being used to their full potential. A butler in a white blazer kept the iced Dom Pérignon coming as the pair regaled one another with epic tales of past matches and got along as though they'd been best pals for ever. Another cause for celebration was the news they'd received that morning. Simone, the nurse who'd been shot by Sadler's would-be assassin in the hospital in Quillan, had come out of surgery and was expected to pull through fine. Flowers and champagne were already being dispatched in bulk for all concerned.

'BEN!' At sound of the cry, Ben turned to see Valentina streaking across the manicured lawn from the château. He barely had time to brace for impact before she piled into him and wrapped her arms around his waist. 'Oh, Ben, I'm so happy you made it home safely.'

'And I'm very thankful to you for all you've done for us, once again,' Ben said.

'But isn't that what dear friends do for one another?' she replied, eyes sparkling and cheeks flushed, clasping both his hands in hers. 'You know how much you're loved here. And you always will be.'

'Let me introduce Roberta,' he said, and the two women eyeballed one another with a certain degree of cold suspicion before Valentina smiled sweetly and said, 'How lovely to meet you at last. I've heard *so* much about you. Do come inside out of the sun, both of you. How long will you be staying? Several days, I hope?'

'I'm afraid we have other engagements,' Ben replied.

Forty-eight hours later, their connecting flight from Paris was landing at Sangster International Airport, Montego Bay, Jamaica. Also aboard the plane were most of the crew from

Le Val as well as a number of former comrades who'd come to see their friend laid to rest and pay their respects to his grieving family.

Ben had attended far too many funerals in his time, and this one was the hardest he'd ever been through. Many tears were shed for Tuesday, even by Roberta, who'd never had the privilege of knowing him. The enlarged image of his face that the family had placed at his graveside, that irrepressible megawatt smile beaming over the proceedings, made the moment more poignant still. As a gospel choir began to sing a lively rendition of the traditional Jamaican funeral song 'Back to the Dust', Ben felt the tears stinging his own cheeks. Beside him, Jeff stood leaning on his cane with his chin on his chest, his face drawn and his eyes shut, struggling to contain his emotions. Ben wrapped an arm around his friend's shoulders and squeezed him hard.

They spent another three days in Montego Bay before Jeff had decided he'd had enough and declared he was going home. 'I'll see you there soon,' Ben told him. But Jeff shook his head. For the last two days he'd been acting on edge, as though there was something he needed to say but had been holding it back, a confession that wanted to come bursting out if only he could find the words to express it.

'I don't mean home to Le Val, mate,' Jeff said in a quiet voice. 'I'm going back to England.'

And in fact Ben had known, deep down, that this was coming. He said nothing, just put a hand on his friend's shoulder. The bond between them had never felt so strong.

'Things won't ever be the same, you know?' Jeff said, shaking his head. 'He was just so much a part of everything that it's like there'll always be a hole where he ought to be.

I don't think I can go on, Ben. I feel like calling it a day. I'm sorry.'

'Don't be,' Ben told him. 'We had a good run. A lot of good times.' And in his own heart, he sensed that this moment was marking the beginning of the new direction that he'd been privately thinking of for some time. At one stage he'd even confided his secret feelings to his sister Ruth, his only living relative. The restless urge to move on had been gnawing at him for months, maybe even years. He just hadn't known what it might entail, and he hadn't had the courage to fully admit to himself that this chapter in his life, which for so long had felt like everything in the world to him, was finally drawing to a close.

But as the wise folks say, with every ending comes a new beginning. With Jeff gone, Ben and Roberta were left alone together and spent the next two weeks exploring Jamaica's north coast. The weather was perfect and each day seemed to last for ever. They wandered along endless palm beaches where the impossibly blue ocean lapped at their bare feet on the white sand. They visited the Green Grotto caves, Dunn's River Falls and Fern Gulley, chartered a cabin cruiser and went diving on coral reefs, grilled fish on the deck, swam for miles in the milk-warm ocean.

And after a while, Ben found himself thinking, *I could get used to this.*

Nothing was said, but Roberta, too, was beginning to feel the subtle change that was coming over them both as they slowly grew closer and closer together until it felt as though they'd never been apart. It was after they'd been walking barefoot along their favourite lonely stretch of beach one evening, hand in hand, enjoying the easy shared silence between them and watching the sunset, that she stopped and looked up into his eyes and asked, 'What's happening with us, Ben? Where do things go from here? Will it work out between us?'

'I always planned everything in my life,' he replied. 'Or I thought I did. But every time I tried to make things go the way I wanted them to, something else would change it all. Now I don't want to make plans any more. We have time. Let's take each day as it comes and see what happens.'

They kissed. He could taste the salty tang of the ocean on her lips and in her hair.

'We have time,' she said.

THIRTY BOOKS . . . AND THE CIRCLE IS COMPLETE

It's sometimes hard for me to believe that so many years have gone by since I first set out to write what would become *The Alchemist's Secret*, introducing the then-new character of Benedict Hope, an ex-SAS soldier turned child rescuer. Back in those days I would never have dared to dream that our hero's maiden adventure would pave the way for a series of thirty novels, plus a few assorted novellas and short stories. Ben has been with me for a long time – and also with many readers who have pretty much grown up with him, starting in their teens and now still following his exploits into their thirties.

But, you know, sooner or later the time was going to come when Ben's story had been told, and after a lot of soul-searching I eventually came to the difficult decision that having survived so many adventures, he was due for a rest.

How do you bring an extended series like this to a conclusion, especially when you've grown so close to your character that he feels like a real person – and more than that, like a dear old friend? I would never have considered letting him die a hero's death, which I don't think my readers would ever have forgiven me for doing. Equally out of the question was the thought of consigning him to a life of domestic bliss.

To a man like him such a fate would have been akin to a bullet to the head. No, I wanted to leave him in a good place; and as the finale of *The Templar Secret* spells the end of a chapter in his life, it also heralds a new beginning for him, one that perhaps offers the chance of happiness that has eluded him for so long. I will leave you, the reader, to imagine what paths he might follow into the future. And who knows, perhaps one day I'll be drawn to catch up with him again.

It's been an honour for me to be able to write these books and create a character that so many readers have loved as much as I always will. And needless to say, it's that love and devotion on the part of Ben's big family of readers from all over the world that has made the writing of the series possible. Thank you, one and all, for the wonderful support you have given it over the years. It's been great to have you with me. We've been together a long time and have come such a long way.

But it ain't over yet. There are always new places to go, new characters to meet and new adventures to be had, and I'd love to have the pleasure of your company as I head towards the next stop on my storytelling journey. Visit my website www.scottmariani.com and find out where the road takes us from here . . .

Scott Mariani

For more unmissable reads,
sign up to the HarperNorth newsletter at
www.harpernorth.co.uk

or find us on Twitter at
@HarperNorthUK